MW01093909

FIGHTING FOR US

A SMALL TOWN ROMANCE

BAILEY BROTHERS
BOOK 2

CLAIRE KINGSLEY

Always Have LLC

Published by Always Have, LLC

Edited by Elayne Morgan

Cover design by Lori Jackson

BN: 978-1-959809-02-1

w.clairekingsleybooks.com

reated with Vellum

To David.
I would have waited, too.

ABOUT THIS BOOK

How long would you wait for the love of your life?

The Asher Bailey who comes home to his quirky small town isn't the same man who put a ring on Grace's finger. He's bigger, harder, haunted. Forced to give up Grace and everything else that was good in his life for a prison sentence he barely survived.

Now that he's home, he finds himself aggressively welcomed by his brothers and gleefully gossiped about by his neighbors. He'd counted on both.

But he never expected to see Grace still wearing his ring.

Grace's fairy tale didn't end. It was interrupted. She's spent the last seven years living her life while waiting for one man. Now that he's back, she's got her work cut out for her. He's scarred and angry, and stubbornly convinced they can't be together. She's more than happy to educate him otherwise.

Every beer, every prank, every kiss brings him closer to

where he's always belonged. In her life. In her arms. In her heart.

Asher fears the darkness inside him can't be contained. But Grace won't give up on him without a fight.

Author's note: A brooding, wounded hero and the woman who won't give up on him. A pack of unruly, prank-loving brothers. A wild neighborhood rumor mill. Spectacular BFF banter. This is a love story about soulmates that delivers the heat and all the feels. The Bailey Brothers series is **meant to be read in order** *and Fighting for Us concludes Grace and Asher's happily ever after.*

1

ASHER

A fist hit my jaw, followed by a swift punch to my kidney. Grunting, I took the blows, absorbing the pain. Didn't have a choice. The guy restraining my arms wasn't strong enough to hold me for long, but these assholes were going to do as much damage as possible while I couldn't fight back.

I growled at the greasy piece of shit in front of me. He had a name, but I didn't give a fuck what it was. The black eye I'd given him last week was fading. I'd have to give him two this time.

He smiled and clocked me again.

Fuck.

I struggled against the grip on my arms. I couldn't see who was holding them behind my back, but he was slipping. The second guy hit me below the ribs again while the first darted closer and punched me on the other side.

None of them could take me one-on-one, so three of them had jumped me in the library. I should have been ready for it. I was always ready, always watching. I had to be.

It was the only way I'd survived prison this long. But they'd gotten the drop on me, and now I was fucked.

"Not so tough now, are you?" the first guy sneered, flashing his yellow teeth.

I met his eyes, locking him in a hard stare. I was going to hurt this guy. Badly. As soon as one of them made a mistake, I was going to unleash on these fuckers. And I was going to enjoy it.

Adrenaline coursed through me, burning everything to ash. My heart pumped fast and my muscles flexed against the arms trying to contain me. Still staring the first guy down, I shifted my body weight. The arms holding mine were tense and rigid. I stayed fluid, ready to strike. Ready to go on the attack.

The first guy's fist smashed into my face again, flooding my mouth with the metallic tang of blood. And I was fucking done.

Throwing my weight forward, I bent my knees and hinged at the waist. The guy holding my arms flipped over my shoulder. I roared, surging toward the first guy, and scored a swift punch to his gut. I didn't have long before they either took me to the ground—it was still three on one—or the guards broke it up. I had to make this count.

A heady sense of euphoria filled me as I rained blows on the first guy. The second jumped on my back, trying to regain control, but I tossed him over my shoulder. He hit the ground with a groan.

Someone barreled into me from the side, wrapping his arms around my waist. We crashed into a table and landed hard on the floor. His body weight smashed the air from my lungs.

Gasping for breath, I fought back, but now there were four. I couldn't take four guys at once. I held my arms up to protect my face while he hit me. Ground and pound. I'd been here before, but in the ring there was a ref to blow the whistle and stop the fight.

Not here. Not in prison.

"Hey!"

Swift footsteps approached. Guards shouted orders. I took a few more punches before someone dragged them off me.

Damn it. That fucking hurt.

Another guard hauled me roughly to my feet, then yanked my arms behind my back and cuffed me. I didn't resist. Just blinked at the blood dripping in my eye and stared daggers at the assholes who'd started the fight, while guards slammed them onto tables and locked them in cuffs.

"Come on," the guard barked, shoving me ahead of him. "Let's go."

I didn't bother pointing out that I hadn't started it this time. That three guys, then four, had jumped me out of nowhere. It didn't matter. At best, I'd be confined to my cell for a while. At worst, they'd throw me in the hole. But nothing I said now would make a difference.

The metal bit at my wrists and I seethed with rage. At those fuckers who'd attacked me. At the guard leading me away. At the concrete and barbed wire that kept me inside. I ground my teeth together, anger pulsing through me, deep as the blood in my veins.

He didn't lead me back to my cell. I decided I didn't care. They could discipline me all they wanted. Throw me in the hole again if that was what they thought would break me. Solitary was brutal, but they couldn't do more damage than had already been done.

I was already broken.

I just hoped whatever punishment those other dicks got was worse than mine.

The guard took me down a hallway and a hint of fear tried to worm its way in through my anger. I didn't know where we were going. Prison life was built on a solid, monotonous routine. I did the same things, day in, day out. It was boring as hell, but at least I knew what to expect.

New or unknown was always bad.

My senses were heightened as I followed the guard into a small room. It had a metal table, bolted to the floor, and two chairs. Probably for attorneys when they met with an inmate. I'd never used this room because my attorney had never been here. No reason for him to come. My sentence was what it was. Eight years. No parole, no chance for time off for good behavior. That was how it worked in this state. I simply had to wait it out until the legal system declared I'd paid for my crime.

Three hundred fifty-two days left.

I crushed that thought to dust before it could take root. I couldn't think about getting out. Not now. Once a day, when I first woke up, I let myself reach for the end. I let all my grief in, and for a minute, I thought about the outside. About my family. Gram. My brothers. Even her, although I had to be especially careful with that.

When that minute was up, I slammed it shut. Blocked it all out. I had to. Anything less made me weak, and I couldn't afford even a hint of weakness in here. I had to be cold and hard as steel. Otherwise they'd have torn me apart years ago.

I held still while the guard unlocked my cuffs, increasingly confused as to what I was doing here. I couldn't have a visitor. This wasn't how visiting hours worked. No one had come to see me in years, but if they had, I'd have been notified and given the option to respond.

I always said no. I didn't see visitors. Which was why they'd all stopped trying a long time ago.

Without a word of explanation, the guard motioned for me to sit and returned the handcuffs to my wrists, locking me to the table.

What the fuck was happening?

The warden appeared in the open doorway. He had a long gray mustache and bushy eyebrows. His barrel chest strained the confines of his shirt and the lines in his face spoke of years of hard living. This guy had seen some shit, and it showed.

"Jesus," he muttered, his voice gravelly. "Why the hell is he bleeding?"

"Fight in the library," the guard said.

"Go get something to patch him up."

The guard left and the warden scowled, tilting his head to examine my face. "You bleeding anywhere I can't see?"

"No."

"Good." He sat down across from me and dropped a folder on the table. "I have some news."

I stiffened, my eyes lifting to meet his. A jolt of fear shot through me like lightning, and a sick feeling spread through my gut. Something horrible must have happened.

Fuck. Please not Gram.

"Is it my family?"

"No. It's not bad news. In fact, I think you're going to find it unexpectedly good."

My brow furrowed. I had no idea what he was talking about.

"You're going home, Bailey. I just received an order for your immediate release."

2

ASHER

*M*y eyes were locked on the floor, although I was well aware of the guard watching me. I sat in a hard metal chair in a holding cell, my wrists cuffed, hands in my lap. Instinctively, I twisted my wrists, seeking the bite of metal against skin, like I needed something to prove this was real.

The cut on my forehead throbbed and my knuckles were battered from the fight this morning. Vaguely, I wondered if my hands would finally heal, or if they'd be perpetually black and blue. Every time the bruises faded, they'd get banged up all over again.

I flexed my fists a few times. The dull pain was still there. I wasn't dreaming.

Another guard came in, and the two of them spoke a few quiet words to each other. Then the first guard nodded to me. "Time to go."

I'd spent the last several hours doing nothing. Just waiting. After meeting with the warden, I'd been escorted to my cell to clean it out, taken to make a phone call, then brought here.

Ripples of confusion had spread in my wake as the other inmates watched. This was out of the ordinary, and it made them uneasy. Hell, I was uneasy too. I'd kept my head down and did as I was told, all the while wondering if this was really happening, or if it was some kind of sick prank.

I followed the guard to a counter protected by a barrier. He motioned for me to lift my hands so he could unlock the cuffs. They came off with a dull clink.

"Asher Bailey," the man behind the counter said. He passed a manila folder with my wallet in it through the opening, then handed me a rectangular box. It was brown and unmarked, about two feet long and a foot wide. The tape on the top barely stuck anymore, but it was better than nothing.

I took my things—the only stuff I had left—and followed the guard through another door.

"Your ride is waiting out in visitor parking," he said.

"Okay." I was surprised my voice sounded so normal. So calm. On the inside, I was reeling.

I was going home.

That should have been good news. I was supposed to have another year. But just like that, a letter from the governor's office had changed everything. They were actually letting me out of this hellhole.

But I wasn't prepared. I had a mental routine, a way I survived each day. And I was having a very hard time processing that it wasn't going to be necessary anymore.

We came to another door and I almost stopped to ask if he was sure. I couldn't shake the feeling that I was being set up—that as soon as I set foot outside, I'd be tackled and restrained. It wasn't that I didn't trust this particular guard. I didn't trust anyone.

He opened the door and I blinked at the bright sunlight.

The early May sky was pure blue without a single cloud. I stepped out and nothing happened. I was still inside the walls, but this was out of bounds. Movement within the prison was heavily restricted, and just a few hours ago, I wouldn't have been allowed out here.

But no alarms went off. No guards came running.

The guard and I walked across the concrete to the tall fence topped with barbed wire. My heart thumped in my chest and my mouth went dry. The guard signaled. A few seconds passed. And then the gate moved.

It rumbled open with a metallic scrape, revealing the outside world—or what I could see of the outside world from here, which was mostly a parking lot. But the mountains rose in the distance, snow still covering their tips.

Those mountains were home.

With a deep breath, I walked through the gate. Still no sirens. It immediately began rumbling shut behind me. They were really letting me go.

The doors of a dark blue SUV flew open and four men poured out. I stared at them, dumbfounded. I'd thought one of them would pick me up, not all four.

Relief slammed into me, so potent I almost couldn't breathe. They swarmed around me, and someone took the stuff out of my hands.

My brothers. They were here. I hadn't seen any of them in so long.

Gavin shoved his way to the front and barreled into me, bear-hugging me with surprisingly thick arms.

"Hey, brother," he said, squeezing me tight.

I hugged him back. How the hell was he so strong?

"Back up, brozinski. Give us a turn." Logan whipped off a pair of aviators and grinned at me. He looked different. His jaw was more square and the stubble he was sporting made him look older.

Of course, he *was* older. He'd been a nineteen-year-old kid the last time I'd seen him.

Gavin let go and Logan spread his arms wide.

"Ash. It's about fucking time."

"Yeah, no shit." I hugged him and he slapped me on the back a few times.

Evan still towered over the rest of us. His hands were grease-stained, like a mechanic's, and he had tattoos I didn't remember. "Good to see you, man."

"You too."

I hugged it out with Evan. Levi hung back a foot or two, eying me with uncertainty, like he wasn't sure what to think. He looked older, like his twin, and he filled out his Tilikum Fire Department shirt in a way he hadn't before.

Seven years was a long time.

Finally, Levi hugged me too. "Good to have you back."

"Thanks."

"You weren't fucking with us," Logan said. "They're really letting you go?"

"I told you it wasn't a prank," Levi said.

My brow furrowed. "You thought I'd call home and say I was being released early as a prank?"

Logan shrugged. "Maybe prison gave you a really dark sense of humor."

Gavin snickered and smacked Logan's arm. "You have to admit, it would have been a good one."

"You guys are fucked in the head," Levi said.

"This place freaks me the fuck out." Logan cast a glance at the prison complex. "Are you clear? Can we get out of here?"

"Yeah, I'm free to go."

"Is this all your stuff?" Evan set the envelope and box in the back of the SUV.

"That's it. I had a few changes of clothes, but I don't want them. And I think I'll burn these." I plucked at the old t-shirt and black sweats I wore. We'd been allowed street clothes if we had them—the prison issued clothes to those who didn't—but I never wanted to wear this shit again.

"Awesome. I'm always down for a little fire," Gavin said. "And by 'a little fire,' I mean a big one."

"Which is ironic, considering you're trying to convince Chief Stanley to hire you on," Levi said.

"Yeah, and I'm a fire expert. I'm perfect for the job."

"Come on," Evan grumbled. "Let's get the fuck out of here."

"Shotgun," Gavin said.

Levi glared at him. "No."

"I called it."

"Let Asher sit up front."

"Oh yeah, good point." Gavin bowed and gestured toward the still-open passenger's side door. "After you, big brother."

"It's good to see you've matured in seven years," I said.

He just grinned at me.

What I didn't say was how hard it was to reconcile this man with the kid I remembered. The last time I'd seen him, he'd been a skinny teenager with hair flopping in his eyes. He'd filled out and grown up. I barely recognized him.

We all piled in the car. Seemed like it was Levi's SUV; he took the driver's seat. Gavin protested at being made to sit in the third row by himself, but Evan growled at him and he shut up.

Some things hadn't changed.

Levi pulled out of the parking lot, pausing at a gate. It

lifted and we drove right through. And just like that, I was on the highway, the correctional facility disappearing in the side mirror.

I was heading home.

"So, can we ask about the elephant in the vehicle, so to speak?" Logan asked.

I looked over my shoulder and pointed to the taped-up gash on my forehead. "Do you mean this?"

"Actually, I was going to say that most of your face isn't broken, but yeah, we can talk about that if you really want to."

"It's nothing. Turned out to be a going-away present."

Levi glanced at my knuckles but didn't say anything. I appreciated that.

"Why did all four of you drive out here?" I wanted to change the subject before they asked more questions about my face. "I figured Gram would only send one of you."

"Are you kidding?" Gavin asked. "Asher Bailey gets out of prison and you didn't think we'd all be there for that? Also, we were fighting over who got to be the one to pick you up, and Gram said if we didn't all get in the car and get moving, she'd turn her peckers loose on us."

I glanced back. "Her what?"

"Gram got chickens," Levi said. "And for reasons none of us can fathom, she calls them her peckers."

The corner of my mouth lifted in what could have almost been called a smile. I couldn't remember the last time I'd done that. "Sounds like something Gram would say."

"So are you going to tell us what happened, or do we have to guess?" Logan asked. "We thought you had another year."

I blew out a breath. It was hard to think; I felt like I was in shock. It reminded me of the first few days after my arrest, when I'd been held at the county sheriff's office. Everything had seemed like a nightmare unfolding before my eyes. Today had a similar dream-like quality.

"The governor intervened and granted clemency," I said.

"Since when do you know the governor?" Logan asked.

"I don't. Apparently the same guy assaulted the governor's niece about six months before..." I trailed off. They knew what I was talking about. "I don't know any details, but I don't think she ever went to the police. Somehow, they found out what happened, and about me. The letter said that given the circumstances of my case, time served was adequate, and I was to be released immediately."

"Holy shit," Logan said.

"Too bad he didn't do that seven years ago," Levi muttered.

"I don't think he was the governor then," Evan said.

"Can we focus on the positive here?" Logan said. "Asher's out. We're taking his ass home."

Home. The truth of that was hitting me hard. Even though I was driving down the highway toward our little town in the Cascades, it was hard to believe.

I wasn't ready. I hadn't prepared.

Fuck.

How was I going to deal with this? I had almost no idea what life had been like back home for the last seven years. Some inmates lived for contact with the outside—visits, letters, updates. Not me. I'd quickly realized that there was only one way I was going to survive my prison term: I had to stay hard. Stay cold. Stay strong.

I'd lost literally everything good in my life—everything worth living for. Reminders of home sliced me open, like I was walking on broken glass. If I'd spent every day bleeding, I would have been ripped to shreds.

So I'd limited contact with the outside world. I'd known I'd pay a price for it later, but the longer I spent there, the harder my resolve had grown. Because I wasn't just protecting myself—doing what I had to do to survive. I was protecting them. I didn't want them to see who I'd become.

I didn't want them to have to know.

But now I was racing down the highway toward home with no time to prepare. No time to get used to the idea of living in the world again.

A world that had changed in ways I couldn't possibly know. Couldn't be ready for.

An odd sense of panic rose in my chest and I clenched my fists. I had no routine. No schedule. No one restricting my movements. I also wouldn't have to worry about three assholes jumping me out of nowhere and trying to beat me senseless, so that would be an improvement. But this was all happening so fast. It felt like I might suffocate.

"You okay, man?" Levi asked.

"Yeah. It's just a lot to take in. It's been a long time."

I paused for a moment, looking out the window. The real elephant in the vehicle wasn't my busted face. It was the seven-year chasm that separated me from these guys. I'd had minimal contact with Gram during my prison term, but no one else. Not even them.

"Look, I know you guys haven't heard from me since I got locked up."

"Don't sweat it, man, we get it," Logan said.

"You do?"

"I was pretty pissed at first when Gram told us we couldn't go see you. But I'll never forget what she said. Do you guys remember that?"

Levi nodded. "She said sometimes when a man goes to war, he has to make himself forget the people he leaves behind. It's the only way he can become the warrior he needs to be to survive."

Damn. Gram always seemed to have a way of getting straight to the heart of things.

"Yeah. That's exactly it."

"The good news is, you can put down your weapons," Logan said. "War's over."

I looked down at my battered hands. Put down your weapons. I wasn't sure if I remembered how.

"Did anyone get a hold of Grace yet?" Gavin asked.

I whipped around and practically snarled at him. "*Don't.*"

"What?"

"Don't fucking talk about her. Don't even say her name."

Gavin's eyes widened and he lifted his hands, palms out. "Sorry."

I didn't miss the look Evan and Logan shared, but I ignored them.

Of all the things I wasn't ready for, hearing about her was the biggest. I'd have to face the truth eventually, but not today. Any day but today. I was already a loose cannon, and just the sound of her name was enough to make me lose my shit.

I couldn't. Not yet.

I'd lost my freedom, my career aspirations, my time, even my dignity. But none of that compared to the pain of losing her. Not even close.

I'd loved her with everything I had, and I'd never get that back.

In those brief moments each morning when I'd allowed myself to think about home, I'd cautiously let my thoughts drift to her. I'd wondered what she was doing. Who she was with and where she lived. What she'd done with her life since I'd been gone. And I'd silently begged God or the universe or whoever might be listening to make sure she was okay—that she was happy and safe.

But I wasn't ready to find out what her life looked like. I wanted happiness for her more than anything, but I couldn't deal with the pain of hearing about it. I needed time to prepare. Time to brace myself for the grief.

3

GRACE

Fresh mountain air blew through my hair as we hugged the hairpin turns in Cara's blue convertible. The weather was gorgeous—sun shining, not a cloud in the sky. We were heading home from a day at a spa. After a delicious brunch, followed by a massage and a facial, I was happy and relaxed.

"Thank you again," I said, glancing at her. "This was great."

Cara's red hair whipped around her face and she smiled, flashing her perfect teeth. "My pleasure."

I'd met Cara when I'd gone back to school at Tilikum College, after Asher had been sent away. We'd both been transfers, and neither of us had fit in with the other students. Although we'd only been in our early twenties, life had knocked us both around enough that we were a little more worldly than everyone else. A little less fresh-faced and naïve.

Being engaged to a man in prison tended to do that to a girl.

I adjusted my sunglasses. "I didn't realize how much I needed the break. And the massage."

"Good. Maybe this will teach you to let me spoil you more often."

I rolled my eyes at her. Cara came from old Hollywood money, and as far as I could tell, she had a nearly endless supply of it. One of her favorite hobbies was trying to spend it on me. I was pretty sure she did it mostly to annoy me.

"I appreciate the spoiling. This time. But don't get any ideas."

"No, my brilliant magical unicorn, now I know your weakness. But next time, we'll spend a weekend at a spa in Napa. Or maybe Paris."

"Stop. You're not taking me to a spa in Paris."

"You underestimate my stubbornness."

"And you underestimate mine."

She glanced at me again. "No, I'm well-versed in your brand of obstinacy."

"I have no idea what you're talking about."

The highway curved and she took the exit toward Tilikum. Sometimes I wondered why she'd stayed in our funny little town. She'd grown up in L.A., among wealthy people and celebrities. Going to fancy brunches and exclusive clubs. I knew she'd moved here to go to college as an act of rebellion, choosing a small school in a small town in the middle of nowhere to piss off her mother. And it had worked. Her mother had been furious. But for some reason, Cara had never left.

For that, I was unceasingly grateful.

"So do you want to go out tonight?" she asked.

"Sure. What do you have in mind?"

"I don't know, as long as it involves dressing slutty and not going home alone."

"Yeah, well, have fun with that."

She stuck out her lower lip in a pout. "Come on, Grace. I haven't had sex in like, forever. I could really use some good dick."

"That's fine. We can go out, and you can dress slutty, and get some good dick."

"What about you?"

"What about me?"

"You think you're relaxed now? You'd be amazed at what some good dick can do for you."

We slowed as we pulled into town and I smoothed my hair down. "I'll pass, but thanks."

She groaned. "At least dress slutty with me. I'll work on getting you laid at some point, but obviously I'm not holding my breath."

"Yeah, don't."

"Why are you so stubborn about this?"

"You know why."

She hit the brakes and stopped in the middle of the road —no stop sign, no cross street. There wasn't anyone behind us, but still.

"What are you doing?" I looked over my shoulder. "Can you maybe pull over?"

She shifted so she was facing me and pulled her sunglasses down her nose to peer over the top of them. "Take it off. Just for tonight."

"Take what off?"

Her eyes moved deliberately to my hand. "That."

My mouth dropped open and for a second, I didn't know what to say. I was used to her teasing me about my lack of sex life; she did it all the time. But take off my ring? "Are you serious right now? No, I'm not taking off my ring."

"Boo, you know I love you more than anything in the entire world, but how long are you going to let this go on?"

"Let what go on? I'm engaged."

"Does he remember that?"

I looked away. "You know this is complicated."

She was quiet for a beat, then reached over to cover my hand with hers. "I'm sorry. You're right, it's complicated. If you don't want to take it off, you should keep it on."

"I know you don't really understand." My voice was quiet. "I don't expect you to get it. You never knew him. You were never around us before."

"I want to understand. You're my girl, and if you want something, I will make it my mission in life to get it for you. It's just... you haven't heard from him in so long."

"I know."

Cara was right, and it wasn't just me. Asher had cut himself off from everyone. He refused visitors, and other than occasional brief messages to Gram to let her know he was alive, contact with him was rare.

I hadn't seen or heard from him in seven years.

"Look, I realize wearing this ring makes me look stupid, or crazy, or both." I held up my hand. I wore several rings on different fingers, but I changed those like I changed my outfits. I never took off Asher's ring. "But I don't care what anyone else thinks. It's nobody's business. Asher asked me to marry him and the fact that he went to prison—for saving *me*, in case you forgot that part—doesn't mean it's over."

"I have not forgotten the fact that he saved you, and you can bet I'm going to give him a big kiss on the lips for it when I finally meet him."

A car pulled up behind us and honked. Cara twisted around and glared at him.

"Oh my god, Cara, get out of the street."

She let her foot off the brake and started moving again. "It's not like there's traffic in this town. He could have gone around me. And I don't think you're stupid, or crazy. Okay, maybe a little bit crazy. But who isn't, really."

"Then why are you suggesting that I take my ring off and dress slutty with you tonight? Where is this coming from?"

"Because the closer it gets to his release date, the more I wonder if you're setting yourself up for some pretty big disappointment. And by disappointment, I mean soul-crushing heartbreak."

I crossed my arms.

"Grace, it's not an unfounded concern. The last time you saw him, he broke up with you."

"Why did I ever tell you that?"

"Because I got you drunk."

I rolled my eyes. "Damn you."

"I'm just worried about you. You have this whole thing built up in your mind, and what if he gets out and you realize he meant it?"

"Do you think I haven't considered that? I think about it all the time. But Cara, I know him. I know us. When he gets out, it's going to be hard. Really hard. He won't be the same, and I'm not either. But he and I..."

"You're soulmates? Meant to be? Predestined? Star-crossed lovers?"

"Not that last one, I hope. Isn't that Romeo and Juliet? They both die."

"True, but it can also refer to lovers for whom the stars aren't aligning. That's definitely you."

"Isn't that the truth."

She hung a left at the post office and slowed so we could wave at Harvey Johnston. His beard was gray and scraggly, and he wore dusty work clothes. His disheveled appearance and befuddled demeanor often led people to believe he was homeless. But he lived in a cabin outside town and seemed to take care of himself well enough. He was just odd.

I liked him. "Hey, Harvey."

With a wide grin, he waved back.

"Look, Asher loves his family," I continued. "He's not doing this to be an asshole or because he doesn't care. He's doing it to survive. That's the only reason he'd cut everyone off like this. Even Gram said so. He wouldn't do it unless he felt like he had no other choice."

"And that's why he said he had to break up with you. He felt he had no choice."

"You know, the way you said that, I can't tell if you're being sarcastic or not. But yes, that's exactly why he said he had to break up with me. And really, it wasn't a breakup, it was an argument. We got in a fight seven years ago and haven't had the chance to finish it."

She laughed.

I nudged her with my elbow. "Why are you laughing at me? Don't be a jerk."

"I'm not, promise. I just had a sudden vision of him coming home and the first thing you do is pick a fight with him."

She wasn't far off. When Asher got home, he and I were going to have words.

After fucking each other's brains out approximately seven million times.

God, I missed him.

She slowed in front of my house and pulled to a stop. "I will say this, I'll always admire your loyalty."

"Thanks."

"I'm sorry I suggested you take off the ring. Let's not fight. I can't leave if I think you're mad at me."

"You're so weird."

"I know. I can't help it, I had a horrible childhood."

I took off my seatbelt and leaned over to hug her. "I'm not mad at you."

"Thanks, boo."

"I'll meet you at the Caboose around eight?"

"Sounds good."

I grabbed my purse and went inside.

Countertop and cabinet door samples were spread across my living room floor. I'd forgotten I'd left those there last night. I'd bought this house about a year ago, and it had been in shambles. Totally unlivable after sitting vacant for years. But it had been nothing some hard work couldn't repair. I still had a long way to go, but the living room, one bathroom, and one bedroom were totally remodeled. The kitchen was usable, although there were no doors on the cabinets and the linoleum floor was hideous. But it worked. I'd been able to move in a few months ago.

There were challenges to living in a construction zone, but I didn't mind. And when I needed a break, I could always go to Cara's for a few days.

Since I'd agreed to go out tonight—which meant I wouldn't be spending my evening on the couch in pajamas with a glass of wine—I showered, did my hair, and put on some makeup. Afterward, I wandered into the kitchen to make myself a quick dinner.

Unfortunately, my fridge was mostly empty. Damn. I'd been planning on roping Cara into running errands with me today, but she'd surprised me with the spa day instead. Not that I was complaining. But now I needed to go to the store.

I grabbed my keys and purse and headed out the door, deciding to swing by my mom's and pick up my little brother. He'd probably like a reason to get out of the house.

And if not, I'd bribe him with candy or something. Moody eleven-year-olds still liked candy, right?

My house was less than a mile from my childhood home. The car bumped along the private drive. Mom's car wasn't parked outside, but Jack's police cruiser was. A few years ago, she'd married Jack Cordero, former Seattle cop turned chief deputy in the county sheriff's office. It had been a bit strange to gain a stepdad in my mid-twenties, especially since my mom had never been married before, not even to my father. But Jack was a great guy who adored her.

I loved that she was finally happy. That she'd found someone who treated her right. Unlike my asshole father—who, in a twist of irony, was also in prison.

On paper, I looked like a girl who ought to be rife with daddy issues. Engaged to a man serving eight years for manslaughter; father in prison for drug trafficking. Yep, that Grace Miles sure had her life together.

But the truth was, my father had never been a big part of my life. There had been brief periods in my childhood when he'd been a regular visitor. But for the most part, he hadn't been around. About five years ago, I'd discovered why: He was married with four other children. My mom hadn't known, and until I'd tracked him down for going deadbeat dad on Elijah, they hadn't known about us.

Now I had three half-brothers and a half-sister who all lived about thirty minutes away. Thankfully, none of them took after the man who'd fathered us. I loved my new family. They were amazing.

Life took unexpected turns sometimes.

I parked next to Jack's car, but my gaze strayed to Gram's house. I wondered if she needed anything at the store. Since I was going, I might as well ask if I could pick up anything for her.

I walked across the grass and up the porch stairs. Gram's house never seemed to change. Same wrap-around front porch that creaked beneath your feet. Front door always painted a cheerful yellow. Yellow shutters to match. Her gardens were legendary, producing more fruit and vegetables than some small farms.

This place felt as much like home as my mom's house did. I had countless memories of sitting at Gram's kitchen table with the boys, my legs swinging while we ate cookies or blueberry muffins. Gram had acres of land and I'd spent most of my childhood roaming with Asher. Playing in the creek, building forts, making up stories and games. It had been a good life.

The front door was unlocked, as usual, so I let myself in and heard water running in the kitchen.

"Hey, Gram," I called as I walked down the hallway toward the back of the house. "I'm going to the store. Do you need any—" Letting out a quick shriek, I stopped in my tracks.

A man stood at the sink. Short dark hair. Broad back and wide shoulders rippling with muscle. Thick, tattooed arms.

I recognized some of those tattoos. But it couldn't be.

He shut off the water and turned, his eyes meeting mine.

Oh my god.

My breath caught in my throat, and for a second, I couldn't speak.

It was Asher.

Or someone who'd once been Asher. This man was thick and hard with a little piece of medical tape over a fresh cut on his forehead. My eyes swept up and down, taking him in. He looked so different.

But it was him. He was standing right here.

He stared at me, a deep groove between his eyebrows,

his eyes flashing with alarm. Why was he looking at me like that? His mouth opened, like he was about to say something, but he closed it again.

Finally, I managed to get a word out. "Asher?"

"What are you doing here?" His voice was gravelly, almost monotone.

"*Me*? What are *you* doing here?"

"I was released."

I faltered again, sputtering for a second before I could get my voice to work. "You were... What? Why didn't anyone call me? When did you get here?"

He didn't answer. Just stared at me like he couldn't believe what he was seeing.

This was not the way I'd always envisioned this moment. I'd planned to be there when he got out so I could meet him outside the prison gates and launch myself into his arms.

Instead, we were standing in Gram's kitchen, staring at each other like neither of us knew what to do.

"Oh my god, what am I doing?" I stepped forward, ready to throw my arms around his neck.

But he held a hand out to stop me. "Don't."

I flinched backward like he'd slapped me. "What?"

"I can't."

"You can't what?"

"I can't do this yet."

"You can't do what? I don't understand."

"Fuck," he muttered. Looking down, he gripped the counter behind him, like he needed to brace himself to keep from falling. "You need to go."

"You can't be serious. Asher—"

"Please," he said through gritted teeth. He closed his eyes like he was in pain. "Please go."

Memories of the last time we'd spoken came rushing

back. When he'd said it was over. When he'd told me I had to let him go.

He was home, and he wanted me to leave?

Sadness and anger warred to be the first to rip free from my chest, and the resulting struggle choked off my reply. Feeling like the world had just flipped upside down, I turned around and walked out.

4

ASHER

I couldn't calm down.

The wood floor creaked beneath my feet as I paced around my old bedroom, trying to ward off the panic. My heart beat too fast and adrenaline singed me from the inside. I balled my hands into fists, trembling with agitation. One step from losing it.

I wanted to hit something.

Why had she come here? Why today?

I'd only been home for a couple of hours. When I'd arrived, Gram had acted like I'd been gone for a long weekend, not spent seven years behind bars. She'd smiled and hugged me tight, then told me to carry my own stuff up to my room.

My brothers had wanted to stay to celebrate, but she'd saved me the trouble of telling them no fucking way. The last thing I needed right now was to have to pretend I was fine. That I was the old Asher they all remembered, ready to jump back into the life I'd left behind.

I felt like I'd been living in another world, and I'd just

been dropped into the middle of this one with nothing but the clothes on my back.

Which wasn't far from the truth.

Once Gram had chased my brothers out, the familiarity of this house had helped ground me. The shutters and front door were still painted yellow. The floors still squeaked in the same places. It still smelled like fresh laundry and baking bread.

Still smelled like home.

The quiet had given me a chance to think. To slow down and get my head together. And I'd come up with a new plan.

My eight-year plan had been tossed out the window with my visit to the warden. That plan had consisted of barriers and mental armor designed to enable me to survive. And when my sentence was almost over, I'd intended to break those down enough to reconnect with my family before I went home. I would read all the letters I'd received to catch up on the details of life in Tilikum. Talk to my brothers on the phone. I'd use the final weeks behind bars to get ready to face life on the outside.

It had never occurred to me that I'd get out early.

So I'd made a new plan. I'd hunker down here for a little while. Take a few days to get my bearings. Catch up on life from the safety of Gram's house. I would read everyone's letters, ask questions, spend time with my brothers. When I was ready, I'd widen my circle. Hear more news. Venture out and see what had changed. Let people find out I was home.

But then Grace had walked in and blown my new plan to pieces.

She wasn't supposed to be here yet. I wasn't ready.

I kept pacing, trying to resist the urge to put my fist through a wall. I craved the pain—wanted to smash my knuckles against something solid.

Wanted to fight.

That urge heightened the sense of panic threatening to overtake me. I wasn't in prison anymore. I couldn't just hit something—or someone. Feeling my fist sink into someone's gut or crack across their jaw might have brought temporary relief. But I couldn't live like that here.

I didn't want to admit it, but deep down, I knew why I was so out of control. For seven years, I'd existed within the confines of a rigid set of rules. I'd had structure. Routine. And the sudden and unexpected loss of that routine had me teetering on edge.

Freedom was supposed to feel good, but right now, it just felt like chaos. Like there wasn't anything solid beneath my feet.

Why did she have to come today, of all days? When I was still reeling from the shock of being released?

I stopped pacing and leaned one arm against the window frame. Closed my eyes and took a few deep breaths, trying to force calmness into my body. To slow my racing heart. But when I opened my eyes, the first thing I saw was Grace's old bedroom window.

Fuck.

I grabbed the curtain in a tight fist and was about to yank it closed—and probably rip it off the wall—when Gram's voice came from the doorway.

"Hey, Bear."

I slowly unclenched my fist, letting go of the curtain.

Her hair was in the same thick braid she'd worn for as long as I could remember. It was mostly gray now. The lines on her face had deepened, but her dark brown eyes were still sharp and clear.

"It's been a day." She sat on the edge of my old twin bed, then patted the mattress next to her. "Come on, now."

The angry, wounded little boy inside me responded to the soothing tone of her voice. I obeyed, sitting on the bed beside her.

"You take your time, Bear."

I leaned forward with my forearms on my thighs and raked my fingers through my hair. "Yeah."

"I mean it. Slow down and breathe."

"I'm trying."

She didn't say anything for a long moment, but her quiet presence helped. My heart rate slowed, and the sense of panic began to recede.

"Sometimes what we need is a place to fall apart. A place where we know our pieces will be safe while we work on putting them back together." She patted my leg. "You're safe here, Bear."

Squeezing my eyes shut, I swallowed back the rush of emotion that welled up inside me—feelings I'd buried for so long. Anger and aggression had been my constant companions—them, and boredom. But things like love and gratitude were foreign—feelings I barely recognized.

Gram didn't say anything while I fought to pull myself together. While my mind reeled and my heart squeezed tight in my chest. I felt guilt for not being happy. Worry that I couldn't handle this. And fear that I was too fucked up to be home.

That I was going to take everyone down with me.

Gradually, my breathing returned to normal. Opening my eyes, I straightened and wiped my palms on my pants.

Now that I wasn't lost in a haze of panic, it dawned on me that my side of the room was full of stuff. Growing up, I'd shared this room with Evan. His side was now empty. There was a comforter on the bed, but it wasn't the quilt he'd used when he lived here. It looked new, with matching pillows, like it had been done up for guests. His shelves and bedside table were bare. No oversize clothes or size thirteen shoes lying on the floor.

My side almost looked like someone lived here. The handmade blue quilt I'd used as a kid was still on the bed. Shelves were filled with sports awards and trophies that I'd left behind when I moved out. There were college textbooks and old spiral notebooks. My volunteer firefighter uniform hung in the closet, next to my old letterman's jacket. Boxes marked *Asher* were stacked against the wall, and my old alarm clock—the obnoxiously loud one Gram had bought me sophomore year so I'd quit oversleeping—sat on the bedside table.

Beside that was a framed photo of me and Grace. It had been in my apartment, before.

"Did you keep all my stuff?"

"Most of it. If I recall, you had some condiments in your fridge that we threw out. But other than that, most of it's here."

"Why didn't you just get rid of it? Or put it in storage or something?"

"I liked having it here."

I wasn't sure what to say to that. I supposed it made sense.

"Grace did, too."

It was hard to hear her name, but I wasn't about to tell Gram not to say it. "What?"

"I think she liked having your things here, too. Now and then, when she was visiting her mom, she'd come up and sit for a while."

Leaning forward again, I scrubbed my hands up and

down my face. I needed more time before finding out the truth about Grace. Time to prepare myself to hear about her life.

She was so fucking beautiful. It had hurt to look at her.

I wasn't ready to talk about her, and yet I couldn't stop myself from asking—from continuing the conversation. "Why would she do that?"

"I suppose it brought her a little comfort. Made her feel like she was still connected to you. It wasn't an easy thing for any of us to live through."

"Gram, I'm so sorry—"

"Don't you dare." She cut me off, and her voice had an edge to it. "Sending you away was wrong, plain and simple. There was no justice in it. So I don't want to hear you apologize to me or anyone in this family. Not for that."

She was wrong. I had a lot to apologize for. But I wasn't going to argue with her.

"You do need to apologize to Grace, though."

I grunted. Great. She'd probably heard everything with her superhuman ears.

"Don't talk to me like a caveman."

"Gram, I can't."

"Can't tell her you're sorry for running her off like that? Of course you can."

"No, I can't see her yet."

She patted my leg again. "It won't be as bad as you think."

Judging by the way I'd felt when I saw her downstairs, I wasn't so sure. "I don't know."

"Well, I do. But you take your time just the same. You've been through more than your share, and no one's going to blame you if it takes a while for you to get your feet under you. But you will."

I wasn't sure about that, either. "Thanks. And Gram?"

"Yes?"

"Thanks for letting me stay."

"Like I said, everyone needs a safe place sometimes. And my cubs can always come home."

5

GRACE

*W*ell, *that* had been a freaking nightmare.

Blindsided and dazed, I left Gram's house, wondering what the hell had just happened. My phone rang, but I ignored it. I didn't trust myself to speak yet.

It rang again before I got home. This time I checked. Levi. The missed call had been Evan. They were probably calling to tell me Asher was home, but I didn't want to talk to anyone with the last name Bailey right now. I'd call them back when I was calm.

I parked in my driveway and when I got out of the car, a memory flashed through my mind, so vivid it took my breath away. Me, standing in front of this house after Asher had told me he was taking the plea bargain and going to prison. After he'd told me I needed to let him go.

Without thinking about it, I'd driven here. Parked outside the then-abandoned house and started throwing things. Rocks, sticks, pinecones. I'd thrown everything I could find, desperate for an outlet for my anger and pain.

I felt like doing it again. Letting my feelings out in a rush and throwing shit at my house. I picked up a pinecone and turned it over in my hand a few times, my eyes locked on the siding.

Then, another memory. The night Asher and I had taken a walk together. He'd held my hand and told me he loved me. Kissed me for the first time in front of this house. We'd said if we stayed together, we'd buy it and fix it up.

Make it a home.

With a deep breath, I dropped the pinecone. I locked my car and went inside. Without bothering to take off my shoes, I fell onto the couch.

Asher was home.

I had so many questions, I didn't know where to begin. How had this happened? Why had no one told me? Most importantly, why was I here, feeling like shit by myself, when Asher was less than a mile away?

He'd said he couldn't do this yet. Couldn't do what? See me? Why?

There was something very wrong about the fact that he was home and I wasn't currently wrapped around him like a pretzel.

I felt sick to my stomach. I'd just been hit in the face with every fear I'd ever had about Asher's homecoming. Every worry I'd tried to set aside—tried to kill with stubborn belief.

The fear that he'd meant it when he'd said we were over, and I'd been waiting for nothing.

My phone binged again. With a groan, I got up to check it.

Gram: *It'll be all right, Mama Bear. He just needs some time. Keep hanging in there for him.*

Letting out a long breath, I sank back onto the couch, staring at her text. I desperately wanted to believe her. Gram never told you what you wanted to hear. Sometimes she wrapped the truth in stories or metaphors that didn't make sense until later, but she didn't coddle anyone. If she said it would be all right, it was because she believed it.

Regardless, contemplating whether I'd just wasted the last seven years of my life waiting for a man who no longer wanted me was too much for my body to contain. I needed to do something with all this anxious energy. I texted Gram back to thank her, then dug out my safety goggles and a sledgehammer. There was a section of cabinet and countertop in the kitchen that needed to be taken out.

So I did what I always did when life was overwhelming. I got to work.

I HESITATED OUTSIDE THE CABOOSE, wondering if this was a good idea.

I'd finished smashing the cabinet and wound up with a few unintended holes in the drywall. But I'd decided not to get bent out of shape over it. Everything was fixable. That was one of the things I loved about remodeling that old house. It didn't matter how broken, old, or damaged something appeared. It could always be made new.

But spending my Saturday night alone with a sledgehammer probably wasn't the best idea, considering how awful I felt. A few holes in the drywall had almost turned into me spontaneously removing a wall—a wall I wasn't actually sure could *be* removed without compromising the integrity of the entire structure.

So I'd put the sledgehammer down and come out to meet Cara.

The Caboose hadn't changed much since I was a kid. It

still had a family-friendly restaurant that closed early on the weekends, and a bar separated by a half wall. Old railroad signs decorated the walls and model trains from Hank's extensive collection were displayed everywhere. And it still had the best onion rings in town.

As usual for a Saturday, it was packed. I spotted Cara at a table in the bar, her red hair loose around her shoulders. She sipped a drink, casually watching the people around her.

Absently, I wiped my hands on my jeans. Was it my imagination or were people staring at me? Had they already heard? Rumors spread through this town faster than summer wildfires, but this was ridiculous. It had only been a few hours.

Trying to ignore the eyes following me, I went to Cara's table.

"There's my sparkling moonbeam." She put down her drink. "But god, what happened to you?"

I dropped like a rock into the chair across from her. "I don't even know where to start."

"How about start with why you're wearing safety goggles. Then we can talk about..." She paused and gestured up and down. "All this."

I brought my hand to my face. Oh my god, I *was* still wearing safety goggles. No wonder everyone had been staring at me. I took them off and set them on the table.

She reached across and started wiping my forehead and running her fingers through the front of my hair, like a mother trying to clean up her filthy child. "Why are you so dirty?"

"I was doing demo."

"And you just dropped your tools and walked out of the

house without looking in the mirror? When are you going to let me hire you a contractor?"

"Never."

She stopped fussing with my hair. "Boo, what's wrong? You look like you saw a ghost or something."

"Asher came home."

"I'm sorry, what?"

"He's home."

"Are you drunk already? You didn't drive here, did you?"

"I'm not drunk."

Her mouth opened, but she hesitated. "Asher as in Bailey?"

I nodded.

"What the fuck are you talking about?"

"I saw him at Gram's."

She pushed her drink across the table. "Drink this, then keep talking, because I'm lost."

I picked up her gin and tonic and took a long swallow. "He's at Gram's house. I don't know why. I saw him and then I went home and almost took out a wall with a sledgehammer."

Leaning back in her chair, she looked over her shoulder toward the bar and wiggled her fingers. "Hank? We need something stronger over here. Immediately."

"He was in the kitchen," I said. My voice didn't sound like me. "And he told me to leave."

Her face went stony. "What?"

"He said he can't do this yet. And then told me to go."

"So you went home and started breaking things?"

"Basically."

"Can't argue with that." She took a deep breath. "Okay, I wasn't prepared for this level of damage control tonight, but we'll improvise."

Hank arrived at our table and slid two shots of what looked like whiskey in front of us.

"Perfect, Hank, you're a gem." She gave him a bright smile, but something behind me caught her attention, and her expression melted into a glare. "Oh great, just what we need. Prince dickhead."

Logan pulled out the chair next to me and plopped down, setting his beer on the table.

"That seat's taken," Cara said.

Logan scowled at her, then shifted so he was facing me. "Has Evan talked to you yet? He said he was going to call."

"I saw Asher."

He held my gaze for a second, nodding slowly, as if he could guess how it had gone. "Well, shit."

"Why didn't anyone tell me?"

"We didn't know until the last minute. Gram got a call this morning and she sent us out to get him. Hell, it wasn't until we were halfway there that I woke up enough to realize what was going on. I'd just gotten off a twenty-four-hour shift when Levi started banging on my door saying we had to go. Anyway, Evan said he'd call you."

"He did, but it was after I'd been there. Levi did too, but I haven't called them back. It was just... I don't know."

Logan winced. "What did Ash say to you?"

"Very little, and none of it good."

"Damn it. I'm sorry, Grace. He's pretty messed up. I think the whole thing caught him off guard and he's not dealing with it very well."

"What happened? How did he get out early? I didn't think that was even a possibility."

"None of us did, even him. But get this. You aren't the only one that scum-bucket attacked. Apparently he assaulted a girl before you, and she happens to be the new governor's niece. I wish I knew how it all went down, but the bottom line is, the governor found out about Asher somehow and I guess he said fuck that, and told them to let Asher out."

"The governor does have the power to grant clemency," Cara said. "Usually it requires a hearing and then a review by a committee. Although technically, he could issue an executive order."

I glanced at Cara, trying to push away the sick feeling I got at Logan's use of the word *assaulted*. I didn't like thinking about that. "How do you know all that?"

"Your fiancé was in prison. I did some research to find out if there were any strings I could pull."

"Of course you did."

Logan looked at Cara with confusion, or maybe surprise. "Anyway, Ash had no idea he was coming home, and the guy's been locked up for years. I mean, you saw him. He looked like he'd been in a brawl right before they let him out."

"Yeah, he was hurt. Did he say anything about not wanting to see me?"

"He wouldn't even let us talk about you. Gavin asked if we'd called you yet and Ash looked like he wanted to break him in half."

"Okay, that's it," Cara said. "Where is he right now, because I'm going to go talk to this guy and—"

"Cara." I reached across the table and put my hand on hers. "Retract the claws, honey."

"No, this is fucked up."

"Stay out of it," Logan said.

"Excuse me? Your asshole brother comes home after seven years of not speaking to my best friend and the first thing he does is tell her to leave? I don't fucking think so."

"Watch who you're calling asshole. You don't even know him."

"I don't have to; I can smell an asshole ten miles away. Speaking of, you're ruining the ambiance with your douchebag cologne. Maybe cool it on the Axe body spray."

He waved his hand in front of his face. "Pretty sure that's you. Even your rich-bitch perfume can't mask the scent of evil."

"Eat my dick, Logan."

"Will you two shut up?" I snapped. "You're not helping."

Logan cast another glare at Cara. She flipped him off.

I rolled my eyes at both of them, although their bickering was waking me up from my stupor.

"Just give him a little time," Logan said. "You saw him. He's fucked up right now."

"Yeah, that's what Gram said, too. The time thing, I mean. She didn't say fucked up." I eyed the whiskey. "I don't know what to do."

"If you can trust anyone, it's Gram," Logan said. "Even Scarlet Fever over there can't argue with that."

Cara rolled her eyes again.

I took a deep breath. He wasn't wrong. I could trust Gram, and if she said it would be okay, maybe it would. Maybe he just needed some time.

Logan rubbed my back a few times. "Hang in there, kiddo. Asher's still in there. He's all big and prison-scary right now, but with a little Tilikum therapy, he'll be fine. Gram will stuff him with pie, we'll go fuck with the Havens a little, then have a few beers around a bonfire. He'll come back."

"I'm sure spending time with *you* will be great for him," Cara said, her voice thick with sarcasm.

Logan swiveled in his chair. "I swear to god, Cara—"

"Shut up, Logan."

"Oh my god, will you two go beat the crap out of each other outside or fuck in the bathroom or something? You're driving me crazy."

Logan smirked. "Nah, bathrooms are gross. Supply closet, maybe."

"I wouldn't fuck you if you were the last dick in a ten-thousand-mile radius."

He put his forearm on the table and leaned toward her. "That's okay. Gram always says don't stick your dick in crazy."

I smacked Logan's arm. "Gram never said that."

"Not in so many words, but the message was there."

Cara reached across the table and took my hand in hers. I could see her pretending Logan was no longer here. "What do you need? Tacos? Ice cream? Or maybe something more direct. Give me an hour, and I can get my hands on a taser."

"No tasers."

"Are you sure? I don't care how big and scary he is, he'll drop like a rag doll."

"Cray-zee," Logan muttered under his breath.

"I'm sure I don't want a taser. I might take you up on the ice cream, though."

She pushed the whiskey toward me. "I'm on it. In the meantime, drink this."

"Fine." I tossed back the shot and winced. It burned going down.

"Good job, boo." She got up, flashing a glare at Logan. With a little flip of her red hair, she shouldered her purse and headed for the door. In search of ice cream, apparently. Knowing her, she'd bring it right in and sweet-talk Hank into letting us eat it here. Of course, he was used to her. He also knew how well she tipped.

Logan's eyes narrowed, but he was totally watching her ass while she walked away.

"She looks good in those jeans, doesn't she?"

Logan chewed his bottom lip, then blinked. "What? No."

"Right."

He shook himself, like he was getting rid of a disturbing image, then patted my leg. "Don't worry. It's the first day. We'll get him back."

"Thanks, Logan."

He leaned closer to kiss my forehead, then ruffled my hair. "You should think about showering before you go out in public, though. You're a mess."

"Thanks for the tip."

"Anytime."

He took his beer and left.

I slumped back in my chair and fiddled with the empty shot glass. My stomach was warm from the whiskey, but the hollow space in my heart was awfully cold. I'd thought Asher's release would mean the end of our ordeal, not the beginning of another.

Apparently, I'd been wrong.

6

ASHER

My eyes flew open and I jerked awake. For a few seconds, I had no idea where I was. Narrow bed, but the sheets were soft. Light peeked in through gaps in a curtain.

Right. I was home.

Sitting up, I swung my legs over the edge of the bed, feeling the cool wood on my bare feet. I took a deep breath and tried to ground myself in the solid wood floor. There would be no cafeteria today. No scuffles or jockeying for space. No fights in the yard.

I could close the fucking door when I went to the bathroom, and it was amazing how much that felt like a luxury.

After a hot shower, I dug through my old clothes and found a t-shirt and some jeans. The jeans didn't fit over my thighs—apparently I'd put on some size. The shirt was tight, but it would work, and I found a pair of sweats that fit.

I needed all new clothes. In fact, I needed just about everything. I didn't have a phone or a car. Everything I owned fit in one half of my old bedroom. Of course, I didn't have any money, either. I'd have to do something about that, too.

Once again, I had the strange sensation that I'd been living in another world and had suddenly been dropped back into this one with nothing.

Downstairs, I found Gram at the kitchen sink. She hung her mug on a hook and gave me a warm smile.

"Morning," I said.

"Did you sleep?"

"Yeah, I did."

"Good. Help yourself to some breakfast if you're hungry. The keys to Grandad's truck are on the hook if you need to go somewhere. Don't be thinking you can take my car."

I chuckled a little. She'd always been adamant that her car was hers alone, and she'd never let any of us drive it. We'd all had to learn to drive Grandad's old truck—a 1960 Ford F-100. It was a beast, and we'd had to become amateur mechanics just to keep it running. But it had gotten us around.

"Thanks. Does it still run?"

"It might. The boys take it out now and again to keep it working." She shrugged, then her eyes narrowed. "You remember how to drive?"

"I think so. I'm sure it'll come back to me."

"All right, Bear. I need to go feed my peckers."

I tried, and failed, to suppress a laugh.

"What?" she asked.

"Nothing. Enjoy feeding your chickens."

She patted my arm, then headed for the back door. "Your shirt's too small."

I cracked a smile as she walked out the back door. "I know, Gram," I said quietly to myself. "A lot of things don't fit anymore."

I poked around the kitchen for breakfast, glad she hadn't been down here cooking for me. Her assumption that I could fend for myself was reassuring. I made some eggs and toast, and the normalcy of that simple task made the ground beneath my feet feel a little steadier.

After breakfast, I went out to the shop next to the house to see if the truck would start.

The shop was big with room to park—and work on—the truck, plus Grandad's old woodworking area. He'd built half the furniture in the house out here.

I opened one of the garage bay doors. Inside, it still smelled like sawdust, wood stain, and engine oil. Tools hung on pegs on the wall and old parts and supplies cluttered the shelves. There was probably half of a second truck in pieces with all the stuff we'd picked up at junkyards over the years.

Grandad's truck was two-tone white and blue. It had some rust and wear, and there were dings on the body. It had always been a working truck, not something for show. I just hoped it ran. Otherwise I was going to need a plan B. Or a better pair of shoes, because I'd be doing a lot of walking.

I got in—the bench seat wasn't any more comfortable than I remembered—and turned the key. The engine roared, the sound vibrating through me. I revved it a few times, enjoying the throaty sound.

It was loud, but it ran.

After turning it off, I spent some time making sure it didn't need any immediate attention. Checked the oil, tinkered with a few things. It had been a long time since I'd gotten my hands greasy under the hood, and it felt good. Normal.

I wiped my hands on a rag and closed the hood. The back of my neck prickled and I glanced over my shoulder. It kind of felt like I was being watched, but I didn't see anyone.

That was weird.

I closed the garage and went inside to clean up. There was a little note stuck to the key hook, Gram's cursive handwriting in blue ink—a note with an address.

I pulled off the note and hung the key on the hook. I didn't need to ask her whose address it was. It had to be Grace.

Subtle, Gram. Very subtle.

But she was right. I needed to go see her. I felt bad for how I'd reacted yesterday. Terrible, actually. It wasn't her fault I was such a fucking wreck.

Ignoring the knot of dread that sat in my gut, I went upstairs to change.

THE TRUCK RUMBLED to a stop and I looked at Gram's note again. Was this the right place? I knew this street well—or I had once—but it looked different. Where was the abandoned house? None of these houses were half-buried in blackberry bushes. Had someone cleared it out? Or was I remembering the location wrong?

Wait. *This* was the abandoned house.

The note said Evergreen Street, but I hadn't thought it meant *this* house on Evergreen Street.

Holy shit. Had Grace bought it? How the hell had she done that?

The overgrown yard had been cleaned up and there were sheer curtains in the big front window. It still needed landscaping and paint, but it was clearly lived in. Which meant she had to have done a shit ton of work on it already.

I hadn't known.

This was a punch-in-the-gut reminder that I didn't know

anything about her anymore. Which was my fault. She'd written to me, but I hadn't read her letters. It had been part of my survival plan. The cornerstone of it, in some ways. Leaving Grace had been the most soul-crushing part of my ordeal. Staying in touch with her hadn't been an option.

Now I had to face her. See for myself what she'd done with her life after we'd ended. And apologize for being such a psycho yesterday.

With no idea what to expect, I got out of the truck, went to her front door, and knocked.

She opened the door dressed in an old Tilikum College t-shirt and jeans with holes in the knees. She had a pencil tucked behind her ear and her blond hair was shorter than it used to be. It looked great on her. In fact, she looked amazing.

Fuck, she was beautiful.

She slipped a tape measure into a tool belt strapped around her waist. "Um, hi?"

Damn it, I was standing here staring at her. "Sorry. Hi."

Her hand was on the door, like she wasn't sure if she was going to let me in. I didn't blame her.

"Can I come in?" I asked.

She eyed me for a second. I couldn't tell what she was thinking. Was she angry? Glad to see me? About to slam the door in my face?

"Sure," she said finally, and stepped aside.

I walked in and glanced around. The hardwood floors shone—they'd clearly been refinished. And the living room looked brand new—fresh paint, white baseboards and trim. She had a couch and two armchairs with a throw rug on the floor. All very cozy. All very Grace.

The rest of the house, from what I could see, was still in progress. She had a little table just outside the kitchen covered with tools and a stack of wood samples. The walls were rough and some had pencil marks on them, like she'd been taking measurements.

But overall, it was amazing. This place had been a shell. She was making it into a home.

It might have been our home, once.

The ache in my chest throbbed like a fresh wound. Fuck, this hurt. I needed to get this over with.

"I'm sure you're busy, so I won't keep you," I said. "I wanted to apologize for yesterday. I was overwhelmed and I obviously didn't handle it very well."

"Okay. Thank you." A little groove formed between her eyebrows as she watched me. "Do you want to sit down?"

I didn't want to sit down. I wanted to scoop her into my arms and hold her. Breathe her in and tell her how much I'd missed her. Tell her how a part of me had died every day that I'd had to spend without her. Soothe this ache with the warmth of her body.

But I couldn't. She wasn't mine anymore.

"Sure."

She gestured to the couch and I took a seat. She took off her tool belt, then sat in an armchair, tucking her bare feet beneath her.

"The house looks amazing," I said. "I didn't recognize it from the outside."

"Thanks. I thought I'd have more of it done before you saw it for the first time. But it's coming along."

"It's beautiful."

She smiled. "I'm sorry I keep staring. I just can't believe you're sitting here. Are you sure you're okay?" She gestured to my forehead. "That looks like it hurts."

I shook my head. "No, it's fine."

Her eyes darted to my knuckles. My hands twitched. Part

of me wanted to shove my hands in my pockets so she wouldn't look. But another part knew she needed to see.

"I talked to Logan last night," she said. "He told me the basics. How you got out early."

"Yeah, no one saw that coming. I was totally focused on making it another year. And suddenly, here I am."

"Here you are."

I glanced away and rubbed the back of my neck. Being this close to her was getting to me. Her voice was so soft, her lips so full. I could still remember what those lips tasted like. What her skin felt like against mine.

Fuck. I needed to stop thinking about getting her naked. What the hell was wrong with me? I searched for a quick way to change the subject.

"So when did you buy this place?"

"What?"

The confusion in her voice made me look up. "I just wondered when you bought it."

"About a year ago." The groove between her eyebrows was back. "You didn't know I bought the house?"

Damn it, what was I thinking? Her letters. She would have told me in one of her letters. God, how was I going to explain this?

"No, I didn't."

"Did they hold your mail, or..."

"No. I got your letters. I just haven't read them yet."

Her lips parted and the hurt in her eyes was like a knife to the chest. "You didn't read my letters? Any of them?"

"Look, I know how awful that sounds."

"Yeah, it's pretty bad. Why?"

"It's hard to explain. Prison was a fucking nightmare and staying connected to the outside world didn't help. It made it worse. I was just doing what I had to do to get through it."

"Is that why you wouldn't accept visitors?"

"Yeah. It was like having a wound scab over, only to rip it open again. I wouldn't have survived in there if I was bleeding all the time. They'd have eaten me alive."

She took a shaky breath. "Okay, so you don't... you don't know anything that's happened in the last seven years?"

"I know some, but not a lot."

"Did you read anybody's letters? Or was it just mine that you tossed out?"

"No, and I didn't toss them. I kept every single one." I leaned forward, feeling frantic. Desperate to make her understand. Desperate not to let this be another way I hurt her. "I had a plan. When my release date got close, I was going to read them, start to finish. I figured it would help me prepare."

"But you got out early."

"Yeah."

"Wow. I feel like such an idiot. I had all these stupid daydreams about you reading my letters and thinking of me, and it never happened. God, I wasn't even close."

"Grace, I'm sorry."

She got up and wandered over to the window. "You know, I didn't want to have it out with you right off the bat, but apparently Cara was right. You get home, and the first thing we're going to do is fight."

"Cara?"

"My best friend."

"Oh."

"I want to understand. I really, really do. I've spent seven years defending you, insisting there's a reason you cut yourself off from everyone you love. I get the survival thing. I can't even imagine what it was like in there, and I don't want to minimize that. But you gave me *nothing*. You walked out of that courtroom without looking back and then, nothing."

"I know, I—"

"No, you don't know. And neither do I. Neither of us have a clue about each other right now. Because you cut me out of your life without giving me a say in it."

"What was I supposed to do?" I stood, fighting to keep from raising my voice, but I was holding onto my self-control by a very thin thread. "Drag myself through the pain of everything I lost, over and over?"

"I could have helped you through it. Damn it, I knew I should have camped outside that fucking prison and gone in every day until you finally got over your stubborn ass and came out to see me."

"Why? So I could have an in-my-face reminder of how fucked my life was?"

"You didn't have to go through it alone."

"Yes, I did."

"You were never alone, Asher. I know I wasn't there, and what you had to deal with was so much worse than me. But I had to live through it too."

I stared at her as the truth dawned on me. All this time I'd been afraid of how it would feel to find out what Grace had done with her life. Because I'd always assumed she'd taken off my ring. That she'd moved on and found someone new. Maybe gotten married and started a family. And I'd never quite known what would be worse—to find out she had or find out she hadn't.

Forcing my gaze down, I looked at her hands. She wore several rings—left thumb, right index finger, both ring fingers. But the one on the ring finger of her left hand...

"You're still wearing my ring."

She lifted her hand, extending her fingers, and looked

down at the ring. Her eyes flicked up to meet mine, her gaze fierce. "Yes."

The weight of that little gold band threatened to crush me. She hadn't taken it off. I'd told her it was over, that she had to let me go, and she hadn't listened.

I was going to have to break her heart all over again. Because she didn't understand. I couldn't marry her. Not now.

"Why?" I choked out.

"Are you serious?" She put her hands on her hips. Before I could answer, she continued. "Go home, Asher."

"What?"

"You saved the letters? You brought them with you?"

"Yeah."

"Then go home and read them."

"But—"

"Go."

I shut my mouth at the sharpness in her tone. I deserved that.

Without another word, I did what she asked and left.

I drove back to Gram's feeling like shit. Anger bubbled up from deep inside. But I wasn't angry at Grace. I was angry at everything but Grace.

Gram's car was gone when I got back. I went upstairs, straight to the box I'd brought home with me. The only thing I'd had worth keeping.

I took it to the bed and sat, leaning my back against the wall, and popped the lid open. I'd kept them in order, always placing the newest one at the front. I trailed my fingers along crisp envelopes. Different sizes and thicknesses. They'd all been opened. Read by prison staff. Then put away in the box.

My occasional calls to Gram meant I'd known the highlights of life back home. Gavin had graduated high school. Evan had moved back to Tilikum. Levi and Logan had been hired by the fire department. There had been wildfires one summer—pretty bad ones—but I'd known everyone was safe. I knew about the fall Gram had taken a few years ago, and that she hadn't broken anything. Knew she'd stayed healthy.

Nothing about Grace, though. I hadn't needed to ask Gram to avoid talking about her. Our conversations had been brief, just enough for me to let her know I was alive. Gram had seemed to understand what I'd needed.

At the very back of the box was the first letter I'd received. I'd kept it beneath my mattress until I'd managed to get the box. Then I'd carefully tucked it inside. Every time I'd gotten a letter, from anyone, I'd added it to the stack. Always torn between the pain of not knowing, and the reality of my need to survive on the inside. The quicker the letters made it into the box, the better. Anything else had made me weak, and weakness had been something I hadn't been able to afford. Not for a second.

With a deep breath, I took out the first letter and pulled it from the envelope. Gently opened it, smoothing out the creases.

My eyes tracked the words on the page, moving over Grace's smooth handwriting. And when I got to the end—it wasn't very long—I could only think one thing.

Fuck.

DEAR ASHER

ear Asher,

I'M STILL NOT sure how to begin this letter. I think I've started it a dozen times. You should see the pile of crumpled paper in the garbage can next to my desk. It's ridiculous. But nothing seems right. What am I supposed to do, ask you how you've been?

I'll just get straight to the point...

Fuck you, Asher.

I'm sorry to pick a fight with you right now, of all times. But you are not breaking up with me.

I understand why you said the things you did. I realize you're trying to do what you think is best for me, and I appreciate that. I really do.

But no, I will not take off your ring. No, I will not find someone else. No, I will not move on. No, I will not let you go.

That's not how this works.

You are what's best for me. I love you, and I've loved you for most of my life. That hasn't changed, and it isn't going to.

This is not the end of our life together. This is a great big, soul-sucking, heart-wrenching tragedy. But it will only ruin us if we let it. And I refuse to let that happen.

Your only job right now is to survive. Don't let them break you. Do what you have to do to get through each day. I'm counting on you to make it through to the end.

I'll be out here, doing the same thing.

And let me be perfectly clear about this, Asher Bailey. I'm not going anywhere. Eight years is an interruption, not a lifetime. We can survive this. I realize nothing will ever be the same. You'll be different, and so will I.

But when you walk out those prison doors, you'll come home to me. I'll be waiting for you, with your ring still on my finger.

LOVE ALWAYS,

Grace

7

ASHER

J sat on the bed, surrounded by envelopes and creased sheets of paper, still reading by the soft glow of a lamp. A breeze of cool night air blew in through the open window, whispering through the pages. I grabbed one before it could fall to the floor and set it carefully back on the quilt.

It was nearly midnight, and I'd been reading for hours, leaving my eyes dry and gritty. But I couldn't stop. Every time I put one down, I found myself taking out the next.

I'd missed so much.

It felt like reaching back through time, each letter offering another glimpse into a world that had kept turning without me. And even though I was sitting in my childhood bedroom, no longer locked behind bars and kept from all the people I loved, reading them still fucking hurt.

I embraced the pain—let the words of the past wound me.

Most of the letters were from the first year or so of my sentence. A lot of people had written to me in the beginning, not just Grace. Friends, extended family, fellow firefighters, guys from the gym. There were notes of support, cards with quotes about struggle and perseverance.

As time had gone on and I hadn't replied to anyone, the letters had slowed. Some people, like Chief Stanley, seemed to have either understood or quickly given up on me. He'd sent me one letter, then hadn't written again. A lot of them had done the same.

I appreciated the notes of support, but Grace's letters were the ones that held me captive, twisting the knife of loss and guilt in my chest.

She'd written to me frequently in the first year. After that, the time between her letters had gradually lengthened. I'd been aware of that, although I hadn't allowed myself the space to contemplate what it meant. In the back of my mind, I'd assumed it was because she was busy living her life. That, and the fact that I hadn't replied. But in those brief moments each morning, when I'd let myself think about the outside, I'd envisioned her moving forward. Happy without me.

I'd desperately needed to believe in those visions. Despite what it had cost me to lose her, I'd needed to believe she was okay.

But nothing had turned out the way I'd thought. And despite the way it made my chest ache, I forced myself to read through the last seven years of Grace's life.

She'd gone back to school at Tilikum College and finished her business degree. Then worked at a couple of different places before taking over the Steaming Mug downtown. From the things she'd written, it sounded like she loved her job. She was the boss now, and had made a lot of improvements to the shop.

Damn, I was proud of her.

Gram had let me know when Elijah had been sick one

winter. I knew he'd been hospitalized with pneumonia, and ultimately recovered.

What I didn't know was that a year and a half later, Grace had gone looking for their deadbeat father to get help with Eli's medical bills, and discovered he already had a wife and four other kids.

It explained a lot, although it was still a shock. I'd never liked her father, but to find out Grace's mom had unknowingly been the other woman, and Grace and Elijah the secret family he'd tried to keep hidden? Holy shit.

And it only got worse from there. Now her father was in prison. Something about drug trafficking.

Jesus.

I hated that she'd gone through all this alone. That I hadn't been here.

She'd spent the last several years getting to know her half-siblings. There was a lot about them in her letters. They owned a winery in Echo Creek, about half an hour from here, and most of them worked there. She'd been a bridesmaid in weddings, and now she visited her nieces and nephews regularly. Her mom had even become friends with their mom, which I had to admit was pretty cool.

Naomi had gotten married to a cop a few years ago, which made me shift uncomfortably on the bed. Grace liked him, and I was glad for her mom. But he wasn't from around here, so I didn't know him—didn't know how he'd feel about me. The ex-con living next door.

Finally, I got to her letter about the house, sent about a year ago. Her excitement shone through the words on the page, and I couldn't stop thinking about the night we'd stood in front of that house together. The night I'd told her I loved her.

Or at least, the old Asher had.

Not that I'd ever stopped loving her. That wasn't possible. I would love Grace Miles until the day I died. But loving her wasn't enough anymore. Not with who—and what—I was now.

I looked down at my bruised hands and flexed my fists. I'd spent the last seven years thinking it was over. She'd spent those same years believing it wasn't.

Her version would have been better. The problem was, she'd been writing to a man who didn't exist anymore.

I wasn't the Asher Bailey who'd kissed her outside the abandoned house. I wasn't the man who'd given her that ring. I wasn't even the guy who'd stood in a courtroom while a judge handed down a sentence of eight years for manslaughter.

He was gone. I was the wreckage that was left.

A COUPLE OF HOURS LATER, I was still awake. I'd put the letters away—tucked them safely back in the box I'd kept them in—but sleep eluded me. I couldn't stop thinking about Grace. Her letters, and all the things I'd missed. That ring still on her finger.

The noise of a rumbling engine drifted through the open window. That was odd. No one else lived out here— just Gram, and Grace's family next door.

It didn't stop, or fade as if someone had driven by. Whoever it was, they were sitting outside Gram's house with the engine running.

I got up and tugged on some clothes, then crept downstairs, instinctively avoiding the spots where the wood floor creaked. The windows down here were shut, muffling the sound, but I could still hear it. I poked my head out the front door.

A pickup truck was stopped on the road out front. Logan leaned out the driver's side window and waved me over.

What the hell was he doing out here?

I had a feeling I might regret this, but I shoved on a pair of shoes and went outside.

"Hey, brosaurus, I'm glad you're up," Logan said, keeping his voice low. Gavin tipped his chin to me from the passenger's seat. "We were trying to figure out how to get your attention without waking Gram."

"It's the middle of the night. What are you doing?"

"Get in." He glanced at Gavin. "Gav, get in the back."

"Why can't he get in the back?"

"Dude, just do it. We'll need you back there anyway."

Groaning, Gavin got out and climbed into the bed of the truck.

"Come on, Ash. Get in."

"Why?"

"We have shit to do. Let's go."

I recognized the slight grin and mischievous gleam in Logan's eyes. He was up to something—which probably meant I should turn around and go back inside. But curiosity won out over good judgment. Besides, I couldn't sleep anyway. I went around to the passenger's side and got in.

Logan cautiously turned the truck around and drove back to the main road.

"Are you going to tell me what we're doing, or is this some kind of hazing thing?"

"Nah, no hazing. We thought you'd want to be in on this, since it's been a while."

"In on what?"

He glanced at me, his signature cocky grin plastered on his face. "You'll see."

Gavin knocked on the back window, so I slid it open.

"I should be driving. It's my truck."

"Quit your bitching," Logan said. "I'm a better driver than you."

"Like hell you are," Gavin said. "And it's cold as shit out here."

Logan glanced at him in the rear-view mirror. "Should have worn a coat, dumbass."

"Okay, mom."

"Do you see what I have to deal with?" Logan gestured behind him. "I handle all the logistics, and I still get crap from that one."

"You can't take credit for this. It was my idea. And a fucking brilliant one, I might add."

"We'll see."

"Credit for what?" I asked.

"Check under your seat," Logan said.

I reached beneath the seat and found a large manila envelope. It was already open, so I pulled out what looked like a stack of bumper stickers, only larger. They were green with white lettering.

"Bailey Street, Bailey Way, Bailey Avenue." I shuffled through them, finding multiples of each. "Bailey Drive, Bailey Court, Bailey Place. What is all this?"

"Street signs," Logan said, like the answer should have been obvious.

I already had a pretty good idea of what they planned to do with them. "I can see that. Why are we renaming the streets?"

"Fucking Havens," Gavin said.

"What'd they do?"

"They changed the *Welcome to Tilikum* signs on both ends of town so they said *Welcome to Havenville*."

"Jesus, it took forever to get that shit off," Logan said.

I chuckled a little. No surprise that the longstanding feud between our family and the Havens was still going strong. It went back generations.

"Obviously we can't let that go unanswered," Gavin said. "So now every street in town is going to be ours."

"Where'd you get these?"

"Etsy," Logan said. "This girl I dated for a while was really into personalizing her shit. So I asked her where she got all her stickers and ordered these."

"He orders something online and thinks he gets all the credit," Gavin said. "Such bullshit."

"Hey, I had to text Layla to get the information. That was risky."

"Yeah, and you ended up hooking up with her a few more times," Gavin said. "Not exactly a hardship."

Logan grinned again. "True. Anyway, these aren't meant to come off. Those bastards will be scraping adhesive off street signs for weeks."

Gavin snickered.

Logan turned and slowed, coming to a stop next to a tall sign. "Pass one back to Gav."

I took a *Bailey Drive* sticker and handed it through the open back window.

"Can you reach?" Logan asked.

"Yeah, I got it." Gavin stood in the bed of the truck and removed the sticker's backing, then smoothed it out over the sign.

I glanced around at the empty street. "I know it's the middle of the night, but aren't you worried about getting caught?"

"Not really. Deputy Cohen is on duty tonight."

Chip Cohen wasn't a Bailey, but if I remembered correctly, his sister was married to one of our cousins. That made him one of us. But I kept eying the street, narrowing my eyes against the dark.

Logan drove ahead to the next block and stopped again. "Dude, it's fine. You don't have to be paranoid; we never get caught."

I handed Gavin another sticker. "I just spent seven years in prison. Everything makes me paranoid."

We drove up and down the streets of Tilikum's little downtown, pausing at every intersection to paste Bailey stickers over the street names. The first few took several minutes, but after a while, we got into a rhythm. Logan would get the truck into position, I'd pass Gavin a sticker, and he'd do the honors.

Realistically, they didn't need a third person to pull this off. Logan could just as easily have done my job. And as weird as it sounded, beneath my paranoia about getting in trouble for this—the last thing I needed was to get on the wrong side of the law—I was kind of glad they'd gotten me up in the middle of the night to deface street signs. Back in the day, we'd done this kind of thing all the time.

We took a left, onto a street that sloped down the hill toward the river that meandered through the center of town. Headlights flashed behind us.

"Shit. Get down," Logan hissed.

I ducked and heard the thud of Gavin sprawling in the bed of the truck. "I thought you said we wouldn't get caught."

"We won't if you shut up."

"The truck's running."

"Good point. Maybe we shouldn't duck. Pretend we're

not up to anything." He slowly sat up and looked in the rear-view mirror. "Never mind, I think they're gone."

Another car turned the corner in front of us, and for a second, I was blinded by bright headlights.

"What the fuck are all these people doing out here?" Logan muttered. "It's the middle of the night."

"We're out here."

"Yeah, but we have a good reason."

The car got closer and I stiffened. It said *County Sheriff* on the side.

Logan leaned out the open driver's side window as the car slowed to a stop next to us. "Hey, Cohen. How's grave-yard treating you?"

"It's not so bad," Deputy Cohen said. "Holy shit, is that Asher?"

Ah, fuck.

"Yep. They actually let the big guy out."

"Ain't that some shit. Hey, Asher. Welcome home."

I nodded to Cohen. "Thanks."

His eyes flicked to the street sign. "Well, I can see you guys are busy. I won't keep you. Hey, Gav."

I glanced back in time to see Gavin's hand lift in a wave. He was still lying flat.

"Just don't leave those sticker backs lying around," he said. "No littering."

"Yes, sir," Logan said. "Night."

Cohen tipped his hat to us, then drove on.

I let out a breath. "Holy shit."

"I told you we didn't have to worry," Logan said.

"You're driving around with a convicted felon, defacing public property," I said. "Of course I'm fucking worried."

Logan just shook his head at me and put the truck into gear. "You ready back there?"

"Yup," Gavin said.

It took us another hour to go through all the stickers. For a small town, there were a lot of street signs. On the way back to Gram's, Logan made sure to stop on the corner by Grace's house so we could replace the Evergreen Street sign with Bailey Way.

Finally, Logan took us down the bumpy road toward Gram's. He parked on the far side of the shop. Gavin jumped out of the back and produced a six pack of beer, seemingly from nowhere. At this point, I didn't bother questioning it.

We walked down a gravel path to a familiar spot out behind the shop, past Gram's well-cultivated gardens. We'd come out here countless times to toast our late-night pranks, although it had usually been with Cokes and candy bars from the Sugar Shack rather than beer.

It reminded me how young my brothers had been when I'd left. How much they'd changed since then.

The clearing had a fire pit lined with smooth river stones, the charred remains of the last fire still piled in the center. It was chilly, but Logan and Gavin both sat down without starting a new one. It was late, and we probably wouldn't be out here long enough to bother with a fire.

Gavin fished a bottle opener out of his pocket and cracked open three beers, handing them out one by one.

"Good work tonight," Logan said, holding his beer out.

Gavin and I clinked our bottles with his.

I took a drink, feeling the hint of a burn as it slid down my throat. "God, I haven't had a beer in years."

"There's probably a lot you haven't done in years," Logan said. "Is it weird being back?"

"Yeah. A lot has changed. I knew life would go on without me, but still. I don't even know where you guys live."

Logan took a drink of his beer. "Levi and I got a place not

far from the firehouse. Then Gavin moved in, even though no one invited him."

"It's a good thing, though," Gavin said. "Your house was boring as shit before I moved in."

"Yeah, kinda. Levi isn't exactly the life of the party. He just works and..." Logan trailed off and paused for a second. "I don't know what else."

"What about Evan?"

"His place is a couple of miles outside town. His shop's out there too. He builds motorcycles and restores cars and shit. He hates people, so it seems to work for him."

"Since when does he hate people?"

Logan shrugged. "Didn't he always? He lives out there with his dog. We see him at Gram's on Tuesdays for dinner, but that's about it."

I took a long swallow, letting it all sink in. Something felt wrong, but I couldn't put my finger on what.

"Are we allowed to talk about her yet?" Gavin asked.

Logan elbowed him. "Dude, no."

"He wants to know where everyone lives and stuff. And it's not like we can keep pretending she doesn't exist."

"It's fine," I said. "I know where she lives. I went over there today."

"Fuck yes," Gavin said. "Hand it over, buddy."

Logan groaned and pulled out his wallet. He handed Gavin a twenty. "Dick."

"It's not my fault I have Gram-level psychic skills."

"What the hell are you talking about?" I asked.

"We had a bet going on how long it would take you to go see her," Logan said. "My money was on tomorrow. I figured you'd hold out at least another day before you cracked."

"What was Levi's guess?" Gavin asked.

"Next week or something."

Gavin laughed. "He's such a cynical bastard."

"You guys are assholes," I grumbled.

"Well, this asshole believes in the power of love, and it just made him twenty bucks richer." Gavin stretched out the twenty and wiggled his eyebrows.

"The power of love?" Logan asked. "You're so full of shit."

Gavin just grinned.

Logan turned to me. "So how'd it go?"

I ignored his question, hoping he'd take the hint and drop the subject.

"That bad?" Gavin asked. "Don't worry, bro, I'm sure she understands. You'll last longer next time."

I shot a glare at him, my hand already balling into a fist.

"Whoa." He put his hands up, one still holding his beer, in a gesture of surrender. "I'm just messing with you."

With a slow breath to tamp down the flare of anger, I unclenched my fist. Of course he was just messing with me. It's what we'd always done. But my first reaction had been to get ready for a fight.

That was fucked up.

"You okay, man?" Logan asked.

"Yeah. I just don't want to talk about her."

"All right. Fair enough. Thanks for your help tonight."

"No problem. Not that you needed me. But thanks for the beer."

"My pleasure," Logan said. "And sure we did. Gotta initiate you back into Tilikum life, bronanza."

I nodded and took another drink. Tilikum life. Pranks. Some things around here hadn't changed. But I had. And I didn't really know whether I fit anymore.

8

GRACE

*T*he shift schedule blurred on the screen. I'd been staring at it for the last hour, making little to no progress. This was ridiculous.

Reaching my arms overhead, I straightened my back and stretched. I was at work, I needed to get my head back in the game. The baristas who worked for me weren't going to want to wait to find out their schedule for next week just because my—sort of—fiancé was out of prison early and our reunion had basically sucked balls. There were perks to being the boss, like my cute little office and flexible hours. But I also couldn't let things slide.

I filled in a few fields on the schedule manager and made sure to hit save. I'd probably have to make changes later, but it would have to do for now. My brain simply didn't want to cooperate today.

My phone buzzed with a text, and I picked it up, already knowing it was probably Cara.

Cara: *I need a status update on the scary prison guy.*

Me: *Where did you get the idea that he's scary?*

It took her a long moment to answer.

Cara: *Damn it. Logan said scary. I retract my statement. If prince dickhead says he's scary, he's obviously a kitten.*

Me: *He's neither, and there's no update.*

Cara: *You have to give me something. I'm dying over here.*

Me: *I already told you everything.*

Cara: *You seriously haven't talked to him since his shitty attempt at an apology yesterday?*

Me: *Nope.*

Cara: *Taser.*

Me: *We're still not going to taser him.*

Cara: *Are you sure?*

Me: *Positive. Are you coming tonight?*

Cara: *Probably. Might as well do something while I'm not having sex because my love life is a joke and men are stupid.*

Me: *They can't all be stupid, can they?*

Cara: *Still waiting for one to prove me wrong.*

Me: *Fair enough. See you tonight.*

Mondays were Stitch and Sip night at the Knotty Knitter, Tilikum's yarn and craft store. Gram had taught me to crochet years ago and invited me to come to the town's knitting group. I'd been skeptical, envisioning a bunch of old ladies sitting around sipping tea with their knitting needles clicking while they gossiped about the rest of the old ladies in town. What could I possibly have in common with them?

But it turned out, Stitch and Sip was a lot more fun than I would have thought. Especially after Cara had joined and started bringing drinks. A few of the ladies still hadn't figured out that Long Island iced teas didn't actually have any tea in them.

It was pretty adorable.

My phone binged with another text, this one from my mom, saying she was out front. I hit save on the schedule— again—and went out to the café.

It always struck me how good my mom looked these days. Her hair was down and she wore a cute open cardigan and stylish jeans. Jack was with her, dressed in street clothes. He was a big guy with a salt and pepper beard and thick arms. He looked like a cop, even without his uniform, and the way he gently placed his hand on the small of Mom's back was just the cutest.

"Hey, you guys," I said. "Do you want to grab a table?"

I hugged my mom and Jack and gestured to an empty table, all before realizing they had my little brother with them. Elijah stood back a few feet, his face buried in a hood and his hands stuffed in the front pockets.

"Oh hey, Eli."

"Hi."

One-word answers were about all any of us could get out of him lately, so I didn't let it bother me.

"Do you guys want anything?" I asked as we took our seats.

"Thanks, but we can't stay more than a few minutes," Mom said. "We were downtown, so we figured we'd pop in and say hi."

"I'm glad you did."

"You don't happen to know anything about the street signs around town, do you?" Jack asked.

I pressed my lips together to keep from smiling. I'd seen them this morning—there was even one on my street—but I didn't know who'd done it. Not that it would be hard to guess. This had Logan and Gavin written all over it. Possibly Levi, too.

"I don't know anything about it."

He raised an eyebrow. "Are you sure?"

Mom put a hand on his arm. "I don't think you should worry about it."

"Do *you* know something?" He glanced at her, his mouth lifting in a smile.

"No, but it's just a bunch of stickers. Someone will take them down."

"This town," he muttered.

I caught Elijah's eye, intending to wink at him. He had to find this funny. But he didn't smile back.

"That's not the reason we stopped in," Mom said. "I spoke with Gram yesterday. She said Asher's home."

"Yeah, I was wondering if you'd seen him."

Mom shook her head. "No, although I saw the old truck parked out front and wondered who was using it."

I tapped my fingers on the table. I didn't particularly want to get into the details with my Mom. She loved Asher, but she also worried about me. Which was understandable, I was her daughter. But at the moment, I wasn't sure what to say. I decided to keep it simple.

"Well, he's home. He was released early, which is obviously great news. Now he's... adjusting."

"I suppose that makes sense. I'm sure the transition can be difficult."

"It'll definitely be difficult," Jack said. "He'll need some time to get used to everything again."

I caught Jack's eye and gave him a grateful smile. He'd never met Asher, but of course he knew the Bailey family. And he knew what had happened to me—why Asher had done what he'd done. He'd never said so explicitly, but I got the impression that he didn't think Asher should have been imprisoned.

He was right. He shouldn't have. But there wasn't any point dwelling on that now.

"Have you seen him?" Mom asked.

"A little bit. I talked to him yesterday. It was good to see him, obviously."

Elijah still didn't say anything. I wasn't sure if he even remembered Asher. He'd been four when Asher had been sent away, and we'd kept most of it from him. I figured he knew by now what had happened, or at least the version appropriate for an eleven-year-old. This probably wasn't all that interesting to him.

"I'm glad to hear it," Mom said. "Well, we need to get going. We have a meeting at the school."

We all stood, and I hugged Jack, then my mom. Elijah scooted toward the door, so I let him have his space. He wasn't into hugs these days.

"If you see Asher before we do, tell him we're glad he's home," Mom said.

"I will."

I said goodbye and watched them go, grateful she hadn't pushed for news about our engagement.

THE KNOTTY KNITTER was just up the street from Lola, the pinup-girl statue outside the Dame and Dapper Barber Shop. I parked my car, and with my tote bag of yarn and crochet projects hanging from my arm, I went inside.

Stitch and Sip was held in the back of the store, past the aisles of yarn and various other sewing and craft supplies. Mismatched armchairs and a couch worn from years of use were arranged in a circle, near a big table where Jessie Montgomery—Knotty Knitter owner and resident crafting genius—held workshops and tutorials.

The large coffee table had a few plates with meticulously laid-out snacks, probably courtesy of Tillie Bailey-Linfield. Tillie was a retired piano teacher, and Asher's great-aunt on his father's side. She loved playing hostess almost as much as town gossip.

She glanced up at me from the pile of knitting in her lap and her eyebrows lifted. She shared a glance with Amy Garrett, who continued the knowing look, passing it to Violet Luscier.

That answered my question. They knew Asher was home.

"Hi, ladies." I set my tote down and took a seat in one of the armchairs.

They said polite hellos, and I nodded to Marlene Haven. She gave me a warm smile.

The most shocking thing I'd learned at my first Stitch and Sip meeting was not that it wasn't a group of little old ladies—Amy Garret was only a few years older than me, and we had other members who were younger still. The attendees varied a bit from week to week. No, the biggest surprise had been that this little group operated outside the Bailey-Haven feud. And Marlene Haven, mother to the notorious Haven brothers—and of course their sister, Annika—was a regularly attending member.

No one had ever confirmed my suspicions, but I was convinced Stitch and Sip had begun decades ago as a way for the women of Tilikum to circumvent the feud, especially when it threatened to interfere with town governance. When things started to get out of hand, the members sat back here on shabby furniture and quietly—and very cordially—set things right.

From the first time I'd come, it had felt like being let in on an important town secret. It was no surprise when Gram had casually mentioned that the sacred rule of Stitch and Sip was simple, but ironclad. What was said at Stitch and Sip *stayed* at Stitch and Sip.

"No Gram tonight?" Violet asked. She was related to Gram, but I wasn't quite sure how. Asher had called her Auntie, but on that side of his family, everyone was either a cousin, auntie, or uncle, regardless of their actual familial ties. Her eyes were like Gram's—so dark they were almost black—and her skin was beautifully smooth, especially considering she was in her fifties.

"I guess not," I said. "I haven't talked to her today."

"I suppose she's otherwise occupied, what with the big news and everything." Violet didn't stop working on the blue baby hat she was crocheting.

"Oh, Violet," Tillie said. "Have a cookie."

"You mean to tell me we aren't going to talk about the biggest thing that's happened in this town in years?"

"Not until everyone gets here."

I just rolled my eyes and started working on the gray and green beanie I'd started last week. Occasionally we worked on projects meant as gifts for friends or family, but most of the time, we made hats, scarves, and blankets for babies and children in need. The winters were cold here in the mountains, so we made sure every kid in town had what they needed to keep warm.

The bell on the front door jingled and Cara swept into the shop. A half-finished scarf—or maybe it was supposed to be a hat; it was hard to tell—hung out of her tote. In her other hand, she carried an insulated cooler bag. Her red hair was down and she wore a fitted black shirt, cropped jeans, and a pair of shiny red stilettos.

She set the cooler down, then tossed herself into a chair, unceremoniously dropping her tote bag. "Ladies."

"Those are quite the shoes," Tillie said, adjusting her wire-rimmed glasses. "I'd fall right over if I tried to walk in them."

Cara pointed her toes. "Aren't they adorable? I found them in my closet today and I swear I have no memory of buying them. But I'm sure glad I did."

"I need to borrow those," I said.

"Anytime, precious baby duckling." She opened the cooler, set out cups, and started pouring from a large stainless-steel tumbler. She added ice from another container and garnished each glass with a slice of lemon, then passed them around.

The room went quiet as we sipped our Long Island iced teas—Cara really did know how to make an excellent cocktail—and worked on our respective projects. Eyes flicked to me now and then, and I knew they were waiting for someone to bring up Asher. He was the current hot topic for gossip in Tilikum. He had to be discussed at Stitch and Sip.

Cara lounged in the chair next to me, her tote untouched. No one asked why she hadn't resumed one of her projects. We all knew she was terrible at it. The craftiest Cara got was staging flat lay fashion photos for her Instagram feed.

"All right, Grace," Violet said, finally breaking the silence, "we need to hear it from the source. Is it true Asher escaped?"

"Of course he didn't escape," Amy said. She had four boys under the age of eight and always looked like she needed a nap. "If he did, he'd be in hiding. I heard he's on house arrest and has to wear one of those ankle monitors. That's why hardly anyone's seen him."

"I heard his brothers found the fabled Montgomery treasure and it was so vast they used it to buy his way out of prison," Cara deadpanned.

I glared at her.

She smirked.

Tillie clicked her tongue. "Everybody knows there's no such thing as the Montgomery treasure."

"Now hold on there, Tillie," Violet said. "Some of the stories have nuggets of truth to them."

"You sound like old Harvey Johnston," Tillie said.

"I don't know. I think Violet might be right," Marlene said. She wore dark blue reading glasses and didn't look up from her project while she spoke. "There's something to that old story about the Montgomery fortune. I don't know if anyone will ever find out what it was, but I think at the very least, it *used* to exist."

"Well, I can't tell you if the Montgomery fortune is, or was, real," I said. "But I can tell you that the Bailey boys didn't find anything, no one bribed anyone, and Asher didn't break out. He was granted clemency by the governor and his sentence declared adequate because of the circumstances of the case."

"Isn't that something," Tillie said. "Has anyone organized a meal train?"

"The man got out of prison, not the hospital," Violet said. "What does he need a meal train for?"

"It's a life transition," Tillie said. "Everyone could use a hot meal during a difficult time."

"That's a nice idea," Marlene said.

"So when's the wedding?" Amy asked. "Are you going to set a date?"

I could feel the color drain from my face and my hands went still in my lap.

"Believe it or not, they aren't in a rush," Cara said smoothly. "I think that's so smart. Some people would jump right into it and get married before they've adjusted to being together again. Holding off for a while and not putting more pressure on your relationship is really the right call."

I smiled at her with unending gratitude. "Thank you."

"That does make sense," Amy said, nodding sagely. "Good for you."

The rest of the circle murmured their agreement.

I knew what people said about me behind my back. Maybe not these ladies—they actually knew me. But other people in town thought I was stupid for waiting for Asher.

Most of the time I didn't care what anyone else thought. But right now, I was feeling pretty raw. And the last thing I wanted was their pity.

Cara leaned close and lowered her voice. "By the way, I started the rumor that he escaped. I thought it sounded badass and I wanted to see if I could get anyone to repeat it."

"You're terrible."

"I know."

My phone binged, so I picked it up to check. I had a text from a number I didn't recognize.

This is Asher. I have a phone now.

My mouth twitched in a smile. It was a little thing—tiny, really. It didn't mean much. There was a big gap between giving me his phone number and setting a wedding date. But it was something. And after the last few days, I'd take it.

9

ASHER

My temporary solution to being a grown-ass man living with his grandma again was to make myself useful. Sitting around would have quickly driven me crazy, so I found ways to stay busy. Gram's house wasn't in bad shape, especially considering it was over a hundred years old. But there were always things that needed attention.

I'd spent yesterday repairing a leaky faucet in the downstairs bathroom and putting up some shelves in the pantry. Today, I'd already put a new coat of stain on the back porch, and started on the logs that needed to be cut and stacked for firewood. It was hot, sweaty work, especially with the spring sun blazing overhead. But I needed it—needed something to keep my feet rooted to the ground.

While I worked, I tried to come up with a longer-term plan. But that was tough. Everything circled back to one central question: What was I going to do with my life now?

I didn't have an answer.

Picking up where I'd left off had never been an option. A felony conviction was an automatic disqualifier for the fire department. I hadn't finished my degree, but it was useless anyway. I could probably find a way to go back to school, but for what? The only thing I'd ever wanted to be was a firefighter. That dream had died a long time ago.

Focusing on the short-term was simpler, but not particularly encouraging. I was starting from zero, with basically nothing. I had no job, no money, I hardly even had any clothes that fit. It felt like I was trying to claw my way out of a deep hole. I was so far down, the sky was nothing but a pinprick of light, high above me.

But there was only one thing I could do. Climb.

And truthfully, I didn't have *nothing*. Gram had put a roof over my head—given me a safe place to land. Grandad's old truck was a beast to drive, but it worked. I had a way to get around.

Yesterday afternoon, an old laptop had mysteriously appeared on the kitchen table. I didn't know who'd left it there, and Gram claimed she didn't know anything about it. My guess was Evan, but he'd come and gone without anyone seeing him. Later, Levi had quietly left a phone with a sticky note warning me not to eat up all his data.

I swung the ax and it sank deep into the wood with a crack. I was still struggling with the sense of gratitude I had for my family. It felt out of place with the anger and resentment—and paranoia—that continuously burned in my gut. I wasn't used to it.

But it was better than the gnawing sense of hopelessness that ate at me. I wasn't going to sit on my ass and wait for someone to fix my fucked-up life, but I hated feeling adrift and without purpose.

My clothes stuck to my skin, so I put the ax down and peeled off my shirt. I hadn't slept well last night and now that it was late afternoon, exhaustion was getting to me. Of course, I hadn't slept well in years, so that was nothing new. But I kept waking up in a panic, not realizing where I was.

I wiped my face on my shirt and tossed it aside. Grace weighed on my mind more heavily than anything else. What did she see when she looked at me? Did she see the truth? Did she understand?

My back prickled and I had the sudden sensation that I was being watched. Adrenaline shot through me, making my heart pound and my hands involuntarily clench into fists. I fucking hated that feeling. I ground my teeth together, ready to fight, even though logically I knew I didn't have to. I wasn't *there* anymore, but my instincts were too strong.

Whipping around, I came face to face with—

A fucking squirrel.

It sat on a log, its bushy gray tail twitching. It was a fat little shit—clearly not hurting for food.

I let out a breath and relaxed my shoulders, feeling like an idiot. What the hell had I expected, a guy with neck tattoos wielding a shank? Jesus.

"What are you looking at?"

It didn't even flinch, just twitched its tail again.

"I don't know what you're waiting for. I don't have any food."

Around here, where there was one squirrel, there were usually a lot more, but I didn't see a gang of furry cohorts lingering nearby. When we were kids, the damn squirrels had made off with our snacks more times that I could count. They were fast little fuckers who could steal your sandwich and be up a tree before you realized it was gone.

The squirrel seemed content to stare at me with its beady black eyes, which was creepy, but probably harmless. I ignored it and went back to chopping wood.

After splitting a few more rounds, I stacked the pieces on

the wood pile. My arms and back were tired and my stomach growled with hunger. I'd probably done enough for one day, so I put the ax and splitting maul away in the shed. Gram's chickens clucked and scratched in the dirt. I paused to eye the coop where she kept them safe from predators at night. The coop wasn't in bad repair, but it was small. I'd have to ask her if she wanted a bigger one. It would give me something else to do.

I went back to the wood pile to grab my shirt, but I didn't see it lying on the ground where I'd left it. That was weird. Had I put it somewhere else? I hunted around for a few minutes, increasingly confused. I'd dropped it right there, and no one else was here.

God, I was losing it.

The back door opened, and Gram strolled out onto the porch. The chickens clucked at her.

"Bear, why don't you come on in and get yourself cleaned up."

"Yeah, I was just about to." I glanced around again.

"Did you lose something?"

"My shirt." I turned in a circle. "I took it off right here and now it's gone. You didn't grab it, did you?"

"No. It was probably the squirrels."

I furrowed my brow and looked back toward the creek. "Why would a squirrel take a shirt? I don't think that's normal."

"Do you really expect normal around here?"

That was a fair point. My stomach gnawed at me with an urgency that overrode the mystery of my shirt, so I abandoned the search and went up the porch steps. "I guess not."

"Maybe Sasquatch needed a new shirt. Yours is probably one of the few that would fit him."

"So the squirrels work for Sasquatch now?"

"It would explain a lot."

Shaking my head, I followed her inside, but didn't bother to point out that Sasquatch wasn't real. I honestly wasn't sure if she believed all the old myths and stories, or just acted like she did to mess with people. But she'd always insisted Sasquatch lived in the mountains outside Tilikum. Although Bigfoot leading an army of squirrels was a new one—and weird, even for Gram.

She pulled a pot out of a cupboard, and I didn't wait for her to tell me I smelled like a wild animal. I went straight upstairs to shower.

The water felt good on my tired body. Relaxing in a hot shower was another luxury I'd never again take for granted. I stood beneath the spray, letting it ease the tension in my back and shoulders.

I finished and dug through a box in my room for more clean clothes. The shirt strained across my back and I had to pull at the sleeves so they didn't cut into my arms.

Voices carried from the kitchen and I wondered who was here. It was more than one person, probably several. I hesitated at the top of the stairs, not sure I wanted to go down there. The last thing I wanted to do was be social.

But the scent of food hit my nose and I was a goner. If that was frybread I smelled, Gram was probably making it on purpose to tempt me into coming down.

It worked.

Fortunately, the kitchen was only full of my brothers. That, I could handle.

Levi and Gavin sat at the table, while Logan leaned his hip against the counter, just within arm's reach of a heaping pile of frybread. Evan stood in the middle of the room, frozen mid-stride, like he'd been doing something and stopped when he caught sight of me.

In fact, they were all looking at me weird.

"What? Did you guys forget I was here?"

"No." Logan reached for a piece and a wooden spoon cracked against his knuckles. "Ow."

Gram slid the plate of frybread away from Logan.

He moved, joining the others at the table, and I realized why everyone—except Gram—was watching me awkwardly.

Grace stood next to Gram, stirring something in a big pot on the stove. She glanced at me over her shoulder but didn't say anything.

Fuck.

I had a flashback to my teenage self, standing in this very kitchen, looking at a younger Grace. The moment I'd realized my feelings for my childhood best friend had changed. I'd worried about what would happen if we dated and it didn't work out. Our families were so close, how would that work? Could I risk it?

The sense of responsibility I felt toward both our families had held me back—until it hadn't. And now I was faced with the very thing I'd feared all those years ago. It hadn't worked out between me and Grace—through no fault of hers—and it wasn't going to. I couldn't drag her through my shit—couldn't ask her to travel the dark road I was on. There was just no way.

But here she was, stirring dinner in Gram's kitchen. It didn't take a genius to realize it was Tuesday, which meant Tuesday dinner, and that Grace had probably been coming every week since I'd been gone.

This was so fucking complicated.

"Good, you're dressed." Gram set a piece of frybread on the pile and wiped her hands on her apron. "Run to the store for me, would you, Bear? I'm all out of heavy cream and I need it for the chowder."

"Yeah, sure."

"Grace can go with you."

I rubbed the back of my neck. "It's fine, Gram, I remember how to get to the store."

"Mm hmm." She took the spoon out of Grace's hand. "Hurry up. Once I let these animals at that frybread, it won't last five seconds. If you don't get back in time, that's your fault."

"Subtle, Gram," Grace said and headed for the door. "Come on, I'll drive."

I blew out a breath and followed.

10

GRACE

*A*sher climbed into my car and adjusted the seat backward. I started the engine and fastened my seatbelt, trying to keep my expression neutral—to hide the whirlwind of emotions swirling inside me.

I'd debated staying home. I almost never missed a Tuesday dinner at Gram's, but I hadn't been sure about tonight. Aside from the text to give me his new number, Asher and I hadn't talked since Sunday. We weren't exactly on a roll, here, and I was struggling with the sickening realization that I might have made an enormous mistake.

Maybe he'd been right, and I should have moved on.

His ring still glinted on my finger. I hadn't taken it off yet, but I wasn't an idiot. At least, not a total idiot. It was very possible everyone who'd ever patted my arm with pity in their eyes and told me they were *concerned* had been right. That Asher's silence had not been an act of self-preservation, but an attempt to drive home the fact that he and I were over. That his prison sentence had truly meant the end of us.

My emotional side wanted to crumple into a ball and

sob. My practical side wanted to reserve judgment until we had a conversation that didn't end with one of us telling the other to leave.

And my stubborn side? That part of me was mostly pissed off.

Asher didn't say anything while I drove to the store, just watched the scenery go by. I wondered how different things looked to him now. Was anything familiar? Or had things changed enough that Tilikum didn't feel like home anymore?

Or maybe he'd changed so much this place would never feel like home.

I cast quick glances at him. At his wide shoulders and broad chest. At his hands resting on his thick thighs. His bruised and battered knuckles. The taped cut on his forehead.

He shifted in his seat and that subtle movement was enough to remind me that there was yet another part of me —a part that wasn't sad, or angry, or interested in problem solving.

That part resided directly between my legs and it craved him like a drug.

The first two times I'd seen him had been emotionally charged and confusing, drowning out my more primal, physical responses. Now I was calm and next to him in an enclosed space. His hair was damp, he smelled clean, and I had to fight down the urge to pull over and climb into his lap.

It occurred to me that I could. I could make up a quick excuse to turn down an empty road where we had a good chance of being alone. I'd be risking a hefty dose of rejection, but what would he do if I stripped off my shirt and put my boobs in his face? Would he really tell me to stop?

I dismissed the idea as quickly as it came. I knew him too well. Asher hated being manipulated, and sexual aggression was not the way to get through his defenses. Even if he gave in, he'd only shut me out harder when the moment had passed, leaving us both feeling worse than before.

And at this point, the fact that I was still physically attracted to him was only making this more complicated for me. Doubt warred with the resolve I'd clung to for so long. As much as I hated to admit it, I had to face the possibility that I'd been holding onto a dream that no longer existed. And wanting him so badly just made this confusing.

I pulled into the Nature's Basket Grocery parking lot and found a spot. The light on my phone flashed with a notification, so I swiped the screen to check. It was a group text from my half-brother, Cooper. As soon as I opened it, I laughed out loud. Asher glanced at me, his eyebrows raised.

"Sorry. It's just Cooper. He's one of my older brothers. Although maybe you don't know that story yet."

"No, I do. I read your letters."

"All of them?"

He nodded.

"Oh. Okay, well... that's good." I angled my phone so he could see. "Cooper and his wife Amelia have twin baby boys and he sent me this."

The photo showed Cooper's babies sleeping soundly in matching bouncy chairs. He'd stacked towers of Cheerios on their foreheads and the message read, *new record.*

"Why do they have cereal on their heads?"

I shrugged. "Because Cooper. You kind of have to meet him to understand."

Another text came through, this one from Leo. It was a picture of his baby boy, also napping, with an even taller stack of Cheerios on his forehead. The message said, *suck it, Coop.*

"And that would be another one of my nephews."

I wondered how long it would take for Roland to send a picture of his baby daughter with a stack of Cheerios on her forehead. I wouldn't have thought Roland would be into this kind of thing—he was the serious one in the family—but the three of them had been trying to outdo each other for weeks. It was both ridiculous and adorable.

"How many nieces and nephews do you have?" Asher asked.

"Let's see... Roland and Zoe have two now. Cooper and Amelia have the twins. Then there's Leo and Hannah, they also have two. And my sister Brynn and her husband Chase are pregnant with their first. So six, soon to be seven."

I stubbornly tamped down the flare of envy that tried to creep up on me. I was happy for my siblings. They all deserved every bit of their happiness, and more. But over the last few years, I'd watched them all get married and start families. And here I was, with a ring on my finger that might not mean anything.

Asher and I probably would have had kids by now. And those kids would have had all these adorable cousins to grow up with.

I put away my phone, trying to chase away that thought. Wallowing in sadness for what I didn't have wasn't going to change anything.

"I guess we should go in so we can get back." I unfastened my seatbelt.

Asher ran his hands up and down his thighs and his jaw clenched tight.

"Are you okay?"

He kept his eyes forward and nodded slowly. "Yeah. Fine."

Before I could stop myself, I laid a hand on his arm. He was not fine. "Are you sure? Because I don't think you are."

"It's fucking ridiculous. It's a goddamn store."

"Is this the first time you've been out?"

Still not looking at me, he nodded again.

I squeezed his arm gently. It was rock solid, knotted with tension. "It's okay. Take your time."

For a second, I thought he might not get out of the car, and a strange sense of panic swept through me. I'd have to go in by myself.

Which of course was fine. I was fine. I wasn't the one who'd spent seven years in prison.

He blew out a breath and unfastened his seat belt. "Let's go."

"Are you sure?"

"Yeah."

We got out of the car, and concern for him pushed aside the spark of relief I felt at not having to go in alone. I'd read everything I could find on the transition from prison life to the outside world, and I knew inmates often struggled at first with everyday things. This was probably to be expected.

Gram had said she needed heavy cream, so I beelined straight for the dairy section. Asher stayed close, scanning the aisles, like he was expecting trouble to pop up any second. I grabbed a carton of cream and we went to the front to check out. There was one person in front of us, so we waited.

Gil Hargrave, a guy in his sixties who owned the Gas N' Grub just off the highway, stopped in his tracks. His mouth dropped open as he stared at Asher.

Asher's eyes narrowed and he stared right back.

"Hey, Gil," I said, raising my voice, hoping to jolt him. "How's Edna?"

Gil startled, finally closing his mouth. "Oh, hi there Grace. Edna's fine."

"Good to hear. I bet she's anxious for you to get home."

His eyes darted to Asher once more, but he nodded. "Yeah, she is. Have a nice night."

"You too." I waved as he continued deeper into the store, then crossed my arms. "What is wrong with people? It's not like he doesn't know who you are."

Asher didn't say anything. Just made a growly noise in his throat.

God, I wished he wouldn't do things like that. There was a fine line between angry noises and sex noises, and he was walking it.

We checked out and drove back to Gram's house. When we got inside, I handed her the carton of cream. She immediately put it in the fridge.

"I thought you needed that for the chowder."

"Oh, I found another one. Seems I actually had plenty."

I raised an eyebrow at her.

She patted my arm. "Dish up, Gracie Bear. It's getting cold."

I glanced at Asher and he shook his head.

We all settled down to dinner at the big farmhouse table. I purposely didn't sit next to or across from Asher. My feelings were all over the place. I needed a little buffer between us.

But it felt good for us all to be together again. No empty chair with an extra place setting. She'd set one for him every time. And every time, it had hurt.

Now he was here.

Dinner was noisy and delicious. We ate Gram's homemade chicken corn chowder and frybread with butter and honey. By the time the meal was over, I was stuffed.

And still unsettled.

I was about to offer to clean up, but without a word, Evan started washing the dishes. Gavin and Levi were already clearing the rest of the dishes from the table. There wasn't anything left to help with, but I couldn't quite make myself go home, either.

I wandered out to the back porch and leaned against the railing, looking out into the darkness. The door shut out the noise from inside, leaving me alone with the crickets and frogs. The faint trickle of the creek down the hill.

Someone else came out and I didn't have to look to know it was him.

He stood next to me and leaned his forearms against the porch railing. When he spoke, his voice was soft and low. "Lot of memories out here."

"So many."

Parties, bonfires, barbecues. Picking berries and digging up weeds in Gram's garden. Climbing trees. Playing down by the creek. Walking hand in hand as he led me away from the twins' graduation party, the night everything changed.

"It's hard to explain," he said.

"What is?"

"Why I freaked out about going into the store. It probably sounds crazy, but I suddenly felt like I didn't know the rules. I didn't know who'd be in there or how I'd get out if shit got bad. And no, I don't know what would go bad in a grocery store."

"It's okay. It wasn't a big deal."

"I guess it's a good thing Gram made you go with me. Who knows how long I'd have sat in the parking lot by myself."

Not for the first time—or the second, or the fifth, or the twentieth—my heart broke wide open for him. "I'm glad I was there."

"Me too." He paused for a moment, still looking out into the night. "I know I'm probably more fucked up than I should be. It's not like it was twenty years."

I wanted to ask why. What had happened to him? But I had a feeling that, whatever it was, he wasn't ready to talk about it.

"I don't think there's a rule book," I said. "You've been through hell. Of course it fucked you up."

He glanced at me, his dark eyes intense. "Why don't you hate me?"

"For what? Breaking up with me without giving me a chance to respond, or cutting me out of your life for so long?"

"Both."

I fiddled with my engagement ring. "I hate what you've been through and that I had to live without you for so long. And don't get me wrong, your silence sucked. But I kind of understood. It wasn't like it was just me—you wouldn't talk to *anyone*. That took some of the sting out of it. It's been hard, but I don't hate you."

He looked away again, still leaning against the railing. "For what it's worth, I'm sorry. I didn't mean to make a shitty situation worse for you."

"I know. I never thought you did it to hurt me."

"I didn't. And I'm sorry I've been acting like a jackass since I got home. I've been living with criminals for the better part of a decade. My people skills are pretty rusty."

I laughed softly. "Yeah, we're going to have to work on that."

"But the thing is, I'm not the guy who gave you that ring anymore. I need you to understand that."

But do you still love me? I let the question die on my lips. I wasn't sure if I wanted to hear the answer. "Well, I'm different too."

"Yeah..." He trailed off and I wondered what that meant. What did he see when he looked at me now? "I can't go back to being who I was, and I honestly don't know where I'm going to end up. And I've seen shit, Grace. I've seen shit, and I've done shit. I don't even want to tell you some of the things—" He stopped mid-sentence and his head dropped.

I kept my gaze on the darkness, my heart lodged in my throat. I didn't think I could reply if I tried.

"I know it hurts to hear this," he continued. "It hurts to say it. But I can't be with you. I'm too much of a wreck."

"Asher, it's only been a few days. Things are going to get better."

"Are they?" There was an edge to his voice. "This isn't about me getting used to life on the outside. I'm not the man you think I am. Not anymore."

Once again, I had a sinking feeling in the pit of my stomach. Maybe he was right.

He turned toward me and in the dim light, his eyes were deep pools of black. I sank into his gaze, searching.

In that moment, I found him.

Asher was a wounded animal, full of anger and pain. Ready to lash out to protect himself. But he was still in there. Not the Asher from before. He was right, he'd never be that man again. No one could come out of what he'd been through unscathed—unchanged.

But he was still Asher Bailey.

And I still loved him.

Blind stubbornness hadn't kept me loyal to him. It was

so much simpler—and so much harder—than that. It was love.

I loved this man. That was why I'd waited. Why I'd accepted his silence, kept his ring on my finger, and remained faithful. We were two halves of the same whole. Two souls meant to be connected to each other. Nothing was ever going to change that.

But like a wounded animal, I couldn't approach too quickly. I had to get past all that anger and fear before I could help him begin to heal.

I'd been patient for a long time. I wasn't about to give up now.

So I softened my expression with a small smile. "Well, for what it's worth, I'm really glad you're home."

His shoulders relaxed. "Me too."

Lifting my eyebrows, I held out my arms. "Welcome home hug? You didn't let me give you one the first time."

"Sure."

I stepped in and draped my arms around his neck. His body was a solid wall of muscle, but his thick arms were gentle as they wrapped around me. I hesitated there for a moment, savoring everything. His warmth, his scent, his touch.

All too soon, he let go. I moved back, dropping my arms to my sides.

We hadn't said our vows—hadn't declared in front of family and friends that we'd be true in sickness and in health, in good times and in bad. But I'd kept those vows anyway, and I didn't regret a single second of it. Because this was love. Messy, imperfect, painful love.

And I wasn't giving up without a fight.

DEAR ASHER

ear Asher,

YOU'RE NOT GOING to believe this. My father has another family.

We haven't heard from him in a long time and my mom was being crushed by all of Elijah's medical bills. So I decided to take matters into my own hands. I tracked him down.

You know how he always said he lived in Seattle and worked in the city? That was a lie. Until recently, he lived over in Echo Creek. That close, the asshole. He and his wife—yeah, his wife—own a winery there.

It gets worse. Not only is he married, he's always been married—even when he was with my mom—and they have kids. Four of them. I have three older brothers and a younger sister, and they didn't have any idea that Elijah and I existed.

I spent my entire life believing my father was just a jerk with commitment issues who chose his career over his family. But we were never his family. We were a mistake he tried to hide.

He's not with his wife anymore. She found out he was having an affair—another one, the piece of shit—and kicked him out. Who knows how many other women there have been. And god, my mom was one of them.

There was a horrible moment, just before I told her, when I wondered if she'd known and kept it from me. But she was even more shocked than I was. She'd suspected there was a lot more going on than he told her, and she knew he was a chronic liar. But she didn't know he was married.

Part of me wishes she'd never had to find out. She's devastated. I've seen her upset before, but I've never seen her look so broken. It's awful. I want to help, but I honestly have no idea what to do.

I guess there is some good news in all this. My half-siblings seem great. Roland, the oldest, totally bailed out my mom. He made sure all Elijah's medical bills were paid, just like that. She argued with him about it. A lot. But he wouldn't budge. I think they're all good people, which means none of them take after the jerk who fathered all of us. So that's something.

Now we have to figure out how to explain everything to Elijah. I don't know how to make a little kid understand something like this. He doesn't have any memories of our dad. But he knows something is going on. The kid is too freaking smart. Honestly, we're probably not giving him enough credit.

I'm not sure what's going to happen now. I'd like to get to know my sister and brothers. After all, we're related. In a weird way, we're family. But I'm not sure how much they want to get to know me. Don't get me wrong, they've been nothing but nice to me. But it's so complicated. They were already dealing with the fallout of finding out their dad had been cheating on their mom, and then I showed up.

I know what you'd say if you were here. You'd tell me it isn't my fault. That I didn't have a choice in the man who fathered me.

And of course you'd be right. But I still feel kind of awful about it. My fault or not, the fact that I exist has hurt a lot of people. I'm not quite sure how to deal with that.

MISSING YOU,
  Grace

11

ASHER

*T*here was something disconcerting about being in a place so familiar when I was so different, even a week after coming home. Maybe Gram was right and I just needed time. But like my old clothes, it felt like nothing quite fit right.

I sat at the kitchen table, scrolling through job openings. Tilikum wasn't exactly a thriving metropolis. Pickings were slim. A handful of the jobs were out simply because of who owned the businesses—hazard of being a Bailey. A Haven wouldn't have hired me before; they certainly wouldn't now. As for the rest, I'd have to take my chances and hope someone would give me a shot.

Not for the first time, I wondered if I should stay.

The news that I was home had already spread through town like a summer wildfire. That part didn't surprise me. This town loved gossip the way some places loved a local sports team. What was surprising was the curiosity about me. It wasn't enough for people to know I was back. They wanted a look at me.

Mrs. Appleton had come down our private drive on

Wednesday, claiming she'd taken a wrong turn. Judge Turner and his wife had done the same thing yesterday. Mabel Wheatley had stopped by with daffodils from her garden, saying she thought we'd enjoy fresh-cut flowers—apparently ignoring the mass of yellow flowers already blooming in Gram's yard.

Gram's fridge and freezer were stuffed full of food people had brought over. Every time, they'd stand at the door clutching a foil-wrapped dish, craning their neck to see inside, trying to get a glimpse of me.

Gram handled the nosy intrusions with quiet amusement. They made anger simmer in my gut, but I tried to ignore them.

I wasn't concerned about the random townspeople showing up unannounced, hoping to get a look at the ex-con. But there were a lot of people from my past that I hadn't seen yet, and I had no idea what to expect from those reunions.

I knew from Logan that Matt and Christian were still with the fire department. Randy had moved away a few years ago. They'd been there that night. All three had written to me shortly after my sentencing, saying they thought it was bullshit—that I shouldn't have gone to prison. Yet I still wasn't sure how I felt about seeing them again. They'd been there. They'd seen it all.

And Chief Stanley. He'd stood by me when I'd gotten into trouble in high school. But that had been a couple of hot-headed kids getting into a fight. This was a lot bigger than that. And I didn't know what he'd think of the man I was now.

The back door swung open and Gram came in. She nodded to me and went to the sink to wash her hands. It helped that she didn't make a big deal out of me being here, nor did she treat me like I was a kid again. She went on with her life as usual, like nothing had changed. It made me feel a little less awkward and out of place.

My phone dinged with a message and I saw Grace's name flash across the screen.

I'd texted her first, when I'd gotten the phone. I probably shouldn't have. I needed to maintain space between us, not encourage more contact. I'd told myself I just wanted her to have my number. Which was bullshit, and I knew it. She could get my number from Gram or my brothers if she needed to get in touch with me.

I wasn't so delusional—or out of touch with my own emotions—that I could deny how I felt about her. I'd loved Grace for most of my life, and I always would. But coming home and slipping back into the life we'd started wasn't an option. I had too many demons inside me. Violent ones. I didn't trust myself, and I didn't know if I ever would.

But I was weak when it came to her. When I'd hugged her Tuesday night, out on the back porch, I'd almost cracked. She'd felt so good, it had taken every ounce of willpower I possessed to pull away. To stop myself from kissing her.

Now she was like a flame I couldn't resist reaching out to touch, even though I knew I was going to keep getting burned.

Grace: *Some of us are hanging out at the Caboose tonight. Probably around 8. Want to come?*

I blew out a breath. I'd quickly realized that avoiding Grace entirely would be impossible. Not as long as we both lived here in town.

Which made me wonder, again, whether I should stay.

Was there a version of this where Grace and I could go back to being friends?

Maybe part of my transition into the outside world needed to be easing into a new relationship with Grace. I'd told her I couldn't be with her. She knew where I stood. Maybe learning to be friends was what we both needed to finally move on.

Someone knocked at the front door, interrupting my thoughts.

Gram glanced at me. "I'll get it. You keep brooding over that text."

"I'm not brooding."

"Could have fooled me," she said as she walked by.

I shook my head and texted Grace, saying I'd be there. Might as well give it a shot.

And if I was being honest—which I didn't particularly want to be—it was hard to resist the temptation of seeing her.

Gram's voice carried from the front of the house. "Afternoon, Rhonda."

"Afternoon. So sorry to bother you, but I was wondering..." Rhonda McDonnel—I'd known her as Ms. McDonnel, the school librarian—trailed off for a second and I could practically hear her trying to look past Gram to see inside the house.

"Wondering what?" Gram asked.

"Oh—well, I was wondering if you could give me some advice about my tomato plants."

"What sort of trouble are you running into?"

I rolled my eyes. Gossip was a town pastime. Subtlety was not. I doubted Ms. McDonnel even had tomato plants. I got up and glanced down the hallway toward the front door. She caught sight of me and her eyes widened. I held her gaze for a moment, my face blank. She wanted a look at the ex-con? Fine, she could look.

Gram said something else, but I tuned out the rest of their conversation and went to the fridge to find something to eat.

Yet another reason I needed a fucking job. I didn't want Gram to go broke feeding me.

The front door shut, and Gram came back to the kitchen, muttering something under her breath.

I closed the fridge. "Ms. McDonnel have a garden emergency?"

"Maybe I should start charging admission." There was an edge to her voice.

"That's not a bad idea. It could offset your grocery bill."

"These busybodies need to come up with better excuses. Tomato plants." She huffed. "My house is not a zoo and you are not an animal on display."

"It's okay, Gram," I said. "They'll get over it soon."

She muttered to herself and picked up a large red bowl off the counter. "I'll be right back. I need to return this to Naomi."

"Why don't I take it?"

She paused with the bowl in her hands and I couldn't quite read her expression. Curiosity, maybe.

Truthfully, I didn't particularly want to take the bowl next door. I hadn't seen Grace's mom yet. But I didn't want Gram to think I needed her to shield me from everyone. And it would probably be better if I just got it over with.

"Thank you, Bear." She handed me the bowl.

I took it with a nod and left to go next door.

The house where Grace had grown up looked different than I remembered. It was blue, instead of faded gray. No more peeling paint, and the porch had been rebuilt.

There weren't any cars out front, but if someone was home, they might have parked in the garage. I stepped up to the door and hesitated with my fist raised in the air to knock. For a second, I could almost believe this was before. That I was still just a kid who'd fallen in love with the girl next door.

It fucking sucked that I wasn't him anymore.

Pushing that thought aside, I knocked.

No one answered.

Wondering if I should leave the bowl on the porch or come back later, I waited another few seconds. It sounded like someone might be inside, so I knocked again, just in case.

I heard the distinct sound of footsteps, and the door opened.

A man in a towel blinked at me, his mouth open like he'd been about to say something, but I wasn't who he'd expected. He was probably in his fifties, with salt and pepper hair and a sprinkling of gray in his beard. Square jaw. A hard edge to his gaze.

Holy shit. This must be Jack Cordero, Naomi's husband. Grace's stepdad.

"Sorry." I shifted the bowl, feeling awkward. "Gram wanted to return this."

He hiked up the towel a little. "Thanks. I thought Elijah lost his key again. You must be Asher?"

"Yes, sir."

I couldn't read his expression. He struck me as a man who was accustomed to keeping his cards close. After all, he was a cop.

What did the chief deputy sheriff think of the ex-con living next door?

"Jack Cordero." He held out a hand and I took it in a firm handshake.

"Asher Bailey. You're Grace's stepdad." I realized a second too late I should have said *Naomi's husband*.

He nodded. "I am. And you're Grace's fiancé."

I rubbed the back of my neck. "I was, yeah."

For a second, he didn't respond. Just looked at me, his eyes sharp and penetrating. "Good to finally meet you in person."

"You too."

I glanced past him, into the house. Even with just a quick glimpse, I could tell the inside was different too. The furniture had changed and there was a large wedding photo on the wall.

I held the bowl out to him, anxious to get out of here. "Sorry to interrupt."

"It's no problem." He took the bowl. "Naomi's at work, so I'll just put this in the kitchen for her."

"Thanks."

My back tightened. There were eyes on me. For all I knew it was just another squirrel, but the rush of adrenaline made my heart race.

Jack looked past me. "There you are. Hey, pal."

Forcing myself to relax my fists, I looked over my shoulder. A kid in a black hoodie stood a few feet from the porch. Dark hair hung in his blue eyes and he had a backpack slung over one shoulder.

Holy shit. Was that Elijah?

He was huge. Relatively speaking, at least. The last time I'd seen him, he'd been four, maybe four-and-a-half. That meant he was eleven now.

The kid's gaze flicked from Jack to me before he quickly looked down.

"Do you remember Asher?" Jack asked.

Elijah shrugged, his eyes still downcast. Without looking up, he swept past me and went into the house.

Jack let out a breath and I didn't miss the flash of frustration in his expression. "I should see if he needs help with his homework."

"Yeah, of course."

"Thanks. Good to meet you."

"You too."

He nodded and shut the door.

I left and walked across the grass to Gram's house with an odd sense of unease in my gut. That was not the kid I remembered. Elijah had been energetic and full of questions, not quiet and sullen.

Maybe it was just his age. I'd probably been similar when I was eleven.

Although when I was eleven, I'd still been recovering from the loss of my parents.

I'd only seen him for less than a minute, but there had been something in his eyes. A flash of anger. I wasn't sure if he remembered me, so I didn't know why he'd be mad. And maybe I'd imagined it. Or maybe he was just an angry kid. I could certainly relate. I had been, too.

So much had changed. And I couldn't shake the feeling that some of it wasn't for the better.

12

GRACE

*C*ara and I got to the Caboose a little early. I'd told her I wanted to make sure we got a table. The funky railroad-themed restaurant and bar was a popular spot, particularly for those of us who didn't want to hang out at the college bars. Saturday nights were usually packed.

But really, I just wanted to make sure I got here before Asher.

I had an admittedly silly fantasy of him walking in, catching sight of me, and thinking I looked good. Not just good. I wanted him to think I looked amazing. I hoped he'd take one look and remember what my body felt like pinned beneath him.

It was only fair. Every time I saw him my mind drifted to that hard, muscled body of his. And what he could do to me with it. I just wanted to return the favor.

I hadn't gone overboard with the outfit. A long, light-weight cardigan over a black tank top, with jeans and low heels. I'd worn this outfit plenty of times when I went out with Cara. If taking off the cardigan meant showing some extra skin, well, it could get warm in here on a spring night.

Cara grabbed our gin and tonics from Hank at the bar and we found a spot near the pool tables. As predicted, it was already filling up. I went ahead and slipped off my cardigan.

"How's everything going, my beautiful little sunflower?" Cara asked. Unlike mine, her outfit wasn't the least bit understated. Her loose silver tank top had thin straps, and it was anyone's guess if she was wearing a bra. Short skirt. Shiny black stilettos. Bright red lips. All very Cara.

I lifted one shoulder while I took a sip. "Not terrible. You?"

"I'm fine. You're still wearing the ring."

"Am I?" I held out my hand. "I hadn't noticed."

"Smartass. So you are still engaged?"

"We don't need to talk about that right now."

She pursed her lips around her straw and took a sip. "Fine. I'll let it go for the moment. But can I rake him across the coals when he gets here?"

"No."

"Why not?"

"Because I don't need you going mama bear on him tonight. Give the guy a break."

"You know what the problem is, don't you? You never should have gotten engaged without my blessing."

"I didn't know you when I got engaged."

"So? You should have waited." She took another sip. "That's okay. I'm willing to evaluate his suitability post-engagement, particularly because you're only sort of engaged anyway."

"Thank goodness for that," I said, my tone wry.

She flashed me a smile. "You look hot. Are you sure this isn't a date?"

"Yeah, I'm sure."

"Weirdest relationship ever."

She had a point. It was weird to be wearing an engagement ring and meeting my sort-of-fiancé at a bar, and yet I had no illusions that this was a date. I'd specifically mentioned *some of us* when I'd texted him, so he wouldn't think I was trying to trick him into something.

No sudden moves.

So tonight was not a date. It was just some friends hanging out in a place where we'd hung out hundreds of times before. And maybe a chance for us to start getting to know each other again. I was hoping the casual environment might encourage Asher to relax and open up a little.

"Just don't make it awkward," I said.

Her eyes widened in mock surprise. "Me?"

"Yes, you."

"Why, Grace, whatever do you mean?" she asked in a fake Southern belle accent.

"I already told him a bunch of us were hanging out, and I don't know if you and I qualify as 'a bunch.' I thought at least a couple of his brothers would be here tonight to help me turn this into a group situation."

She pointed toward the bar. "Evan's here."

Evan *was* here. He sat on a stool, nursing a beer. Despite the fact that the Caboose was filling up, the stools on either side of him were empty. He was imposing, and not just because of his size. His dark brow was perpetually furrowed in a glare that tended to create a halo of space around him.

"Confession," Cara said. "I'd totally fuck Evan."

I glanced at him, then back at her. "Really?"

"Oh yeah."

"Since when do you like Evan?"

"I don't. He's a total dick. I'd fuck Levi, too. He's also a dick, but I'd still bang him."

My mouth dropped open. "You'd sleep with Levi? You realize he and Logan have identical DNA?"

"So?"

"Logan is so much nicer. And more fun to be around."

"I can differentiate between prince dickhead and his brothers, even his twin. I'm not saying I'm *going to* sleep with either of them. Just that, theoretically, I would."

"Why are we talking about which Bailey you'd theoretically fuck?"

She shrugged. "Because Evan's over there looking all mean and it made me think of sex."

"You need so much therapy."

"I've had lots of therapy, but you're probably right, I—" She stopped, her mouth still open, and her eyes went wide. "Holy shit."

"What?"

I looked over my shoulder, and in an instant, I knew exactly what had caught her attention. Or rather, who.

Asher stood just inside the door, his eyes scanning the restaurant. Although it looked like he'd finally gotten some clothes that fit, his tattooed arms still threatened to pop open the seams of his shirt. His brow creased, his eyes narrowing, as if he were assessing everyone's potential as an adversary.

"Is that him?" Cara asked.

"Yeah."

"You didn't tell me he was so fucking intimidating. I think the guy in blue over there just peed his pants."

Glancing back at her, I laughed. "Shut up."

"I get it now. If you've been waiting seven years for *that*, it was worth it."

"It's worth it because he's my best friend and I love him."

My eyes traced the hard lines of his body. "But yeah, the rest of it's not bad either."

She was right, he was intimidating. Like his brother, it wasn't just his size. He exuded something—power and strength, even danger. His posture said he was ready for anything, and his piercing eyes and chiseled jaw sent a distinct message. *Don't fuck with me.*

Evan got up to meet him and the two exchanged a quick hug. That was interesting. Evan wasn't a hugger. They spoke for a moment and the people around them shifted nervously in their chairs, which almost made me laugh. Most of the people in here were locals. Even if they didn't know Asher and Evan personally, they probably knew someone who did. What were they afraid of?

Asher's eyes swept the bar again, landing on me.

Electricity crackled between us and the butterflies in my tummy took flight. I hadn't felt this kind of tingly anticipation in a long time.

It felt good. Really good.

He crossed the distance to our table, his gaze locked on me. Evan peeled off and went back to the bar, but I hardly noticed. This place could have been going up in flames around me, and I wouldn't have had a clue.

"Hey." His eyes smoldered, but he seemed to catch himself. He glanced away and when his gaze returned, he was back to being guarded.

But I'd seen it. And that little glimpse of desire was enough to feed my resolve.

"Glad you made it." I reached back across the table and nudged Cara, who was staring at him open-mouthed. "This is my friend, Cara Goulding."

"Hi."

"So this is what all the fuss is about," Cara said, openly looking him up and down.

I pushed the chair next to me away from the table. "Do you want to sit?"

"Sure."

He took the seat, resting his forearms on the table. Cara looked him over like she was analyzing the lighting for an Instagram photo—head tilted, finger tapping her lips.

"Will you stop?"

She raised her eyebrows. "What am I doing?"

"Scrutinizing."

"Grace, this is the mysterious Asher Bailey. I've waited years for this. I have to say, the women of Tilikum should be jealous. It's quite possible you picked the best brother."

Asher glanced at me, his brow furrowed. He looked confused.

"Don't mind her. She'll tell you she has no filter, but really she just loves to say provocative things to surprise people. Or to get attention."

Cara sat back and took a sip of her drink. "It's so nice how you love me for me."

Evan came over with two beers and set one in front of Asher, then unceremoniously turned a chair around and straddled it. He gave me a quick chin tip.

"Hey, Evan."

"So, Asher, how was prison?" Cara asked.

I shot her a glare.

"Who the fuck are you?" he asked.

Her lips curled in a smile and she twirled her straw between her thumb and forefinger. "Grace's best friend. Confidante. Shoulder to cry on."

Asher held her in a hard glare, but Cara didn't flinch. They stared for a long moment, as if they were sizing each other up. The tension made my back tighten. It felt like two of the most important people in my life were about to decide whether or not they were going to hate each other.

"Prison was shitty," he said finally.

"Then I'm glad you're out." Cara held up her drink. After a second's hesitation, he clinked his beer against her glass and they both took a sip.

I let out a breath. That was a relief. I hadn't really thought about what would happen if Asher and Cara didn't get along, but it was a complication I did not need. I wasn't sure what had just passed between them, but if it meant they were willing to accept each other, I was grateful.

He set down the bottle and glanced around. "This place looks the same."

"It hasn't changed much," I said. "Hank might have added a new model train or two."

"Onion rings are still good," Evan said.

"Was the food in prison terrible?" Cara asked.

I started to tell her to shut up, but Asher didn't seem fazed.

"It was pretty bad."

"What was the worst part? Not the food, I mean overall."

He hesitated, like he was contemplating whether to answer, then took a drink of his beer. "You don't want to know."

Evan watched his brother, but his expression was impossible to read. He didn't say anything. Just set his beer on the table.

A cute blonde in a pink cardigan came up to our table, stopping next to Evan. She scrunched her shoulders and nibbled her bottom lip. "Hi. Sorry, I don't mean to interrupt, but you're Evan Bailey, right?"

Evan's eyes flicked up and down, like he was quickly

taking her in. He glanced away and took a long drink of his beer. "Yeah."

She looked over her shoulder. Three other girls at a table across the bar watched—probably her friends. They nodded with encouragement and one gave her an enthusiastic thumbs up.

"Um..." She fiddled with something in her hands. "You probably don't remember me, but you did some work on my dad's car. I came with him when he picked it up last week. I'm Jill."

Evan didn't look up. Just grunted.

Her smile faltered, but only for a second. Her eyes brightened and she took a deep breath. "I've never really done this before, but I thought maybe you'd want to hang out sometime."

She slipped a small piece of paper onto the table in front of him, her eyes nervously darting to the rest of us. Her finger pressed against the paper for another second, like it was a game piece and she wasn't quite ready to leave it there and end her turn. With another quick breath, she let go and straightened.

"So, that's my number. Text me, or give me a call?"

Evan barely acknowledged the scrap of paper. He took another drink and set his beer down. "Uh-huh."

I felt bad for the poor girl. She looked so sweet and hopeful. I didn't know what Evan's problem was, but I'd seen him shut down girls before. Especially when they looked like this—someone a guy could actually date.

"Okay, well, thanks. You guys have a good night." With another bright smile, she waved, then practically skipped back to her friends.

"She was cute," I said.

He half-shrugged, like he was bored with the whole thing. "Sure."

"Are you going to call her?"

His forehead creased and he looked at me like I'd just suggested something idiotic. "No."

"Why not? She seemed nice."

"They all seem nice." He set his beer down and stood. "I gotta get going. See you, Ash. Grace."

Without another word, he walked out.

I darted a quick glance at the girl. She was staring at our table, her expression stricken. Not only had Evan left her number sitting in plain sight, he'd set his beer on the other side of it, as if to make sure she'd see that he hadn't taken it with him.

"Nice, Evan," I muttered.

"What was that about?" Asher asked.

"I don't know. Apparently he's too broody and mysterious to even be nice to a girl."

"Huh."

Cara pursed her lips around her straw, then looked at her drink with annoyance. "I need another one. Anyone else?"

"I'm good for now," I said.

Asher shook his head, so Cara got up and went to the bar.

"Your friend is weird."

"Cara? Oh, I know. She takes some getting used to. But underneath her antics, she has a heart of gold. She just doesn't let many people see it."

As if on cue, Cara caught my eye. She gave me a dramatic wink before pointing toward the pool tables.

Giving me some alone time with Asher. God, I loved her.

"Was it just me, or did it seem like she and Evan couldn't see each other?" he asked.

"You noticed it too? Oh my god, it's the weirdest thing."

"Did something happen between them?"

I shook my head. "No. They've always been like that, since the first time they met. And she's the same with Levi. It's like they passively ignore each other. I guess it's better than Logan. They actively hate each other."

"Really?"

"Oh yeah. They can't go ten seconds without fighting. I think he's around here somewhere, so hopefully they can both behave themselves."

"Does she get along with anyone besides you?"

I laughed. "Yes, she does. She and Gavin get along okay. She doesn't ignore him, at least, although he's like a puppy who won't leave you alone until you scratch behind his ears. He doesn't let people ignore him."

Asher's mouth turned up in a hint of a smile. "That kid."

Just that twitch of his lips made my heart swell. "I know. He's crazy, but we love him."

The noise in the bar grew as the tables filled. Asher's gaze wandered and I fidgeted in my chair. People were staring at him. Not everyone, but enough that it was noticeable. It made me want to go toss drinks in all their stupid faces.

"Easy there, tiger," Asher said.

"People are staring."

"Yeah." He took another drink. "Figured they would."

"It doesn't bother you?"

He shrugged. "Not much I can do. It's not like I can drag them outside and beat the shit out of them."

I started to laugh, but his face was so serious. I wasn't sure if he was kidding.

"So is this a typical Saturday night for you?" He set his empty on the table.

"More or less. I don't always go out, especially since I bought the house. I've spent a lot of nights with a hammer or a paint roller instead of a drink."

"You've had help, though, right?"

"Yeah, some, particularly with the big stuff. Gavin still insists he has scars from clearing blackberry bushes."

He was quiet for a moment, his eyes intent on his beer bottle. He idly turned it around a few times. "If you need help with anything, let me know."

My heart did a little victory dance, but I tried to keep my expression measured. "That would be great. Thanks."

His eyes swept the bar again. "I should probably call it a night."

My momentary rush of happiness fell just as fast. "Are you sure?"

"Yeah. I know it's early, but I haven't exactly been sleeping well. I'm kinda worn out."

"Okay. Well, it was good to see you."

"You too." He stood, and I followed. "You're okay to get home?"

"Yeah, I came with Cara. She's around here somewhere."

He nodded. "Good. Night, Grace."

"Goodnight."

He hesitated for a second and I thought maybe he'd change his mind. But he turned and walked away.

I slowly sank back into my chair, not quite sure how to feel. He hadn't stayed long, but at least he'd come. And it hadn't been strained or awkward.

But it had been awfully *friendly.*

"Hey, G."

I gasped as Logan dropped into the chair next to me. "Damn it. You scared me."

"You had such a great *staring off into the distance* thing going on, I couldn't help myself."

"Thanks." I rolled my eyes.

"Anytime. So what happened? You scare him away already?"

"He said he was tired. Plus half the assholes in here kept staring at him."

Logan cast a random glare around the room. "Fuckers. I'm disappointed he left. I was about to come over here and start flirting with you to make him jealous."

I laughed. "Oh yeah. Great plan."

"You don't think it would work?"

"No."

"You vastly underestimate my flirtation skills. I could have had him fuming with jealousy. Make him go all caveman possessive."

I glanced away, hoping my cheeks weren't flushing. Asher going caveman possessive over me sounded all too good right now. "Yeah, well, I'm pretty sure he's trying to friend-zone me."

"God, prison fucked him up more than I thought."

"I know, right? Who wouldn't want all this?" I gestured at myself.

"That's what I'm talking about. I know you're getting up there, but you're not bad for your age."

I punched him in the arm. "Jerk."

He just grinned at me.

"You owe me a drink for that."

He groaned, like I'd just asked him to fix a hole in my roof. "Fine. What're you drinking?"

"Gin and tonic."

"All right. I'll fill in for the Bailey who should be buying you drinks tonight. And I won't even expect you to put out."

"That's good because I prefer men, not little boys."

"Ouch." He put a hand on his chest. "And damn it, I can't even brag about how big my dick is, because it's you and that's too weird."

I laughed while he went to the bar. Maybe tonight hadn't ended with Asher walking me to my car, giving in to his feelings, and kissing the hell out of me. Not that I'd been fantasizing about that all day. But it hadn't been bad. We'd hung out. Talked a little. It had been nice.

I wasn't sure I could call it a step forward, but at least it wasn't a step back. And at this point, maybe that was a win.

DEAR ASHER

 *ear Asher,*

*I*F *I* E̲V̲E̲R̲ T̲E̲L̲L̲ Y̲O̲U̲ *I have plans to go backpacking with your brothers again, please paste this letter to my face. Five days in the wilderness with four Baileys? Unbelievable. Your brothers are animals under the best of conditions, but in their natural habitat they're utterly ridiculous. Gram tried to warn me, but of course I didn't listen.*

Actually, our trip was amazing, despite the fact that your brothers are gross. I'd trained to carry my gear, so that wasn't a problem. My feet hurt like crazy, though, especially on the second day. I woke up and my feet already ached, so putting in another ten miles was brutal.

But at the end of that day, I felt like kind of a badass. I kept up with them and I didn't quit.

I think something happened to all of us on the second day. Day one, our spirits were high; there was talking and joking around. Day two, we were quiet. Even Logan and Gavin, which was so weird. It was like we were all digging deep to see if we had what it took. On day two, you still feel like you have so far to go, but you're already tired and sore, and you wonder if you're really cut out for this.

But on the morning of day three, something was different. I think partly we all felt a little better. Like we'd pushed through the initial soreness and our bodies were adapting. But there was a mental shift, too. I almost can't explain it.

Evan smiled. He actually smiled. More than once. I can't remember the last time I saw him do that.

I saw it in Logan too. He sort of chilled out. It was like he didn't need to fill in every silence or make sure someone was always looking at him.

Gavin was the calmest I've ever seen him. It was eerie, actually. Not that we didn't have to stop him from killing himself at least a dozen times. He tried to catch a rattlesnake, Asher. Why does he have a death wish? But overall, he was way more mellow than normal.

Speaking of smiling, when we stopped for lunch that day, Levi cracked a joke. Can you believe it? I didn't think he remembered how. I forgot how funny he could be.

I don't know what it was. Maybe being away from everything with no distractions. Out in the fresh air under that huge blue sky, the mountains all around us. Or maybe Gram's right and you are all a bunch of wild animals. Maybe I was seeing the Bailey men as they're meant to be, wild and free.

Whatever it was, there was some magic out there. It was a grueling hike and sleeping on the ground sucks, but I'd do it again in a heartbeat, especially if you were there. I'd love to see what the wilderness would do to you. If it would open you up and set you free the way it did for them.

Maybe someday we'll experience that together.

In any case, I not only survived, I conquered. Now I'm happy to be home, and a bed has never felt so good.

LOVE YOU,

   Grace

13

ASHER

*S*ometimes it was annoying as hell how fast word could spread in this town. Although the number of people stopping by Gram's to gawk at the ex-con slowed, I couldn't go anywhere without being followed by whispers and stares. The gossip train was rolling. Rumors ranged from a prison riot leading to my escape—no idea how they'd come up with that one, since I wasn't in hiding—to my family being secretly rich and bribing the governor.

My favorite was the speculation that I'd never been in prison at all—that I was actually a spy and had been on an extended covert mission overseas.

People around here had always loved spinning tall tales, so I wasn't sure if anyone actually believed all that bullshit. But it fed the town's curiosity.

However, sometimes word getting around could work in a guy's favor. Case in point, after Gram loaned me out to my great-aunt Tillie to fix a few things she claimed had been on my great-uncle Fred's honey-do list for a decade, I started to get calls. A week later, I had enough work that I could consider myself employed.

Becoming the local handyman hadn't exactly been the plan. But it was a way to get back on my feet, and I liked that there wasn't too much commitment. As hard as I was trying to adapt to life in Tilikum again, I still had doubts. Big ones. I didn't want anything tying me down right now.

I'd spent most of the day at Mitch and Darcy Benson's house, installing a new sliding door. Mitch had come home partway through the day and had eyed me warily for a while. I wasn't sure whether he was threatened by the fact that he had an ex-con in his house, or didn't like that his wife had called someone else to do a job. A few hard stares back at him and he'd left me alone. But it hadn't exactly been comfortable.

Maybe I'd stick with little old ladies for clients. The worst they did was gawk at my tattoos and try to feed me cookies.

My route home took me through town. Dark clouds were rolling in and the air smelled like rain. I passed the Steaming Mug and my gaze lingered on the coffee shop as I slowly drove by. Just a glimpse of the place where Grace worked, and my mind was suddenly filled with her.

She was the moon to my ocean. I couldn't escape her gravity.

But I was sure as hell fighting it. I had to.

The other night at the Caboose, I'd come dangerously close to giving in. Again. Sitting next to her, hearing her voice, our legs touching beneath the table, I'd almost caved. I'd been a heartbeat away from hauling her out to my truck and fucking her right there in the parking lot.

It had been such a long time.

Instead, I'd left. And it had been the right call. I couldn't let that happen. I'd only wind up hurting her more than I already had.

Since then, I'd kept my distance. She was at Gram's for Tuesday dinner, but I stayed in the kitchen—surrounded by my brothers—the whole time. I didn't want to risk being alone with her. The two of us out on the back porch again would be a recipe for temptation I didn't know if I could resist.

Other than that, I hadn't seen her. We texted back and forth a little, but I avoided making plans with her. I still didn't know if what I was attempting was possible—if we could live separate lives, side by side in the same town. And maybe it was wrong of me to stay. Maybe I was making it harder for her to let go, just by being here.

Something in the middle of the road caught my attention and I slammed on the brakes to avoid hitting it. I jerked forward against the seat belt and my hands clenched the steering wheel.

Harvey Johnston slowly stood and adjusted his cowboy hat. He grinned and held his hand up in a wave.

I rolled down the window and leaned out. "Harvey, what are you doing in the street?"

He turned in a slow circle. "Am I?"

"Yeah, buddy. Did you lose something?"

His brow furrowed and he patted himself down, like he was looking for something. A smile crossed his face. He reached into the pocket of his leather vest and pulled out a small spray bottle. "Found it."

"What is that?"

"Squirrel repellent," he said, triumphant. He tipped his hat to me and wandered over to the sidewalk.

Chuckling, I shook my head and kept driving.

I would miss this place if I left.

I drove by the gym where I used to train and, on a whim, I pulled over and parked. I'd passed it at least a dozen times, but I hadn't gone in. My life as a fighter had developed there. For a kid with a lot of anger to work through, it had been a much-needed outlet.

But the skills I'd learned there had also been one of the reasons I'd faced jail time.

I looked down at my hands, flexing them a few times. My knuckles were mostly healed and the cut on my forehead was barely a scab. The marks I bore from years of fighting had faded, the scars becoming harder to see. Unfortunately, the ones on the inside hadn't gone anywhere.

Clenching my fists again, I thought about the last time I'd hit something. It had been a while, and as fucked up as it was, a part of me missed it.

The demons wanted to be let out.

Which was why I was not going into that gym to ask to start training again. My days as a fighter were over.

But I did need a place to work out. There was another gym over by the college, but it was one of those chain places. I didn't need rows of treadmills and repetitive pop music played over the speaker system. I needed a place to lift.

I went inside and was greeted by the familiar smells of rubber and metal. One side of the gym had a weight training area, with squat racks, benches, and free weights. That was what I was after. I'd worked out a lot in prison, and I didn't want to lose my strength.

The other side had open practice mats, a roped-off boxing ring, and an MMA cage toward the back. Punching bags hung from steel chains. A coach worked with a small class on one of the grappling mats and a couple of guys sparred in the ring.

I'd never thought of MMA as anything other than a hobby, even when I'd entered tournaments. I'd just enjoyed the physical and mental challenge, and it had taught me a lot.

But in prison, fighting had become something different for me. Something dark and dangerous. Something I no longer trusted.

I tore my gaze away from the mats and found someone who worked there. He set me up with a membership so I could come in and lift. And even though I wasn't putting on gloves again, it felt like a step in the right direction to do this for myself. It wasn't much, and I was still living with Gram for the time being. But it was something.

Dusk was falling when I left. The clouds covered any trace of the darkening sky and the first drops of rain pattered against the asphalt. Felt like we were in for a storm.

I walked up the block to my truck, fiddling with the keys in my pocket. The street was empty, as if everyone had scurried inside at the threat of rain. But before I'd made it halfway, my back tightened and a chill shot down my spine.

Eyes. Someone was watching me.

I slowed my pace, straining to listen. Were there footsteps behind me, or was that just the rain? Huge drops splashed across my arms, dripped into my hair. My heart raced and my body tingled with adrenaline. I clenched my fists, digging my fingers into my palms.

I stopped next to my truck and whipped around, my arm already cocked and ready to lay a motherfucker out.

Nothing. The street was empty. Not even a fucking squirrel.

Thunder rumbled in the distance and rain pelted me, falling hard now. Squinting in the waning light, I searched, but I didn't see anyone. Had I imagined it? Or had someone been watching? Slowly, I lowered my arm.

Feeling unsettled, I got into my truck and drove home.

The windshield wipers could hardly keep up with the sudden downpour. My eyes alternated between watching the road, and checking the mirrors, looking for any sign that I was being followed.

No headlights flashed behind me. I tried to relax my grip on the steering wheel, but my heart still beat too fast. My instincts screamed at me. You had to have eyes in the back of your head in prison, especially when you were a constant target. I hadn't seen anyone, but I'd felt the all-too-familiar sensation of being watched.

I didn't know what it meant, but it couldn't be good.

The windows glowed with light when I got to Gram's. I sat in the truck for a few minutes, my eyes glued to the rear-view mirror, just in case. But no one else came down the road.

And there she was again, filling my thoughts out of nowhere. Grace.

I had a sudden vision of knocking on her door, dripping wet from the rain. Of her pulling me inside and stripping off my soaked clothes to get me warm. Her hands all over me. Her skin pressed against mine.

My heartbeat slowing to match hers.

Jesus. Where had that come from?

With one last glance in the rear-view, I got out of the truck. I ran up to the front porch to get out of the rain and almost stepped on a box sitting on the welcome mat. That was weird. It didn't look like a package that had been shipped—too flimsy. And there was no address label. Just an envelope with my name on it taped to the top.

Something made me reluctant to touch it, but I picked it up and took it inside.

"Hey, Gram?"

Her voice came from the kitchen. "Hi there, Bear."

"Do you know who left this?" I asked as I walked in. I set the box on the counter.

Gram sat at the big farmhouse table with a mug of tea and the remnants of her dinner. She wore a pair of reading glasses and had a thick novel open next to her plate. "Left what?"

"This box. It was on the porch."

"No, they must not have rung the bell."

Eying the box with suspicion, I pulled off the envelope and opened it. A slip of paper was tucked inside. It read, *It's not your birthday, but we thought you might enjoy some cake.*

I set the note aside and popped the tape on the top.

Sure enough, inside was a small cake. Had to be homemade. The chocolate frosting was uneven and someone had attempted to write *Asher* in blue. But it was mostly a jumbled mess of smears.

"What the..."

"What is it?" Gram asked.

"A cake."

"Who's it from?"

I turned both the note and envelope over to see if I'd missed something. "I don't know. It doesn't say."

"Is it actually cake, or is something else with frosting on it?"

"That's a very good question."

Without knowing who'd left this, it could be anything. Once we'd sent a box of donuts filled with hot sauce and mayonnaise to one of the Haven brothers. This cake smelled good, but there was no way I trusted it.

I grabbed a knife and sliced through the middle. It felt like cake until I hit something hard. Thick chunks fell away, crumbling around an object, like it had been baked right in.

Oh for fuck's sake. I picked through the crumbs and pulled out a metal file.

Someone had left me a cake with a file baked into it.

I held it up to show Gram. "This was in it."

She eyed it over the rim of her glasses. "That would have been more helpful before they let you out of prison."

I couldn't help but laugh. "Really, Gram?"

She just shrugged.

This had to have been one of my brothers. Probably Logan, the fucker. I was going to have to get him back for this.

"Do you want any of it?" I asked.

Gram raised her eyebrows. "You realize it was probably one of those animals you call brothers who baked that, don't you?"

"Yeah." I leaned closer and inhaled. "It smells like chocolate."

"Suit yourself, but I wouldn't chance it."

"You're probably right. Are you sure you don't know who left this?"

She didn't look up from her book. "Sure don't."

There wasn't even a hint of humor in her voice. No indication that she knew and was keeping it from me. But I still wasn't sure. Gram was crafty. She might have been in on it. She never owned up to a prank, but I'd caught an amused twinkle in her eye more than once.

I pulled out my phone and took a quick picture before tossing the cake in the trash. I was going to text my brothers and see if the perpetrator would fess up, but I felt the sudden pull of Grace's gravity.

This would make her laugh. I could send it to her just to make her laugh, right? That wouldn't hurt anything.

Me: *Found this on the porch.*

Grace: *Is that a file? Oh my god, that's a terrible joke. I can't stop laughing.*

Me: *My money is on Logan, but I'm not ruling out Gavin.*

Grace: *Probably both. Or Levi. He's quiet about it, but he won't hesitate if he sees an opening. What are you going to do to get them back?*

Me: *I'll have to think of something.*

Grace: *Better make it good.*

Me: *I will.*

My thumbs hesitated above the keys, ready to type, *maybe I can come over and we can plot their demise together?* But I stopped. Set my phone down.

That wasn't a good idea. Until I was sure we could just be friends, I needed to be careful. Anything else wasn't fair to her.

And hell, it wasn't fair to me either.

14

GRACE

*A*s much as I loved my little house—particularly for what it meant—Cara had the coolest house in town. When she'd first moved here, she'd bemoaned the lack of what she called *adequate housing options*. I guess when you'd grown up in a literal mansion, small-town living took some getting used to.

She'd found a house built on the hillside overlooking the river, just on the north edge of town. The owners hadn't been looking to sell, but she'd offered them a ridiculous amount of money for it. Then she'd gutted it and completely remodeled every inch.

Or, more accurately, she'd sipped drinks and ogled the construction crew while they remodeled every inch.

Fine. *We'd* ogled the construction crew.

That had been a fun six months.

I'd texted her this morning to see if she wanted to run some errands with me. She hadn't answered yet, but I'd decided to come over anyway.

I parked in her driveway and let myself in. "Cara?"

The main floor had an open floorplan. From the entry, I

could see all the way to the back of the house, where floor-to-ceiling windows offered an incredible view of the river. Dark wood beams across the ceiling contrasted beautifully with her light furniture and cabinetry.

"Cara?" I called again. "Are you home?"

She appeared at the top of the wide staircase carrying a white suitcase. "Hey, fluffy love bunny. I didn't hear you come in."

"Are you going somewhere? Or did I invite you over for a slumber party and forgot?"

"I have to go to L.A." She came down and set the suitcase at the bottom of the stairs.

"Is everything okay?"

She sighed. "Not according to my mother, but she's insane, so who knows. She's going through a crisis. Again. I'll be back in a few days."

"I hope she's all right."

"She's probably fine. If you think I'm dramatic, she makes me look like a weed smoking surfer who meditates. Anyway, I'm so sorry to leave you right now."

"Why are you sorry?"

"Because we're on a mission to get your fiancé back."

"We?"

She rolled her eyes in exasperation. "Yes, we. You're my person, Grace. You want something, I help you get it. That's how this works. You want Asher Bailey to marry you? I'm going to get that stubborn tattooed son-of-a-bitch to the fucking altar."

I stepped in and hugged her. "You're crazy, but I love you."

"I know. I love you too." She squeezed me and planted a kiss on my head. "I got your text, but what errands did you need to run? Do you want me to come with you? I can call and get them to hold the plane for a couple of hours."

Cara rarely flew commercial, especially when she made quick trips home. She preferred to charter small private planes.

"Don't be silly," I said. "I need a few groceries and some stuff at the hardware store. But it's no big deal."

"Are you sure?"

"Positive."

She eyed me for a second, like she wasn't sure about leaving me alone. "Okay. Keep me updated on any and all developments with Asher. If that man so much as smiles at you, I want to hear about it."

"Yeah, of course. Do you want a ride to the airfield?"

"No, I'll just leave my car there."

I walked her outside so we could hug and say goodbye. The clouds were finally clearing up after last night's storm. I drove back into town and stopped at a drive-through ATM, then popped into work to see how things were going. If Cara had been with me, we would have grabbed lunch somewhere downtown, but since I was alone, I just poured myself a cup of coffee to go and headed out.

I'd planned to stop for some groceries, but that could wait. I did need to swing by the hardware store. Since buying my house, I'd become a regular customer. Unlike Cara, I didn't have a limitless bank account, so hiring a contractor to come in and do all the work in one fell swoop was out. She'd offered to bankroll it for me, but there was no way I could accept that kind of money from her.

The hardware store was a short drive from the Steaming Mug. I slowed at an intersection shortly before the turn. Two guys stood in the bed of a pickup truck. I got closer and sure enough, it was Luke and Zachary Haven. They were scraping a Bailey Avenue sticker off the street sign.

I chuckled as I drove by. They had their work cut out for them. Those stickers were everywhere. I wondered if they knew about the one on my street. I'd have to ask Logan and Gavin if they had any more stickers so I could replace it if someone took it off. Although they hadn't admitted to putting up all the Bailey street signs, it had obviously been them.

That reminded me, I needed to crochet another beard to put on Lola, the pinup girl statue. It had been a while since any of us had bearded her.

A handful of cars were parked outside the hardware store. Asher had worked here back in college. It was so strange. It didn't look any different. Still the same faded red building with a big sign that read *Tilikum Hardware* across the front. I could remember meeting Asher here after he got off work. Hopping into his car and driving into town to get burgers and ice cream at the Zany Zebra. Or going back to his apartment and straight to his bed.

The front doors opened, and someone walked out pushing a full cart. What was it I'd needed here? Suddenly I couldn't quite remember. I tapped the steering wheel and my engine still hummed. I hadn't turned the car off yet.

My chest felt strangely tight and a nervous ache clawed at me from the inside. I hadn't eaten much today. Maybe the coffee wasn't sitting well in my empty stomach.

I backed out of my parking spot, deciding food was more important than whatever I'd been meaning to get. I'd just have to come back later.

At home, I fixed myself a quick lunch. About half an hour later, there was a knock on my door. I answered it to find a grocery delivery sitting on the step. That was weird.

The delivery person was already pulling out of the driveway. I went outside and tried to wave him down—he must have had the wrong address—but he didn't see me.

I eyed the bags sitting in front of my door, not sure what to do with them. Maybe they were for one of my neighbors. I crouched down and unfolded the receipt stapled to the first bag. It had a handwritten note at the bottom.

Deliver to Grace Miles. From Cara Goulding.

Oh my god. Cara had ordered me groceries.

I brought them inside, then sent her a text.

Me: *Why did you send me groceries?*

Cara: *You said you needed some.*

Me: *That doesn't really answer my question. I can buy my own groceries.*

Cara: *I know but I felt bad for bailing on you before we could run errands. So now you don't have to.*

Me: *You're so silly. What if I'd gone to the store already?*

Cara: *You didn't.*

Me: *You're very sure about that.*

Cara: *I know you.*

Me: *I guess you do. Anyway, this is really sweet. Thank you.*

Cara: *No problem, boo. Love you!*

Me: *Love you too.*

I put the groceries away—she'd ordered my favorite of everything—and pondered what to do with the rest of my day. I could turn on a mindless show and crochet. That would at least keep my hands busy. But I was craving a more intense activity.

With a house to remodel, there was no shortage of things to do. I changed into an old t-shirt and cutoffs so I could get to work.

The kitchen was still half demolished, but I wasn't ready to dive into that project any further. However, there was the old rec room next to the garage. I hadn't touched that space yet.

I wandered over and stood in the doorway with my hands on my hips. Dusty rose. That was probably what they'd called this shade of carpet. Over the years, the pink had faded into a sad gray-tinged mauve. I could practically smell the decades of dirt ground into the fibers. No wonder I hadn't tackled this room yet. Gross.

The flooring needed to go, so I'd start there. With a deep breath of resolve, I started pulling up the baseboards. The thin oak popped off the walls in long strips. Once I'd taken all the old trim out to the debris pile in the garage, it was time to tackle the carpet.

I loosened one corner and pulled it back, hoping to see the same original hardwoods that I'd found throughout most of the house. But it looked like there was a layer of linoleum underneath. That was odd. And hideous. I didn't know what was worse—the yellow, brown, and olive-green pattern on this floor, or the dusty rose carpet someone had put over the top of it.

The linoleum seemed to be glued down. I sliced a piece of it with a box cutter and ripped it free. Particle board. Groaning, I tossed the floor scrap aside. One of the other rooms had been like this—a layer of particle board topped by glued-down linoleum. And it had been a nightmare to get out. This was going to be a lot more work than I'd thought.

I went back to the garage to get a crowbar when a thought crossed my mind. I could really use some help, and Asher had volunteered.

Had he meant it? I didn't think he would have said it otherwise. Maybe that had been a hint that he wanted to be involved. I certainly wanted him here, and not just so I could spend time with him—although that was also true. But I wanted him to have a hand in restoring this place. Give him a chance to put his mark on it.

And now that the thought was in my mind, I couldn't get it out. I'd been trying to give him space—it was clear he needed it—but right about now, I'd give almost anything to have him near me. Prison bars no longer separated us, but there were barriers just the same. I just needed a little bit of him. Enough to keep me going.

I brought the crowbar inside and found my phone so I could text him.

Me: *Hey. Remember when you said to let you know if I need help with the house?*

Asher: *Yeah, what do you need?*

His quick reply made me tear up. No questions, no excuses. Just, what do you need? I wished everything with him could be this easy.

Me: *I'm ripping up flooring and ran into a snag. I could use those big muscles of yours. Are you busy?*

Asher: *I'll be right over.*

15

GRACE

*L*ess than ten minutes later, Asher was on my doorstep. I opened the door and for a split second, I couldn't move. He was dressed in a tank top that showed the full span of his shoulders and the tattoos covering most of his right arm. He was so solid and thick, yet his deep brown eyes hinted at softness underneath all that muscle. At a piece of the Asher I'd once known.

He was standing right here. And even though he was only a foot away, I still missed him so much it hurt to breathe.

"Hey." I tried to keep my voice light. "Thanks for coming over."

"Sure. You didn't say you needed any tools, but I have a bunch in the truck just in case."

I stepped aside so he could come in. "Thanks. I think we're good for now. I thought this room just had carpet, but there's a layer of linoleum glued down to particle board underneath."

"Sounds shitty."

"Yeah, pulling up particle board is no fun."

I handed him a crowbar and led him to the room. He wrinkled his nose.

"I know, it smells dirty in here," I said. "This is one of the few rooms I haven't touched yet. In fact, I had a bunch of stuff stacked in front of the door for a long time. I almost forgot this was here."

He pulled a pair of work gloves out of his back pocket and put them on. "I can see why."

"I figure once we get the carpet out, we'll have a better idea of what we're dealing with. I'm hoping there's hardwood underneath the particle board, but it's hard to say. I don't know if this room is original, or if someone added it after the house was built or what."

"There's definitely a level change when you walk in here. This floor sits higher than the rest of the house. That's probably a good sign."

"Yeah, that's what I was thinking too."

He clapped his hands together. "All right. Let's get this dirty pink shit out of here."

"Amen to that."

The carpet came up without too much trouble. We sliced it so we could roll it up in sections, and haul them out to the debris pile. Then we pulled up the carpet strips so we didn't have to worry about all the sharp tacks getting in our way.

Asher took a crowbar to a section of particle board. With what looked like almost no effort, he loosened a large section of floor and freed it. We peeled back the linoleum and moved the particle board out of the way.

Just what I'd been hoping for. Hardwoods.

"Look at that, Gracie Bear. A hidden treasure for you."

Biting my lip, I kept my eyes on the floor. I didn't want

him to see me tearing up again. But he'd called me Gracie Bear.

I was so stupidly in love with this man.

"That's exactly what I was hoping to see."

"We'll need to be careful, but I don't see a lot of damage here. Hopefully the rest of it's the same."

"Yeah, I hope so too."

We got to work, gently freeing sections of particle board from the hardwood underneath. We were getting through it pretty fast, and I almost wished it was harder. Maybe I could find something else for us to do when we finished. Working side-by-side with him felt like a dream. I didn't want it to end.

"Did I tell you I met Jack?" he asked.

"My mom's Jack?"

"Yeah."

"No, you didn't. How'd that go?"

He tossed a chunk of flooring aside. "Awkward. I think I interrupted his shower."

I laughed. "Oops."

"What's he like?"

"He's a great guy. He can come across as kind of serious, but he's really a big sweetheart. He's so good to my mom."

"Yeah?"

"Definitely. She was hesitant about dating, and who can blame her after my father? But Jack was really patient. I think he just knew, and he was willing to wait for her to come around."

"How is he with Elijah?"

"He's great with him."

"Really?"

"Yeah. Mom wouldn't have kept dating him otherwise. It was always important to her that we got along with Jack."

Asher straightened and wiped his forehead with the back of his arm. "I saw Elijah, too. He came home while I was talking with Jack."

I could imagine how that had gone. "Let me guess. He had his face buried in a hoodie and he muttered three or four words you couldn't understand."

"I don't think he said anything."

"Yeah, he's like that lately. Not just with Jack. He barely talks to anyone."

"Why? What's wrong with him?"

I shrugged. "According to him? Nothing. According to the school counselor? Puberty. According to the therapist mom took him to? A latent reaction to the introduction of a new parental figure."

"How long have they been married?"

"A couple of years."

Asher's brow furrowed. "You're sure Jack is okay with him?"

"If you're wondering if Jack did something to hurt Elijah, there's no way. Jack's a good man. I think Eli's just been through a lot, the poor kid. When he was seven, he found out he had four other siblings by the father who'd basically abandoned him. Then our dad went to prison, and he had a million questions about what happened and why. It was tough. Meanwhile, Levi and Logan moved out, then Gavin. He loves those guys, but they're adults with their own lives, you know? They can't exactly be his playmates. Add in a new stepdad, and that's a lot for a little guy."

"Yeah, I guess it would be."

"Mom's doing everything she can for him. But you can't make someone open up, even when they're eleven."

"No, you can't. He was just so different when he was little."

"He was. Do you remember the dinosaur phase? Were you around for that?"

The corner of his mouth turned up. "Yeah, I remember. He was like four and he knew all those long names."

"Yep. He was so cute."

We took a quick break to get some water, then got back to work. The rest of the flooring came up without too much trouble—for Asher, at least. He was so strong, he made it look easy. I needed a lot more leverage. But in the end, we got the room cleared out.

I grabbed a broom and started sweeping up the dirt left behind while Asher inspected the hardwoods.

"These are in good shape," he said. "The nail holes can be patched. I think if you get these sanded down and refinished, they'll look nice."

"I'm so glad. One thing I've learned, you never know what you're going to find when you start pulling a house apart."

He paused in the back corner of the room and tilted his head, then crouched to get a closer look.

"Something wrong over there?"

"No." He traced his fingers across the floor. "But there's a seam here."

I leaned the broom against the wall. "A seam?"

"Yeah, like someone cut into the floor." He brushed more dust away. "It's a rectangle."

I crouched next to him and ran my fingers along the line. "Are the boards loose, or is it nailed down?"

"I'm not sure."

He found a flathead screwdriver and gently worked the end into one of the cracks. The whole section shifted. He worked his way down, gradually loosening the floorboards.

With a soft crack, the section came loose. We lifted it and set it aside.

Below the hardwood, someone had cut straight into the subfloor, leaving a hollow underneath. It was dark and dusty, but it wasn't empty.

"Oh my god, it's like a hidden compartment beneath the floor."

His brow furrowed. "Yeah, it actually is. I thought it might just be access to the crawl space. But someone built this after the fact."

I reached down but Asher grasped my wrist. "What? There's something down there."

He scowled at me. "Careful. I'll get it."

I was about to ask what on earth he was worried about, but stopped myself. His concern was so sweet, I didn't want to ruin it.

He pulled out a dust-covered box. It wasn't very big, not much larger than a shoebox. Cobwebs clung to it, but it seemed to be in good shape.

I brushed off the top. "It's wood. What do you think is in it?"

"Only one way to find out."

The hinges were stiff, but the lid opened. Inside was a cloth that might once have been white, but had faded to a dull cream color. I lifted it and set it aside.

Beneath the cloth, we found a stack of yellowing envelopes. I picked up the top one, handling it gently. The paper felt brittle and the outside was blank. No name or address. For a second, I was disappointed. Were there just a bunch of old, empty envelopes in here? Why would someone have put these beneath the floorboards?

But I opened the envelope and found a folded piece of paper inside.

"There's a note."

"What does it say?"

"Oh my god, I think it's a love note. Listen to this: 'My dearest E, I watched you from afar today, as I am inclined to do each time our paths cross. It is both a supreme delight and exquisite torture to see you, as I am unable to touch you. Our present situation frustrates, yet motivates me, for surely a solution can be found. My love for you is too great to set aside. I long for the time when we can be together in the bright light of day, as we are in the stolen moments we share under the cover of night. But fear not, my love, our time will come.'"

"Wow. That's romantic as hell."

"Isn't it? I wonder who they were. It's only addressed to E, but not signed. And there's no date, either."

I carefully folded the note and placed it back in the envelope. The rest were similar. Love notes written to someone named E, all lamenting their inability to be together, promising that their love would be worth the wait. Two were shorter, hastily-scrawled requests to meet in secret.

"I wish I knew who'd written these," I said. "I'm dying to know what happened. Who were they? Were they ever able to be together? This is going to drive me crazy."

"I think there's something else in here." He lifted an object and slipped it from its cloth wrapping.

It was a small hand-held mirror. The silver was dull and tarnished, but even without its original shine, it was beautiful. Detailed scrolling decorated the edges, and it had an intricate floral design on the back.

"Is that an inscription?" I asked. He handed me the mirror and I brought it closer so I could read it. "Eliza Bailey.

Oh my god, Asher, this belonged to a Bailey? I bet you're related to her. Have you ever heard of her?"

"No. But this looks old."

"It does look old. I bet she's E. These notes must have been for her. But why would someone have hidden them?"

"We could ask Gram, or one of my aunties. See if anyone knows who Eliza Bailey was."

"Good idea." I set the mirror gently in the box. "Do you want to take it? It looks like it belongs in your family. And I'm..." I trailed off, not finishing that sentence. *I'm not a Bailey.*

Because damn it, I should have been.

"No, you keep it. You found it, you should hang onto it."

"Okay. Thanks. I'll take good care of it."

He helped me replace the floorboard, making sure it sat securely in place. I took the box to my room for safekeeping and when I came out, Asher was waiting near the door.

I didn't want him to go, but I had a feeling he wasn't going to stay, even if I asked. I could still feel the distance he was keeping between us.

"Thanks again for your help."

"Anytime."

He opened the door and stepped outside. I leaned against the door frame, feeling both glad that he'd come and sad to see him go.

Turning, he hesitated. His eyes dipped to my mouth and a tiny spark of hope flared in my chest.

Go ahead, Asher. Come closer and kiss me. You know we both want it.

He looked up, meeting my gaze. "I'll see you later."

Trying not to let my disappointment show, I smiled. "Yeah. See you."

He went out to his truck and I shut the door behind him.

Feeling a little forlorn, I went back to my bedroom. The box was sitting on my bed, so I opened it and took the mirror out again. I traced my fingers over the name. I felt a connection to Eliza. Based on the notes, she'd probably been in love with a man she couldn't have. Although my situation wasn't the same—Asher and I had never had to meet under cover of darkness—I still understood what that felt like.

It basically sucked.

16

ASHER

I came home from work in the late afternoon, tired and sticky with sweat. I'd replaced a set of front porch stairs, which had put me in the full sun for most of the day. Gram wasn't home. I wasn't sure where she'd gone, but that was typical. She kept herself busy.

The floorboards creaked beneath my feet and I wondered if it would be worth trying to fix them. On the other hand, there was a certain charm to it. The floors had always creaked in this old house. I went upstairs, passing the photos Gram had on display. Pictures of us boys. An old photo of her and Grandad. My parents' wedding portrait.

I understood why she kept them there, although I found them hard to look at. Especially the photo of my parents. She had several photos of Grandad around the house— pictures of him alone as well as some of the two of them together. Their faded wedding photo hung on her bedroom wall, and there was a picture of him in the kitchen. I'd heard her say that it helped her keep him with her all the time.

More than once, I'd wondered how she'd weathered the

losses in her life with such grace and still seemed to find so much joy in living.

I peeled off my sweaty clothes and got in the shower. Despite the hot water, I couldn't relax. My back tightened and my heart thumped in my chest. I kept glancing out into the bathroom, checking the door, as if someone would come in. Logically I knew I was alone in the house, but the compulsion was too strong to ignore.

Finally, I stepped out of the shower and quickly locked the door.

Frustrated at my irrational reaction, I got back in and turned up the heat. Closed my eyes and took deep breaths to slow my racing heart. Repeated to myself, over and over, that I was home. I was fine.

I'd felt calm for most of the day, so this sudden flare of panic made me angry. Rage felt better than fear, so I gripped it tight. Let it smolder in my gut and flood my veins like fire.

God, I was so fucking mad.

The worst part was, I had nowhere to put all this anger. Or maybe I had too many places to put it. I was angry at the world, looking for a fight I couldn't have.

Angry at the inmates who'd constantly fucked with me.

At the prison guards who'd looked the other way.

At the judge who'd handed down the sentence. At the fucking prosecutor who hadn't given me a break. At the attorney who'd convinced me the plea deal was my only option.

And at that piece of shit who'd attacked Grace.

Memories flashed through my mind. I couldn't stop them. Blood and pain. The sound of bone crunching. I felt pinned down. Helpless. Too many arms holding me in place.

A surge of rage and fear ripped through me, and for a

second, I had no idea where I was. Reacting on instinct, I struck out with my fist, punching something solid.

But my knuckles didn't sink into flesh over ribs or crack against someone's jaw. Gasping for air, I reached out with my other hand to brace myself, finding cool tile against my palm. Hot water streamed over me, the low hum of the shower the only sound.

Opening my eyes, I looked down at my right hand. Goddammit, I'd just punched a shower tile. I slowly flexed my fingers, hoping I hadn't broken anything. I could move them, but my knuckles were already bruising.

That was going to be fun to explain.

But that wasn't the worst part. The real bitch was, I felt better. My hand began to throb with pain, but my head was clear, my heart rate returning to normal. I opened and closed my fist a few more times. Apparently when I got out of control like that, I just needed to hit something.

Fuck.

I still felt the itch. The desire to unleash my anger and fuck someone up. The fact that hitting things—or people— was so cathartic was not a good sign. I'd been hoping that urge would go away once I got out. But so far, it hadn't.

Careful of my newly bruised knuckles, I finished up in the shower and got dressed. There was plenty of time before it got dark, so I decided to go work on the new chicken coop. Gram had mentioned at dinner last week that a new home for her peckers—god, why did she have to call them that?— was a great idea. And I needed to keep busy—do something with all this pent-up energy.

And anger.

I went out to the shop, strapped my tool belt around my waist, and walked out back.

Gram came home not long after I got started and poked

her head out the back door. "Bear, you be careful of my peckers. Watch your step."

"Don't worry, I won't step on a chicken."

She narrowed her eyes, like she wasn't quite sure she trusted me around her poultry. I chuckled softly and shook my head.

I heard a vehicle pull up out front and a minute later, Levi came around the side of the house. He wore an old t-shirt and jeans and had a tool belt around his waist. He carried a measuring tape and had a pencil tucked behind his ear.

I stood, pocketing the nail I'd been about to hammer in. "Hey. What's going on?"

"What are you doing?"

"Building Gram a new chicken coop. You know, for her peckers." I nodded toward the chickens scratching in the dirt nearby.

His jaw tightened, and his defensive posture triggered a hit of adrenaline. I didn't actually think he was about to come at me swinging, but I'd been in enough fights to recognize the hostility in his eyes.

"I came over to do that," he said.

I paused, the hammer dangling from my hand. "Okay. I've got it, though."

"Did you measure everything properly? Do you have the dimensions?"

"Getting locked up didn't make me an idiot," I snapped. "Yes, I measured everything."

"I didn't say you were an idiot."

"Fine, but why are you looking at me like I just pissed in your toastie flakes?"

"I just want to make sure it gets done right."

What the hell was his problem? "I've got it, Levi. If you want to help, go bring some lumber around."

"Asher, you—"

Gram opened the back door and stepped onto the porch, cutting him off with a sharp look. She crossed her arms, her eyes moving between the two of us. "Boys. I'm sure I don't need to get the old boxing gloves out."

In the early days after our parents had died, all five of us had harbored a lot of aggression, and we'd taken it out on each other. One day, Gram had come home with two pairs of boxing gloves. From then on, if our fighting got out of control, she'd have us put the gloves on and go at each other in the backyard. After we'd thrown some punches and gotten it out of our system, she'd made us take the gloves off and hug it out. We'd called it the Arena.

I flexed my fists. There was no way I was boxing with my brother, no matter what we'd done as kids. "No, Gram. We're good."

"Are you sure? Because I still have them."

Levi's eyes flicked to me. "Nope. We're fine."

"Good," she said with a smile, then went back inside.

Levi and I eyed each other for a second. I didn't understand why he was being such a dick. Why did he care if I built a new chicken coop? I was about to ask why it mattered, but with a scowl, he turned around and left.

17

ASHER

*M*y job Thursday took me downtown, to the Art of Manliness, a barber shop still owned by Gerald McMillan. His old-fashioned barber pole had stopped spinning and he'd called me to see if I could fix it. Totally outside my wheelhouse, but I told him I'd see what I could do.

As I stepped back and watched it spin, I couldn't help but congratulate myself. Not bad for having no clue what I was doing.

Gerald came out wearing a white apron over his broad chest. He was bald on top, but sported a thick auburn beard. "Looks great, Asher. Thank you."

"Hey, no problem."

We shook hands and he paid me, then I gathered up my stuff and went back to my truck.

The firehouse was just up the hill. I put my tools in the truck and revisited the same internal debate I'd had with myself at least a dozen times since I'd been home. Chief Stanley. Should I go talk to him?

It seemed like half the town had wanted to gawk at me.

But I hadn't heard from the chief. Of course, I hadn't reached out either. But this was a tough one. He'd been my mentor. Given an angry kid a place to stay out of trouble. Encouraged me to follow my dream.

And watched me get hauled away to prison after pleading guilty to manslaughter.

But avoidance would only work so long in this town. Sooner or later, I'd run into him. It would probably be better to go see him now. Get it over with. The firehouse was a short walk from where I'd parked, so I pocketed my keys and started up the hill.

As I crossed the street, voices down by the Zany Zebra caught my attention. A bunch of kids were outside the black-and-white-striped burger joint, but it didn't sound like they were joking around or having fun. It looked like three of them were ganging up on the fourth.

The victim's head was buried in a hoodie, so I couldn't see his face. But the way he backed away from the others, I could tell he didn't want to be there. One of the other kids stepped forward and shoved his shoulder. He staggered and clutched his backpack strap to keep it from falling. His hood slipped back and I got a glimpse of his face.

Oh hell no. That was Elijah.

"Hey," I yelled. "Assholes. Get the hell away from him."

Fixing the little shits with a hard glare, I stalked down the street toward them. They were just kids; I wasn't going to hurt them. But it did give me a great deal of satisfaction to see their eyes widen with fear and their faces go pale. They looked like they were about to piss their pants. One took off running in the opposite direction. That seemed to jolt the other two into action, and a second later, all three were sprinting down the street.

Elijah's hoodie was still partly off his head, so I could

actually see his face. He looked so different—so much older. I hardly saw any of Naomi, or even Grace, in him. He must have taken after his dad, which probably kind of sucked for him. He was old enough to realize that if he didn't resemble his mom, he might look like his father. The father who'd abandoned him and was now in prison. Not that I was one to judge a guy for being in prison—obviously. But Grace and Elijah's father was a piece of shit regardless.

"Hey buddy, are you okay?"

Elijah stared at me, his blue eyes piercing. He looked angry, but maybe he was just upset. Or embarrassed. Getting picked on sucked no matter who you were.

Grace had said he didn't talk much, but I still wanted to know if he was all right. So I tried again. "Do those kids pick on you a lot?"

"Why do you care?" He adjusted his backpack on his shoulder.

At least that was a response. "Because I do. You're Grace's little brother. I'm Asher. I don't know if you remember me."

"I know who you are."

"Okay. Do you need a ride home or anything?"

"No."

"Buddy, I live right next door to you. It's not a big deal."

The groove between his eyebrows deepened. "I'm not your buddy. Just leave me alone."

He hiked his backpack up his shoulder and walked away.

I thought about following him, but I didn't want to be creepy, so I let him go. Still, I had that same unsettled feeling I'd had when I saw him the first time. Was Elijah being bullied? Was that why he was so silent and sullen? I wondered if Grace knew anything about this.

Of course, I might have witnessed a random encounter. I

had no idea if those kids picked on him all the time, or if they'd just decided to be assholes because it had been three against one. Maybe he'd even started it. It was hard to say.

I turned around and headed for the firehouse but stopped again at the intersection. My back tensed with the familiar feeling of eyes on me.

Someone watching.

Fuck, I hated this feeling.

It had happened a couple of times since the other night at the gym. Not every time I went out, but enough that I was either being followed, or I was really fucking paranoid.

Honestly, I wasn't sure which would be worse.

I'd been home for about three weeks and was trying to hold it together. My mental state wasn't as steady as it probably appeared. I'd been able to fake it so far, but the truth was, I was hanging on by a thread. I had a hard time sleeping, and it was a rare night that I didn't wake up in a cold sweat from a nightmare. I'd started barricading my room at night, and I couldn't take a shower without locking the bathroom door, even when no one was home.

The other day, I'd shut all the curtains in Gram's house. She'd opened them all again, muttering about it being too dark inside. I still couldn't explain it, but I'd felt so exposed. Like I needed a place to hide.

And every time I left her house, I took roundabout routes wherever I was going, in case I was being followed. I watched the rear-view mirror as much as the road in front of me, always half-convinced someone was back there.

It was fucked up, and I knew it. But realizing it didn't do anything to change how I felt.

My heart pounded in my chest. I scanned the road, but I didn't see anything suspicious. Elijah had cut through Lumberjack Park and disappeared. People were out and about, a car drove by, and a squirrel scurried past, racing up a tree. If someone was watching me, they were doing a good job of staying out of sight.

Telling myself I probably wouldn't be attacked in the street in the middle of the afternoon, I kept walking.

The feeling subsided by the time I got to the firehouse. Either that, or the sensation of being watched was edged out by the dread of going in there. Of facing this part of my past.

Just looking at the building made my chest ache. It had been a second home to me, the crew an extension of my family.

It was where I'd proposed to Grace.

Fuck.

One of the garage bays was open, but the engine wasn't there. A couple of guys were working on the ambulance. There'd be others inside. I wondered if my brothers were on duty. The fire chief's truck, with its Tilikum Fire Department emblem on the door, was in the parking lot, so Chief Stanley was here.

Time to do this.

I went in the side entrance and waited, shoving my hands in my pockets. Everything looked the same. The TFD emblem painted on the wall. Chief Stanley's portrait with his name and title underneath. Another wall had a bulletin board with community notices and posters on fire safety. And a table held stacks of red plastic fireman's helmets for when kids came in for field trips.

Reminded me of Elijah. I'd brought him a bunch of those hats so he'd always have one.

I avoided looking at the memorial wall. Wasn't really prepared to face the photo of my dad.

"Holy shit." Christian came down the stairs, dressed in street clothes. "Asher?"

Seeing Christian hit me hard—kicked some of the breath from my lungs. He'd been there. "Yeah. Hey, man."

"Goddamn, it's good to see you." He gave me a quick, back-slap hug. "I heard you were out already. How are you doing?"

"Not bad, considering." That wasn't exactly a lie, and I certainly didn't want to dig too deep into that question. "Is Chief here?"

"Yeah, he's upstairs. Hey, can I just say something?"

"Sure."

He paused for a second. "I just wish there'd been something else I could have done. Something I could have said differently to the cops, I don't know."

"There wasn't. You just told them what happened, same as everyone who was there. It wasn't your fault."

He scratched his jaw. "Yeah, I suppose. You know, no one here blames you for what happened. We all would have done the same thing."

I nodded. "Thanks."

"Sorry, man. You probably don't want to revisit all that shit. Chief's upstairs. You can go on up."

"Thanks. And Christian?" I held out my hand. "Thanks for having my back."

Meeting my eyes, he took my hand and shook it. "Anytime."

He dropped my hand and headed for the garage. I went upstairs in search of the chief.

I found him in his office, seated behind his desk. He was on the phone, so I waited nearby. A few seconds later, his eyes caught mine and he held up one finger, indicating for me to wait.

The passage of time showed on Chief Stanley's face. The differences were subtle, but I could see them. A little more gray in his dark hair. A few more lines around his eyes.

A twinge of nervousness hit me as he ended the call and set down his phone.

He stood and came out of his office, so I waited where I was. I couldn't read his expression. His jaw worked the way it did when he was about to say something. He stopped in front of me and held out his hand.

"Asher. Good to see you."

I shook his hand, relief washing away most of my nerves. "Hey, Chief. Sorry it took me so long."

"That's all right. I knew you'd come around. Coffee?"

"Sure."

I followed him to the kitchen. He took out two TFD mugs and poured us both a cup of something dark that resembled coffee.

"There were some donuts in here earlier, but you know how long those last." He gestured to an empty box on the counter.

"It's no big deal."

He took a seat at a table and I sat in the chair across from him.

"So I figure the one about you escaping is probably just a rumor." There was a glint of humor in his eyes.

"Yeah, I have no clue where they got that one."

"I'm just surprised nobody's figured out how to work a Sasquatch sighting into it. He could have been the one to distract the guards."

"Good point."

"No, I've talked to Gram. I know the real story."

I nodded, glad I didn't have to go into the details. It was easier not to think about prison if I could avoid it. I dreamed about it too much already.

Chief stared into his coffee for a moment. When he finally spoke, his voice was quiet. "You did your time, Asher. You faced the consequences. I wish things could have been different, but I'm proud of you."

Looking away, I blew out a breath. I hadn't expected that. He casually sipped his coffee, giving me a minute to pull myself together.

I fucking needed it.

When I thought I could speak again, I cleared my throat. "Thanks, Chief."

"So, what's next?"

"I honestly don't know."

He nodded slowly. "You know my hands are tied—"

"I know," I said, cutting him off. I didn't want to talk about the fact that I couldn't be a firefighter with a felony conviction. I knew it, he knew it, we didn't need to discuss it. "That is what it is. Nothing either of us can do about it."

"Maybe not, but I don't have to like it."

"Yeah, life is like that." I glanced down at my mug. "I'm still trying to figure things out. How are things here? What'd I miss?"

"Ah, hell. What's it been, seven years? We had wildfires a couple of summers. Nothing that got close to town, but the smoke was bad. Obviously you know I hired the twins. Still deciding whether that was a smart move."

I chuckled at that.

"We have a couple of new guys, and we've got Gavin on volunteer duty. Don't tell him this, but he's in the running for a career spot. I'm making him sweat it for now, though." He grinned. "As for the rest of the town, you know how it is. Doesn't change a whole lot. College kids come and go over on the south end. Gets a little busier in the summer with tourists in town to hike to the falls or camp in the foothills. Baileys and Havens still take shots at each other."

"Yeah, that's for sure. What about you?"

He shrugged. "I'm still a grumpy old bachelor. Skylar graduated high school, same year as Gavin. She still lives over in Spokane. I'm proud of her. She grew up into a beautiful young woman."

"I'm sure she did."

A guy I didn't know poked his head around the wall. "Hey, Chief, we need you downstairs when you have a minute."

"I'll be right there."

"Sorry, I should let you get back to work."

He stood, and I followed suit. "I'm glad you stopped by."

"Me too. Thanks again, Chief."

"Asher, if you need anything—a place to stay, a referral —be sure to let me know."

"I will."

We shook hands again and went downstairs. I got out of there quickly, before I could get caught up in a conversation with someone else. My chest was too choked with emotion. I couldn't get over the way Chief had said he was proud of me.

Sure, I'd faced my sentence and served my time. I'd done what I had to do. But I'd come out of it a fucking mess.

And walking out of the firehouse felt like I was finally closing the door on this part of my past. Which was probably a good thing. I needed to put it behind me and move on.

But if closing a door was supposed to mean a new one opening, I had no idea how to find it, or where it would lead me when I did.

DEAR ASHER

ear Asher,

MY MOM DID IT. *She got married to Jack Cordero today.*

It was honestly one of the most beautiful things I've ever witnessed. I cried through the entire ceremony. I've never seen her so happy. And the way he looks at her. God, Asher, I can't even describe it. He loves her so much.

Neither of them wanted a big wedding, but I think they underestimated how many people they have in their lives who wanted to share that moment with them. You know my mom doesn't have a lot of family, and none who live nearby. And Jack's family isn't large either.

But there's Gram and your brothers. Shannon and Ben, and all my half-siblings and their families. Not to mention Mom's friends from work, and the neighbors and people in town who've known her forever. Jack's colleagues at the sheriff's office.

Their "not big" wedding turned into a big deal fast.

It was beautiful, and so much fun. Mom and Jack were

happy, and everyone was happy for them. Elijah looked so cute in his suit, I couldn't stand it. Everyone had a great time.

It wasn't too bad being at yet another wedding. I feel like I've been to a lot of those in the last few years. My sister and brothers have all gotten married. I went to their mom's wedding, too. And yes, it stings a little. It's hard to wait for my turn.

But what really made me ache was the simple fact that you weren't there.

Every time there's a party or a big celebration, or even sometimes when nothing special is happening at all, I find myself wandering outside or to a window. I look up at the big sky, whether the sun is shining or the stars are twinkling or it's blanketed with clouds. And I remember that you're looking at the same thing.

Maybe it's cheesy, but it makes me feel a little better. I like to imagine you staring up at the same spot as I am. That even though we haven't spoken in so long, we're still connected.

We're beneath the same sky.

I LOVE YOU,
   Grace

18

GRACE

*S*titch and Sip was quiet this week. Tillie and Violet were there, but Amy's kids were sick so she'd stayed home, and Cara was still in L.A. with her mom. The rest of us sipped our drinks—without our resident bartender, it was just wine I'd brought—while we chatted and worked on our respective projects.

I was attempting a beard for Lola the pinup girl. I'd made one before, but I wanted this one to be bigger—and more obnoxious. Marlene Haven politely pretended she didn't know what I was doing. I would have done the same for her. It was the Stitch and Sip way.

Gram sat with a lap full of knitting. I wasn't sure what she was working on, but the colors were pretty—soft yellow, lavender, and pale blue.

"Those are nice colors," I said, gesturing to her project.

"I thought so. It's for your sister."

"My sister Brynn?"

"Mm hm. She's expecting a baby, isn't she? I haven't heard if she's having a girl or a boy, but I thought these worked either way."

"Thanks, Gram. That's really sweet. She'll love it."

She smiled.

"Hey, Gram. I have a question. Have you ever heard of someone named Eliza Bailey? Maybe someone from the early part of the twentieth century?"

I'd done some research. Although I hadn't found much —no mentions of an Eliza Bailey in Tilikum—based on the style, I was fairly certain the mirror was at least a hundred years old.

"That doesn't ring a bell."

"What about you, Tillie? Has anyone on the Bailey side done a family tree?"

Tillie paused, her forehead creasing. "I don't recall an Eliza Bailey. I've traced the family history, but that's not a name I've come across."

"Could there have been other Baileys in Tilikum? It can't be that unique of a last name."

"It's possible, but not likely," Tillie said. "A Bailey was among the founders of our town. I'd imagine anyone with that last name would have been related somehow. Why do you ask?"

"I found an old chest under the floorboards in my house. It had a silver handheld mirror in it, and the name Eliza Bailey is engraved on the back."

"Well I'll be," Tillie said. "Maybe Eliza was her middle name but that's what people called her. Records would list her first name. That might be why I've never heard of her."

"Or maybe she's a distant cousin," Violet said. "Not someone in the direct family line."

Tillie nodded. "True. Now you have me curious, Grace. Did you find anything else?"

"I did, actually. Anonymous love notes."

A collective *aw* went around the circle.

"Are they written to Eliza?" Tillie asked.

"I think so. They're addressed to E, but none of them are signed. They're old. And it's obvious from the way they're written that it was two people who couldn't be together for some reason. Some of them talk about meeting in secret at night, or finding a way for them to be together all the time. They're terribly romantic."

Tillie put a hand on her chest. "So romantic. What a lovely thing to find. I wonder who her beau was."

"Maybe he was a Haven," Marlene said, and all eyes snapped to her. She shrugged. "Don't you think it's possible?"

"Does the feud go back that far?" I asked. "From what I can tell, Eliza probably lived in the early nineteen-hundreds, before the First World War."

"I don't actually know when the feud started," Marlene said. "It could be that old."

It felt a bit strange to talk so openly about the feud with Marlene. After all, she was a Haven. By marriage, but still. She'd grown up in Tilikum; she'd always been on the Haven side.

But getting to know the Stitch and Sip ladies had taught me a lot about how things really worked here. Although the rivalry was very real, and women weren't immune to it— case in point, I was crocheting a beard to put on Lola—the women also tended to be the ones to go around it when necessary.

"I don't think anyone knows when it started," Gram said. "People mostly care about who did what, and how they're going to answer back."

Violet rolled her eyes. "A bunch of nonsense, if you ask me."

Gram chuckled.

I wondered what Gram really thought of the feud. Despite being a Bailey herself, as far as I knew, she'd never participated in it. When her grandsons played pranks on the Havens, she usually just rolled her eyes, and occasionally reminded them not to do anything illegal.

"Gram, were you always on the Bailey side?"

Her hands didn't stop working. "Not exactly. When I was a girl, my family called the Bailey-Haven feud a white-man problem. In those days, we Indians had plenty of our own troubles without borrowing theirs."

"Aren't we supposed to say Native Americans?" Tillie asked.

Gram snorted. "You can say what you'd like, it makes no difference to me. But I've been an Indian my whole life. I'm too old to be bothered changing what I call myself now."

Tillie smiled. "Fair enough."

"As for the feud, I didn't pay much attention to it," Gram continued. "But then I went and married a Bailey. I knew what it meant to marry into that family. The Baileys became my people the day he put that ring on my finger. Still, the feud didn't matter too much to us. Frank and I had bigger concerns than what the Havens were doing."

"Like what?" I asked.

"In those days, white men didn't marry Indian girls."

"Wow. Were people against your marriage?"

"There was resistance on both sides. Not that Frank cared a lick about any of that."

"He wanted to marry you no matter what?"

Her hands fell still and her mouth turned up in a smile. "Oh yes. He wouldn't be swayed. Of course, it's a well-known fact that Bailey men are the most stubborn creatures in existence."

Marlene sighed. "And Haven men are right there with them."

"No wonder this town keeps feuding," Tillie said, shaking her head.

"Bailey men are ridiculously stubborn," I said. "I can attest to that."

"Don't you worry about that, Mama Bear," Gram said. "He'll figure it out. Might take him longer than it should, but he'll come around."

I let out a sigh. "I hope so."

"A man needs to know his mission," Gram said. "Without that, he's adrift. It's why so many young men act like idiots. They haven't found their mission yet; they don't have anything guiding them. Some men, like Asher, find their mission early. It's what made him so steady when you two were younger. But he doesn't have that anymore, and he's going to struggle until he finds it again."

"Let me guess. He needs time?"

Gram nodded. "He does. And when that isn't enough, he'll need a good smack upside the head. But you'll know when that's necessary."

I laughed. "Thanks, Gram. I'll keep that in mind."

The conversation turned to other things and I made good progress on Lola's beard. I was going to make this one extra special.

I said goodbye to the ladies and took my tote bag out to my car. We'd ended a bit early, and there was still half an hour before closing time at the Steaming Mug. I'd left a few things in my office that I'd meant to bring with me, so I decided to pop in before I went home.

Alexa, a college student and one of my most reliable baristas, was closing tonight. Her light brown hair was in a knot on top of her head and she wore a gold hoop in her nose.

"Hey," she said with a smile. "Just stopping in, or did you need something?"

"I just wanted to grab a few things off my desk."

"Do you want some tea? We got more of that black currant tea that was so good."

"That sounds great, actually. Thanks."

I grabbed what I needed from my office and brought it to one of the empty tables.

Alexa brought my tea. "There you go."

"Thanks."

She went back to the front counter and I sat. I brought the tea close so I could inhale the fruity aroma.

Thinking about what Gram had said about stubborn Bailey men made me crack a smile. She wasn't wrong. And she'd know—she'd been married to one for decades.

I remembered Grandad Bailey well. Tall, with bright blue eyes and an easy smile. He'd possessed a knack for making anything fun. Chores or projects around the house had always become a game.

He'd passed away when I was still in my teens, but he'd been as much a part of my childhood as Gram. My mom's parents hadn't been around, and my father's family—if he had any—probably didn't know I existed. But Gram and Grandad Bailey had filled that gap so completely, it had never bothered me that I didn't have biological grandparents in my life.

A noise startled me out of my reminiscing, and I glanced up.

"Sorry." A man lowered himself into a chair at the table next to me. "I didn't mean to scare you."

"It's okay. I guess I was lost in thought for a second."

He was striking, with short blond hair, green eyes, and bone structure that could have been sculpted from marble. His button-down shirt had the sleeves cuffed and he had tattoos almost everywhere I could see. On his forearms and hands, peeking out from his shirt collar, and running up his neck.

"Are you from around here?" he asked.

"Yeah, I am. Are you in town visiting?"

He grinned. "Is it obvious I'm an outsider? Yeah, I came to look up an old friend. Cute town."

"I like it."

He shifted in his chair, so he was angled toward me. "So what do you do?"

"I work here, actually. I run the shop."

He glanced around. "It's a nice place."

"Thanks. What about you?"

"Family business."

I waited for him to elaborate—family business could mean a lot of things—but he didn't. Which struck me as a little bit odd. Was he waiting for me to ask? I couldn't tell if he was flirting with me, or just making conversation. Either way, I didn't particularly want to encourage him by asking questions.

"So, what do people around here do for fun?" he asked.

"You know, small-town stuff. There's a bowling alley, and a movie theater, but it's old and tiny. Good popcorn, though."

"What if a guy wanted to get a drink?"

"There are a bunch of bars down by the college. Or the Mountain Goat Tavern is decent if you don't mind sticky floors. And there's a place called the Caboose that has a full bar."

Nodding slowly, he held my gaze while he listened. I

couldn't place why, but he was making me a bit uncomfortable. Was it his appearance? I didn't want to be judgy, but
with all those tattoos, he was intimidating.

I wished Asher were here.

"Excellent. I'll check those out. Thanks."

"Sure." Shifting away, I took a sip of my tea, trying to
make it clear I was done with the conversation.

He paused for a moment and drank some of his coffee.
"What if a guy wanted some company with his drink?"

"Sorry, if you're looking for an escort," I said, making air
quotes, "I can't help you there."

He laughed. "That's not what I had in mind. What about
you? Are you free tonight?"

Wow, he was bold. "I'm actually not available any night."
I held up my left hand and wiggled my ring finger.

"Ah. Got it. Sorry, I didn't see that."

"It's okay."

He nodded again and stood. "I should stop bothering
you and let you get back to your tea. Enjoy your evening."

"Thanks. Have a nice visit."

"I will."

I watched him leave. He'd left his mostly-full coffee
sitting on the table.

Something about that had been strange. Not the fact
that he'd struck up a conversation with me, nor that he'd
asked me out for a drink. Despite the ring on my finger, I
was approached by men occasionally. I couldn't quite place
why, but my instincts were telling me something was off.

Gram—and my mom, for that matter—had always said
to trust my instincts. And at the very least, I didn't want to
leave the shop alone in the dark. He probably wasn't out
there waiting for me. But I also knew all too well that the
unthinkable could happen.

I really wanted to call Asher.

Maybe that wasn't a good idea. Our relationship was... complicated. Did I really need to ask him to come down here? I could wait for Alexa to finish up and we could walk out to our cars together.

But my fingers twitched with the urge to text him. I was anxious and uncomfortable, and maybe it was all in my head.

I texted him anyway.

19

GRACE

*N*ot five minutes later, Asher's truck rumbled outside. I let out a relieved breath, feeling better already.

I stood and gathered my things. "Are you good to go tonight, Alexa?"

"Yep, I'm just about done and my boyfriend is parked out back."

That was a relief. I didn't want her to be alone. "Great. I'll see you later."

"Thanks, Grace."

I went outside to meet Asher and locked the shop door behind me. He got out of the truck and our eyes met. I bit my lip against the rush of heat in my veins. *God, look at him.* I wanted to climb him like a tree.

Calm down, Grace.

"Hey, thanks for coming."

He glanced up and down the street. "Is everything okay?"

"Yeah, it's probably nothing. Something a little weird

happened. I don't know why, but it felt like I should tell you."

"What happened?"

He had a groove between his eyebrows that did terrible things to my insides. It reminded me of what he used to look like when he was inside me. I could practically hear him groaning in my ear.

"What? Oh." I tucked my hair behind my ear. God, I was making myself all flustered. "Sorry. A guy came in a little bit ago. I was at a table inside and he sat at the one next to me. He struck up a conversation and—I can't really explain it, but something felt off. I probably didn't need to call you, but I felt weird leaving the shop alone."

"I'm glad you did. What did he say?"

"Not anything unusual. He asked if I was from around here and wanted to know what there was to do. He asked if I'd get a drink with him, but obviously I told him no."

Asher's eye twitched. "Was he pushy about it?"

"No. That's the thing, he was fine. He wasn't rude or anything. Maybe a little aggressive, but not in a bad way. Once I said no, he apologized and left."

The furrow in Asher's brow deepened and he clenched and unclenched his fists. He kept glancing up and down the street while I talked, and I wondered what had him so distracted.

"But something about it bothered you."

"Yeah. I can't explain it, but little things felt off. Like he said he worked for his family business, but he didn't say what that was. He was dressed almost like he had a corporate job, but he was covered in tattoos. I'm talking down his arms, over the backs of his hands. All the way up his neck. I'm probably a jerk for letting that make me nervous, but his appearance was intimidating."

Asher's gaze snapped to my face and his body stilled. "What kind of tattoos?"

I shrugged. "I don't know. I didn't look at them long enough to really make out what they were. He had a lot."

"Did he tell you his name?"

"You know, he didn't. Maybe that's why it was weird. He asked me to go get a drink with him, but he hadn't given me his name, or asked for mine."

"So he doesn't know who you are."

"No."

"Did he say why he's in town?"

"Yeah, he said he was visiting an old friend. Or maybe he said *looking up* an old friend. It was something like that."

"Fuck," he muttered, then leaned closer. "Grace, I need you to try to remember. What kind of tattoos did he have?"

The edge in his voice made my stomach flip with sudden anxiety. "I don't know what the designs looked like."

"What color?"

"Mostly black, I think? I don't know, why does that matter?"

"What about red? Was there a lot of red?"

"I don't remember."

"What did he look like?"

I tucked my hair again and shifted the stack of paperwork I'd grabbed from my desk. "Short hair. Blond, maybe? He was very striking. Different-looking, but that might have been all the ink."

He didn't look away, his eyes holding mine captive. The intensity in his expression made my heart beat harder.

"Asher, you're kind of freaking me out right now. What's wrong?"

"Nothing."

"Don't lie to me. Do you think you know who he is?"

"Maybe."

I hesitated for a moment, wondering what was going on in that head of his. The tension in his body was almost palpable, but it was the wildness in his eyes that made me nervous. He seemed so agitated, like the slightest provocation would make him snap.

Maybe I shouldn't have told him.

"Do you think he's someone from prison?"

"I hope not. But if he is, I don't want him anywhere near you." He grabbed my hand. "Let's go."

"Where are we going?"

"Home. Or maybe Gram's. You'll be safe there. Where's your car?"

"I parked in back."

He tugged me toward his truck. "We'll come back for it later."

"What? Why?"

"I need to get you off the street."

"Asher—"

He didn't give me a chance to argue. Looking up and down the street again, he opened his truck door and pushed me inside.

I decided to cooperate. Although I didn't understand why, this had rattled him. Either there was a lot he wasn't telling me, and he had reason to believe I could be in danger, or he was seriously paranoid.

I wasn't sure which was worse.

He got in and checked our surroundings again. The veins in his forearms stood out as he held the steering wheel in a tight grip. He didn't say anything, just drove down the street, checking the rear-view mirror constantly.

"Take me home, okay?" I asked. "Not to Gram's. It's getting late and she goes to bed early."

His jaw hitched, but he nodded.

We got home and he parked in the driveway, then came around to the passenger side and took my hand. He was hyperalert, his gaze darting all around, as if he expected someone to jump out of the bushes.

I fished my keys out of my purse and unlocked the door, but he held out his arm to block the way.

"Let me go in first. Wait here."

He left me outside, gaping at his back. He needed to search my house? What did he think he was going to find in there?

"Asher, I don't think the tattooed guy is waiting for me inside. He doesn't know who I am."

No answer.

So much for trusting my instincts. I was starting to regret having told him anything.

When he reappeared, he didn't look any less frantic. I came in and he shut the door behind me, locking it quickly. Then he closed the curtains on the front window.

"What's going on?" I asked. "Are you going to barricade the door, too?"

"I just want to make sure you're safe."

"From what? What aren't you telling me?"

He moved to stand in front of me, his dark eyes meeting mine. "There are just some people out there I don't trust. And if one of them is here..."

I shifted closer, my body aching with the desire to hold him. To comfort him. But I wasn't sure if he'd let me.

"Just let me find out if there's a problem," he continued. "Stay here tonight, okay? Don't go anywhere."

"Seriously?"

"I know you think I'm crazy."

"I don't think you're crazy, I just wonder if you're over-reacting."

The hardness in his expression fell away, as if the tight grip he kept on himself faltered. His eyes pleaded with me. "Grace, please."

A rush of emotion tightened my throat and I nodded. "Okay. I'll stay here."

He let out a breath. "Thank you."

I couldn't resist him anymore. Whether he wanted it or not, I was hugging him. I stepped into his space, wrapped my arms around him, and closed my eyes.

Please, Asher. Just let me do this. Let me hold you for a moment.

For a second, he didn't move.

Neither did I.

Then he folded his arms around me. Unlike the last hug we'd shared, he didn't immediately pull away. He tucked me in closer, his arms tightening. Turned his face into my neck and took a deep breath.

His heart was pounding in his chest and his skin was covered with a sheen of sweat. He was so tense, he was almost shaking.

God, he wasn't just worried. He was terrified.

I gently rubbed the back of his neck, wishing desperately that this didn't have to be so hard. That he would let me in. Let me help him.

He took another deep breath, then slowly let go. Reluctantly, I dropped my arms and stepped back. My body buzzed from the contact and my heart ached at the turmoil raging in his eyes.

"I won't go anywhere," I said softly. "I'll stay right here. Promise."

He nodded. "Good. I have to go. Keep the doors locked."

"Okay."

With one last long look, he left. Through the peephole in the door, I saw him pause outside. He didn't leave until he heard me latch the deadbolt.

Letting out a slow breath, I went into the living room and collapsed onto the couch.

What had just happened?

The unsettled feeling was back, but it wasn't because of the tattooed stranger. Asher had been telling me since he'd come home that prison had messed him up. But until now, I hadn't really believed him. I'd known he would have to adjust to life here again, and that could be bumpy. And I was certainly aware that he was different in many ways.

But maybe he was right. Maybe prison had fucked him up, more than I'd wanted to admit.

20

ASHER

*I*t was killing me to leave Grace alone. I fought the urge to turn around and go back to her house. But I had to find out who'd been in her shop tonight. A knot of fear sat in the pit of my stomach, like a smoldering rock. If I'd put her in danger...

I couldn't let anything happen to her. Not again.

But I couldn't stay, either. I didn't trust myself.

The moment her arms had gone around me, I'd nearly collapsed. I could still feel her. The warmth of her body in my arms, every inch pressing against me. For that brief moment, I'd almost felt calm, as if her soothing touch could chase away all my demons.

She'd felt so fucking good.

But I had to protect her, even if that meant protecting her from *me*.

I couldn't stop checking the rear-view mirror as I drove into town. My thoughts were a whirlwind and my heart raced. Who was out there? Was it someone with a score to settle? Would he try to get to me through Grace? Had he known who she was?

Going to Jack Cordero crossed my mind. Grace's stepdad was a cop. Maybe he could help.

Except what was I going to say? That I thought I was being watched, and a guy with tattoos had talked to Grace? I wasn't totally irrational. I knew that was too vague, and the guy hadn't done anything wrong.

But it wasn't *what* Grace had said that had me fighting to keep control of myself. It was *how* she'd said it. Something about him had triggered her instincts—had been enough to make her tell me about it. I didn't know if I could trust myself, but I trusted her. If she thought something was off about the guy, I trusted that she was right.

And even though it was a leap to assume he had anything to do with me, in my fevered brain, that leap wasn't very far. It was possible. I'd known it was possible since the day I'd come home. I just hadn't thought it would come so soon.

Fuck.

I wasn't sure what to do, so I went to the only place I could think to go. My brothers' house.

Logan, Levi, and Gavin shared a place not far from the firehouse. It was a ranch-style with a big garage. I parked on the street and went to the front door, hoping at least one of them was home.

Levi answered, dressed in a t-shirt and sweats, and his eyebrows drew together. "Asher?"

I pushed past him and went inside, my body too jittery to keep still. "I have a problem."

He shut the door behind me, and Logan looked over from the couch in front of an enormous TV mounted to the wall. The coffee table was littered with wrappers, beer bottles, and soda cans, and there was a laundry basket in the corner piled high with clothes.

Logan paused his video game. "Hey, Ash. I was just owning Levi in the face. Wanna play?"

"No."

He scowled. "Fine, you don't have to be a dick about it."

"I'm not being a dick. I said I have a problem."

"Yes, Grace is too good for you, but you should still totally hit that."

The knot of fear exploded into anger. "Don't fucking talk about her."

"Jesus," Logan said. "What the hell is wrong with you?"

I took a breath, trying to calm down. Levi still stood near the door, watching me with his arms crossed.

Gavin appeared in the hallway, buck naked, rubbing a towel over his wet hair. "Hey, Ash."

"Dude," Logan said. "We've talked about this. Put some fucking clothes on."

"That's what I'm doing." He walked over to the laundry pile and bent over to sort through it.

Logan let out a disgusted groan and held his arm up over his face. "God. Seriously. What the fuck. No one wants to see that."

Levi pinched the bridge of his nose and shook his head.

"It's not my fault you guys are in my room," Gavin said, still digging through the clothes.

"This isn't your room," Levi said. "You don't live here."

I glanced at Levi, then Logan, trying to avoid looking at my little brother's bare ass. "I thought he did live here."

Logan still shielded his eyes with his forearm. "It's only a two-bedroom, so he sleeps on the couch."

"We told him he could crash here once and he never left," Levi grumbled.

"I pay my share of the bills." Gavin thankfully pulled on

a pair of boxer briefs. Scrubbing the towel over his head again, he grinned at me. "What's up, bro?"

Logan tossed the game controller onto the cluttered coffee table and leaned back, stretching his arm over the back of the couch. He was only half-dressed himself, in a t-shirt and boxer briefs, his white socks pulled up to his shins. "Sit, man, make yourself at home."

The couch looked questionable, so I went to the armchair.

"Whoa," Gavin said, holding up a hand. "Hang on, don't sit down yet."

I stopped with my legs bent. "Why?"

He winced. "I might have poked some thumbtacks through the seat so when one of these dorks sat down, they'd get stuck in the ass. But I have a feeling you won't find that funny and you'll probably hurt me, so let me make sure they're all gone."

Levi scowled at him. "I saw them earlier, dumbass. I would have put them in your bed, but you don't have one because you don't live here."

Gavin ran his hand across the seat, ignoring Levi.

"I'll grab another chair."

Their dining area had a surprisingly nice wooden table —beautiful compared to the rest of their furniture—with four matching chairs. I dragged one over to the living room and sat. Gavin flopped into the armchair sideways, but Levi remained standing.

"Lay it on us, bronoculars," Logan said. "What's going on?"

"A guy showed up at Grace's coffee shop tonight and he gave her a weird vibe. I think I might know who he is. And if I'm right, it's not good."

"Who is he?"

"A guy who was in my cell block for a while. He's known as Reaper."

"Reaper?" Logan asked. "That sounds like a gang nickname or some shit. Why would a guy like that be out here?"

"Holy shit," Gavin said. "Did you make prison enemies? Were there gang members?"

I shot him a glare. "Where the fuck do you think I was? White-collar prison with a bunch of guys in for tax evasion? *Yeah* there were gang members. And drug dealers, and guys doing time for assault, armed robbery, murder. Yeah, I made enemies. I got in there and I was just some fucking kid. Word got around what I was in for, and everyone wanted to test me. See if I was really tough enough to kill a guy with my bare hands, or if it was just adrenaline."

"Jesus, Asher," Levi said under his breath.

"I didn't go in there looking for a fight, but it's kind of hard to avoid when half of them want to fuck with you. A couple guys who have ample reason to hate me are out. So I've got that hanging over my head for the rest of my life."

Logan sat forward on the couch, his forearms resting on his knees. "So this Reaper guy has it in for you and you think he's here."

I stood, fear and anger punching through me again. Was Grace still okay? "Yeah. Maybe. Grace said the guy had a lot of ink. Arms, hands, neck. She couldn't remember what the tats looked like, but that could be him."

"So, just a tattooed guy," Levi said. "That's what you're basing this on."

I whirled on him. "How often do you see a guy with fucking neck tattoos in Tilikum?"

"I don't know, but that seems like a stretch."

"He didn't ask for her name," I said. Why didn't they get it? "He asked her out for a drink, but didn't say his name or get hers. Would you hit on a girl without finding out who she is? What if that means he already knew exactly who she was?"

"How would he know who she is?" Logan asked, then held his hands up. "Hold on, don't jump down my throat. It's not a dumb question. It's not like you and Grace have been hanging out a lot since you got back."

"I don't know. But I'm pretty sure someone's been following me."

"Shit," Gavin said.

"Why?" Levi asked. "Have you actually seen anyone?"

"You really want to get punched in the teeth, don't you?" Gavin asked.

"No, but he comes rolling in here talking about someone coming after him for revenge and I want to know how real this is. If it's real, it's fucked up and we need to do something about it. But this could still be a coincidence."

"It's not a fucking coincidence. I know when I'm being watched. I had to or they would have sent me home in pieces." I paused to take another deep breath. "Look, it might not be him. But I think someone's been watching me, and Grace's description matches a guy who'd happily tear me to shreds if he could. Plus, something about him bothered her enough that she felt like she needed to call me. That means something."

"I can respect that," Logan said. "So what do we do?"

"Protect Grace." The words came out of my mouth before I could stop them. I couldn't help it. My first—and strongest—concern was her.

Gavin shot up out of the chair. "On it."

"More clothes, Gav," Levi said.

"Good point. I don't want to make Grace fall in love with me. That would be awkward."

Logan snorted. "You wish."

"Hold on." Levi held his hands up. "If it's him, and he's that dangerous, what the fuck are you going to do? And how are you not getting killed in the process?"

I didn't have a good answer to that. The thought of Grace in danger had me so panicked, I couldn't think clearly. "I won't do anything stupid. Just don't let her out of your sight until I know what's going on."

"We could just put Evan on her doorstep," Logan said. "His grumpy ass would scare anyone away."

Gavin laughed, but Levi held up a finger. "No, don't put Evan at Grace's house. He should go with Asher."

"Good luck with that," Gavin said. "Isn't he still hibernating or something?"

"He'll help," Levi said.

"Maybe." Gavin sounded skeptical. "You can always try bribing him with food."

"Just call him," Levi said.

"Shouldn't two of us stick with Ash?" Logan asked. "If he's the target?"

"No," I said. "You guys go to Grace's house. Watch the outside and don't let anyone in."

Logan stood and clapped me on the back. "We've got this. Don't worry. Come on, broritos."

Levi tossed a balled-up sock at Logan. "Dude, pants."

"I fuckin' hate pants."

I left my brothers while they put enough clothes on to leave the house. I trusted them, which was a weird feeling. It had been a long time since I'd really trusted anyone.

But I had to. I needed to leave Grace in their hands until I figured out what the hell was going on.

21

GRACE

*M*y alarm jolted me awake. Groaning, I smacked the bedside clock. Or tried to. I missed. Cracking my eyes open, I found the button and jabbed it a few times for good measure.

Turning over, I pulled the covers up. I wasn't ready to be awake. I'd gone to bed early last night, listening to a meditation app for a while to help me relax. But I'd still slept restlessly. Memories of holding Asher in my living room had invaded my dreams, mixing with memories from before. I'd woken up several times and stretched my arm across the empty side of the bed, reaching for him. Believing in my half-awake haze that he was here, sleeping beside me.

I would have given just about anything for that to be true.

A few minutes later, my alarm went off again. Apparently I'd hit snooze. I rolled over and hit the correct button this time. But I was awake now, and I had to work, so I reluctantly peeled myself out of bed.

I straightened my tank top and rubbed my eyes.

Caffeine. I definitely needed caffeine. I opened the bedroom door and almost tripped over something in the hallway.

A large green lump lay on the floor. It moved and I jumped backward, shrieking.

Dark hair poked out from one end and an all-too-familiar face turned toward me. Gavin. He was curled up in a green sleeping bag. "Is it morning?"

"What the hell are you doing?"

"Sleeping, until you kicked me." His voice was gravelly, and he blinked his eyes slowly.

"I didn't kick you, I almost tripped over you."

Another voice carried from the living room. "Shut up over there."

I put my hands on my hips. "Seriously? How many of you are in here?"

"Three." Gavin closed his eyes and nestled back into the sleeping bag. "Evan went with Asher. We're on Grace duty."

"Grace duty? What does that mean?"

Without waiting for an answer, I stepped over him and went out to the living room. Sure enough, I found two more Baileys. Levi had the couch and Logan had improvised, pushing two armchairs together to make a bed.

"When did you guys get here?"

"Last night. You were already in bed, so we let ourselves in," Logan said. The chairs were too short for him to stretch out, so he had his legs tucked up and his hands beneath his cheek. Groaning, he sat up and rubbed his neck. "I slept like shit."

My meditation app must have drowned out the sound of them coming in. Except—

"How did you get in?"

"Key."

"Who gave you a key?"

Logan's forehead creased, like I'd asked a weird question. "I've always had a key. We made copies when you moved in."

"Wait, what? Who else has one?"

"We all do." He rubbed his neck again. "Obviously."

Levi groaned. "I hate all of you."

"He's grouchy when he doesn't get his beauty sleep," Logan said. "Actually, he's grouchy all the time."

"Fuck off."

"See?"

I put my hands on my hips. "We'll come back later to the part where you all have keys to my house and I didn't know. What are you doing here?"

"Before we leave the key discussion, should I make a copy for Asher?" Logan asked. "Or is that like a relationship thing and you'll take care of it?"

"Logan."

"Sorry, I'm just asking."

"Asher sent us," Gavin said from the hallway.

My hands dropped to my sides. Asher had sent them? "Oh my god. Are you supposed to be bodyguards?"

"Yep," Logan said. "But if this is going to continue, we need to talk about better sleeping arrangements."

Levi sat up. "Or maybe you need to not suck and you'd get the couch. This was comfortable."

"You want a rematch? I'll pin you right now."

"Did you guys wrestle for who got the couch?" I asked.

"Yeah, out front. But he cheated," Logan said.

"I didn't cheat. You're just pissed that I'm better than you."

Logan scowled. "Cheater."

Gavin came out of the hallway, dragging his sleeping bag across the floor. He paused and cleared his throat. "Uh, Grace?"

"What?"

His eyes darted back and forth, like he wasn't sure where to look. He dropped the sleeping bag and headed for the kitchen. "Nothing."

"You might want to put some clothes on, G," Logan said. "You're giving Gavin confusing pants feelings. Now someone's going to have to give him the talk."

I looked down at myself. I was dressed in nothing but a tank top and panties—and no bra. Lovely. "I didn't know you guys were out here."

"We should have known you'd go to bed at eight. You do look hot for your age, though."

"Oh for fuck's sake. I didn't go to bed at eight. And you're a child."

"I know, but you love that about me." He winked.

I spun around and headed for my room. "You guys better make me some coffee."

"Already on it," Gavin said from the kitchen.

Damn Baileys.

I went back to my room to put some clothes on and check my phone. No messages. What was going on with Asher? He'd obviously gone to their house last night after he'd left here. I appreciated that he was concerned. His protectiveness stirred a deep longing inside me. But was it necessary to send his brothers over here to sleep at my house?

Closing my eyes, I sank onto the edge of my bed, remembering the way he'd felt last night. His body had been so tense, his heart hammering. Was he right? Was this man dangerous? Or was Asher paranoid?

Both options were disturbing, if for different reasons.

I came out dressed in a t-shirt and yoga pants—and bra—and was greeted by the smell of coffee and bacon. The armchairs were still shoved up against each other, and blankets and dirty socks were strewn around the living room, along with a random t-shirt. But the bacon meant I'd probably forgive them for being animals.

It wasn't their fault they were barely housebroken. Gram had done her best, but there was only so much she could do.

Gavin was at the stove cooking bacon, wearing nothing but his boxer briefs. Logan was similarly dressed, although he had one white sock pulled up to his shin. I didn't even bother asking why. It was Logan.

He handed me a cup of coffee.

"Thanks." I cradled the cup in my hands. "Did Levi go home?"

"Nah, he's out doing a lap. Making sure everything's all clear out there."

It was interesting that they were taking this so seriously. "Are you guys here just to indulge Asher, or do you really think there's something going on?"

Logan shrugged. "I don't know. Asher's convinced, but let's be honest, he's a little out of it."

"I believe him," Gavin said.

I sank down into a chair at the kitchen table. "Why?"

He turned over a piece of bacon and jerked his hand away. "Ow, hot. I just don't think he'd get all freaked out over nothing. And he was freaking the fuck out last night."

"Yeah, he was. What did he say to you guys?"

Logan grabbed a piece of bacon off the plate and brought it to the table. "Basically that a tatted-up guy hit on you and sent up enough red flags that you lit the Asher-signal. He thinks it's some guy named Reaper who wants revenge. Probably because Asher beat his ass in prison."

My eyes widened. "What?"

"I gotta be honest, I'm kinda pissed I got put on Grace

duty," Gavin said. "No offense, Grace, but I wish I could have gone out with Asher last night to hunt this guy down."

"I swear to god, Gav, you have such a death wish," Logan said.

"Dude, a guy with neck tattoos named Reaper? I need to see that. Was he scary as fuck, Grace?"

A sick feeling spread through my stomach. "He wasn't scary so much as unsettling. But I need you to back up. Asher thinks this guy's tracking him down for revenge? Has anyone talked to him this morning?"

"Yeah, he texted when you were getting dressed," Logan said, his voice nonchalant. "He said no luck last night, stay with Grace."

I gaped at him. "Why didn't you tell me?"

"Sorry, I slept like shit last night. You need better guest accommodations."

"You're killing me right now, Logan."

He just grinned.

"Can you be serious for a minute? Be honest with me. Do you think Asher's right? Is he in danger?"

"Here's the way I see it," Logan said. "I'm sure he tangled with a tatted-up dude named Reaper in prison. He said he got into it with a lot of guys in there."

"Oh my god."

"As for whether the guy you met is him—who knows? It seems crazy, but what the hell do I know? Asher said the guy creeped you out, he's worried you're not safe, so we crash here until we're sure." He shrugged, like that was all any of us needed to know.

I let out a breath, trying to take it all in. It wasn't like I didn't know Asher had been in fights in prison. As much as I'd hoped he'd been spared that sort of violence, I'd seen him when he'd first come home. He hadn't gotten the cut on his forehead or the bruises on his knuckles from tripping over his shoelaces. But someone tracking him down for revenge... that was terrifying.

"Should we call Jack?" I asked.

"Maybe, but let's wait to hear from Asher first," Logan said. "Plus, he might just be losing it and paranoia is taking over."

"I still don't think so," Gavin said. "Do you think they found Reaper already? Maybe I can meet them and get in on this."

"That dude would probably rip you in half."

"I bet I could take him," Gavin said.

Logan rolled his eyes. "Right."

"Asher kicked his ass."

"Yeah, but Asher's like ten times the badass you are."

Gavin put the last piece of bacon on the plate to drain and turned off the stove. "I could take Asher."

Levi came in the front door and shut it behind him. "No you couldn't."

"You don't even know what we're talking about," Gavin said.

"Doesn't matter. You couldn't take Asher in any scenario."

"Yes I could. I'm not saying I'd win every time. But I bet I could make him tap out five matches out of ten. Maybe six since he's out of practice."

Logan got up and grabbed another piece of bacon. "Have you ever beat Asher? Even once?"

Gavin glared at him. "No, but I was a kid the last time we grappled. I hadn't even finished growing yet."

"I wouldn't want to go toe to toe with him," Logan said, half a piece of bacon sticking out of his mouth. "Not now."

"That's because you suck," Levi said.

Logan bit off the piece of bacon and dropped the rest on the counter. "Okay, brotato. Rematch. Let's do this."

He lunged and Levi widened his stance.

"Stop! Not inside." I put a hand to my forehead. "God, why do you guys make me act like I'm your mother?"

Amazingly, Logan listened. He stopped and flashed me a grin. "We're just giving you practice for when you have your own pack of Bailey cubs."

"I'm not having any Bailey cubs at this rate. In case you haven't noticed, your brother isn't exactly interested. And I'm certainly not having them with any of you."

Logan opened his mouth like he was going to say something, then closed it again and paused. "Nope, that'd be too weird. I definitely can't give you my Bailey sperm. You're going to have to keep wearing Asher down. He's your only hope."

I didn't reply. Just took a drink of my coffee.

Gavin stuck a plate of bacon in front of me, then sat down. Levi poured himself a cup of coffee but didn't join us. He leaned against the counter and looked out the window.

"Hey." Gavin rubbed a few circles across my back. "Don't worry. He'll quit being dumb sooner or later."

"This is why, isn't it?" I asked. "Why he keeps saying we can't be together. He thinks he has to protect me from something."

"Well, yeah," Logan said, dropping into a chair. "You know how he is with that protector shit. In high school he broke Josiah Haven's arm for fucking with Evan."

"That time at the Caboose," Levi said, his voice quiet, "he was ready to drag those two dicks outside for mouthing off to you."

"Yeah, I remember."

"And then, you know..." Gavin trailed off.

I did know. And I did *not* want to talk about it right now.

"Jesus, Gav," Levi said. "Of course we know. You don't have to say it."

The front door burst open, sparing me the need to shift the subject away from one of the worst nights of my entire life. Levi dropped his mug in the sink, Logan stood so fast his chair tipped over, and Gavin jumped up and leaped over the table, landing in a half crouch on the other side.

Cara stood in the doorway with her white rolling suitcase, her bright red lips parted. Her red top matched her lipstick and she wore white capris with a pair of strappy high-heeled sandals. "Hello, my wild tropical mermaid. Wow, what's going on here?"

"Shut the fucking door," Logan barked.

She whipped off her sunglasses, as if to make sure he received the full force of the hate in her glare. "Excuse me?"

Gavin went over to shut and lock the door. "Scary ex-con might be in town to get revenge on Asher and he talked to Grace last night, so she's on lockdown."

"What?" Cara shrieked. She dropped the suitcase handle and her sunglasses clattered to the floor. She was in the seat next to me so fast, it was like she'd teleported. "Oh my god, are you okay?"

"Yes, I'm fine." I grabbed her wrists so she'd stop pawing at me. "A guy weirded me out and I told Asher. And now I don't know if there's a guy in town who wants revenge, or if Asher is having a paranoid meltdown."

"God, Grace, I don't know which is worse."

"I know." I threw my arms around her. "I missed you."

She hugged me back. "I missed you too."

"Where you been, Cara?" Gavin asked. He flipped a chair around and straddled it.

"Hold on, Gavin." She pulled away and held me by the upper arms. "Are you positive you're okay?"

"Physically? Yes. Emotionally? I've been better."

"Did an ex-con seriously threaten you?"

"No, you're getting the wrong idea. He just talked to me, no threats at all. Actually he asked me out for a drink. But something seemed off, so I told Asher. Next thing I knew, Asher was dragging me home, shutting the curtains, and begging me to stay here for the night. And then I woke up to these guys trying to stand guard or something. Although they were sleeping."

Cara's mouth dropped open again. "Why didn't anyone call me?"

"Why would we call you?" Logan asked.

She shifted in her chair to face him. "Because I'm her best friend and if anyone tries to hurt her, I'll murder them, dump the body, then lead the fucking search party."

Logan glared at her. Levi went back to the kitchen to pour more coffee.

"For the record, I suggested we call you." Gavin smiled, looking smug.

"I'm serious, Grace, if you need protection, I'll get you protection," Cara said. "One phone call and I'll have a goddamn team surrounding this house with a sniper positioned in your attic and—"

"Whoa." I held up a hand. "Slow down. I don't think we need to call in Special Forces."

"Technically, they'd be paramilitary contractors."

"Still."

Gavin pushed my plate of bacon in front of Cara. "Breakfast?"

She absently took a piece. "Wait, what's Asher doing? Why isn't he playing bodyguard?"

"I guess he went looking for the guy? I don't know, he didn't tell me before he left last night. He texted Logan this morning and told him they didn't have any luck and to stay with me."

She wound her arm around my shoulders. "Thanks for covering for me, guys, but you can all clear out now. I've got this."

"Nice try, evil Ariel," Logan said. "We're not going anywhere."

"As if I'd trust you with my bestie. You fell asleep on the job."

"It was night."

"You could have at least taken shifts. What kind of a bodyguard are you? Oh, right—a terrible one."

He narrowed his eyes. "What kind of a best friend are you? You weren't even here."

"Oh, I'm sorry I had to fly to L.A. to deal with my crazy mother's latest meltdown. How selfish of me to be there for my family."

The argumentativeness in Logan's expression melted away. He cleared his throat. "I didn't know that."

"Then get your facts straight," she said, although the edge in her voice had softened. She turned her attention back to me. "Do you have to work today?"

"Yeah."

"I'll go with you."

"Me too," Gavin said.

"Really?" Logan asked. "I thought you wanted in on the Reaper action."

"I do, but the girls need someone to go with them. You stay here and keep an eye on the house. Levi can catch up with Asher and Evan to give them a third."

Cara and I glanced at Gavin. Maybe we were both surprised. His plan wasn't terrible.

"I guess that might work," Cara said slowly.

"Of course it will." Gavin flashed a wide grin. "As much as I'd love to get face to face with the scary prison guy, if you're going to sit around the coffee shop all day, you'll want company. And it's not like you're going to hang out with *him*." He gestured toward Logan. "And if Reaper shows up looking for Grace again, I'm not even worried. You'll claw at least one of his eyes out and then I can subdue him until the cops get there."

"I like it," Cara said. "Gavin comes with us. Although I still think I should call in professionals. Can I send them with Asher? We can't let anything happen to him." She put a hand on her chest. "Oh my god, that's so weird. I think I'm actually worried about him."

I grabbed her hand and squeezed. "No contractors. At least not yet. But I appreciate the offer. And I know, I'm worried too."

Truthfully, I wasn't just worried, I was terrified. But not for myself. I was scared for Asher.

22

ASHER

*G*asping for air, I was awake and on my feet in an instant. The room was dim, and I didn't recognize my surroundings. Where was I? My heart beat hard, making my pulse throb in my neck.

Who was here? Where were they?

I tracked movement to my left and my body tensed, ready to spring into action, but I stopped short when I realized what it was.

A dog.

I let out a long breath. A huge German shepherd stood a few feet away, watching me. He seemed to be waiting to see what I did, as if he were still deciding whether he was going to allow another animal in his territory.

That's right. I was at Evan's house.

"Hey, Sasquatch." I sank down onto the couch where I'd been sleeping. "Did you wake me up, or was it the other way around?"

He sat, his keen eyes fixed on me. Apparently he'd let me stay for now, but he wasn't finished watching me.

I rubbed my face and ran my hands through my hair. I

must have been having a nightmare. Again. I wondered when I was going to get over that shit. I'd woken up so disoriented, I'd forgotten where I'd gone to sleep last night.

After sending my other brothers to watch over Grace, I'd come out here to pick up Evan. By the time we'd gotten back into town, there'd been no sign of Reaper. Or whoever the guy was. We'd checked a bunch of places—asked around to see if they'd seen a man with a bunch of tattoos. No one had seen him.

Eventually we'd given up. Most places had closed, and we'd already checked the ones that hadn't. Walking around the streets looking for him didn't make much sense. So I'd taken Evan home. He'd suggested I crash here and we could go out and look again in the morning.

Which was how I'd wound up almost jumping out of my own skin and coming face to face with Evan's guard dog, Sasquatch.

Leaning back against the cushions, I waited for my heart to slow down. I still felt on edge—ready to jump up and defend myself.

Evan came out of his room and Sasquatch stood, his tail wagging furiously.

"Hey big guy," Evan murmured, his low voice scratchy. He rubbed Sasquatch between the ears, then glanced at me. "Morning."

I nodded. "Morning."

"We still on?"

"Yeah."

"I'll throw some clothes on and we can head into town. You want a shower or anything?"

"I'll take one later." I rubbed my hands up and down my thighs. The anxious energy running through me made it hard to stay still. I wanted to get going.

"Sasquatch, let's go outside," he said, patting his thigh.

His dog's gaze swung back to me.

"He's okay, big guy. He can stay."

Sasquatch looked unconvinced. He didn't move.

Evan shrugged. "He's really territorial."

"He scared the shit out of me this morning."

"Yeah, he was probably watching you sleep off and on all night. Sasquatch, outside. Now."

At the sharp tone of command in Evan's voice, the dog finally obeyed, walking to the back door to be let out.

While I waited for Evan to take care of Sasquatch and get dressed, I texted Logan, telling him to stay with Grace. He replied with a shirtless selfie in Grace's kitchen. Gavin was in the background grinning and flipping me off.

At least they were there.

When Evan was ready, we left, me in my truck and him on his bike. He lived a couple miles outside town, up a steep dirt road that I wouldn't have seen if I hadn't known where to look. He'd fixed up a small cabin and built a huge shop on his property. After dropping out of college, he'd moved home and started working on old cars and motorcycles. He'd turned it into a full-time business, building custom motorcycles and restoring classic cars.

I didn't have much of a plan, other than checking breakfast places—and bars—to see if anyone had seen a guy with neck tattoos. We got one hit, but it was someone who'd seen him yesterday afternoon. Other than that, no luck.

After a while, Evan talked me into taking a break for breakfast. My head didn't agree with him, but my stomach did, so we stopped to grab some food at the Bigfoot Diner. Plus, as he pointed out, this was the busiest and most popular breakfast spot in town, and it had a view of the Steaming Mug.

CLAIRE KINGSLEY

I kept a vigilant watch on the street outside, as well as the front door, while we ate. No sign of Reaper.

But I did see Grace.

She was with Gavin and her redheaded friend. She was dressed for work, in a black shirt and cropped pants. Her hair a little wavy. God, she was so beautiful. Every time I saw her, even just a glimpse, it hit me how different she was. We'd been so young before, and she was all woman now.

But why was Gavin the only one with her?

"Grace just went into work and I saw Gav, but where are Levi and Logan?" I pulled out my phone to see if I'd missed an update.

"Logan's at her house. Levi just texted asking where to meet us."

I had the same text. I didn't like that she only had Gavin with her, but it was smart to leave someone at her house. And her friend Cara was probably as good a bodyguard as one of my brothers. She was kind of scary.

I replied to the group text, telling Levi to go check on Gram.

No guys with neck tattoos came into the diner, so we finished our breakfast and left.

Something across the street caught Evan's attention, and he paused, narrowing his eyes. A couple stood chatting outside the Steaming Mug. I knew the guy—knew who he was, at least. Luke Haven. The girl looked familiar. She was blond, wearing a pink cardigan. Why did I recognize her? Then she smiled at Luke and I remembered. She was the girl who'd tried to give Evan her number that night at the Caboose.

Luke was clearly flirting with her, although it was hard to tell how she felt about it. Grinning, he said something and shifted closer, but she took a small step back.

Evan eyed them for a second, then started walking across the street toward them.

I took a couple of quick steps to catch up. "What are you doing?"

"Cockblocking that asshole."

"Why?"

"Because he's a dick and he deserves it."

I stopped a few feet away while Evan approached Luke and the girl. Her eyes widened when she noticed him coming, and she crossed her arms.

"Hey," Evan said, his low voice rumbling. He acted like Luke wasn't there. "I was hoping I'd run into you again. You gave me your number a while back and I don't know what happened to it."

She blinked and the defensiveness melted from her expression. Her arms dropped to her sides. "Oh. You lost it? I thought you weren't interested."

Luke looked dumbfounded. He held out his hands. "Dude, seriously?"

Evan ignored him, subtly shifting closer to the girl. "Not interested? Are you kidding?" He made a show of looking her up and down, as if he liked what he saw. "No, I lost it and I've been kicking myself ever since. So what do you say? Can I have another shot? I'll take good care of it this time."

Her eyes flicked to Luke, then back to Evan, and her mouth moved like she wasn't sure what to say. "Um... yeah. Sure, why not?"

Evan took out his phone and handed it to her. "Here. Put it in my contacts. Then I can't lose it."

She nibbled her bottom lip as she typed. Evan inched closer to her.

I couldn't tell if Luke was about to hit Evan or not. His hands clenched into fists, but his gaze moved to the girl and back again. I had a feeling he didn't want to start a fight in front of her.

But he definitely wanted to punch my brother in the face.

I didn't blame him.

The girl handed the phone back to Evan, and when her gaze lifted to meet his eyes, she sucked in a little breath. He'd moved closer, towering over her, and his face was fixed on hers.

She bit her lip again and gave him a shy smile.

Without breaking eye contact, Evan pocketed his phone. They stared at each other, and I wondered if he was going to kiss her.

Instead, she popped up onto her tiptoes and kissed him, a quick brush of her lips against his cheek. Her eyes widened again, and she looked shocked, like she couldn't believe she'd just done that. "Oops."

Evan shrugged, as if in resignation, grabbed her by the waist, hauled her against him, and kissed her back.

Only his kiss wasn't light or quick. He invaded her mouth, kissing her deeply, like he was checking her fucking tonsils. Luke stared at them, open-mouthed, rage burning in his eyes. If Evan hadn't already made a personal enemy out of Luke Haven, he certainly had now.

He broke the kiss slowly and pulled away.

The girl's eyes fluttered open. She looked drunk. Her cheeks were as pink as her cardigan, and she blinked slowly, like she was coming out of a trance. Her legs trembled and I wondered if she was going to need help to remain standing. "Whoa."

"See you around," Evan said. He cast one quick glance at Luke, then nonchalantly walked back toward me.

I fell in step beside him. "What the fuck was that about?"

"Nothing."

"Are you actually going to call her?"

He cast me a sidelong glance. "No."

"Dude, that's cold. She seems like a nice girl. Why would you fuck with her just to cockblock Luke Haven?"

"She'll live."

"I know she'll live, but that was a dick move."

He stopped and faced me. "Luke Haven's an asshole who deserves worse than me stepping in when he's trying to hit on some chick. And why do you care? Most girls *seem nice*. Doesn't mean they are. You just don't get it because Grace is a fucking unicorn. Not that you realize it."

I was about to bark at him not to talk about her when someone approached us, slowly clapping.

A guy covered in tattoos.

23

ASHER

I stared at him for a second while he approached, slow clapping with a grin on his face. Short blond hair. Button-down shirt with cuffed sleeves. Tattoos everywhere. On his forearms, down over the backs of his hands. Covering his chest and crawling up his neck.

I'd done time with him. But he wasn't Reaper.

"Holy fuck," I said. "Declan?"

"I don't know who that guy is or what he did to you, but that was impressive," he said.

Evan was tense, eying him like his dog had eyed me this morning.

"You son of a bitch, what are you doing here?" I nudged Evan with my elbow. "It's okay. I know this prick, but he isn't Reaper."

Declan laughed. "Reaper? Why the hell would that crazy asshole be here? Nice town, though." He took a deep breath. "I've been enjoying the fresh mountain air."

I should have been relieved—if Declan was the tattooed guy, it meant Grace wasn't in danger—but I wasn't convinced yet. I had to be sure. "Did you talk to a woman in that coffee shop last night?" I gestured toward the Steaming Mug.

His forehead creased. "What's with the interrogation?"

"Did you?"

"Yeah, I guess I did. She turned me down, though. I take it you know her?"

"Ash, what the fuck is going on?" Evan asked.

I gestured toward Declan. "This is Declan Wallace. We did about five years together. He got out—what, two years ago?"

Declan nodded. "About that, yeah."

"What are you doing here?"

"I heard you got out. Figured I'd look you up."

There was something in his voice. He wasn't here just to *look me up*. Declan had been the closest thing I'd had to a friend in prison, but not someone I'd expect to come find me so we could catch up and shoot the shit.

"Give me a minute." I nodded to Evan to follow and we moved a short distance down the sidewalk.

"So this isn't the guy?" he asked.

"No. Declan's fine. I have no idea why he's here, but he's harmless."

Evan's expression didn't change, and I couldn't tell what he was thinking. He simply looked like he didn't give a shit. About anything. "You better call off the rest of the wolf pack. Gavin's probably driving Grace crazy."

"Yeah, I'll let them know."

He cast one more glance at Declan. "Okay, I'm out. Work. I'll see you."

"Thanks, man," I said as he started to walk away. I was going to say more—try to tell him that I appreciated him having my back—but he just lifted a hand and kept walking.

Evan had changed. I felt like I didn't know him anymore.

I turned back to Declan and he grinned at me again. "Can I buy you a beer?"

"Now? It's morning."

"So?"

I shrugged and pulled out my phone. "Sure, what the hell. I just need to text someone first."

Declan waited while I texted my brothers, letting them know I'd found the tattooed guy and it was someone else. I sent Grace a text too, although my quick message didn't seem close to adequate. I'd probably scared the hell out of her.

But this had scared the hell out of me too.

We weren't far from the Caboose, so we walked over and found a table. The waitress gave Declan a funny look when he ordered two beers, but didn't comment. She left with our order and Declan glanced around.

"Is this town even fucking real? You've got an old-school barber shop, and that little corner store that looks like it's straight out of the fifties—"

"The Sugar Shack?"

"Yeah. And this place. A railroad restaurant? I swear to god, this place is fucking adorable. No wonder you came back."

I wasn't interested in talking about my hometown. "Declan, why the hell are you here? I've been going out of my mind."

"Did you really think I was Reaper?"

"What was I supposed to think? I hear a guy with tattoos like that," I said, gesturing up and down, "is here in town. Yeah, I thought it was Reaper, here to finish what he started on the inside."

"I don't think you need to worry about him. A guy like that has bigger problems than some kid who fucked him up a few times. Besides, he'll do something stupid and get himself locked up again sooner rather than later. If they're smart, they won't let him out next time."

"Yeah, well, I hope you're right."

"Don't lose sleep over it."

I glanced away. "That's assuming I can sleep."

"It's tough, isn't it?"

"What?"

"Coming back. Making the switch to the real world."

The waitress came back with two beers. He politely thanked her, then took a drink.

I nodded slowly and took a swig of my beer. "Yeah. It is tough."

"That's kind of why I'm here."

"You mean it's not because you missed me?"

He chuckled. "Don't flatter yourself."

I narrowed my eyes at him. "Have you been following me?"

"Following you? Nah, man. I saw you go into a gym yesterday, but you didn't see me. I figured I'd run into you sooner rather than later, so I didn't go in. Like I said, this town is nice. I thought I'd spend a couple days here regardless."

He hadn't been following me?

Shit. That should have been good news. Obviously I didn't want to be followed. But it meant my instincts were so out of whack, I was basically losing it.

"I'll just level with you, Bailey. I'm here with an opportunity."

"No offense, but if it's something that might land me in prison again, I can already tell you the answer is no."

He put his hands up in a gesture of surrender. "Hey, give a guy some credit. I'm one hundred percent legit now."

I raised my eyebrows.

"I'm serious, man. I'm with you, I'm never going back."

"All right. Good for you. So what are you doing now?"

"It's a funny story. When I got out, I did the same as you. Went back to my hometown. Didn't take me long to figure out that wasn't going to work. I have a brother in Phoenix, and he told me if I came down, he'd have a job for me. So I took him up on it."

"If you're in Phoenix now, what are you doing up here?"

"Visiting my grandma."

"Are you serious?"

"Dead fucking serious, man. She's in a nursing home, so I come see her when I can."

"And then you coincidentally happened to hear I was out early?"

He shrugged. "Not exactly a coincidence. I looked you up. Inmate information is all online. It's not hard to get."

"Why?"

"Like I said, I have an opportunity for you. My brother owns a gym and they train some of the top MMA competitors in the world."

My back stiffened and my grip on my beer bottle tightened.

"I saw what you could do when we were on the inside," he continued. "You don't just have skills, you have instincts. With the right trainer behind you, you could compete against the best. Fuck, you could crush the best."

I ground out the words. "You want me to be a fighter?"

"My friend, you *are* a fighter. Some people are good because they have training and skill. But guys like you? They're born with it. Granted, anyone who gets in the ring needs skill. You still have to train. But I'm telling you, there aren't many people out there who have what you have.

Some guys can fight, and some guys are fighters. You're a fighter."

I looked away, still gripping my beer in a tight fist. He was right, I was a fighter, but I hated it. And I hated that he'd seen it so clearly. Although how could he not? I'd literally fought my way through my sentence. I'd spent most of my seven years with a big fucking target on my back—the guy everyone wanted to prove themselves against.

I didn't want to be that guy anymore. The urge to fight was a demon inside me, and I had to keep it locked away. Anything else was too dangerous.

"Look, I appreciate the offer, but I don't think that's a good idea."

"I get it. It means relocating and you've got family here." He narrowed his eyes. "And maybe a girl?"

I glanced away again. "Not exactly."

"Coffee shop girl flashed a ring at me. Was she yours once? And maybe someone else put that ring on her finger while you were gone?"

"I don't want to talk about her."

He put his hands up again. "Fair enough. But seriously, man, think about it. What are you going to do out here? What kind of job are you going to get now? I know what it's like—I grew up in a small town, although mine was more of a shithole than this place. Still, no one looks at you the same. And this could mean huge money."

"I'm almost thirty. Aren't I already getting too old for this?"

"Not at all. A lot of fighters don't peak until their mid-thirties. We've got guys still winning into their forties. You train properly, take care of yourself, you'd have a solid ten years, maybe fifteen. Things go well, that's more than enough time to make you a shit ton of money. I'm talking set-you-up-for-life kind of money. Set your family up for life, if you want."

Take care of my family. That was the crack in my armor, and he'd just wormed his way in. Right now, I could barely afford to take care of myself. I didn't have a plan or any other opportunities. Ever since I'd gotten out, I'd been asking myself what I was going to do with my life. This could be the answer to that question.

I sat back in my chair. Declan didn't say anything. Just settled in with his beer, like he could tell I needed to think.

The money was tempting. I wasn't going to lie to myself about that. Not because I gave a shit about being wealthy, but because I needed to be productive. I needed purpose. Maybe getting in the ring and beating the shit out of people would be worth it if it meant I could ensure Gram never had to worry about money. If I could take care of my family and know they always had what they needed.

Maybe it would start to make up for the time I'd missed. For how I'd pushed them away.

But I couldn't ignore what else it would mean. Leaving Tilikum. Leaving my family.

Leaving Grace.

I took a drink, the hint of bitterness sitting on my tongue. I wanted her so badly, I ached with it. And there was a voice in my head trying to tell me that I didn't just want her, I *needed* her. That she was good for me.

But I couldn't ignore the fact that regardless of what I wanted, I wasn't good for her. I barely slept. I had nightmares almost every night. I constantly felt like I was being watched. I was always on high alert, always ready to respond. Ready to fight.

I'd been convinced someone was following me, and as much as I wanted to tell myself I wasn't crazy—maybe there had been someone—deep down, I knew. It had been in my head.

It wasn't normal.

That also meant my initial instinct was right. I needed to stay out of the ring. No MMA training. No sparring. And certainly no fucking fighting. Not even if it would make me a shit ton of money. I couldn't take that risk.

"I appreciate you coming out here." I set my bottle down. "It's a good offer. But I can't take it."

He regarded me for a few seconds, his expression thoughtful. "Tell you what. Give it some time, see how things play out. If life here works for you, that's great. If not..." He pulled out a business card and slid it across the table. "Call me."

I took the card, pinching it between my thumb and forefinger. "Okay. Thanks."

He pulled out his wallet and tossed some money on the table. "It was good to catch up with you. Take care, man. Stay out of trouble."

"You too."

Still holding his business card, I watched him stand and walk out. My body ached with fatigue. I was coming down from all that adrenaline and I felt like shit. Almost hungover.

And all I could think about was Grace.

My defenses were whittled down to almost nothing. If she hadn't been at work, I would have gone straight to her house, knowing what would happen if I did. Knowing I'd be powerless to resist her.

I was stuck between a rock and a hard place. I couldn't have her. But fuck, I couldn't leave her, either.

DEAR ASHER

ear Asher,

I FEEL like if I wrote this to anyone else, they wouldn't believe this story was true. But you know Tilikum.

Yesterday while I was at work, there was a commotion out on the street. I could hear it from my office in the back. It sounded like someone yelling. When it didn't die down right away, I went outside to see what was going on.

On the next block over, Harvey Johnston was outside Happy Paws, the pet supply store, yelling at... something. I wasn't sure what, and you never know with him. He was on the sidewalk, shaking his fist, and shouting a barely coherent stream of expletives.

A few people stood around gawking at him, but they seemed reluctant to get close. I didn't blame them—he was really worked up. But you know Harvey, he's harmless, even when he's ranting about something.

So, there he was, yelling at someone or something, and I realized the big Happy Paws sign that hangs over the sidewalk was swinging. None of the other signs in front of the other shops were moving, so it wasn't the wind. Not only was it swinging, it looked like it was about to fall. And Harvey was standing right under it.

I ran across the street and grabbed Harvey by the arm. That surprised him enough that he stopped yelling, but he didn't move. I yanked him out into the street and he kept asking, "Did you see them? Did you see?" over and over.

About three seconds later, the Happy Paws sign crashed to the sidewalk, right where Harvey had been standing.

I looked up, and what did I see? Two gray squirrels scampering away across the roof.

Squirrels, Asher.

Harvey kept pointing and saying, "There they go! After them!"

Did they actually loosen the sign so it would fall? Can squirrels DO that?

I honestly don't know.

I do know Missy Lovejoy (if you don't remember Missy, she owns Happy Paws) has been embroiled in an all-out war with the squirrels this year. She says they steal her pet treats and splash in the dish of water she leaves out for people's dogs.

Harvey's always saying they're organized. I know he's not exactly all there, but maybe he's not as crazy as he seems.

I told Gram about it later and she said Missy Lovejoy needs to strike a deal with the squirrels. How does one strike a deal with small mammals? I asked her that very question and she just shrugged and said it's not up to her to solve everyone's problems.

What is with this town? Is this normal? I don't think this is normal.

Anyway, I just thought a little slice of life here in Tilikum might make you smile.

. . .

I LOVE YOU,
   Grace

24

GRACE

*F*ortunately, my Bailey bodyguards were called off fairly quickly. I loved those guys, but the thought of them "guarding" me twenty-four/seven was a little much. Cara had stayed over last night, but by morning she was no longer trying to talk me into letting her hire mercenaries. Everything seemed to have settled down.

I was hoping the end to the perceived crisis would mean a calmer Asher. I hadn't seen him yesterday—we'd both ended up working late—but he'd texted several times to see how I was doing. Although I didn't want to get my hopes up too much, it felt like maybe that hug we'd shared had been a breakthrough.

Who was I kidding? My hopes were up.

"Huh." Cara looked at me over the top of a book. "Peachy pants, did you know only thirty percent of the earth's land is forest?"

"Nope." I barely glanced at her.

"Me neither." She shut the book and unceremoniously dropped it on a pile next to her chair.

We were in a chilly back room in the Tilikum Library.

The dry air smelled dusty, like an old crypt no one had opened in centuries. I'd dragged Cara here with me so I could do a little digging into the town's history. See if I could find any trace of Eliza Bailey.

Partly, I was curious about the mirror, and who Eliza Bailey might have been. But I was also off work today, and needed something to keep my mind occupied for a while. Seven years without Asher had made me an expert at creating distractions for myself.

I'd already looked online but hadn't come up with anything about an Eliza Bailey. In fact, there wasn't much to be found about Tilikum in general prior to the 1920s. Libby Stewart, one of the library volunteers, had solved that little mystery for me. About a hundred years ago, Tilikum had suffered a devastating fire, and huge portions of the town had burned down. Records and artifacts from anything prior to that were scarce and hard to find.

Still, I was nothing if not stubborn. I'd been hoping the library would have a database, maybe one that wasn't available online. What they actually had was an ancient microfiche reader and old newspaper articles on sheets of film.

Cara sat in an armchair she'd dragged in here herself, earning a horrified look from Libby. She'd grabbed a few books, seemingly at random, and thumbed through them while I squinted into the eyepiece, skimming for any references to someone named Eliza Bailey.

"I can't believe they don't have a second one of those," she said. "This would go twice as fast if I could help."

"Why would they have two? I didn't even know these things existed. I think I'm lucky they have this one."

"True." She picked up another book from her random stack. "Do you really think you're going to find anything?"

"I don't know, but I'm curious enough to try."

She flipped a page. "But why would newspapers help?"

"There might be marriage or birth announcements. Or even an obituary. That would have information about her family."

"Yeah, I get that, but what if she had a secret lover and they never married, and no one ever knew?"

"I know I won't find that in the newspaper, but if I can find out anything about her, it might give me a clue. Those love letters are so poignant and sad. I want to find out who wrote them and what ultimately happened. Did they find a way to be together?"

"God, you're such a romantic. You're hoping you find out they lived happily ever after."

"Of course I am."

She closed the book and sat forward in the chair. "Because if they had a happy ending, maybe you will too?"

I turned toward her. "I know this doesn't have anything to do with me and Asher. Even if Eliza Bailey's story has a sad ending, it doesn't mean we will."

"But it would still make you feel better."

"Fine. Yes, it would make me feel better. I'd love to find out those love notes led to a happy ending."

"Are your eyes tired yet? If you need a break, I can take over for a while."

"Thanks, but I know you're bored. You don't have to stay."

"I'm bored as hell, but we both know I can't go."

"What are you talking about? Of course you can."

Her forehead creased. "You mean if I go, you'll stay here by yourself and keep searching?"

I opened my mouth to say of course I would, but the thought of being left alone back here made a thread of anxiety uncurl in my stomach. I actually didn't like that idea. At all.

"See?" she asked. "Don't worry, boo. I've got you. I'm used to it."

"Used to what?"

"That you can't go anywhere in public by yourself."

"What? Yes I can."

She raised her eyebrows. "No, you can't. Except work. You've been that way since I've known you."

I felt oddly defensive, like she was flinging an unfair accusation at me. "That's crazy. Of course I can go places by myself."

"Yeah? When was the last time you went grocery shopping alone?"

"I..." I had to stop and think. When *was* the last time I'd gone grocery shopping alone? I usually went with Cara or picked up my little brother and bought him cookies or candy while we were out. "That's just because we like going together. And sometimes I want to get Elijah out of my mom's hair."

"Okay, but it's not just grocery shopping."

"I go to Stitch and Sip alone."

"No, you don't. You might drive yourself there, but you're meeting people you know."

"Still."

"Do you ever go to the Knotty Knitter when it's not Stitch and Sip night? By yourself, just to buy yarn or whatever?"

"No, but I don't need to. I'm already there almost every Monday."

She tilted her head, regarding me for a long moment with a bewildered expression. "You really don't know this about yourself, do you? I always assumed you were aware of it."

"There's nothing to be aware of, because you're wrong."

"Grace, I've known you for years, and while I'm sure there are a few exceptions, I'm positive you almost never go places alone. Why do you think I always need to run errands or get groceries when you do? I've never run my own errands or shopped for my own groceries in my life. But I know you're always going to need someone to go with you, so I do. Why else would I set foot in a hardware store? I cannot possibly think of a more boring place to lose an hour of my life."

I stared blankly at the microfiche screen. Oh my god. Was she right? I couldn't remember the last time I'd gone into a store or restaurant by myself. Not unless I was meeting someone. I went to work, but otherwise, I was always with someone else—usually Cara. We went everywhere together, and I'd never really thought about it. We were close. We both needed someone. But was that really the reason?

"Oh my god, Cara, I think you're right. I don't know how to feel about this right now. How could I be unaware of something so unhealthy?"

"Probably because of me," she said, her voice nonchalant.

"You? Why?"

"You know how some people totally spoil and enable their children? That's me. I'm people. I can't stand the thought of you being unhappy, so I do whatever I have to do to make sure you're not."

I swallowed back the tightness in my throat and my eyes misted with the threat of tears. "Why are you so good to me?"

"Let's be honest, good to you is debatable. A little tough love might have been better. But I just can't. I want you to be happy. I care about maybe two people in the entire world, which I realize is kind of fucked up. But no one else has ever given me a reason."

"Aw, honey."

She smiled. "Normal people spread out their love and attention, but I don't have anyone else, so you get it all. Which I realize probably sucks for you because I have no idea how to actually love someone."

"Now that's definitely not true."

"It really is. But I'd like to think I'm learning. Next I have to learn how to share you."

I turned sideways in my chair so I was facing her and leaned forward. "If Asher and I figure things out, that's going to be hard for you, isn't it?"

Glancing away, she fiddled with a lock of red hair. "Yes, but I'm also okay with it, because if it's what you want, then it's what I want."

"You really mean that, don't you?"

"Of course I do. I'm probably a terrible friend in a thousand different ways, but I wouldn't lie to you."

"That's love, Cara. *That's* how you really love someone. You want what's best for them, even if it means you have to lose something."

She shrugged, and I could see her trying to remain nonchalant. Cara didn't dig into her feelings very often.

"You're my person," I said. "You're never going to lose me. Even if I marry Asher."

"Shut your beautiful face."

I laughed, but my smile faded. "Do I have a problem? You'd tell me if I have a problem, right?"

"Honestly, I don't know. If you weren't even aware of it, I bet it's just a habit. We got so used to doing literally everything together back in college, and now you don't think about it. Besides, it's a totally codependent relationship. I get a lot out of you needing me."

"Yeah, maybe it's just habit." I chewed on my bottom lip, not sure whether I believed that. "Tell you what, give me thirty more minutes here and we'll go get lunch. Anywhere you want."

"You know what I really want?"

"What?"

She looked off into the distance, her expression dreamy. "There's this place in San Diego that has the most unbelievable coconut shrimp you'll ever eat in your life. If I can get a flight, do you want to go?"

"Today?"

"Yeah. It would have to be more like dinner, but I still think we could make it happen."

"I'm not going to San Diego today."

"Why not? It's not a long flight."

Shaking my head, I laughed. "I was thinking something a little closer. Like here."

She slumped back in the chair and groaned. "Fine. We can go to the Caboose, but I'm definitely day-drinking."

"Me too, for sure."

"Are you sure you don't want to go to San Diego?"

"Cara, the last time you took me on one of your crazy spontaneous trips, we were supposed to be gone for eight hours. Two days later, I'd almost lost my job."

A wide smile spread across her face. "Yeah, but we had fun."

"We did have fun," I reluctantly admitted.

"That's okay, I'm over the San Diego idea. Hank makes really good gin and tonics and that sounds better than food anyway. Even coconut shrimp."

My phone dinged with a text and as soon as I saw his name on the screen, I was smiling.

Asher: *Would you believe me if I told you three squirrels stole my lunch?*

Me: *Actually, yes I would.*

Asher: *It was in my truck, but I left the window down. I saw the little fuckers running away and my lunch is gone.*

Me: *That was your mistake. Can't let your guard down around those little guys. They're shifty.*

I glanced at Cara. She was pretending not to watch me, but I knew she was curious. For a second, I thought about asking her if she'd mind me inviting Asher to have lunch with us.

But as much as I'd have loved an excuse to see him, I quickly decided not to. Cara would say yes, but I didn't want to alter our plans. My friendship with her was important to me, and I couldn't get in the habit of making her feel like a third wheel.

Asher: *No kidding. I'll grab something in town, I just thought you'd enjoy laughing at my misfortune.*

Me: *It definitely made me smile.*

Asher: *Then it was worth it. I love your smile.*

Yep, my hopes were officially rising. Fast.

"What's that all about?" Cara asked.

"Just Asher. Squirrels stole his lunch out of his truck. He thought it would make me laugh."

One corner of her mouth hooked in a subtle grin. "Texting you just because?"

"Yeah."

"Hmm. Interesting."

I nibbled my bottom lip again. "He also said he loves my smile."

She raised her eyebrows. "Boo, slow down. You're taking

this relationship way too fast."

"Shut up."

"I'm serious. He's already texting you nice things? What's next, tea on the porch with a chaperone? Be careful not to show any ankle. You might damage his esteem for you."

I laughed. "Stop."

"I'm not the one being all slutty and showing too much ankle. Hussy."

"Oh, I'm the hussy? That's hilarious coming from you."

"I know, I'm such a hypocrite. But seriously, I'd really like to start shopping for bridesmaid dresses, so if you two could hurry it up, that'd be great."

"I'll be sure and do that just for your convenience."

She flashed a big smile. "You're such a good friend."

Libby Stewart poked her head in the door. "Um, Grace? Ms. Montgomery sent me to tell you your time's up."

Lorraine Montgomery was the head librarian.

"Really? Sorry, I didn't know there was a time limit."

"I didn't either, but that's what she said."

Cara and I shared a look. That was... weird. It wasn't like browsing through old newspaper articles on microfiche was a popular library activity.

"Okay." I turned off the machine. "We were pretty much done anyway."

"Did you find anything? Ms. Montgomery was asking about it."

"Not really. Do you want me to put these somewhere?" I gestured to the stack of film.

"No, that's okay. I'll take care of it."

"Thanks, Libby."

Cara and I grabbed our purses and left Libby in the storeroom.

"Was it just me, or was that strange?" Cara asked.

"Kind of. Although maybe that old microfiche machine can only take so much use. It was getting pretty warm."

We passed the front counter where several people were checking out books. Lorraine Montgomery eyed us. She looked like the consummate librarian, with her floral dress, tan cardigan, and wire rimmed glasses. She even wore her graying hair in a loose bun.

She'd always been stern, but I had no idea why she was watching us like she thought we were sneaking books out of her library.

"Well, whatever," Cara said. "I'm ready for gin."

"Aren't you always?"

"Basically."

Cara held the door for me and I cast a glance over my shoulder—at Lorraine Montgomery, still watching me.

25

ASHER

The familiar smell of rubber mixed with a hint of sweat greeted me as I walked into the gym. An industrial-size fan hummed in a corner and the clink of weights echoed from the high ceilings. Two guys grappled on one of the open floor mats and another pair sparred in the cage, their grunts adding to the sounds of movement and activity.

Jack Cordero stood near the front, talking to a guy wearing a Tilikum Fire Department t-shirt. He was dressed in street clothes and carried a duffel bag—looked like he'd already worked out. A lot of the guys from the sheriff's office worked out here, and so did most of the firefighters. They'd always had a good-natured rivalry. Back when I'd been a volunteer firefighter, I'd often sparred with the deputies. The TFD guys had put me up against them because I was good. I usually won. TFD pride and all that.

The firefighter—I'd seen him before, but I didn't know his name—laughed at something Jack said. Jack glanced over and caught my eye. Gave me a chin tip greeting. I returned it.

I liked Jack. Prison had admittedly made me predisposed to distrust authority, especially cops. But Jack seemed like good people.

I stopped at the front desk and signed in. I was about to veer toward the side of the gym with the weights, but someone on one of the open mats caught my eye. I stopped and did a double take. It was Grace.

She was dressed in a tank top and a pair of black shorts that showed off her athletic legs. Her hair was pulled back and her feet were bare.

One of the trainers—I thought his name might be Diego —squared off with her. He wore a t-shirt and shorts and his long hair was secured in a man-bun. They circled each other slowly and I noticed Grace never let her feet cross, always keeping a good stance. Her center of gravity was low, her knees slightly bent.

She was totally focused on her opponent, her eyes watching his. He feinted to one side, and she flinched, but didn't take the bait. A beat later, he shot on her, wrapping his arms around her waist. She sprawled instantly, leaning her body weight into him, her legs stretched behind her.

Damn. That was a good move.

He couldn't take her down with such a hard sprawl, so he pulled back. They locked up, heads together, both fighting for position. I had an urge to shout out instructions —*change levels, Grace*—but I kept quiet.

Moving fast, she went for his inside leg with hers. Half a second later they were both on the ground. At first it looked like she'd made a mistake and he was going to turn things around on her. But she rolled to her back, pulling him on top of her, and got him in her guard. Her legs were wrapped around his waist, her feet locked.

In wrestling, being on your back was always bad. In

Brazilian jiujitsu, however, it was a position of strength. Grace had him right where she wanted him.

Diego coached her as they grappled, giving her quick—and increasingly breathless—instructions. He tried to sit up, moving his upper body away from hers, but she followed, keeping her legs locked tight. Twisting at the waist, she threaded her hand around his opposite arm and wrenched him forward, pulling his face into the mat. Without letting go of his arm, she shifted her weight beneath him, twisting his bent arm backward at a painful angle.

Push up on his wrist, Grace. Push up.

She squeezed her legs tighter against his attempts to break her hold, and pushed up on his wrist. He smacked the mat with his other hand, and she let go.

Nice move.

Diego stood and helped her to her feet, then shook out his arm. They exchanged a few quiet words. She nodded; he was probably critiquing her form, letting her know what she'd done well and where she could improve. He patted her shoulder and walked off the mat.

It was about then that I realized I was standing in the middle of the gym, staring at her.

She caught sight of me and the smile that lit up her face almost broke me wide open. She was sweaty and flushed, her hair falling out of her half-ponytail. Her tank top and tiny shorts showed a hell of a lot of skin, all glistening from her workout.

God, she was beautiful. Sweaty, messy, and absolutely perfect.

"Hey you." She walked toward me, rooting my feet to the spot. I couldn't have moved if I'd tried. "I didn't know you were training again."

"I'm not, actually. I'm just here to lift."

"Really? You don't want to get back on the mat?"

I shook my head. "No. You looked great, though. That was a nice submission."

"Thanks." She paused for a second. "Do you want to at least warm up a little?"

"With you?"

Her eyes held mine and her lips turned up in a slow smile. It wasn't a friendly smile. It was full of heat, dripping with suggestion. "Yeah. Come on. I promise I'll go easy on you."

I jerked my thumb over my shoulder, vaguely in the direction of the weights. "That's okay. I'll just go do my thing."

"That's fine, I understand. It's been a while. You're probably worried you're rusty."

With that look in her eyes, I wasn't sure if we were talking about grappling anymore. "I'm not worried about being rusty. At anything."

"You sure about that, big guy?"

She was goading me, and I knew it. I still took the bait. "Yeah, it's not an issue. Some things you never forget."

"Like riding a bike?"

I stepped up to the edge of the mat and looked down on her. "No, not like riding a bike."

"Show me."

Every muscle in my body tensed. It was all I could do to hold myself in check. I wanted to drag her somewhere private, rip those shorts in half, pull out my cock, and fuck her up against a wall.

The worst part was, I knew that look in her eyes. She wanted it as much as I did.

I couldn't fuck her here—obviously. There were other people around. I wasn't an animal. But more than that, I couldn't fuck her anywhere. Not while I was still such a wreck.

But goddamn, she was hard to resist.

"I'm not grappling with you, Grace."

"Why not? Are you afraid I'll win?"

I looked her up and down. "I probably have eighty pounds on you. Maybe more."

"So?"

"I'd crush you."

"You think so? Since you're so confident, how about we make it interesting?"

"How?"

"I bet I can make you tap out. If I win, I get what I want. If you win, you get what you want."

"What do you want?"

"A date."

Fuck. I was unraveling so fast, my brain could hardly keep up. A date. Take Grace out on a date. I was supposed to be keeping my distance. Giving us both a chance to move on.

But god, roll around on the mat with her? Touch all that skin? Get her sweat on my clothes? I wanted to do the right thing, but every man's willpower has limits. I was definitely reaching mine. And it wasn't like she could win. She'd looked good against Diego, but I was a trained fighter, and bigger than her. The risk was minimal.

That's what I was telling myself, at least.

"Fine. You make me tap out, you get a date."

That sly grin of hers slid across her face again and she caught her lower lip between her teeth. "Good. Let's do this."

"Hang on. What if I win?"

She walked to the center of the mat and looked back at

me. "If you want to pick something, suit yourself. But you're not going to win, so it doesn't matter."

"Is that so, tiger?"

"Yep."

"No, we need to set the full terms beforehand. I don't want you backing out when you lose."

She put her hands on her hips. "I won't back out. But if it'll make you feel better, what do you want if you win?"

Oh shit, now I had to think of something. It was occurring to me that she was already several steps ahead. She'd goaded me into this from the start, and I was still trying to catch up. "Chocolate cake."

"That's it?"

It wasn't very good, but I couldn't say if I won, I got to take her back to her place and fuck her until neither of us could see straight. And that thought was taking up too much space in my brain. It was hard to think of anything else.

"Do you know how long it's been since I've had cake?"

She shrugged. "Okay, Bailey. If you can make me tap out, I'll bake you a cake. Now get over here and show me what you've got."

I took off my shoes and socks and stepped onto the mat. The pliable smoothness was familiar beneath my feet. Damn, it had been a long time.

Grace fixed her hair, pulling it back and retying it. She shook out her arms and bounced up onto her toes a few times. Then she widened her stance, gave me a smirk, and gestured for me to come at her.

The sounds around me fell away. No more voices, clanking weights, humming fan. My focus narrowed to the space of the dark blue mat. To my opponent.

To Grace.

Lowering my center of gravity, I reached for her, testing

her defenses. She batted my arm away. I tried again, shuffling closer. She deflected, avoiding my grip. But this time, she surged in, going for a trip on my inside leg.

I'd seen her use that move on Diego, so I was ready for it. I moved my leg before she could get hers wrapped around it and took advantage of the shift in her balance. Grabbing her thigh, I pulled up on her leg and drove my body weight forward.

We hit the mat with Grace on her back and I moved to side control, circling so I was perpendicular to her, my chest on top of hers. I should have been able to end it here, but she was fast. And determined. She resisted my efforts to get my arm beneath her neck, and used her lower body strength to shift her hips.

"You sure you're not rusty?" she asked, her voice strained with effort.

I grunted and swung my body around, going for control on the other side. Careful not to put too much weight on her ribcage—I didn't want to hurt her—I tried to hook one of her legs.

She shoved her knee into my gut, using me as leverage to get her hips free. I grunted again, scrambling to regain control. Damn, she was fast. And slippery. Not because she was sweaty—she moved like a cat. Every time I thought I had a solid hold, she contorted out of it somehow.

Suddenly, she went on the offensive. Pushing against me again, she moved her hips backward. I tried to counter, but she used my momentum against me. Her body twisted and she hooked an arm around one of my legs. Next thing I knew, my face was smashed into the mat and I was rolling onto my back.

Using my surprise to her advantage, she straddled my hips, sinking her body weight onto me. She planted her palms in the center of my chest and before I could react, she twisted off, her ass landing on the mat right beside me.

And she had my arm.

Clamping my upper arm between her thighs, she threw herself backward, stretching it out as she went.

I had no leverage in this position. I needed to turn into her so I could keep a bend in my elbow, but it was too late. Her legs pushed my upper body down while she quickly increased the pressure on my arm.

Holy shit. It didn't matter how much bigger I was. She could break my arm like this.

I didn't give up, still trying to shift my weight and give myself some room. But she redoubled her efforts, squeezing her thighs and bending my arm in the wrong direction. It hurt like a motherfucker. I gritted my teeth, growling against the pain.

And hit the mat with my other hand, tapping out.

Instantly, the pressure eased. She released her thighs and let go.

I stared at the ceiling for a second, breathing hard. She'd actually made me tap out.

She scooted back and sat up, crossing her legs.

I turned toward her. "Since when do you know how to do an arm bar?"

"Since I do. I told you I'd win."

Surging forward, I shoved her onto her back and sank my weight over her hips. She wrapped her legs around me and locked her feet. I held her wrists pinned above her head, but she didn't resist. Just fixed her blue eyes on mine.

All the reasons I couldn't have her tried to barrel through my mind. But it was so hard to pay attention to them when I had her pinned to the ground with my groin pressing against hers. My cock hardened between us. I knew she could feel it. Without breaking eye contact, she moved her hips. It was just an inch, but it was enough. That subtle rub against my dick set off a chain reaction of sensation. I pushed harder against her, making her eyelids flutter and her lips part with a soft exhale.

Just that look on her face was almost enough to make me come all over myself.

Someone cleared their throat, reminding me where we were. Even with that, it was hard to make myself move. She felt so fucking good. A low groan rumbled in my throat, but I let go of her wrists, moving my hips back.

We both got to our feet and I took a step away to create some distance. I felt out of it, like I was drunk. And maybe I was. Drunk on her. I could smell her all over me. And the way her skin glistened made me want to lick her.

She brushed a tendril of hair off her forehead. "Looks like I get a date."

"That was the bet. What do you want to do?"

"I'm sure you'll figure something out. You know me. I'm not fancy."

I did know her. Seven years had changed us both—me more than her—but she was still Grace. Still the girl I'd fallen for all those years ago.

"Thank god you two are done," a woman's voice said behind me. "I was wondering if I'd have to pull the fire alarm to clear this place out and give you some privacy."

Grace laughed and I glanced behind me. Her friend Cara stood to the side of the mat with her arms crossed. She was dressed in a tank top and even tinier shorts than Grace's.

"You know that's illegal, right?" Grace asked.

Cara shrugged, like she didn't care. "Are you ready, or do you want me to come pick you up later?"

"I'm ready." Grace started to walk off the mat, but paused in front of me and met my eyes. "So..."

"How about tomorrow. I'll pick you up at six?"

Her lips twitched in a seductive smile and her eyes flicked down to my groin, then back again. "Perfect. See you then."

Fuck, she was going to kill me.

Letting out a breath, I glanced at Cara. She gave me a quick wink, like she approved. Then she followed Grace toward the locker room.

I stepped off the mat and grabbed my shoes, feeling oddly calm. In fact, I couldn't remember the last time I'd felt so even. Like my mood wasn't in danger of crashing. I was turned on as hell, the pressure in my groin annoyingly strong. But there were people all around me and my back wasn't clenched. The ever-present sense of impending danger was still there, but it was muted, like it had moved to the background.

It felt good.

I took my stuff to the other side of the gym and set my bag down. My phone buzzed with a text from a number I didn't recognize.

It's Cara. If you need a date idea, I can help.

That was interesting. I hadn't taken Grace on a date in a long time. Maybe I could use some advice from her best friend.

I still didn't know if I should be doing this. A little skin contact with Grace wasn't going to suddenly fix me; the sense of calmness I felt was undoubtedly temporary. I had to be careful.

But I couldn't deny the ways Grace and I were connected. It was hurting both of us to be apart. I'd been home for almost a month, and that pain wasn't easing. It was getting worse. The ache in my chest kept growing, and if she felt anything like I did, it was probably close to unbearable.

I couldn't win. If I gave in, there were so many ways this could go wrong. So many ways I could fail her. But my efforts to keep us apart, to somehow be friends, were turning into a slow form of torture.

Gram's voice crept into my mind. *Take your time, Bear.*

Maybe I didn't have to make a decision about the future right now. I could take Grace out and let that be what it was. A date.

And maybe with time, there'd be a way I could make it work. I was all kinds of fucked up inside, and I still didn't think she realized the extent of the damage. Maybe when she saw it—truly saw how many scars I had—she'd decide she couldn't handle it.

But I couldn't keep fighting this. Not when I had so many other demons to keep locked away. And not when Grace's pull on me was so strong.

26

ASHER

*A*fter punishing my body at the gym for an hour or so, I went home to Gram's. The smell of frybread hit me as soon as I opened the door, making my mouth water. As much as I wanted to get my own place—and I was getting closer—there were perks to living here. Particularly Gram's cooking.

"Hey, Gram." I set my stuff down and went to the kitchen at the back of the house. Something savory, almost spicy, hit my nose when I got closer.

"Hi, Bear." She presided over an enormous stack of frybread and a cast iron skillet filled with simmering meat. "I hope you're hungry. I felt like we needed Indian tacos."

"Starving. But that's a lot of food, even for me. Who else is coming?"

She flipped a piece of frybread to brown the other side. "I didn't invite anyone, but you know how my cubs are. They can smell my frybread all the way across town. Now when they come barreling in here, I'll have plenty."

"Smart."

"With experience comes wisdom. There's a package for you. It's on the table."

I took a seat and slid the rectangular box closer. The tape popped off easily and I pulled out a plastic food container with the lid on. It was turned upside down so the bowl portion was on top, and I tilted my head to look through the plastic. "Is that Jell-O? Who left this?"

"I don't know. It was on the porch when I came inside after feeding my peckers."

I snapped the seal on the lid and lifted the bowl. Sure enough, it was a lopsided dome-shaped glob of green Jell-O. And inside...

"Oh my god. They put a shank in Jell-O."

I laughed, because what else could I do? First the file baked into the cake. Then someone had put one in the glove box of the truck. I'd ordered a pizza for me and Gram the other night and there had been a fake shank made from a toothbrush in the box. I had no idea how they'd pulled that one off. Now another one in bright green Jell-O.

"Someone must think you're going to need those someday. Is there something you're not telling me?"

"Yeah, Gram, I'm dealing drugs. Don't go out to the shop. The less you know, the better."

She chuckled.

I pushed the container away. "When I find out which one of them is doing this, I'm going to make them pay."

"Why do you assume it's only one of them? Sometimes they still roam as a pack."

"Good point."

"All that aside, how was your day?"

"It wasn't bad, actually."

"How's Grace?"

I eyed her with suspicion. "How did you know I saw her today?"

She took the piece of frybread out and set it on the wire rack to drain. "I didn't."

"Then why did you ask about her?"

"Why wouldn't I ask about her?"

I shook my head. "She's fine. I'm taking her out tomorrow night."

She cast a glance at me over her shoulder, then turned off both burners and gave the meat a quick stir. "Are you, now?"

"Yeah. I kind of lost a bet."

"Oh, I see. So she's making you do it."

"No. Sort of. I saw her at the gym and she bet me she could make me tap out." I stretched my arm and rolled my shoulder. "She basically schooled me."

Gram chuckled. "That's our Mama Bear."

"I didn't even know she'd learned to grapple. Some of her letters mentioned going to the gym, but I thought she meant working out to stay in shape."

She took the seat across from me. "Does it surprise you?"

"A little bit, yeah. She was never interested in martial arts before."

"Trauma changes people. Makes them see things differently. You have to remember, she got hurt that night too."

I looked away. "I know. Believe me, I've never forgotten that."

"She's very good at making sure she seems all right on the outside. It's a skill you two have in common. But it can also be a weakness."

"You don't think she's okay on the inside?"

She tilted her head. "Normally I don't like to point out the obvious. If someone's going to insist on being stubborn or thick-headed, far be it for me to intervene. Reality will smack into them eventually. But no, Bear, she's not. Neither of you are okay on the inside."

I paused, letting that sink in. Feeling like a selfish asshole for not thinking about it before.

"Gram, I don't know if I can be with her. Because you're right, I'm not okay on the inside."

"Of course you aren't. Nobody expects you to be, least of all Grace."

"I know she doesn't. But the life we were planning before doesn't exist anymore. I'm not the same. I wish I was, but I'm not. I've got a lot of..." I trailed off, not quite sure how to explain. "I have a lot of bad stuff inside. I don't want to take her down with me."

She nodded slowly. "The spirit of a protector is strong in you. Always has been. It's up to you to figure out how to use it. It takes wisdom and good judgment to know who needs your protection, and to recognize what you're meant to protect them from."

Before I could reply, the front door banged open. I could tell without looking that at least two, if not three, of my brothers had just arrived. I met Gram's eyes and she winked.

"See? Let's eat."

THE EARLY JUNE sun had dipped beneath the mountains, but the sky was still light. My brothers and I had made quick work of Gram's dinner. They'd said they had no idea she was cooking. They'd all gotten off a shift at the same time and decided to come over. Gram had just smiled with a knowing look in her eyes, then told us not to break anything while we fought over who had to clean up after dinner, because she certainly wasn't doing it.

They'd gone home already, and I went out to check the truck's oil. Grandad had always said his truck would run forever if you treated her right. I wasn't sure about forever, but I wasn't letting her die on my watch.

I popped the hood and lifted the bar to hold it open. The faint sound of voices carried on the breeze. Jack was outside in front of their house talking to Elijah. I couldn't hear what they were saying, but even without seeing his face, I could tell Elijah wasn't happy. His hood was down, but his arms were crossed and he dug his toe in the gravel.

Jack was dressed in his uniform and he looked frustrated. Not quite angry—there was nothing aggressive in his posture. But he put his hands on his hips and shook his head. He said something else, waited, then got in his car and left.

Elijah shuffled around toward the back of the house with his hands stuffed in his pockets.

I hesitated, my hand still on the raised hood. He had parents—two of them now. I'd asked Grace if he ever said anything about being picked on. She'd said no and assured me she'd talk to her mom about it. This wasn't any of my business. Wasn't my responsibility.

But still.

I cut through the yard, veering for the back, and found Elijah sitting on a tree stump, his back to me.

"Hey, Eli. What's going on?"

He looked over his shoulder. "What do you want?"

I didn't really know how to talk to kids. Especially now. What was I supposed to say?

Suddenly, I had a vague memory of my grandad working on his truck. I was eleven or twelve, and I'd gotten into trouble at school. Instead of punishing me, he'd brought me out to the shop to help. I'd handed him tools and helped him tighten bolts. All the while, he'd talked to me. Not like a grownup talking to a child. Like a person talking to another person. Patiently nudging me until I finally told him what had happened.

"Have you ever worked on a car?" I asked.

He looked back again, a little groove forming between his eyebrows. "No. Why?"

"I was working on my truck and could use another set of hands."

"I just said I don't know how."

"That's okay. I can show you."

He watched me and the suspicion in his gaze hit me square in the chest. This kid did not trust me. Which was fine, he barely knew me. But I had a very strong feeling that he didn't trust anybody.

I nodded toward the shop, then turned around and started walking. If he followed, he followed. If not, at least I'd tried.

I heard his footsteps behind me.

We got to the shop and I rooted around for a stool. I brought it, and a rag, around to the front of the truck and motioned for him to climb up.

"Pull on that, right there. It's the dipstick. It's how you check the oil." I held the rag while he pulled it out. "Now we need to wipe this off and put it in again to make sure it's accurate. Stuff moves around in there when you drive, so you can't tell the actual level of oil on the first try."

"Wipe it on that?"

"Yep."

He slid the dipstick along the rag, then put it back in. "Now?"

"Yep, go for it."

He pulled it out again.

"See that mark? You want to make sure the oil is above that. This is looking good. Looks clean enough, too. Dirty oil isn't good either."

He nodded and replaced the dipstick. "Is that it?"

"That's all there is to checking the oil, yeah. But the truck's been making a weird noise. I need to poke around in here and see if I can figure out why."

I wasn't exactly making that up. I'd only come out here to check the oil, but this truck always made weird noises.

Made me wonder how often Grandad had worked on it because he needed to, versus as an excuse to get one of us boys to talk.

I went back into the shop and grabbed a few wrenches. At the very least, I could loosen and tighten a few things. Let Elijah do the same.

"I guess Jack doesn't need to work on his car at home." I handed him the tools.

"No."

"Most people probably don't these days." I gestured for one of the wrenches and he passed it to me.

I waited, resisting the urge to fill the silence and ramble at him.

Finally, he spoke. "He's let me turn on the siren before."

"Yeah? Pretty loud, huh?"

"Really loud. He said you get used to it."

"Does having Jack around make you think about being a cop someday?"

"I don't know. Maybe."

"Here, can you tighten this for me?" I pointed to a bolt and watched while he leaned in to tighten it. "I remember when you wanted to be a firefighter."

He stiffened, pausing for a moment, then twisted the bolt one more turn. "Yeah."

I held my hand out for the wrench and checked the tightness. "Nice job. This is perfect."

Except for my handful of quiet instructions, we worked in silence for a while. Checked the distributor cap. Tinkered with the carburetor. We did find a bolt that seemed a little loose. After a while, I took the tools and gave him another rag so he could wipe off his hands.

"Did you know there's a secret fridge out here?"

"No."

"Yep. My grandad put it there. He always said Gram didn't know about it, but I think she probably did."

"She knows everything."

"You know what, I think you're right."

"What did he keep in it? Beer?"

I chuckled. "Nope. Same thing my brothers and I keep in it now. Cherry Coke."

"Cherry?"

"Yeah, it was his favorite. Gram always said soda rots your teeth. Which, to be fair, it does. So he kept his stash out here. Once in a while he'd let us have one. There should be some in there. Want one?"

He shrugged. "Sure."

I went into the shop and grabbed two cans of Cherry Coke while he jumped off the stool. He sat on an old railroad tie and I found a log round that would work as a seat. His soda popped and fizzed when he cracked the can open.

"So are you glad school's almost out?"

"Yeah."

I took a drink, feeling the bite of carbonation on the back of my tongue. "Will you still hang out with your friends?"

He shrugged.

I didn't want to make him clam up, but I felt like I had to try. "I know you probably don't want to talk about it, but do those kids pick on you a lot?"

He stared at the dirt, unmoving, his elbows resting on his knees. I waited again, leaving the ball in his court. I wanted to say something else—let him know he could tell me—but I also knew if I just stayed quiet, he might speak up.

"Yeah," he said finally.

Fuck.

"Your mom and Jack know about that?"

"Not really."

"Why not?"

"It's not like they can do anything."

"Sure they can."

He looked up, his eyes fiery. "What? Anytime something happens at school, they just have a meeting. It doesn't change anything."

"What would happen if you just punched one of the little shits in the face?"

His eyebrows drew together, and I glanced away. I shouldn't have said that.

But a thought took root in my mind. It was a bad idea. The last thing I should do with an eleven-year-old kid. There was a reason I wasn't training anymore. Same reason I'd turned down Declan's offer. I didn't belong on the mat, or in the ring. So this idea that hit me? It was not good.

"Are you kidding?" he asked. "If I did that, they'd destroy me."

That was it. Fuck this. "You want me to teach you how to make sure that doesn't happen?"

His eyes widened.

"You don't have to hit anybody. But I can show you how to neutralize an opponent."

"What do you mean?"

"If someone comes at you, I can teach you how to take them down to the ground and make it so they can't move. Control them. Trust me, you get some dipshit punk in an arm bar or a rear naked choke, they'll think twice before they touch you again."

He fidgeted with his Coke.

"If you're not interested, no pressure. But it can help a lot if you know how to take control of a situation. It sucks to feel powerless."

"I know. I hate it."

"Me too."

He met my eyes and nodded. "Okay."

A warm feeling spread through my chest. "It's getting dark, so maybe tomorrow? I don't have a mat, but we can use the grass. Just don't wear something that'll get you in trouble if you get grass stains on it."

He cracked a smile. Almost. "Yeah, okay."

"Awesome." I stood and he handed me his empty can. "Thanks for your help. I'll see you tomorrow, then?"

He got up and brushed his hands on his pants. "Yeah."

I nodded and turned to go back into the shop.

"Um, Asher?"

"Yeah?"

"My mom doesn't let me have Coke."

The corner of my mouth lifted, and I winked. "Don't worry, kid. I just spent seven years in prison. I ain't no snitch."

And for the first time since I'd been back, I saw Elijah smile.

27

GRACE

Six o'clock couldn't come fast enough.

I'd been living in a state of tingly anticipation since yesterday afternoon at the gym. Grappling with Asher had riled up my hormones something fierce. It was the most physical contact we'd had since he'd been home. And when he'd gotten on top of me? God. He'd pressed his solid erection against me and I'd almost died.

For a brief moment, he'd let his guard down. I'd seen it in his eyes. I was just hoping I could convince him to do it again.

Preferably multiple times while we were both naked.

Cara lay stretched out on my bed, one hand behind her head while she flipped through something on her phone. "Stop touching your hair."

I slowly lowered my hand. "I wasn't."

"You've been messing with it for the last ten minutes."

"I can't help it."

Turning back to the mirror, I smoothed down my black dress. It skimmed my curves, giving me a nice silhouette without being too tight. I'd bought it on sale a couple of years ago when Cara and I had been out shopping, but I hadn't had a reason to wear it yet.

"You should go commando," she said.

"Why?" I turned and looked over my shoulder to see the back of the dress. "You can't see a panty line at all."

"No, but it'll give him easier access."

I sighed. "Don't get my hopes up. It's taken me this long just to get a date with him. And I had to put him in an arm bar to get it."

"A girl's gotta do what a girl's gotta do."

My phone buzzed and a jolt of worry hit me. *Please don't be Asher saying he has to cancel...*

Mom: *Are you going to see Brynn soon?*

My half-sister had just had her first baby—a girl they'd named Lily—a few days ago.

Me: *Definitely. Just waiting to hear when it's a good time for them.*

Mom: *Can you take Elijah with you? I think it would be good for him to see them.*

Me: *Of course.*

Mom: *Thanks honey.*

Cara lowered her phone and looked at me with raised eyebrows. "If he canceled, I don't care what you say, I'm getting a taser."

"No, it was my mom. She wants me to take Eli with me when I go visit my sister."

"She had her baby, right?"

I nodded. "A girl."

"You are so going to get baby fever. I reiterate my suggestion to go commando."

"Cara, I'm not going to tempt him into sex so he can get me pregnant. Even if I do get baby fever—which I won't—that's a terrible thing to do to someone."

"Do you really think I'd suggest you get knocked up on purpose? I'm an awful person, but I'm not that evil. Besides, if I thought that was a good idea, I'd have been pushing you to get his D inside you from the start. I just mean if your lack of panties tonight escalates the situation, it could get you to the fancy white dress faster. And then you can have all his babies. Since we're on the subject, do you have condoms?"

My lips twitched. "No, but I went back on birth control already."

"That's my adorable warrior princess. So responsible."

I shrugged. "It might not be necessary for a while, and I'm not kidding when I say I don't expect anything to happen tonight. But when it does, I don't want to have to worry about whether or not one of us has a condom handy."

"Smart. As soon as that man cracks, you want that dick."

"Amen, sister."

She clutched her hands to her chest. "Aw. I really hope it's tonight, though. You deserve it a million times over. Plus, one of us needs to be getting some."

"That reminds me, you haven't been out with anyone in a while. Is everything okay?"

"Yeah," she said on a sigh. "I'm in a rut. It's so hard to find a guy with the right attributes. Fuckboys share my general skepticism toward commitment, but they always think they're so much better in bed than they really are. And the ones who are amazing in bed are inexplicably looking for a long-term relationship."

"You're complaining because you've met men who are both amazing in bed and want commitment? You realize how insane that is, right?"

She shrugged. "I never said it was healthy. But that's not even the real problem. They're all so boring. Both fuckboys and bedroom stallions who want real girlfriends. I haven't even bothered in forever. And believe me, my vagina isn't pleased. Modern technology is great, but there's just no substitute for the real thing. Which reminds me, when you do finally get that big Bailey of yours to take you to pound town, I want all the details. And I'm also going to be insanely jealous and probably not speak to you for about twenty-four hours. I apologize in advance."

"Advance apology accepted."

She smiled.

There was a knock on the front door and Cara and I gasped, looking at each other like a couple of kids who'd just heard a sound on the roof on Christmas Eve.

Cara put a hand on her chest. "Why am I so excited? The only date I have tonight is with Lady Delilah."

"What's that?"

"Lady porn. It's classy but still super hot."

"Classy porn?"

"It's a thing. Now go. Have a fun date with your almost-fiancé. Don't worry, I won't be here when you get back."

I leaned down and hugged her. "Thank you."

She squeezed me back. "I really hope you get laid. Love you."

"Love you, too."

My heart fluttered with excitement as I straightened my dress and went to answer the door.

The specimen of rugged sexy manliness that greeted me when I opened the door sent a jolt of arousal straight between my legs. My entire body reacted to the sight of him. His piercing dark eyes. The scruff on his square jaw. The width of his shoulders and powerful frame.

He was so different from the Asher I remembered, but if anything, I was more attracted to him now than I'd ever been. Scarcity might have played a small part—I wanted him so badly I could taste him—but it was deeper than that. I responded to his raw masculinity on a biological level.

My heart and mind adored this man, and my body desperately wanted him.

His eyes roved up and down and I caught the quick drag of his teeth across his lower lip. "Wow. You look beautiful."

"Thanks. You look great too."

He really did. He wore a dark jacket over a button-down shirt and slacks. His shirt hugged his muscular chest just enough that you could imagine exactly what he had underneath it, and his pants strained against his thick thighs.

"Ready?"

I grabbed the little clutch I'd bought a few years ago, thinking it would be fun for date nights, and slipped my phone inside. Asher gestured for me to walk ahead of him.

His hand touched the small of my back and I nibbled on the inside of my lip. This night was off to a great start already.

"Do you mind taking the old beast?" He gestured to Grandad's truck.

"Not at all."

Actually, I loved the old truck. It wasn't exactly comfortable, and it was hard to drive. But it was home to a lot of good memories.

We got in and the engine roared to life. He backed out of my driveway and headed toward town.

"So what are we doing tonight?" I asked.

"Dinner. And then I have tickets to the theater over in Pinecrest."

"Really? How did you get theater tickets on such short notice?"

The hint of a smile played on his lips. "I had a little help."

Did he mean one of his brothers? Which one of them would have suggested the theater? I'd gone to a show with Cara last year—it wasn't really her thing but she'd indulged me—and I'd been wanting to go back ever since. It was a small community theater, but their productions were fantastic. Even Cara had admitted it was fun.

But I didn't think any of his brothers would have known about that. Had he talked to Cara? I glanced at him, but he just winked and his dimple puckered.

God, his dimples.

He'd chosen the Greek place in town for dinner. It was a newer restaurant—and happened to be one of my favorites. He had to have talked to Cara. How else would he have known?

Wherever he'd gotten the idea, dinner was amazing.

Not just the food—although that was good. The whole experience. Asher was more relaxed than he'd been since he'd come home. He did check the restaurant carefully when we went in, and his eyes darted around periodically, like he was being cautious about his surroundings. But we talked—even laughed—and it was so easy. The comfort I remembered feeling with him was returning.

This new Asher wasn't the same man. I knew that. He'd probably never be as easygoing as he'd once been. Prison had stripped him of that. And I hoped—for his sake—that his hypervigilance would ease and the anger I could see simmering beneath the surface would fade.

But the more I got to know him again, the more I knew I truly loved him.

They hadn't stolen his compassion. He hadn't lost his desire to protect the people he loved. His once-easy smile had become harder to earn, but it wasn't gone. And he still had his sense of humor. He would always be intelligent and hard-working, and his loyalty ran deep.

The question wasn't whether I still loved Asher. I did, from the very bottom of my heart and soul. The question was whether he still loved me.

Physical attraction aside—it was clear we still had that—did he still want me? How much of his guardedness and reluctance to reestablish our relationship was because he didn't feel the same way about me anymore?

That sobering thought hit me as he led me out to his truck. After all, I'd been the one chasing him since he'd come home. The only reason we were on this date was because I'd goaded him into it.

At some point, I was going to have to bring it up. He'd told me, more than once, how he felt about being with me—given me reasons for the distance he was keeping between us. But he hadn't told me how he felt about *me.*

Specifically, whether he still loved me or not.

But tonight wasn't the time. I wanted to enjoy this date for what it was—a pleasant evening with a sexy-as-hell man.

The drive out to Pinecrest was about thirty minutes along a curving highway through the mountains. Dusk fell and the clear sky was tinged with pink and orange. We only passed a handful of other cars—not surprising for a week-night out here. It would be busier at the height of summer, when outdoorsy tourists flocked to the Cascades. For now, we rolled down the empty highway, idly chatting, no sense that there was any hurry.

When we got to the Starlight Community Theater, Asher found parking a couple of blocks up the street. Like the gentleman he'd always been, he opened my door and offered a hand to help me out. He once again walked beside me with his hand lightly brushing the small of my back. I wasn't ashamed to admit I was so starved for his touch that this small gesture filled me with giddy warmth. It was almost disappointing to get inside.

Until we found our seats. Then I wasn't disappointed at all.

The theater was housed in an old building that showed its age. There were cracks in the wallpaper and the thick velvet curtains hiding the stage from view were a faded shade of burgundy. It was small enough that there probably wasn't a bad seat in the house. But the seats themselves were tiny and set very close together.

I lowered myself into the upholstered chair and Asher took his seat beside me. There was no way for us to sit without touching. Especially because Asher was not a small man.

An older couple made their way down our row and nodded to Asher. Their seats were right next to him, forcing him to lean in my direction so he wouldn't crowd them. A few minutes later, the seats beside me filled. With a contented sigh, I shifted to my left. Squish beside Asher? Gladly.

His shoulders were so much wider than the seat, I had to tuck myself partially behind him. He put his arm on the arm rest, taking up his and mine, but I had a feeling he'd be more comfortable if he laid his arm over my thigh. If he didn't do it on his own, I decided I'd give him a nudge once the play started.

With nowhere to put my arm, I slipped it around his. There was stiffness in his posture, like he was trying to create space between us where there was no space to be had. But I embraced the closeness, relaxing against him. Enjoying his warmth.

The lights dimmed and the curtains parted. Asher

shifted in his seat and moved his arm, gently draping it over my leg. My lips twitched with a smile. This was even better.

It didn't take long before I had no idea what was happening on stage.

The audience laughed. I rested my cheek against his arm. The audience sighed. I turned my face slightly so I could inhale his scent. The audience gasped. It sounded like a good show, but I was lost in the feel of him pressed so close against me.

As the play went on, he relaxed. He splayed his palm over my thigh. Then his fingers idly shifted the hem of my dress and he traced circles over the skin just above my knee. Without really meaning to, I tipped my legs apart another inch and I felt his sharp intake of breath.

But he didn't pull away.

Toward the end, he tilted his face toward me and inhaled deeply. God, he was smelling my hair. I nuzzled my cheek against him, reacting to his touch and attention. I smelled him again, not even trying to hide it. He was the human equivalent of a potent drug—deliciously intoxicating and completely addicting.

The play could have lasted hours longer as far as I was concerned, but eventually the cast gathered and took a bow while the audience applauded. Maybe it was a little bit sneaky, but I kept my arm wound around his while I clapped so he wouldn't move too soon.

The house lights turned on. We stood and I wondered if my left cheek was more flushed than my right from leaning on him for so long. I felt dizzy, like I'd been jerked awake unexpectedly and was having trouble coming to. Two hours squished in too-small seats with Asher had shaken my equilibrium.

He led me out through the lobby and as soon as the cold

night air hit my skin, I grabbed my bare arms. The temperature had dropped, and I'd spent the last two hours wrapped in Asher's body heat.

"Cold?" he asked, already sliding his jacket from his shoulders. He put it around me, and I grabbed the lapels to keep it on.

"Thanks. Will you be warm enough?"

"I'll be fine."

He walked me up the street to where he'd parked the truck. I hoped he wouldn't ask too many questions about the play. I couldn't have guessed what it had been about. The audience had seemed to enjoy it, but I'd been engrossed in enjoying him.

We got in the truck and he glanced at me. "The play was... good."

"Yeah, I really enjoyed it." *Or, more accurately, I enjoyed sitting so close to you.*

"Me too."

We headed for the highway beneath a sky blanketed with stars. It reminded me of summer nights when we were kids, spent lying in the bed of this very truck, pointing out the constellations and making up our own.

The headlights cut through the thick darkness. There weren't any streetlights out here. Just the jagged rock face jutting high above the road on one side, the land descending toward the river on the other. Suddenly, the truck jolted, almost like we'd run over something.

"Oh no, that wasn't an animal, was it?" I asked.

Asher slowed and pulled over to the shoulder. "I don't think so. I didn't see anything. But I want to check and make sure everything looks okay."

He turned off the engine and got out, then reached beneath the seat to get a flashlight. I waited while he circled the truck, the light a narrow beam in the darkness. After coming around the other side, he got back in and shut the door, then tucked the flashlight back under the seat.

"Everything looks fine."

He turned the key to start the truck, but nothing happened.

His brow furrowed and he tried again. Still nothing. "That's weird."

Pushing the clutch down, he wobbled the gear shifter. Then he took the key out completely, reinserted it, and tried again.

Still nothing.

"Well, fuck. I should have left the engine running. I'm sorry about this."

"It's okay. Maybe it just needs a minute?"

"Yeah. I have no idea what's going on. It's been running fine."

"Do you remember the night we climbed out our windows and Grandad caught us? We were in the truck pretending we were bank robbers fleeing the scene of the crime."

He laughed softly. "He was in his shop sneaking a Cherry Coke with the light off so he wouldn't get caught."

"We thought we were dead. But instead he took us for a drive."

Asher nodded slowly. "He turned the radio up. It was that old-school country station he loved. We rolled the windows down and cruised the back roads listening to Waylon Jennings."

Recalling such a happy memory filled me with warmth. I let out a sigh.

Asher shifted so he was partially facing me and when he

spoke, his voice was soft. "We have a lot of good memories, don't we?"

"So many."

I was tempted to take off my seatbelt, scoot across the bench seat, and kiss him. But I'd been making all the first moves. It would just leave me wondering if it was what he wanted, or if he was only following my lead. He knew where I stood. If anything was going to happen between us tonight, I needed him to take charge.

He stared at me. We were blanketed in darkness, shrouded in the silence of the empty highway. My heart sped up, pumping in my chest with steady beats of hope. He reached out and tucked my hair behind my ear, then trailed his fingertips softly along my jaw and brushed his thumb over my lower lip.

For a brief moment, everything stilled. Neither of us even blinked.

Then he moved.

In an instant, he popped the latch on my seatbelt and hauled me across the seat. I let his jacket slip from my shoulders. His tongue wet his lips and he pressed his palm to the side of my face, brushing his nose against mine. With blood roaring in my ears, I waited, my mouth parted, ready for him.

He surged in to capture my lips with his. My eyes fluttered closed and I exhaled, sinking into his kiss. Oh my god, finally. It felt so good, I thought I might melt away into nothing. His fingers slid into my hair and his mouth moved against mine. Every nerve ending fired, lighting me up with a heady sense of euphoria.

His other arm hooked around my waist and he pulled me closer. He delved his tongue into my mouth, and I opened for him, letting him taste me. I couldn't get enough; I wanted him to devour me whole.

Twisting into him, I slid my leg over his lap. He pulled me on top of him, gripping me tight with his strong hands. A low groan rumbled in his throat as I pressed down, my legs straddling his hips, my dress hiking up my thighs.

I braced myself on the seat behind him, ignoring the steering wheel digging into my back. I couldn't have cared less. Asher kissed me hungrily, his tongue sliding against mine, increasingly frantic. He slid his hands beneath my dress and cupped my ass, squeezing hard.

The pressure between my legs was both exquisite and unbearable. He rubbed me against him through his pants, sliding me along his solid erection. I whimpered into his mouth, desperate for more. His hips jerked, pushing his hardness against me, right where I needed him.

If he kept this up, it was going to be the fastest orgasm I'd ever had in my life.

I wanted more. I wanted him inside me, but I couldn't stop to unfasten his pants. He held my ass in a firm grip, his fingers digging into me, and rubbed me up and down his hard length. Tilting my hips, I moved with him, chasing the climax my body desperately wanted.

He grunted hard and tried to speak, but we were both lost in a frenzy. I didn't know if he meant to tell me to stop, keep going, or wait so he could free his cock and do this properly, but I was too far gone. Totally overwhelmed by the intoxicating sensations flooding through me. The sharp pleasure jolting through my sensitive clit with every stroke. The bruising pressure of his hands. The wet warmth of his mouth tangling with mine, our kisses demanding and messy.

"Yes," he growled.

Heat and pressure built so fast, I was blinded by it. Rhythmically rolling my hips, I let go—gave in and let it happen. Moaning and gasping into his mouth, I hit the peak, that earth-shattering point right before everything explodes.

I threw my head back and cried out as I came apart. Waves of pleasure crashed through me, filling my entire body.

"Fuck," he grunted, almost breathless. "Fuck. Fuck. I—"

His voice cut off with a strangled growl and his fingers dug deeper into my skin. He closed his eyes, his brow furrowing deeply, and grunted again. And again.

And again.

My clit continued to throb and pulse while I rode out the final crest. I watched him come, too enraptured to care that we hadn't even undressed. My skin flushed with warmth and my core tingled with undeniable satisfaction.

He opened his eyes and loosened his grip. Blinking with what looked like surprise—and maybe even a hint of embarrassment—he glanced down at himself.

"Fuck. I didn't mean to..."

I touched his face, drawing his eyes back to mine. "It's okay. That was amazing."

He let out a breath and opened his mouth to say something, but headlights flashed behind us, lighting up the cab of the truck.

His eyes widened. "Shit."

I slid off his lap. There was a wet spot on the front of his pants—as much from me as him. My panties were soaked. But I felt so good, I couldn't find it in me to care.

Until it occurred to me that it might be Jack who'd just parked behind us. That would be awkward.

Asher looked down again and I shoved his jacket at him.

He pulled it over his lap right as someone tapped on the driver's side window.

Oh, thank god. It was just Evan.

Clearing his throat, Asher rolled the window down.

"You all right?" Evan asked.

"Yeah. Fine." There was no mistaking what was in Asher's voice. He sounded like he'd just finished coming. Which he had, obviously.

I bit my lip and tried not to giggle. It was possible I was still feeling euphoric.

Evan's eyes flicked to me, then to the jacket covering Asher's lap. He winced slightly and leaned back. "Sorry. I recognized the truck. Figured something must be wrong if you were just sitting here on the side of the highway."

"We pulled over to check something and the truck wouldn't start again," I said.

Asher turned the key. Still nothing.

"Hmm." Evan looked up and down the truck. "Did you already call for a ride?"

"No," Asher said.

"I've got my car, so I can take you home if you want. We can come back out tomorrow and see if we can get it started. Not much we can do tonight."

"Yeah, thanks."

"You guys need a minute, or...?"

Asher shook his head. "No. We're good."

Evan nodded and walked back to his car.

Nibbling on my bottom lip, I stifled another giggle while Asher rolled up the window.

He glanced down into his lap again. "I didn't mean to... That shouldn't have... Damn it, Grace, it's been a long fucking time."

I reached over and rubbed the back of his neck. "You have nothing to apologize for."

We both got out and apparently he decided to just own it. He put the jacket on instead of using it to cover his groin. Not that you could see much in the dark anyway.

Evan waited outside his restored sixty-eight Camaro and gestured for us to climb in back through the driver's side. Sasquatch sat proudly in the passenger's seat, watching us with his tongue lolling out as we got in.

We drove back to town in silence and the momentary high of my orgasm faded. Asher didn't reach over to touch me or hold my hand, and I started to wonder what had just happened and what it meant.

Was he throwing his guard up again? How hard was I going to have to try to get him to lower it now?

By the time we pulled up to my house, I felt like I'd been dunked in cold water. I had no idea what was going on in Asher's head, and I couldn't exactly ask. But the space between us felt like a crevasse.

Evan let us both out and Asher walked me to my door. I needed him to stay. I needed his arms around me, to soothe the fear simmering in my belly. To hold me after what we'd just done. I craved his touch with a fierceness that surprised me, even now.

But I couldn't seem to make my mouth form the right words. Couldn't bring myself to ask.

I was too afraid he'd say no.

My keys dangled from my fingers and I hesitated, giving him space to ask to come in. Or giving myself time to get over my fear and just tell him what I wanted.

"Sorry about... all of it," he said.

"There's nothing to be sorry for."

He nodded and lowered his eyes. "Goodnight, Grace. I'll talk to you tomorrow."

Disappointment ripped through me, making my throat tighten and my eyes burn. I bit the inside of my lip—hard—before I managed to get a word out. "Goodnight."

He hesitated there, like he was wrestling with something. Then he touched my arm gently, and with a soft exhale, he turned and walked away.

28

ASHER

*F*uck.

I walked back to Evan's car, feeling like a storm was about to break inside me. What the fuck had just happened? I'd decided I could handle this date if I took it slow, and I'd wound up coming in my goddamn pants.

My head was still swimming and by the time I shooed Sasquatch into the backseat and climbed in, I knew I'd just fucked up. Badly. She'd given me every opportunity to ask to come in and I hadn't taken it.

And why the hell not? We'd just made out in the truck and dry humped so hard we'd both come through our fucking clothes. Why not just go in and finish what we'd started? Do it right this time?

Evan didn't say anything as he pulled out of her driveway and headed to Gram's. I'd never been more grateful for his tendency toward silence. Raking my fingers through my hair, I struggled with what to do. I didn't want to hurt her. That was why I'd tried to stay away. Why I'd told her to let me go all those years ago and resigned myself to losing her.

But I couldn't stay away. It was killing me, and I knew it had to be killing her too.

God, I was such an idiot.

"Stop," I said, my voice rough. "Go back."

Without a word, Evan whipped the car in a tight U-turn, right in the middle of the street. The engine roared as he hit the gas and sped us back to Grace's house.

He stomped on the brake to stop in front of her driveway and gestured to his glove box. "There's condoms in there."

I glanced at him and the corner of my mouth twitched. "Thanks."

He just shrugged, like it didn't really matter, his hands still on the steering wheel.

I grabbed a strip and shoved them in my pocket before getting out of the car. He drove off before I could say anything else.

Grace's porch light was off and her curtains were closed. Resolve and desire roared to life inside me. I stalked up to her door and pounded on it. Hard.

A second later, she answered. Her cheeks were flushed pink and anger burned in her eyes. She opened her mouth —probably to yell at me—but I didn't give her the chance.

I barreled inside, kicking the door shut behind me, and didn't stop until I had her backed up against a wall. I caged her in with my arms, leaving her no choice but to look at me. "I love you."

Her lips parted and she gasped.

"I'm so sorry." Picking her up, I held her against the wall and cut off whatever she was about to say with a kiss. She wrapped her legs around my waist and threw her arms over my shoulders, kissing me back with as much intensity as I felt.

"I fucking love you so much," I growled into her mouth.

She responded with what felt like a sob, her body shuddering. It sliced me right through the chest, but instead of flinching away from the pain it caused, I dug into it. Let it hurt. I deserved it.

But maybe tonight I could help ease it for both of us, at least a little.

Without bothering to put her down—or stop kissing her—I carried her down the hall. I didn't know which room she used, but she pointed to a door.

We tumbled onto the bed, ripping off our clothes like they were on fire. I pushed her onto her back and climbed on top of her, ready to thrust in.

Goddammit. Condom.

"Hang on," I said. "I have a condom. Pocket."

"Wait." She put a hand on my chest. "I'm on birth control. You don't need one."

"Are you sure?"

"Positive. It's fine. And I've never been with anyone else."

I gazed into her blue eyes, feeling so fucking unworthy. I hadn't meant to suggest I thought she might not be safe. "I love you so much."

"I love you too. Now please fuck me before I die of anticipation. I've been waiting for this for such a long time."

"I know, baby. I have too."

Leaning down to kiss her, I shifted my hips to line up the head of my cock with her opening. She was already slick and wet. Coming in my pants hadn't been ideal, but at least I didn't have to worry I'd fire off like a rocket on the first thrust.

After all, it had been a long fucking time.

Groaning, I slid inside her. She didn't just feel good. She felt unbelievable. Her inner muscles tightened around me, tiny pulses that sent shockwaves through my body. She was going to make me lose my mind.

"Don't move yet," she whispered.

I held still, my cock buried deep. She clung to me, her arms around my back and her legs locked around my waist. Inhaling deeply, I breathed her in. Felt every inch of her warm skin against mine.

"I missed you so much," I said low into her ear.

Her hand moved up the back of my neck. "I missed you too."

Gliding through her wetness, I pulled out, then thrust in again. I meant to take it slow. To savor this. But she felt too fucking good.

I sped up my rhythm, fucking her harder. Growling into her neck. She held on tight, soft moans escaping her lips.

Making out in the truck hadn't done anything to dampen our frenzied desperation for each other. She drew her knees higher and dug her fingers into my back. I kissed her neck and sucked on her skin, thrusting my cock deep inside her.

"Fuck, I missed this pussy," I growled, reaching down to grab a handful of her ass while I drove into her again.

"You could have had it a long time ago."

I lifted up to look at her and thrust in—hard. "Oh yeah?"

"Yeah."

"I have a lot to make up for. Is this helping?" I drove in again. "How's that, baby?" Another hard thrust. "Does my cock help?"

"Oh my god, yes."

Driving hard with my hips, my back and arms flexing, I plunged in and out of her wet heat. Her face flushed pink, the color creeping down her neck. She was so goddamn sexy. I dipped my mouth to her lips, lapping my tongue against hers. I wanted to taste every bit of her. Devour her whole.

I licked my way down her neck and flicked my tongue over the hard peak of her nipple. Her tits were so beautiful. So feminine. Round and sweet and delicious in my mouth.

It was all coming back to me. Everything she loved. I sucked on her nipple, still relentlessly fucking her. Her back arched and she draped her arms over her head, whimpering. Letting go. Losing control.

I rolled us over so I lay on my back and she straddled over the top of me. She was a goddess. Blond hair loose around her face. Beautiful round tits and pink nipples standing erect. Narrow waist curving into hips that rolled against me.

"That's it, beautiful," I said. "I want to see you."

She planted her hands on my chest as she rode my cock, her eyes half closed. I held her hips and thrust up into her, letting her set the pace. She could do this all night if she wanted. I couldn't get enough of her.

Her body's slow waves turned into faster jerks, up and down my cock. She was hot and tight around me, her rhythm making the pressure in my groin build fast.

"Ride that cock hard, beautiful. As hard as you want it."

Her fingernails dug into my chest and she moaned, closing her eyes. I thrust my hips, driving my cock into her while she rolled, grinding her clit against me.

Faster. Harder.

"Fuck yes, Gracie. That's my girl. So beautiful."

Her pussy tightened around me and she threw her head back, moaning with the rhythm of my thrusts. I watched her come, mesmerized as she rode out her orgasm. As her silky inner walls pulsed around my aching cock.

She blinked her eyes open and her hair fell into her face. I reached up to tuck it behind her ear.

"Oh my god," she breathed.

I slid my hand to the back of her head and brought her mouth to mine. Kissed her hungrily.

But I wasn't finished with her yet.

"On your knees."

Smiling, she slid off me. I sat up quickly and got behind her. Pressed her shoulders down to lift her ass in the air.

"Mm, Gracie." I ran my thumbs along her opening. "Look at this beautiful pussy."

"You want more?" she asked.

I grabbed my cock in one hand and drew the tip up and down her wet slit. "Yeah, I want more. I want to come deep inside you."

She arched harder. "Fuck me then, Asher."

I stroked my cock a few times, letting the tip rub against her. "You need more of this too, don't you, beautiful?"

"Yes. Please."

Holding her hips tight, I thrust inside and unleashed.

I drove in and out, slamming into her, losing myself in the feel of her. In the drag of my cock through her slick walls. In the heat of her pussy surrounding me. She was hot and perfect and I loved her so fucking much.

The pressure grew, but I didn't hold back. I fucked her until my back clenched and the pulsing tension hit the breaking point.

And then I let go.

I exploded inside her, groaning as I came hard. For that one delirious moment, nothing else existed. Just my throbbing cock as I poured myself into her. My hips jerked with every pulse, the ecstasy staggering.

When I finished, I pulled out, breathing hard. She rolled

onto her back and pulled me down. Our bodies tangled together and we held each other tight, catching our breath, our hearts racing. I planted soft kisses anywhere I could find skin, murmuring how much I loved her.

Because I did. I always had. And in this moment, nothing else mattered.

29

ASHER

I came awake slowly, drifting from the depths of sleep like there was no reason to rush. Sunlight peeked through the curtain. I'd actually slept all night. I couldn't remember the last time I'd done that.

The sheets moved, softly dragging against my bare skin. Still half-asleep, I turned onto my side and hooked an arm around Grace's waist. Hauled her closer. She made a little noise in her throat, then nestled in against me. Inhaling deeply, I smelled her hair. Her skin. Her scent settled in my lungs, triggering a deep response in my brain. Contentment. Satisfaction. Relief.

I didn't know what came next. My reasons for keeping us apart hadn't gone anywhere. Being with Grace like this made me feel better, but the blissful peace wasn't permanent. The darkness inside me still crept around the edges, looking for a way in. A way to poison everything good in my life. I still had to protect her from that, although I didn't know how.

For the moment, I simply held on.

My cock hardened against her, but there wasn't any

urgency to my arousal. I'd happily fuck her again as soon as she was ready, but I was also content to drift like this for a while. Half-awake. No stark memory of a nightmare behind my eyes. Just Grace, in my arms, her warm skin touching mine.

I'd missed her so fucking much.

She inhaled deeply, her ribs expanding, and tilted her head back. "Morning."

I kissed her temple. "Morning."

"I like waking up this way."

Pulling her in tighter, I nuzzled my face against her. I couldn't get close enough. "Me too."

We lay in silence for long moments. I gently caressed her skin and idly planted soft kisses on her neck and shoulder while she murmured her approval.

Eventually, I felt her shift. Not so much physically, although she drew her arms up and stretched. But I could tell she was fully awake and probably wanted to talk.

We certainly had things to talk about.

I loosened my hold on her so she could roll onto her back, and propped myself up on an elbow.

Her lips twitched in a smile. "How'd you sleep?"

"Good. Great, actually. Better than in a long time. Must be the comfortable bed." I winked.

"I'm sure that was it," she said, her tone wry. "Although I'm not surprised you like the bed. It was yours."

"What?"

"This was your bed. I took it when we cleaned out your apartment."

"You've been sleeping on my bed all this time?"

"Yeah. You don't want to know how long I went without washing the sheets you had on it. It's probably gross, but I don't care. These ones are new, though." She nibbled her bottom lip. "Can I tell you an embarrassing secret that no one else knows? Not even Cara?"

"Sure."

"I sealed your old pillowcase in a plastic bag and it's hidden in my closet. Sometimes I'd get it out and put it up to my face so I could still smell you."

I dipped my forehead to hers. "Oh my god. You're so fucking cute."

"You don't think that's gross?"

"I would have done the same thing if I could have."

"I thought you didn't think about me when you were in prison."

It hurt to hear her say that, but I wasn't surprised. "No, I thought about you every day. Every morning when I woke up, you were the first thing on my mind. And when I had to put you away, you didn't go very far. I couldn't always keep you up here." I tapped my temple. "So I held onto you in here." I put my hand on my chest.

She placed her hand over mine and curled our fingers together. "Thank you for coming back last night."

"I'm sorry I walked away in the first place."

"It's okay, you made up for it."

"See? Told you I'm not rusty."

"No, not at all. Although I think your grappling could still use some work."

I smiled. "Wow. How do you know I didn't let you win?"

"Did you?"

"No, not really."

She laughed.

"When did you start training? I don't remember you mentioning it in your letters."

"I probably didn't. It felt weird to bring it up, because of why I'd started."

"What do you mean?"

"I took my first class a few weeks after you left. I decided I never wanted to feel helpless again."

Hearing her say that sent a flash of memory through my mind. I could still see it all so clearly, still feel the sickening realization hit me. *They had Grace.*

"Hey." She touched my face. "Are you okay?"

"Yeah, sorry." I brushed a tendril of hair off her forehead. "Are *you* okay? I don't mean right now, I mean in general. After what they did to you."

Her eyes darted away and her features clouded with sudden tension. "I think so. I don't like thinking about it. And everything that happened to you was a much bigger deal."

"Maybe. But it still happened to you, too. I mean, I saw it. They—"

"I know," she said, quickly cutting me off. "We don't need to relive it."

"Okay." I brushed her hair back again.

She was quiet for a moment, then took a deep breath. "I've never been back to the bar where it happened. A few people have told me I should go, like it would give me closure or something. But I've never wanted to. I pretty much avoid that whole street. And Cara thinks I have a problem going places by myself. Public places. She said I can't go anywhere alone, except for work."

"Is she right?"

"Kind of? Maybe? I don't know, she also said I might have just gotten used to going everywhere with her and it became a habit to call her when I have to go shopping or something. We were roommates for a long time and we literally did everything together."

"She seems like a good friend. I'm glad you have her."

"Me too. She's a very good friend. I'm so glad you don't hate her, because that would have been awful."

I smiled. "No reason to hate her. I still think she's weird, but she's good to you, so that's enough for me. By the way, you can thank her for the theater tickets. And she gave me the tip about the restaurant. Said it was your favorite."

"I knew it. When did she talk to you?"

"She texted me when we were still at the gym."

"That sneaky bitch. I love her."

"I don't know how she got the tickets. She just said 'give me twelve hours.' I met her outside City Hall yesterday morning and she slipped them to me like we were doing a drug deal."

"Typical. I don't know how she does it either, but that kind of thing is basically her superpower." She paused, tracing a finger across my chest. "So, speaking of last night, can we talk about it?"

"Yeah, of course."

"I meant what I said about never being with anyone else. I just want to make sure you know that."

"I know. I haven't done anything to deserve your faithfulness, but I've never doubted you." I kissed her forehead. "I hope it goes without saying that I haven't been with anyone else either."

"You sure you didn't get a little too close with one of your cellmates?"

"No. Definitely not."

She laughed. "Good to know."

"I'm sorry if I made you doubt that I love you. I never stopped. And I know it's probably hard to understand, but everything I did was because of how much I love you. Maybe it was all wrong. But I'm not..." I trailed off, struggling to find the words to explain.

"You're not the same."

"I'm not, but it's deeper than that." I glanced away. It was hard to look at her and talk about this. "It was rough in there. Maybe it makes me weak that everything that happened fucked me up inside like it did. But I'm just trying to keep it together. It's harder than you think."

She touched my face again, caressing my rough jaw with her soft fingertips. "I know. And it's okay."

"Grace, last night meant everything to me..." I trailed off again, searching for what else I was trying to say.

"I can hear you hesitating. I know you're not ready to say we're officially engaged again. That's okay. I haven't taken your ring off, but not because I think we're going to start planning a wedding. I still wear it because taking it off would feel like giving up. And I can't do that."

The sting of tears hit my eyes and I swallowed hard against the lump in my throat. I wasn't just unworthy, I was lower than the dust beneath her feet. "I don't know why you still love me. I haven't done anything to deserve it."

"Maybe that's not how love works. Nobody's keeping score. I love you because I do. Because of who you were, and who you are now. Because something deep inside me is connected to something deep inside you. And whatever that is, I think it's worth fighting for."

Leaning down, I brought my mouth to hers. Savored her soft lips and tasted her tongue with mine. When I pulled away, she smiled.

"Do you remember what you said to me the night you first told me you loved me?" she asked.

I nodded. That had been one of the most important nights of my life. I'd never forget a moment of it.

"You said it was okay if I didn't say it back yet. You just wanted a chance. And then you asked me for a summer."

"I remember."

"Well, that's what I'm asking for now. It's okay if you aren't ready to give me forever. I understand you have things to work out for yourself first. So give me a summer. If we're still together at the end of it, then..." She caught her bottom lip between her teeth. "We see where it goes."

Relief flowed through me like a wave. I could give her this. It would allow me some time to get my shit together. To see if I could calm down. Time to make sure my demons were safely locked away. To be sure I'd never put her in any kind of danger.

No matter what she said about love, I didn't deserve hers. But maybe I could try to change that.

Rolling onto her, I kissed her again. Her hands splayed across my back and my cock thickened between us.

"Is that a yes?" she asked, giggling between kisses.

"Yes." I buried my face in her neck and breathed her in. "That's a yes."

After letting her up so we could both use the bathroom, I hauled her back into bed with me. And when I climbed on top of her and slid inside, she felt so good, it was almost like none of it had ever happened. That we'd been together all these years and this was just a typical morning. The two of us, tangled in the sheets, our bodies joined in pleasure.

She'd given me a summer, once. The least I could do was give her the same. I just hoped her faith in me wasn't misplaced, and I could hold the fractured pieces of myself together.

DEAR ASHER

*ear Asher,*

YOU'RE NOT GOING *to believe what I did today. I closed on the house.*

I swear, I spent a solid hour signing documents. My hand got so tired and by the end my signature was barely legible. But after writing a terrifyingly large check and basically signing my life away, I am now the proud owner of a house.

Sort of.

It's a house in the general sense. You've seen it, of course. It has a roof and walls. Those are actually intact. It smells like dust and dirt—but not mold—and I don't think anyone should go inside who hasn't had a tetanus shot recently.

But it has good bones. I'd always hoped it did, and when I talked with the home inspector, he confirmed everything I'd been wanting to hear. The roof is solid. The walls are stable. The electrical is old, the plumbing remains to be seen, and the cosmetic stuff? Well, there's a lot.

It won't be a total gut job. The walls don't have to be taken down to the studs, although there will be a lot of patchwork to do. Plus flooring, paint, trim, doors, windows. The list goes on and on, and that's before I start thinking about the really big (and expensive) projects like the kitchen and bathrooms.

But think of how great it's going to be when it's finished. I didn't walk through the house and see the mess, I walked through and saw the potential. I saw what hard work could do. It's on that nice quiet street, the neighbors are lovely, and the lot is fantastic. Or it will be when we get all the blackberries and weeds cleared out.

Levi thinks I'm nuts. So does my mom. But I think this is one of the most sane things I've ever done. Plus, we have two more years of this not being together bullshit, and let's be honest, I need something to do. Work is going well, and I have family and friends. But lately, it's not enough. I need a project.

Now I've got one. A big one.

It feels like a lifetime ago that we said someday we might buy that old house on Evergreen Street together. This isn't exactly what we meant. Me buying it alone while you're serving a prison sentence wasn't what either of us had in mind. And I thought about waiting until you come home.

But I'm already waiting for so many things. I'm waiting for you, waiting for my life to begin again. It would be easy for me to get stuck in one place. I don't want to let that happen. So far, I've kept going. I haven't stopped living, even when things have been hard and I've wanted to.

So I'm not going to stop now, and I'm not going to wait. Who knows, when you come home in two years, the house might be finished. Don't worry, I promise I won't pick any colors you'll hate. And if I do, we can fix it when you get home.

For now, I'm off to the hardware store to start looking at...

everything. Paint, lighting, cabinets, flooring. It's time for me to get started on the future and make this a home.

MISSING YOU EVERY DAY,
    Grace

30

GRACE

*A*sher slipped my hand into his as we walked through town. I smiled up at him and he squeezed. Such a simple thing, to wander down the street hand in hand. I'd missed it so much. I'd never take it for granted again.

Summer had barreled its way into Tilikum almost overnight. We'd gone from warm days with light breezes to scorching heat and still air. Today, the sun blazed overhead in the clear blue sky, but a little heatwave hadn't done anything to deter the town from celebrating.

It was the first day of the annual Mountain Man Festival. A banner spanned the street, claiming it was the 108th year running. I doubted it had really existed that long. But people around here liked to believe that our traditions dated back to the time when this had been little more than a railroad depot with a sawmill, and a pit stop for prospectors and adventurers.

For a moment, I wondered if the Mountain Man Festival had existed in Eliza Bailey's time.

Downtown was closed to traffic and vendors lined the

streets, like a big farmers' market. Everything led toward Lumberjack Park, where the real action was held. Individuals and teams competed in contests and feats of strength—everything from archery and ax throwing to wood chopping and log pulling. Nearby were more booths and tents, home to the Tilikum chili cook-off and the all-important Blue Ribbon Pie Contest.

Gram was probably busy setting up her pies now. To the chagrin of the Havens, and the surprise of no one, Gram Bailey won every year.

Asher had been home for nearly two months, and it had been several weeks since our second first date. We were getting to know each other again, and it was easier now. He was slowly opening up to me, relaxing his defenses. He was still wary, still vigilant about his surroundings. I could see him doing it now while we walked—keeping an eye on people, maintaining space between us and others.

And he had nightmares.

He hadn't officially moved in with me, but he slept over often. And more than once, I'd awoken to find him jolting awake—his heart racing, his body covered in sweat. He wouldn't talk about his dreams, and I didn't know if it was because he couldn't remember them when he was awake, or if he didn't want to tell me. I had a feeling it was the latter.

I hoped that time would help. And that maybe soon he'd be willing to see a counselor. I'd gently brought it up, but he'd said a counselor would just make him talk about things he wanted to forget.

We slowed our pace so I could stop at a booth and glance at the handmade jewelry. The pieces were beautiful, adorned with polished gems and stones. Next to it was Chuck Bailey's booth. Along with his *I believe in Bigfoot* merchandise, this year he was selling bottles labeled *Squirrel Repellent*.

We kept wandering down the line, glancing at the things people were selling. Homemade soaps. Jams and jellies. Beef jerky and smoked salmon. Handmade purses, aprons, and scarves. We passed Lola, the giant pinup girl, and Asher paused to look up at the dark brown crocheted beard hanging from her face. It was long, reaching all the way to her ample cleavage, and dotted with a rainbow of crocheted flowers.

"Wow. Someone outdid themselves."

"Lola does look very fancy."

He turned to me. "You wouldn't know anything about who did that, would you?"

I blinked innocently. "I have no idea. But whoever made it did a lovely job."

Asher grinned and shook his head.

I eyed Lola with satisfaction. The beard I'd made was huge and the flowers were a nice touch, if I did say so myself. It was always important to make sure Lola was bearded on the first day of the festival, but it was also diffi-cult because of all the people setting up their stalls the night before. I was glad Gavin had managed to put it on her without getting caught.

By tradition, Bruce Haven—owner of the Dame and Dapper Barber Shop and the one who'd put up the giant pinup girl statue in the first place—wouldn't take the beard off until the festival was over, if we managed to get it on before it began.

Mission accomplished.

"Hi, honey," my mom called from further up the street. She stood with Jack and Elijah. Her hair was down and she wore a pretty floral sundress and sandals. Jack's barrel chest was barely contained by his uniform and he had his thick arms crossed.

Elijah was miraculously without his hoodie—probably because of the heat—but he stood with his head down a few steps away from both Mom and Jack. I hoped he wasn't still having trouble with kids picking on him. Mom and I had both tried to talk to him about it—as had Jack—but he'd insisted everything was fine now. I worried about the poor kid.

I waved to my mom. Asher seemed tense beside me as we walked closer. I hoped he didn't feel uncomfortable because Jack was in law enforcement.

"Hi, Mom, Jack. Hey, Eli."

Asher greeted them with a nod. Jack returned it and Mom smiled.

Elijah looked up at Asher and a flicker of a smile crossed his features.

"Hey, buddy," Asher said.

Elijah's smile grew a little. "Hi."

"Are you two having fun?" Mom asked.

Asher let go of my hand and slid his arm around my shoulders.

"Yeah, it's a great day so far," I said.

A voice came over Jack's radio. "We have multiple reports of gang activity over on Bailey Way."

Jack pressed the button and turned his head to speak into his radio. "Bailey Way?"

"It was Cedar Avenue, but the Bailey sign is still up."

He shook his head slightly. "I'm a couple of blocks from there, but are we sure this warrants a response? Can't they just shoo them away?"

"A series of thefts have already been called in. I think there's a coordinated effort here."

"Thefts of what?"

"Primarily snacks. But Mrs. Carter said they stole her sun hat."

"Why would—? Never mind, I'll go check it out." He let go of the button and rolled his eyes. "Damn squirrels."

He gave my mom a quick kiss and left.

"Well, I won't keep you two," Mom said. "I promised Elijah we'd get scones."

"Have fun."

I glanced up at Asher and caught him winking at Elijah. Eli seemed to be trying to hide a smile, and he waved goodbye.

"What was that about?" I asked.

He tightened his grip on my shoulders, pulling me in closer. "Nothing."

I wound my arm around his waist, enjoying the closeness. It certainly wasn't nothing to see Elijah looking almost happy. But I decided not to press him on it. For now.

We made our way to Lumberjack Park. Contests were already underway in the grassy areas, with spectators cheering on the contestants. Levi was about to go head to head with Luke Haven in a wood-chopping contest. They'd already drawn a huge crowd. Any time a Bailey faced off with a Haven, the whole town got riled up. There were too many people for us to see much, so we kept walking.

The off-duty firefighters had set up a grilling station at the park's edge. Logan, along with half a dozen others, stood shirtless in the heat, grilling bratwurst and hamburgers. The line to buy was long—and mostly women.

"That's definitely the way to do a fundraiser," I said.

Asher laughed. "That guy loves any excuse to take his clothes off."

"Is that Gavin?" I asked, pointing to a tree next to the grill. "What's he doing?"

Gavin hung upside down from a tree branch with a long stick in his hand. He was pointing the stick toward the grill. Logan tried to bat it away with the metal tongs in his hand.

"Are those marshmallows?" Asher asked.

"I think so." I shook my head. "He's *so* going to fall."

The most ridiculous fencing match I'd ever seen broke out, Gavin wielding a long marshmallow topped stick—while hanging upside down from his knees—and Logan fighting back with barbecue tongs.

"Sometimes I really wonder how he's still alive," Asher said.

We moved on, crossing the grass. Cara waved from a folding chair. She was attracting more than a few eyes with her string bikini top and cutoff shorts. A picnic blanket was spread out next to her with a cooler and two grocery bags. A small folding table held a pitcher and cups. Half a dozen more chairs surrounded the blanket, and an umbrella staked in the ground provided shade.

She lifted her drink. "There you are. I was wondering when you'd show up."

"This is something." I gestured to her setup.

"I figured if I'm going to be out here all day, I might as well be comfortable."

"How'd you get all this stuff down here?"

"I paid Gavin. Help yourself to a margarita. There's more ice in the cooler."

Asher poured us each a drink and we took a seat.

"Paid Gavin how?" I asked, raising an eyebrow.

Cara lowered her sunglasses. "With money. The Bailey boys are your territory. Besides, he's cute, but like a puppy cute."

"Why are they my territory? I'm only dating one of them, I don't need all five."

She adjusted her sunglasses and waved off my comment. "Still."

I took a sip of my drink and winced. It burned going down. "God, Cara, is there anything other than tequila in this?"

"Whatever, boo. You're not an amateur."

Asher took a drink, glanced at his cup, shrugged, and took another sip. "It's good."

Cara beamed at him. "Thank you."

Logan sauntered over, all toned muscle and hard abs. It looked like he'd added to his tattoos recently. I didn't remember them going so far down his arm. His shoulder and upper arm had a beautiful flame design, full of oranges, reds, and blacks.

He carried a plate piled high with grilled bratwurst stuffed in buns. "Who needs some meat? It's on the house."

Cara pulled off her sunglasses—probably to make sure he'd see her roll her eyes. "Nobody needs your meat, Logan."

"That's definitely not true. When you're hungry, nothing beats Logan Bailey's meat."

"Gross. We don't need to hear about how often you beat your meat."

"Believe what you want, sweetheart, but this guy's meat is in high demand."

"Yeah, we saw the line, and I'm sure your dick is impressive, too," I said, rolling my eyes at him. "I'll take one. I should eat something with this tumbler full of tequila Cara gave me."

Logan winced. "Don't talk about my dick, Grace. You always ruin everything."

"Then don't wave it around in our faces," I said. "If you need to prove to Cara that your dick is so great, take her back to your place."

"He wishes," she said.

He shuddered. "No thanks. I choose life."

Logan started peeling off paper plates from the bottom of his pile and handing out bratwursts. Looking reluctant, he held one out toward Cara.

She glared at him and he pulled it back, like he was flinching away from something hot.

Levi wandered over, shirtless and sweaty. Logan handed him a plate and he piled two more bratwursts on top of the first.

"Fuck, did I miss it?" Logan asked. "Did you win? Tell me you won, bropocalypse. The pride of the entire Bailey family rests on you."

He scowled, but I caught the hint of a smile at the corner of his mouth. "Of course I won."

Logan pumped his fist in the air, then high-fived his brother. "Fuck yes."

Asher leaned toward me. "Where's Evan? I haven't seen him today."

"Oh, he never comes out for these things."

"Really?"

I shook my head. "No. I mean, he basically hates everyone, so he doesn't come into town all that often. But especially not when it's crowded."

Asher's brow furrowed, like that surprised him.

Maybe Evan had changed a lot since before Asher had gone to prison. It was easy to think he'd always been the surly recluse he was now. But back in high school and early college, Evan had been a lot less angry. A lot nicer to everyone, too.

"Heads up!" Gavin barreled in, doing a back flip onto the picnic blanket. He stuck the landing, straightened, and took a bow. "Thank you, folks, I'll be here all day."

Levi rolled his eyes while shoving a bite in his mouth.

"Hey, brodeo." Logan pushed a plate of bratwurst at him. "Hungry?"

"Always." He took the plate and glanced around the circle, then offered it to Cara. "Hey, gorgeous. Hungry?"

She paused, like she might refuse but didn't want to hurt his feelings, then exhaled. "Sure. Why not. Thanks, Gav."

He grinned. "No problem. Logan, I need another one."

Logan glared at Cara, but handed Gavin another plate. As if to punctuate his defiance, Logan plopped down into one of her chairs, grabbed the last bratwurst, and took a big bite.

Cara shifted in her seat so she was facing away from him.

"I'm glad you beat Luke," Logan said around a mouthful of food. "Otherwise we'd never hear the end of it."

"You could have entered," Levi said.

"I was grilling."

Levi glanced at his plate and tilted his head as if to acknowledge that his brother had indeed been doing important work.

"Speaking of the Havens, has anyone else noticed they haven't answered back yet?" Asher asked. "For the street signs. Those went up a while ago, but they haven't done anything."

"Shit, you're right," Logan said. "I bet they're planning something big."

"We need to be ready for them," Gavin said. He'd sprawled out on the picnic blanket and without looking, reached into one of Cara's grocery bags and pulled out a bag of chips. "The street signs were awesome, but it wasn't a prank to end all pranks. They're going to try to get us back."

"No doubt," Logan said.

"Don't you guys ever get tired of pulling pranks on people just because your parents and your grandparents and your great-grandparents were doing the same thing?" Cara asked.

Everyone's gaze swung to her. All four Baileys—even Asher—looked at her like she'd just suggested gravity was a myth.

She put a hand up. "Sorry."

"If they want to surrender, we'll gladly accept," Logan said. "But the Baileys will not be the ones to wave a white flag."

"Shit, no," Gavin said. He tossed the bag of chips at Levi, who caught it like he'd been expecting it.

"Maybe we should meet up and strategize," Logan said. "Beers at our place tonight?"

"Nope," Gavin said, popping the *p* with his lips. "I have a date."

"Shut the fuck up," Logan said. "With who?"

Gavin grinned at him. "None of your business."

Logan tore off a piece of bun and threw it at his face. "Liar."

"I'm not lying. I don't think you know her. College girl. She's staying over the summer to catch up on some credits. I met her at Grace's coffee shop. By the way, that's the best place ever to meet girls. You guys should hang out there more often."

"What the fuck is the world coming to? Gavin has a date." Logan shook his head and gestured toward Asher. "Jailbird over there has his girl back. Next you're going to tell me Levi has a girlfriend."

Levi glared at his brother.

"We all know that's not true," Gavin said, and everyone murmured their assent.

Asher glanced around. "Why not?"

"Levi's saving himself for that Instagram model," Logan said. "What's her name? Marika something? She is hot."

"I thought we decided he was trying to get on a reality TV dating show," Gavin said.

"I still think he met a girl online, but in a twist of tragedy, they can't be together," I said, winking at Levi. "Maybe because she lives in Australia or something."

We'd been teasing him about how rarely he dated for years. It wasn't that he *never* dated. But his girlfriends were few and far between, and his relationships never seemed to last. So we messed with him by coming up with theories.

Levi threw a chip at me.

But I caught something in his expression. Was it possible we were hitting close to home? Was there a deeper reason he didn't date very often? His brothers never had serious girlfriends, either, so I'd always brushed it off as a Bailey thing. Asher had always been the only brother drawn to a long-term relationship—other than Evan when he was younger, but he hadn't had a real girlfriend since college. I had no idea whether he dated now, but if he did, I doubted it was ever serious. We certainly never heard about it. And Logan and Gavin both dated casually, but were basically allergic to commitment. Those two had always been that way.

But was something else going on with Levi? Maybe I'd imagined it, but I thought I'd seen a hint of sadness in his eyes.

"Oh!" Cara sat straight up in her chair. "Grace, I almost forgot. I got you something." She pulled her phone out of her tote and started typing. "I didn't send it yet because I wanted to see your face when you opened it."

"Uh oh. Should I be scared?" I asked.

"I would be," Logan muttered.

My phone binged and I opened her message. It was a picture of an old newspaper, similar to what I'd been searching through in the library. But this wasn't an article. It looked like an ad or a notice. And right in the middle was the name I'd been looking for.

"Oh my god." My eyes widened as I read. "You found her. You found Eliza."

Asher leaned over. "No shit?"

"Who's Eliza?" Gavin asked. "She sounds hot. Only I'm thinking intense and goth hot, not cute and wears pink hot."

"She's a Bailey," I said. "I found an old silver mirror with her name engraved on it. Someone had hidden it in a box with a bunch of anonymous love notes underneath the floorboards of my house."

"Cool," Gavin said.

"I know. Listen to this. 'Cash reward for information about the disappearance of Eliza Bailey. Reward doubled for her safe return.' There's more here at the bottom, but it's hard to read."

"The film was damaged," Cara said. "That was all there was."

Narrowing my eyes, I tried to make out what it said. "This looks like it might be a list of people they want found for questioning. I can't read the first one, but it looks like Montgomery—or mont-something at least. And, oh my god, you guys. I think this is a Haven. John Haven maybe."

"A Bailey girl goes missing and a Haven was involved?" Asher asked. "That could explain a lot."

"Holy shit, Grace," Gavin said, sitting up. "Did you just solve the mystery of the feud?"

"Not really. We don't know if this is how it started. If the families were already feuding, this could have been part of it, not the way it began."

"True."

"And who knows if the Haven guy had anything to do with it," Levi said.

"Dude, don't defend him," Logan said.

"I'm not defending anyone, I'm just saying."

I gazed at the clipping. "At least this is more confirmation she was real. I was starting to wonder if the mirror meant anything. But I still don't know who sent her those letters."

"Anonymous love notes, then she goes missing?" Cara asked. "Maybe she and the guy who wrote them ran away together."

"Or maybe she was supposed to marry the Haven guy and he found out about the notes," Logan said. "He killed them both and hopped a train out of town."

"If he did, I hope her ghost haunted him, making his dick go soft every time he tried to fuck another woman," Cara said.

"There's something seriously wrong with you," Logan said.

"I wonder if she was ever found," I said, ignoring Cara and Logan.

Cara shrugged. "I'll have Libby keep looking."

"Libby?" I asked.

"Yeah, I paid Libby down at the library to keep searching for any mentions of Eliza."

I laughed. "And here I was thinking you went back to that dusty room by yourself to surprise me."

"Do you even know me?" she asked. "Why would I do that when I can pay an under-appreciated library volunteer too much money to do it? Tsk tsk."

"Well, either way, thank you. This was really sweet."

She smiled. "You're welcome, boo."

Gavin shot up to his feet. "I think the pie judging is over."

Logan popped out of his chair and Levi crumpled his plate. The three of them eyed each other for half a second, then all took off running in the direction of the pie booth. Once the judging was over, people were free to purchase slices of pie, with the proceeds going to the Tilikum food bank. None of it lasted long.

Cara took her time unwinding from her chair and replaced her sunglasses. "Pie does sound good."

I glanced at Asher while she walked away, leaving the two of us alone on her picnic blanket. "You don't want a slice of pie?"

The corner of his mouth hooked in a grin and his tongue darted across his lower lip. "I want something sweet, but it isn't pie."

A pleasant tingle ran down my spine and heat bloomed in my core. He helped me to my feet and as we quick-walked back to my car, all I could think was that we couldn't get back to my house fast enough.

31

GRACE

Gram's house smelled like blueberries and sugar. I peeked into the living room and glanced up the stairs but didn't see anyone. The kitchen was similarly empty, although there were muffins sitting on the counter. They looked fresh.

Asher and I were both off today—whenever he could, he arranged his schedule so he didn't have any jobs on my days off—and he'd asked me to meet him here. I wasn't sure what he had planned, but I was looking forward to finding out.

Gram came in from the back, carrying a basket of eggs on her arm. "There's our Gracie Bear."

"Hi, Gram." I gave her a quick kiss on the cheek.

I heard footsteps coming down the creaky stairs and Asher appeared, looking freshly showered with damp hair. He beelined for me, scooping me into his arms. I turned my face into his neck and inhaled deeply. He smelled so clean and delicious. I was positively addicted to this man.

"Ready?" he asked.

"What are we doing?"

"You'll see. I already have stuff out in the truck, so we can get going."

"Are you sure we shouldn't take my car?"

"Why? The truck's been running fine."

I lifted my eyebrows.

"It has. I don't know why it wouldn't start that night."

I'd heard the story. He went out to get the truck the next day and it started on the first try.

"Mm hmm," Gram hummed from behind the refrigerator door.

Asher glanced at her. "What was that for?"

"What?"

"That *mm hmm*. Do you think I sabotaged the truck so it would break down?"

I playfully smacked his chest. "Did you?"

He put his hands up. "No. I swear."

"No, I certainly don't think you did," Gram said, closing the fridge. "Someone else might have, though."

"Who would sabotage the truck and then fix it again in the middle of the night?" he asked. "I don't think that's possible."

She shrugged. "Maybe it was a coincidence. Maybe not. But it sure did work, now didn't it?"

My cheeks warmed and I shared a quick look with Asher. She didn't know what we'd done in that truck when it had been broken down on the side of the road, did she? She just meant Asher and I were together now. Right?

Gram didn't say anything else, just grabbed a steaming mug of tea and headed for the sitting room. On her way out, she paused to gently touch the photo of Grandad that hung in the kitchen.

"Wait, does she think Grandad sabotaged the truck so we'd break down?" I whispered.

Asher shook his head slowly, gazing at the photo. "Maybe?"

"Do *you* think Grandad sabotaged the truck?"

A little smile played on his lips. "I don't know. Honestly, I wouldn't put it past him. Anyway, should we get going?"

"Sure."

He grabbed two warm muffins from the basket. I paused just inside the kitchen doorway and glanced at the photo. It had been taken just before he'd fallen ill. He was standing on the bank of the river holding up a fish, a wide smile on his face. His mischievous blue eyes sparkled in the sunlight.

For a second, I could have sworn he winked at me.

"Thanks, Grandad," I said under my breath, then followed Asher outside.

THE TRUCK BOUNCED along the dirt road and the sun shone high in the summer sky. A thunderstorm had blown through yesterday, briefly drenching everything, and the landscape seemed to have bloomed again overnight. Wildflowers covered the clearings, bathing the ground in color.

At this point, I knew exactly where he was taking me. This road led out to a spot on Lake Tilikum, just north of town. There wasn't much out here. A few faded *No Trespassing* and *Private Property* signs that the locals ignored. Around the east side of the lake were some cabins, but as far as I knew, they were long abandoned.

The lake and its surrounding area wasn't public land, but no one seemed to be sure who actually owned it. That left it as a kind of hidden wonderland. Visitors who came to the area to hike and camp left it alone, partly because of the signs, and partly because the trails weren't on any maps or guides. Locals enjoyed the beautiful lakefront scenery or hiked out to the twin waterfalls at the north end. But the only roads to get out here were bumpy and often hazardous, keeping all but the very determined away.

It had been a favorite spot of mine and Asher's, even long before we'd dated.

Grandad had taken all of us out here as kids many times. We'd climbed in the back of the truck and laughed as we bounced along the poorly-kept road. Sometimes we'd stopped to cut back blackberry bushes with machetes just so we could get through.

When we could see the clear blue waters of the alpine lake, Asher pulled off the road and parked, positioning the truck so the back faced the view. He got out and spread two thick quilts in the bed of the truck.

"We can hike out to the falls if you want," he said. "Or swim, although I remember it being cold as fuck. I also brought a picnic."

"This is amazing." I took his hand and he helped me into the back. "I just realized I haven't been out here since the last time I was here with you."

He climbed in and we both settled on the blanket, sitting cross-legged. "You haven't?"

"No." I glanced around, taking in the fresh warm air, the clear sky, the sound of the water gently lapping against the bank. "I missed it."

"Me too."

We dug into the picnic he'd packed. Cheese, salami, and crackers. Fresh berries from Gram's garden. The blueberry muffins were to die for. We chatted as we ate and it felt so... normal. Just the two of us on a day off, talking about work, funny things his brothers had said, and musing over how

Gram managed to keep the resident squirrel population from stealing the nuts from her walnut tree every fall.

It was truly a mystery.

Last night's storm had left a light breeze behind, cutting through the summer heat. Still, I stripped off a layer, shedding my t-shirt so I was in a tank top and shorts. Asher took off his shirt and there was no part of me that was complaining.

We leaned against the back of the bed and I shifted so I was facing him. He'd come home with more tattoos than when he'd left, and he'd recently had more work done, filling them in and adding to the designs. Now they stretched across one side of his chest, onto his shoulder, and down his arm. It all matched the Native American design he'd started with on his upper arm, a traditional rendering of Bear, like you might find on a totem pole.

"This is turning out beautifully." I gently traced the black and red design on his chest.

"Thanks."

I gazed at it for another long moment. "It tells a story, doesn't it? It's not just random designs."

The corner of his mouth lifted. "Yeah. You can see it?"

"I think so." I moved so I could get a better look and touched the bear on his upper arm. "Bear represents you."

"Right."

I ran my fingers down past his elbow to his forearm. "Here I see a lot of things. This looks like fire. And is this an eagle?"

"Raven."

"Are these faces inside Raven?"

"Yeah. Some of the old stories say one of the things Raven did was fly the souls of the dead back to the creator."

I touched the faces. "Your mom and dad."

He smiled and although there was sadness in his eyes, he didn't seem overwhelmed by it. "Yep."

"This looks like... another bear face, maybe? With an owl above it."

"That bear represents Grandad and the owl is Gram." He pointed to another part of the design. "This is water. I added it as a counterpoint to fire."

"So this is where you come from." I moved my attention back to Bear on his upper arm, then to his shoulder. There were more animal faces, almost hidden in the intricate tribal design. "What are these?"

"Can you guess? There's four of them."

"Your brothers. Oh my god, how did I never realize that before?" I carefully traced from his shoulder to his chest. This was where the ink was freshest, although it was healing well. Within the design, I could see what looked like a bird holding its talons out to grab a fish. Below that was another animal. It looked like they might be fighting over prey. "What's all this?"

"It's an eagle and a bear both trying to take the same fish. It represents strife. I guess it's my reminder to keep fighting."

"And what's this face?" I asked, softly touching a spot toward the center of his chest. This one was almost hidden among the rest of the design.

"Another bear." He paused for a moment. "It's you."

"Really?"

"Yeah. Remember Declan, the guy with all the tattoos? He's the only reason I let someone do ink on me in prison. I didn't want to come out with a bunch of prison tats, but he actually knew what he was doing. He designed it based on the bear I already had. If you look closely, he wrote your name."

I stared at the tattoo on his chest. I'd looked at it before, but I hadn't examined it carefully. We tended to be distracted by other things when we had our clothes off. But he was right. Hidden in the design, just below the bear's face, the lines made my name.

"Oh my god. Asher."

"I told you—when I couldn't have you up here," he said, tapping his head, "I kept you here."

I splayed my palm over his chest. "I love you so much."

"I love you too, beautiful."

He ran his fingers through my hair and brought my lips to his. What started off as a soft kiss quickly transformed into more. His tongue delved into my mouth, hungry and insistent. I couldn't help but smile while he kissed me. It felt so good to be wanted—to be wanted by him.

His hand slid down and I gasped when he brushed across my nipple. I was so sensitive to his touch. He trailed his hand lower, over my belly, to the waistband of my shorts.

Birds chirped and the sun blazed above us. We were outside in the full light of day.

"Here?" I murmured against his mouth as he slid his hand into my panties.

"We're alone," he said, his voice low.

I tipped my legs open, welcoming his touch.

"That's my girl," he murmured. His hand fisted in my hair, holding my head with his mouth next to my ear. "You're wet already."

His fingers gently explored, his breath hot on my neck. I let my eyes flutter closed, surrendering to him. Letting him take my body where he wanted.

"I love this pussy," he growled, dipping the tip of his finger inside me. "So soft and wet. So perfect."

I trembled as he slid his finger in deeper. He pressed his

body closer to mine, still keeping a tight grip on my hair. He was both demanding and gentle. The contrast was intoxicating.

He traced his wet finger around my clit, and I moaned in pleasure. He knew every inch of my body—knew exactly how to touch me to make me feel good. His fingers teased my hot bundle of nerves with quick strokes.

"That's it, Gracie." His growly voice alone was enough to make me wet for him. "You like that, don't you?"

I nodded, sighing out a soft yes.

Shifting slightly, he drew me closer and slid his fingers back to my opening. He dipped a finger inside, then another, slowly pumping them in and out. His palm rubbed against my clit, giving me the perfect amount of friction and pressure.

I let out another moan.

"Yes, beautiful. That's it. No one can hear you."

"Oh my god, Asher."

He kissed my neck, his tongue lapping against my skin. "You want me to make you come, don't you?"

His fingers moved faster and I nodded, opening my legs wider. God, he was good at this. His cock, his tongue, his fingers—it didn't matter. He knew how to drive me absolutely crazy.

"Mm, Gracie. Your pussy's so hot. I can't wait to fuck you."

I reached for his cock, intending to shove my hands into his pants to get to it, but his grip on my hair tightened.

"Not yet, beautiful. I'm going to make you come first. This is just for you."

I could hardly complain. There was something about him fingering me with my clothes on in the back of the truck under the bright summer sun that felt naughty and erotic. Especially with the way he kept talking dirty in my ear, his voice so growly and low.

I loved it.

Moving my hand down, I held it over his, moving with him.

"That's it. You're going to come right here, aren't you, baby?"

"Yes. Please."

A deep growl rumbled in his chest and he kept his rhythm steady. His hand stroked my clit and his fingers gently curled inside me, rubbing right where I needed it.

"Give me what I want, Gracie," he murmured in that dangerously low voice. "Come for me, love."

His fingers were relentless, moving faster. Harder. The world around me seemed to swirl as the heat and pressure peaked. The metal of the truck dug into my back, but I barely noticed. All I could feel was Asher's touch, his deft fingers demanding I come for him. Now.

With one more perfect stroke, I obeyed.

I cried out as I came apart, my body melting in his arms. He murmured soft encouragement as the hot waves of climax crashed through me, groaning as if he enjoyed this as much as I did.

I'd barely finished when he growled again, a deep animalistic sound. With rough hands, he ripped off my shorts and hauled me into his lap so I straddled his thighs.

Still breathless from coming, I braced myself against the cab behind him as he pulled out his cock. It was thick and swollen, drops of moisture beading on the tip. He rubbed my wetness down the shaft and pumped it with his hand a few times.

"I'm going to come in you so fucking hard," he said through gritted teeth. "Get the fuck over here."

He hooked one arm around me and hauled me closer. With his hand still gripping his cock, he lined it up with my very slick opening, and pulled me down on top of him.

Groaning, he held my hips and moved me up and down his length. His brow furrowed and he grunted with every hard thrust. I could feel him thickening inside me, his cock pulsing with the need for release. He was ready—now.

"Fuck, you feel so good," he said, his voice strangled. "I can't fucking take it."

My barely finished orgasm exploded again as his cock throbbed. He grunted, slamming me down onto him, his hips jerking as he came. I rode it out with him, euphoric and breathless.

We both slowed as we finished and I dropped forward against him. With his cock still inside, he wrapped his arms around me. I felt so safe. So loved. And so in love with him.

32

ASHER

*a*n unexpected surge of nervousness hit me as we turned off the highway into Echo Creek. It was a nice little town, about half an hour from Tilikum. I'd been down here before—many times—but it had been a while. And today we weren't just looking for a new place to eat or going out for a drive because the weather was nice. We were going to visit Grace's other family—the Miles siblings she'd met while I was in prison.

I wasn't sure why I was suddenly nervous. Her sister Brynn had recently had her first baby, and when Grace had asked me if I'd like to come meet the family, I hadn't hesitated to say yes. These people were a part of her life now, so of course I wanted to get to know them.

But now that we were almost there, I felt edgy. Worried.

I held on to Grace's assurances that they were all good people and were anxious to meet me.

She turned at a sign that read *Salishan Cellars Winery*. The long drive led past rows of grapevines, and there were more in the distance. Several buildings were surrounded by beautifully manicured gardens and a grove of pear trees.

The place was bustling with people and the parking area was full.

We passed the public areas, driving deeper into the grounds. Here there were more trees and a path winding through them, but no people in sight. A white cat darted across the road ahead. Finally, Grace turned and parked in front of a large house with a big wrap-around porch. The front door was wide open and several other cars were parked outside.

My heart beat fast and my arms and hands tingled with adrenaline. It felt a lot like the night Gram had sent me and Grace to the store. I'd taken one look at the entrance and a deep sense of panic had erupted in my chest. I felt it again now—the fear that I was walking into uncharted territory. I didn't know what to expect in there. Who I could trust. What I'd need to look out for.

It was irrational, and I knew it, but that didn't do anything to make the feeling of impending doom subside.

"Hey." She reached over to rub my arm. "Are you okay?"

I stared straight ahead, trying to get a hold of myself. She slid her hand to the back of my neck and gently stroked my skin, running her fingers up into my hair and down again. Letting her touch soothe me, I took deep breaths, hoping the sense of dread would subside.

Why the fuck did this keep happening? I was stronger than this.

"Take your time." Grace's voice was soft, calming.

The panic started to recede. I still felt edgy, but my heart rate slowed to a more normal pace and the feeling that I was about to walk into a hostile situation—where I needed to be ready to fight my way out—faded.

"Sorry," I said, my voice rough. "I fucking hate that."

"It's fine." She kept stroking the back of my head. It felt good. "No rush."

I closed my eyes for a moment, focusing on her touch. Her nearness. She was so good to me. I loved her so much, and I hated that she had to help me like this. That I couldn't just be normal—get out of the car and walk into the house. I knew there was nothing to fear, and yet this irrational part of me insisted there was. I could practically feel the skin on my knuckles splitting from a fight I wasn't going to have.

When I thought I felt calm enough, I opened my eyes. "I'm good. We can go in."

"Are you sure? It's totally fine if you need a few more minutes."

"No, I don't want to make it weird."

"Trust me, Asher. Everybody has issues of one kind or another. They're all well aware of that. You won't make it weird."

I took her hand and brought it to my lips. Kissed the backs of her fingers. "Thank you."

She smiled. "You're welcome. Let's do this."

Was I ready? I had no idea. I'd just have to grit my teeth and handle it—do it for Grace.

Elijah poked his head out the open door and lifted his hand in a wave. Naomi and Jack had come by earlier and let him stay. Grace and I would take him home when we left.

"Hey, Eli," Grace said. "Is everybody here?"

"Yep. Everybody. I mean, really everybody."

Seeing Elijah look so calm and happy did a lot to ease the tension in my chest. He even smiled a little.

A man who had to be one of Grace's brothers—the resemblance between him and Elijah was unmistakable—poked his head out the door. His eyes landed on Grace and a wide smile crossed his features. Opening his mouth, he started to speak—until he looked at me. Then his jaw dropped and he stepped out onto the porch, his eyes widening. He wore a double baby carrier with two babies, one strapped to each hip. One was asleep with his head against the guy's shoulder and the other played idly with a baby toy hanging from the guy's neck.

"Holy shit. Gracie, you said he was coming and I don't think I really believed you, but you weren't making shit up. Damn it, I'm trying not to swear in front of my kids. Eli, you're supposed to poke me when I do that."

Elijah grinned and stabbed him in the ribs with a finger.

"Ow. Thanks buddy." He took a breath. "Sorry, I'm just a little bit in awe right now. Because I'm guessing this is the infamous Asher Bailey and oh my god we've been waiting so long to meet you. Jesus, this is really happening."

He darted back inside—he moved fast for a guy carrying two babies—and I could hear the semi-muffled sound of him calling people's names.

Grace slipped her hand in mine as we walked up the porch steps. "Don't mind him. That's just Cooper. He gets really excited about... everything."

Elijah smiled. "He's really fun."

"Chase, where the hell, I mean heck are you? Gracie's here with the prison guy!"

"Oh god," Grace said, putting a hand to her forehead. "Asher, I'm sorry."

Strangely, hearing Grace's half-brother shouting *Gracie's here with the prison guy* made me feel better.

"It's okay, you get used to them," Elijah said. "Cooper freaked me out when I first met him, too, but he's actually really nice."

"Thanks, bud."

Grace tugged on my hand and I followed her inside.

The entryway opened to a great room with a living area and a long dining table next to the entrance to the kitchen. Food was spread out on the table, and several people sat in chairs and on a long bench. Others occupied the couch, armchairs, or the floor.

It was a lot of people. And every single one of them stopped what they were doing to look at me.

"Hey, everybody," Grace said. "Um... so, this is Asher."

I felt like I was on stage and the curtain had just opened —and I had no idea what I was supposed to do. I lifted my hand. "Hi."

A woman stood from her place at the table and rushed forward to greet us. She hugged Grace, then offered me a hug too. "Asher, it's so nice to finally meet you. I'm Shannon."

"Nice to meet you too."

"I'd do introductions all at once, but I don't want to over-whelm you. But... this is our family." She gestured to the room full of people. "Chase and Brynn are in one of the bedrooms with Lily. I'm sure they'll be out soon."

I'd studied Grace's photos of her family so I'd be familiar with who they were. Shannon was her father's ex-wife, and the mother of her half-brothers and -sister. She was now married to Ben, a rugged looking older guy with a lot of gray in his beard. He gave me a polite nod from his spot at the table.

Grace's siblings were all here, too. We spent some time making the rounds and saying hello. I was introduced to her oldest brother Roland, who held a little girl in his arms. His wife, Zoe, was on the floor playing with their son, a boy of about four. Cooper's wife, Amelia, offered us dessert several times before apologizing for being overly excited.

Her brother Leo and his wife sat on the couch with two

young kids who seemed to want to do nothing but crawl all over their dad. The little girl smushed her face against his beard while he tried to talk and their younger child, a boy, kept trying to climb him like a jungle gym. His wife Hannah had to do most of the talking for the both of them, but Leo didn't seem to mind.

Cooper wandered around with his two babies—identical twin boys, I was told—snacking on cookies and picking up dropped threads of conversation every time he got close, as if we'd never stopped talking in the first place. He got particularly excited about my tattoos. I showed him my forearm and moved my t-shirt sleeve so he could see my shoulder. He reached for my shirt, like he was about to lift it to see the ink on my chest, but Amelia jumped in and stopped him.

"What?" Cooper asked, then looked down at his two— now sleeping—babies. "I'd show you mine, but I can't exactly while I'm wearing my boys."

Amelia kissed the top of one of her babies' heads and rubbed Cooper's earlobe. "Next time, maybe."

Another couple came down the stairs—Chase and Brynn, Grace's half-sister and her husband. Chase held a newborn baby wrapped in a pink blanket against his chest.

I heard Grace's sharp intake of breath and she squeezed my hand.

Brynn smiled when she saw Grace. I let go of Grace's hand so she could go hug her sister.

Ben quietly offered me a seat at the table and a beer, both of which I took gratefully. He gave me another nod, as if to say he understood. Thankfully, I didn't feel panicked anymore, but it was hard not to be a little overwhelmed.

Kids ran around, laughing and playing with toys. A dog named Scout, who I later learned belonged to Brynn and

Chase, seemed to appear out of nowhere to play with the kids. Dads bounced babies while they drank beers or glasses of wine. Moms congregated on the couch and chairs with wine and snacks. Elijah played with the other kids. Shannon sat next to me and struck up a conversation while Ben gently rested a hand on her shoulder.

Grace chatted with her family, looking toward me often, raising her eyebrows with a clear message. *Are you still okay?* I gave her a nod each time.

And I was, for the most part. This side of her family was big and noisy, but I could see why she loved them so much. And they clearly loved her, and Elijah. Given the circumstances—Naomi had been the other woman, and Grace and Elijah their father's illegitimate children—it said a lot for the kind of people they were that they'd welcomed Grace and Elijah into their family.

They loved Grace. That was enough for me.

Grace sat on the couch and Chase gently placed his sleeping newborn in her arms. Suddenly, I couldn't take my eyes off her. The look on her face as she gazed at the tiny baby did very strange things to me.

The erection was probably the most surprising. Watching her cradle a baby made me hard for her in a way I'd never experienced before. It was like tapping into a primal urge, so deep it was only semi-conscious. It made me want to get her home as fast as possible so I could fuck her. Repeatedly.

God. This whole scene was messing with my head. Was watching Grace hold a newborn baby giving me the urge to get her pregnant?

It made no sense, but that was what the most caveman part of me wanted.

But another part of my brain was having a very different response.

She looked absolutely beautiful with that baby in her arms. Like she'd been made for it.

Because she had.

And as I watched her older brothers and brother-in-law expertly caring for their small children, a profound sense of doubt settled in my gut.

I didn't know if I was cut out for this.

Grace wanted a family. I'd known that already, but watching her hold her new niece brought that into sharp focus. Before I'd gone to prison, having kids with her had been a foregone conclusion. I'd wanted it as much as she had.

But now? Did I have any business being someone's father?

And what did it mean for me and Grace if I didn't?

I tried not to let that somber realization ruin the afternoon. I talked to her family, had another beer, ate some food. I answered questions honestly, although most everyone was polite and didn't ask me anything too intrusive. No one pushed about wedding plans or where she and I stood on getting married, and for that I was grateful. The only mildly inappropriate comments came from Cooper, but the guy was pretty likable, so I didn't mind. Eventually, I even lifted my shirt so he could inspect the rest of my ink.

He showed me his, too, once he'd been relieved of his babies by Amelia. He had a brightly colored unicorn across his ribs, and after knowing him for less than two hours, it didn't surprise me in the least.

No one else in the family appeared to be anywhere close to leaving, but Grace seemed to sense I was starting to get antsy. I liked these people, and I loved them for loving my girl. But it had been a lot to take in. After she cuddled the baby for a while, and spent some time playing with her other nieces and nephews, she said we needed to go.

Saying goodbye to everyone took a solid half-hour. I'd hugged more people today than I had in the last month combined. But eventually, we made it out the door.

"I'm sorry if that was crazy overwhelming," Grace said when we got in the car. "I hope I didn't make you stay too long."

"No, they were all really great."

She glanced at me and smiled. "Everyone loved you."

Elijah finally made it out and he climbed in the back seat.

"Have a good visit?" Grace asked, looking at him in the rear-view mirror.

"Yep."

It was only a one-word answer, but his tone was light. He'd had a good day, and that made me appreciate this side of their family even more.

"Awesome," Grace said. "Let's get home."

We left the winery and drove out to the highway. I watched the scenery go by, a chaotic mix of emotions running through me. Grace and I had been having a good summer. Being with her was such a relief, it was easy to imagine this going on forever. I wanted to kick myself for pushing her away so hard when I'd first come home. If I'd handled things differently, I could have spared us both a lot of pain.

But days like today made me wonder if I was kidding myself. Because I wasn't like her brothers. Calm and assured, men who'd obviously been ready for fatherhood. I wasn't ready. Not even close.

Would I ever be? For every good day—where I felt

steady—I had two where I was on edge and panicky. Grace seemed so confident that I'd be fine, but I couldn't help but wonder if that was wishful thinking. If it was what she wanted to believe, rather than what was true.

I wanted to believe it too, but I didn't share her confidence. And I didn't know what it would mean for us if she was wrong.

DEAR ASHER

ear Asher,

YOUR BROTHERS *just pulled off one of the best pranks in the history of Tilikum. I know, that's a huge claim. But I'm not kidding. It was epic.*

A few months ago, we heard that the Havens were planning a big family reunion here in town. Obviously that was too much temptation for the Bailey boys to resist. They were determined to prank the whole family, although I had no idea how they were going to pull that off. The Havens were going to be ready for them. Can you imagine if there was a Bailey family reunion? Your brothers would be on high alert the whole time. So I didn't think they'd be able to orchestrate a good prank without getting caught.

I underestimated them.

The Havens had reserved space in Lumberjack Park, and for most of the day, your brothers just went about their business. The twins got off their shifts and went home. Evan came into town and went to the store. Gavin hung out at my shop for a while, flirting with my baristas. They knew they were being watched— the Havens were taking turns making sure the Baileys were all accounted for. So they acted like it was a normal Saturday.

I don't know if the Havens were lulled into a false sense of security or what, but the boys struck later that night.

The sun went down and the party in the park was still going strong. Somehow, Gavin crept in among the entire Haven family and put red dye in all the drinks. They had punch bowls and lemonade and bottles of wine and beer. Gavin got to almost all of it.

It wasn't just dye. It was a special formula—a tasteless, edible, and very persistent stain.

It's possible I had something to do with that part. But if anyone asks, I'll never admit it.

What did this stain do, you might ask? Almost every Haven at the big Haven family reunion looked like they'd been feasting on the blood of their enemies.

For a week.

Yep, it took a solid week for their mouths, lips, and teeth to start to look normal again. I kid you not, everyone who had a dyed drink looked like a vampire who'd never been taught manners. It was like that powdered drink mix we used to get when we were kids—the kind that stained your upper lip—only so much worse.

Because it was dark, none of them realized how bad it was during the reunion. If they noticed people's mouths turning blood-red, they obviously didn't think much of it. Everyone kept happily drinking their Bailey specials.

The Haven brothers are pissed. I saw Josiah and Zachary downtown and they glared at me so hard it probably gave them a headache. Of course, I probably deserved it. I asked them why their teeth were so red. They weren't amused.

I still can't believe the boys pulled that off. On the surface, it might not seem like the prank of the year, but think about what went into it. I know how much work went into making that dye (you really can learn anything on YouTube, by the way), and even then, none of us expected it to work so well. Or be so bright red.

The real question is, how did Gavin get in and out without getting caught? I swear, he's secretly a ninja. I thought for sure he was going down.

I'm still amazed it worked, but it's been good for a laugh. And let's face it, we need a good laugh these days.

I MISS YOU,

Grace

33

GRACE

I drove home from Salishan feeling warm and squishy inside. I'd looked forward to introducing Asher to that side of my family for such a long time.

Even though he'd started out edgy, he'd relaxed as the afternoon had turned to evening. He'd handled everything without a hitch—from the introductions, to all my nieces and nephews, to my brother Cooper. Of course we had a long way to go before he felt comfortable enough to consider them family the way I did. But we'd get there.

And god, I could still smell baby Lily on my shirt. I'd always liked babies, but holding her today had felt different. My ovaries positively ached.

Maybe Cara had been right. I *was* getting baby fever.

Asher was quiet, but I didn't press him to talk. Even after we dropped Elijah at my mom's house, I let the silence linger. He didn't seem on edge, just contemplative—staring out the window as we drove. I was curious to hear his thoughts, but I didn't want to force it, especially if he needed time to decompress.

Dusk was falling and the light was dim when I turned onto my street. Something was outside my house, partially in the yard. Something large.

And where was Asher's truck? It had been parked in the driveway.

"What the hell?"

I stopped and Asher flew out of the car. I turned off the engine and followed, trying to make sense of what I was seeing.

He stood in front of a huge rectangular block of crushed metal. It was half in the yard, half on the asphalt, like it had been unceremoniously dumped there.

"What is that? And where's your truck?"

Asher didn't answer. He circled the metal block and picked something up off the street. A license plate.

"Those pieces of shit," he growled.

A sick feeling spread through my stomach. The block looked like the remnants of a car—or truck—that had been crushed at a junkyard. And Asher's truck—Grandad's truck—was gone.

Oh god. They couldn't have.

He pulled out his phone and called someone—probably one of his brothers. "We have a fucking problem."

I did a slow lap around the block of metal, not really listening to what he was saying, although I was vaguely aware of him ending one call and making another. The Baileys and Havens had pulled some crazy pranks on each other over the years, but this? They never destroyed each other's property. Would they really have done something so awful? So personal? Everyone in town knew this had been Grandad Bailey's truck, even them.

Asher pocketed his phone. The veins in his forearms and neck popped out and his jaw was set in a hard line. But it wasn't the tension in his body or the way he stalked to my car, like a predator going on the attack, that scared me. It was his eyes.

He turned and fixed me in a cold glare, sending a shiver down my spine. "Keys."

I knew he wasn't angry at me, but the rage in his face was terrifying. I'd never seen him look like this before.

"Asher, I don't think—"

"Give me the fucking keys, Grace." He pressed his lips together and glanced away for a second. "Sorry. Please give me the keys."

"I'm coming with you."

"No—"

It was my turn to hold him with a hard stare. "Yes, I am."

He acquiesced with a slight nod and I tossed him my car keys.

I didn't ask where we were going or why. I already knew. So it was no surprise when we pulled up in front of the Timberbeast Tavern. It was the Havens' equivalent to the Caboose, the place where people on that side of the feud hung out. I'd never been inside.

It was also no surprise when Levi's SUV screeched to a stop next to us and he and Logan got out, nor when Gavin drove up seconds later. Evan's motorcycle roared as he parked next to Gavin. He must have driven fast to get here so quickly.

"Is this a joke?" Logan slammed his truck door shut. "Because this better be a fucking joke."

Asher tossed the license plate at him.

Logan's eyes widened and he showed it to Levi.

Evan popped his knuckles, his eyes narrowing. Even Gavin looked pissed, and almost nothing made him mad.

This was going to be bad.

"Hold on, boys," I said, holding up my hands. "You guys can't just walk in there and start hitting people."

"The fuck we can't," Logan said, tossing the license plate back to Asher. "They took it too far this time."

Oh no.

Asher led the way, bursting into Timberbeast with his brothers right behind him. Feeling helpless, I followed them in. I didn't know what I was going to do if this got ugly—and it sure looked like it would—but I couldn't wait outside and do nothing.

Timberbeast had a similar shabby quality to the Caboose, although instead of railroad décor, it was filled with vintage logging photos, axes, and old business signs. A giant saw was mounted on one wall and a faded Haven Timber Company sign hung in the lobby. The Timberbeast logo, a cartoon drawing of a burly, bearded, hairy-chested logger with a huge ax, greeted people as they walked in.

Our abrupt entrance made the entire bar go silent. It was like something out of a movie. I half expected to hear a record scratch, which was such a weird thing to think when we might be seconds away from a full-on bar fight.

Several of the Haven brothers were indeed here. Josiah and Luke stood near the bar and Zachary sat at a table with a few other people. Unfortunately, I didn't see their sister, Annika. I didn't know her very well, but there was a chance another female voice could help calm this situation before it got out of hand. As far as I knew, none of the Haven brothers had wives or serious girlfriends, so with no sister in sight, I didn't see any potential allies.

Luke squared his shoulders and his eyes narrowed, full of hostility. Josiah's posture was less aggressive, but his confidence was undisguised as he watched Asher and his brothers walk in. Zachary leaned back in his chair, a half-grin on his face, like he found five Bailey men walking into his bar mildly amusing.

This was their territory and it showed.

Asher tossed the license plate on the floor near Josiah and Luke's feet. It landed with a metallic clink.

"This was too far, you pieces of shit."

Luke's upper lip twitched. He reminded me of a growling dog being held back on a leash, anxiously awaiting the moment his owner's hand would slip and he'd be free to surge forward and attack.

I moved closer to Asher.

Josiah scoffed. "We didn't start this."

Asher took a step forward. "Maybe not, but we're going to finish it."

Several more men stood from their chairs and stools, squaring off with the Baileys. Zachary stayed where he was.

"Let's take it outside, then." Luke's eyes were fixed on Evan.

Josiah put a steadying hand on his brother's shoulder.

"What the fuck were you assholes thinking?" Logan asked.

Zachary put a hand to his mouth to suppress a laugh.

"You think this is funny?" Gavin started to surge toward him, but Levi grabbed him before he could pounce.

Josiah took a step. "You guys seriously want to brawl over this?"

Asher started to move but I put a hand on his chest. "Josiah, what the hell? They put stickers on street signs and you destroy their grandad's truck? What did you expect was going to happen?"

"What are you, the Bailey ambassador now?"

Asher growled, clenching his fists, and I threw myself in front of him.

"Stop!"

Zachary started laughing again and this time Levi let Gavin go. He lunged at Zachary, pushing an empty chair out of the way so it clattered to the ground.

"Hold on," Zachary said, jumping out of his seat and retreating toward the bar. He held his hands up. "The truck's fine. We didn't crush it."

Gavin didn't stop stalking him.

"What?" Asher asked, his voice dangerously low.

"We didn't crush the truck. It's out on the old forestry service road. We broke in, put it in neutral, and towed it out there. All we did is hide it and take the license plate off. Calm down, you fuckin' psychos."

"Don't tell me to fucking calm down," Gavin said.

"Gavin, please." I turned to Josiah. "Is that true?"

"Of course it's true," he said. "Their shitty truck is fine."

I started to breathe out a sigh of relief, but the tension in the bar only heightened. I kept my body squarely in front of Asher, my back against his chest. I could feel the rage pouring through him. Gavin twitched, like he was two seconds from jumping Zachary, regardless of what they'd actually done to the truck. Evan and Luke stared each other down, a fierce hatred burning in their eyes.

"Let's go get the truck," I said, not sure which of the Baileys I was really talking to. Maybe if one of them broke the standoff, the rest would follow.

I had a feeling it wasn't going to be Asher.

"Come on, you guys, let's go. If they're lying... I don't know. But let's not do this right now."

Asher moved closer again, forcing me forward in front of him. "Get your shit off my girl's property. I want it gone."

Luke snarled but Josiah's expression remained impassive. "We'll get to it."

"Now," Asher said through gritted teeth.

"I said we'll get to it, Bailey."

"How about I break your other arm," Asher said.

I braced my feet against Asher's push, knowing I couldn't stop him if he decided to go after Josiah and Luke. I just hoped my body in front of his was enough of a deterrent. I couldn't let this happen. "This was low, you guys. It wasn't funny."

"Seriously?" Zachary asked. "It's fuckin' hilarious. You guys have no sense of humor."

"That truck means something, dumbass," I shot back. "You guys still have your grandparents, and your parents. Stuff like this is off limits, and you know it."

"Where's the rule book?" Zachary asked. "Or did you just make that up?"

"Don't talk to her like that," Asher growled.

"Oh for fuck's sake." My patience was gone. "Why make this ugly? Don't you have enough shit to deal with in your own lives without being assholes for no reason? So they put up a bunch of stickers. So what? You guys did it on the big town signs. And before that, we did something ridiculous, and before that it was you. Who cares? It wasn't hurting anyone. But this was personal. You guys should have known better."

For a second, no one moved. Silence hung in the air.

Gavin caught my eye and nodded. He turned for the door, like he was satisfied. I glanced back and saw Levi and Logan shoot glares around the room before turning to follow Gav.

Leaning against Asher, I turned my head and lowered my voice. "Let's go."

He took a step back, so I crouched down to pick up the license plate. Evan backed toward the door slowly, his eyes never leaving Luke Haven. Luke glared back.

Silently hoping no one would speak—if any of them so much as breathed wrong, all hell could break loose—I made sure Asher's brothers got out the door. He tried to guide me in front of him, but I took his hand so he couldn't turn around after I'd gotten outside.

Going back in there alone would have been dangerous and stupid. A rational Asher would have known that. But right now, I didn't trust him to be rational. Not with the tension coming off him, the rage burning in his eyes.

He stopped next to my car and stared at the door, like he was contemplating going back in. His hands twitched and the muscles in his arms flexed.

"Let's go get the truck," Gavin said, his voice casual. He seemed to have let go of his anger already. "If they so much as scratched it, we can come back and fuck shit up."

One by one, they all got in their vehicles. Evan's motor-cycle roared to life and he sped away. Logan and Levi pulled out onto the street, followed by Gavin.

Finally, Asher got in my car. I climbed in, feeling anxious and jumpy from all the adrenaline flooding my system. I stared at the dashboard. I couldn't even look at Asher.

My heart beat uncomfortably fast. That had almost turned into a bar fight. And the last time Asher had gotten into a fight in a bar...

I swallowed back a choking sob that threatened to over-take me. I didn't want to do anything to make this worse, and if he thought I was hurt or upset, it might spark his rage. So I held it in, pushing it deep into the pit of my stomach.

But the fear was overwhelming. If Asher got in a fight and was arrested... or worse, if the fight went terribly wrong...

I couldn't live through that again.

34

ASHER

*W*e found Grandad's truck hidden out on the forest service road, a dirt road that went up into the hills, popular with dirt bikers and teenagers looking for a place to make out. True to their word, they hadn't damaged it—just removed the license plate. But rage still churned hot in my gut. Whether they'd damaged it or not, they'd stolen my truck. And Grace was right—the prank was too personal.

I had too much anger and aggression rippling through me. I wanted to hit someone—preferably a Haven. To fight until my knuckles were bloody.

The urge was almost overwhelming. It scared me.

So I didn't go back to Grace's house. I'd never hurt her—not in a million years. But I still didn't trust myself to be around her right now. I'd probably wind up snapping at her, and despite how out of control I felt, I had enough presence of mind to know I didn't want to do that. She deserved better.

I was also smart enough not to go back down to the

Timberbeast. Or go looking for the Havens. I really fucking wanted to. But I didn't.

Instead I drove out to the lake and sat in the bed of the truck, hoping the quiet and solitude would help me calm down.

I still wanted to hit someone. I flexed my hands into fists and idly knocked my knuckles against the metal of the truck. Not hard enough to injure myself. Just hard enough so I could feel something else. Something other than rage.

Eventually, I went home to Gram's. I had a worried text from Grace, asking if I was okay. I let her know I was fine, I just needed to be alone. Thankfully, she seemed to understand.

I woke up the next morning feeling calmer. More even. I was still pissed at the Havens for what they'd done, but I didn't feel like I was one step away from punching a hole in a wall.

Although if they hadn't gotten that block of fucking metal out of Grace's yard, I'd revisit my resolve not to get violent with those dicks.

Thinking of Grace, I sent her a text.

Me: *Morning. I have to work today. Call you when I'm done. Miss you.*

Grace: *I miss you too. How are you feeling?*

Me: *Better. I'll be fine.*

Grace: *Good. I have to work too so I'll see you tonight. Love you.*

Me: *I love you too.*

Gram was out feeding her chickens when I came downstairs. If she'd heard about the Havens' prank yesterday, she didn't say anything. I left with promises that I'd finish her new chicken enclosure soon and went to work.

I was busy enough that the day went by fast. Jobs were

still coming in—more than enough to keep me busy—but I was growing increasingly restless. I didn't mind the work, but it wasn't exactly fulfilling, either. I'd always been a goal-oriented guy—once I'd matured enough to realize how much I needed to be, at least. Even though I was making money, it wasn't giving me a sense of purpose beyond getting paid.

I still lacked direction. If I kept doing what I was doing indefinitely, I'd do okay for myself. Maybe grow it into a larger business. Hire some employees. And there was nothing wrong with that. People needed guys like me to build their fences and fix their porch swings and install new windows.

But it wasn't enough.

It was late afternoon when I finished up, and the first thing I did was text Grace. I felt depleted, like I was running on empty and I needed her to fill me up again. She was stuck at work dealing with a minor emergency—one of their refrigerators had died, so she was waiting on the repair guy and trying to decipher the warranty paperwork. Fixing refrigerators was not in my skill set, so I told her I'd bring her some dinner later if she wasn't finished yet.

When I got home, I saw Elijah sitting outside by himself. He'd been coming over most afternoons or evenings so I could teach him some grappling moves, and he'd been picking it up quickly. I was proud of the kid. I didn't know whether it was making a difference in his confidence—he still moped around with his head down most of the time—but I hoped eventually it would.

He didn't come over when he saw me, so I went inside to change. When I came downstairs, he was still sitting out there. We weren't planning on grappling today. I'd worked him pretty hard for the last several days, and even young kids needed rest. But maybe something was wrong. I went outside and wandered across the grass between our houses to find out.

"Hey, bud. What's going on?"

He shrugged. "Nothing."

"You okay?"

"Yeah, I'm fine."

I wasn't sure if I believed him, but I decided not to push. Yet. I might be able to get him talking if we were doing something else.

"So I've been building a new chicken enclosure for Gram. There's still plenty of daylight left. Want to help me make some progress?"

He shrugged again. "Okay."

We veered through the shop to grab some tools and supplies. I gave him a tool belt to wear and we went out back.

He was such a smart kid. Every time I taught him something new, whether it was a grappling move or how to use a tool, he picked it up fast. Despite his quiet and often standoffish demeanor, he seemed to soak up the attention I gave him. He was lonely, and I knew it wasn't Naomi and Jack's fault. I had no reason to believe they ignored him. Hell, I'd seen Jack trying to engage with him plenty of times. What I didn't know was why Elijah resisted him so hard. If Elijah needed someone, and Jack was reaching out, why weren't they connecting?

We worked in silence for a while. He didn't offer anything and I took a page from Grandad's book and didn't talk right away. He helped me stake out the perimeter for the new enclosure and we hauled some of the scrap wood I was going to use, stacking it nearby.

I watched him from the corner of my eye. Maybe martial

arts could be a way for him and Jack to bond. I liked hanging out with him, but I could see how strained his relationship was with both his mom and stepdad. I wondered if he knew Jack worked out at the MMA gym downtown. Maybe they'd never talked about it.

"How are things with Jack?"

Elijah shrugged. "Okay."

"Did he ever do something to make you not like him?"

His brow furrowed, like he was surprised—maybe even confused—by my question. "No. He's fine."

"That's good. He seems like a decent guy."

"My mom likes him."

I chuckled. "That's also good. She deserves it. You know, he trains at the MMA gym in town. I've seen him there. I bet if you asked, he'd teach you some things."

He dropped a piece of wood in the dirt. "You don't want to teach me anymore, do you?"

Damn it. Poor kid assumed I was trying to bail on him. "No, buddy, that's not what I mean. I just thought since Jack's your stepdad, maybe you could hang out more if you found something in common."

He shrugged again. The bit of openness I'd been seeing in him quickly faded, like he was curling in on himself. "There's no point."

"No point in what? Hanging out with Jack?"

"Yeah, why bother? He'll just leave."

"I don't think Jack's going to leave."

His face lifted and I could see the anger burning in his eyes. "Everyone leaves."

"What do you mean?"

"Just what I said. People always leave. It's what they do."

"That's not always true."

"You did."

I flinched, like he'd just kicked me. "You remember that?"

"Yeah. I was little, but I wasn't dumb. You didn't say goodbye or anything."

Fuck. I started to reply, but he wasn't finished.

"My dad left. I don't even remember him. Then you were gone, and nobody would tell me why. I found out what you did when I learned how to Google stuff. Logan and Levi moved, and so did Gavin, and I hardly see them anymore. Everybody leaves. Jack will too someday. And so will you. You were supposed to marry my sister and now Mom says she doesn't know if it's going to happen."

Fuck. Again.

"Eli, I'm not leaving. And things with your sister are... complicated. It's not that I don't want to marry her, I just—"

"I don't care," he said, his voice sharp. "It doesn't matter. I gotta go."

"Eli, wait."

He didn't. He unfastened the tool belt, letting it drop to the ground. Then he turned on his heel and quickly walked back home.

I rubbed my chest, feeling like I'd just been kicked in the sternum. I'd assumed he'd been too little to remember me going to prison. Clearly I'd been wrong. And when he laid it all out like that, it was no wonder he acted the way he did. In his eyes, every man who'd ever been an important part of his life had left him, starting with his own father.

He still had his other brothers, and I'd seen how happy he was when he visited them. But they were all busy with their own young families. And although they were only half an hour away, it wasn't the same. They hadn't filled the hole Elijah had inside him.

A hole I'd had a hand in creating.

35

ASHER

*F*or the next week or so, Elijah avoided me like the plague. I saw him sometimes when I was at Gram's, but he'd quickly disappear. I wasn't sure what to do —whether I should wait it out and let him decide to talk to me again, or push harder and try to patch things up. My inexperience with kids left me feeling indecisive and frustrated.

The thing was, I understood how he felt more than he realized. I knew how hard it was to lose people. And I knew what it was like to carry a hot coal of anger around all the time. I'd been like that as a kid, and I struggled with it now.

I was trying to let that anger go and ease back into life here. But it was fucking hard.

I'd left the enclosure half-finished, thinking I'd try to coax Eli into helping me with it again. But eventually, I decided to just get it done. I wasn't going to live here with Gram much longer and I didn't want to leave any projects unfinished.

I went out back and got to work, my head full of unanswered questions. About Elijah, my job, my living situation. About whether I could move forward with Grace.

Where I went next after staying with Gram had become a silent question looming over everything. Grace hadn't pushed for me to move in with her, but I knew it was what she wanted. Which wasn't unreasonable. She'd bought the house on Evergreen Street for us. And every time I thought about that, I was hit with a volatile mix of emotions. I loved her for it, and I was so proud of her.

But I wondered if that house represented a future that didn't exist anymore. I didn't quite feel like I belonged there. It was more hers than ours.

I hadn't talked to her about that yet. I didn't know how to bring it up without hurting her feelings. She'd been nothing but patient with me, and I loved her so fucking much. But living with her in that house represented every one of my fears. That I couldn't be the provider and protector she needed—and deserved. That I might never be ready to be a father.

But I knew how much it would hurt her if I moved into my own place once I left Gram's. She'd probably tell me she understood. That she could be patient—again. Or still. But would time spent living on my own make a difference?

We were giving things a summer, but as the season went on, I didn't feel like I was any closer to knowing what was right. Whether I was cut out to be the man she needed in her life or not.

The back door opened and Levi came out onto the porch.

"Are you fucking kidding me?" he asked.

I straightened and shot him a glare. This was not what I needed right now. "What?"

"I said I was coming over to do that."

For fuck's sake. This was the third or fourth time Levi had showed up and bitched at me for working on Gram's house, like I'd put him out of a job. "Jesus, Levi. She's let me live here for months, the least I can do is help her out. I've got this. You don't need to keep coming over here and getting pissed at me."

"You already knew I was coming over to build that. You should have left it alone."

"There's other stuff to do if you need a side gig so bad. Go check the leaky faucet in the upstairs bathroom."

"Dude, don't tell me what to do. You don't get to start giving orders."

"It's not an order, it's a suggestion. Why are you acting so territorial?"

"I'm not territorial, I just don't understand why you keep jumping in on shit that I already said I'd do."

Gram pushed the back door open, walked out, and crossed her arms. "Language, boys."

Levi didn't stop staring me down. "Sorry, Gram."

"You two have an issue?" she asked, her voice sharp. "Because this isn't the first time I've heard you two arguing lately."

"Apparently he thinks he needs to be in charge of the projects around here," I said, trying—and probably failing —to sound like a grownup instead of a petulant kid.

He rolled his eyes. "No, I just don't appreciate you messing with my plans. I already bought all the supplies for the enclosure, and then I show up here and you've started the damn thing?"

I opened my mouth to fire back, but before I could say a word, Gram turned and marched back inside, leaving the two of us staring at each other. The back door banged shut behind her.

"Look, if it's so fucking important that you build a goddamn chicken fence, build it." I dropped my hammer with a thud. "I already worked all day anyway, so have at it."

"What am I supposed to do with all the shit in my truck? I said I'd take care of it. But you're too fucking self-absorbed to listen to anyone."

"What the fuck are you talking about?"

"At Tuesday dinner week before last—"

Levi's answer was drowned out by a sudden noise, like a small engine. Gram appeared, walking around the side of the house, wielding a chainsaw. The cords in her thin arms stood out, but she handled it with ease. She set her mouth in a thin line, pointedly refused to make eye contact with either one of us, and marched to the porch steps.

My mouth dropped open and I gaped at her in shock. She stopped in front of the porch, planted her feet, bent her knees, and sawed right through the first step. The chainsaw roared as it sliced through the wood, like a knife through butter. Sawdust flew up around her. She made another cut, then another, randomly hacking into the steps that led down to the yard.

Straightening, she turned off the chainsaw and lowered it. She studied her work, then gave a short nod. "There. Now there's plenty of work for both of you." She put the chainsaw on the ground. "Put that away for me, will you, Bear? It's heavy."

I watched, dumbstruck, as she brushed her hands together and walked back around the side of the house.

"Holy shit," Levi muttered.

Our eyes met and it was like we'd been doused with cold water.

"Beer?" Levi asked.

I nodded. "Fridge."

He went inside and came back with two cold beers. After glancing at the ruined stairs, he jumped the short distance down, his feet sending up a puff of dirt. He handed me one of the bottles. One of Gram's chickens, apparently nonplussed by the noise, pecked and scratched her way around my feet.

Careful not to trip over the chicken, I sat on a log round and took a long swig of my beer. "So do you want to take the steps, or the enclosure?"

He shook his head and sat on another log. "Sometimes I think she's crazy and has us all brainwashed into believing she's wise."

"Maybe. Or maybe we drove her crazy."

"True."

"Look, I didn't realize you were bringing shit to build this," I said.

"I thought I said something, but maybe you weren't at the table."

We sat in silence for a long moment, just drinking our beers. I wasn't sure if we'd actually resolved anything, but at least we weren't arguing for once.

"Grandad taught me to build stuff," he said out of the blue. "I know he taught all of us, but I spent a lot of time with him by myself. After Logan and I moved out, I started coming over to do projects for Gram. It wasn't much, but at least I was doing something."

I nodded in understanding. "I hear you, man."

We lapsed into silence again. We'd all been close to Grandad, but Levi had probably been the closest. Losing him had been rough.

"Elijah was getting picked on," I said, not quite sure why I was bringing this up. But it weighed heavily on my mind, and maybe he'd have some old Grandad tricks I hadn't thought of. "I saw it happen in town once and coaxed him into talking to me."

"No shit?"

"Yeah. I started teaching him some grappling skills so he'd have the tools to neutralize an opponent. Make him feel more confident."

"That's good."

"I thought so, but it kind of went south. I said maybe Jack could show him some things too, and he got pissed." My brow furrowed as I stared at my beer, as if it somehow held the answers. "He said there's no point because Jack will just leave like everyone else."

"Ouch."

"Yeah."

Levi took another drink. "He's right, though. Not about Jack leaving—he's a good guy. I don't think he's going to leave Naomi or anything."

"But he's right about everyone else?"

"In a way."

"I know, I get it. His piece of crap father abandoned him."

"You left too."

"Yeah, he threw that at me. But what was I supposed to do? I didn't leave on purpose. I was handcuffed and led to a prison bus."

"Yep. And then you severed contact with everyone except Gram, and refused visitors."

"Jesus, Levi. Really?"

He shook his head. "You just don't get it. Everything went to shit when you left. No one wants to admit it, or maybe it's been long enough that they don't really remember. But we fell apart."

"What are you talking about?"

"Gram did her best, but there was only so much she could do. Evan dropped out of college and moved home, but nobody knows why. He still won't talk about it. Not like it matters because he's always hiding out in his shop, avoiding everyone. The only thing Logan takes seriously is work, and sometimes even that's a stretch. We barely got Gavin through high school, and I have no idea how he hasn't accidentally killed himself. Do you know what it's like to respond to an emergency call and it's your little brother? That time it was a broken leg, but I'm just waiting for the time when it isn't."

"What do you want me to do? Go back in time and change something?"

"I just want you to realize that this whole thing sucked for us too."

"I know it did. But there wasn't anything I could do. Would it have made it any better if I'd sent letters home, telling you all about how fucked up it was in there? How I had to fight my way through a constantly rotating group of inmates? How I became the guy everyone wanted to fuck with?"

"Maybe you shouldn't have fucking killed the guy."

His words stung like a slap and I stared at the dirt for a long moment. I wasn't waiting for him to take it back. I knew he wouldn't. He was simply the first one to say what they'd probably all been thinking.

I lifted my eyes to meet his. "Maybe he shouldn't have tried to rape my fiancée."

"You could have stopped."

My jaw tightened and tension rippled through my neck and shoulders. "That's why I got locked up, isn't it? The court determined I should have known when to stop."

"But you didn't."

"What's your point? That it's my fault things were hard? That's life. None of us asked for this. We didn't ask for Mom and Dad to die either, but it happened. I did what I did to save Grace, and if I had to, I'd do it again. I'd sacrifice anything to keep her safe. Maybe if you ever love someone, you'll understand."

I regretted saying that as soon as the words left my mouth. But I was too pissed and defensive to do the right thing and take it back.

"Fuck you, Asher."

"No, fuck *you*, Levi."

I stood and walked away.

DEAR ASHER

ear Asher,

LOGAN WAS OFFICIALLY HIRED full-time by the TFD. Levi's offer came through already, so now Chief Stanley is stuck with both of them.

Everyone wound up at Gram's that night, including at least half the fire department. And because she's Gram, she sent four fresh pies to everyone who was still on duty and couldn't come over. They built a fire, people brought food. You know how it is. They partied well into the night, long after Gram went to bed.

It should have been fun. Everyone else seemed to be having fun. But not me.

All I could think the entire time is that you should have been there. It was yet another milestone you had to miss.

The more of those that pass, the harder it is to put aside my grief and enjoy them. I want to remember that there will be plenty of important moments in the future and you'll be here for *those. But right now, all I can think about is the unfairness of it all.*

It's so fucking unfair.

I hate this. I hate that you're being punished. That you're losing this time. I hate that I was assaulted and you have to pay the price. How is that justice?

I hate that they took you away from me.

Most of the time, I can handle it. There's an end date, and although it feels like it might as well be a million years from now, it's going to happen. You didn't get life in prison, you got eight years.

But god, Asher, right now eight years seems like a lifetime.

I'm starved, like a little bit of me, deep inside, shrinks smaller every day I have to live without you. I'm holding it together the best I can. Putting on a happy face for the world. But on days like today, my smile is a big fat lie. I'm not happy. I'm not okay. I'm dying inside.

I probably shouldn't tell you things like this. You're fighting your own battle, and it's far worse than mine. At least I'm surrounded by goodness. Even in my darkest moments, there's light. I have my family, and Gram, and your brothers. I have my friend Cara. They're carrying me through this, more than any of them know. But you don't have anyone.

Which makes it hurt all the more.

I don't know what I'm trying to say. But if the only letters I ever sent you were all sunshine and rainbows, you'd know I was hiding something. I don't want you to worry about me—I'll be okay—but I can't hide this from you, either. This is real.

My heart hurts. There's a hollow space inside me that won't be filled until you come home, and sometimes I can't ignore the ache. I can't deny it's there.

. . .

I MISS YOU,
Grace

36

GRACE

The rumble of the truck outside made me smile. I set down the plate I'd been about to wash—I couldn't wait to get this kitchen finished so I'd have a dishwasher again—and dried my hands. Asher had texted, asking if he could come over, and just the sound of the engine coming to a stop sent a little tingle of pleasant anticipation thrumming through me.

Since the stupid Haven prank, Asher had been edgier, vibrating with a constant undercurrent of tension. Whenever we were together, I could feel it, and it made me anxious.

He needed more help than I could give him. I'd known that for a long time, but he always pushed back when I suggested therapy. He said his counselor in prison hadn't done anything for him, and he didn't want to pay to talk to someone who'd just make him dredge up all the things he wanted to forget. It wasn't surprising, really. He'd always resisted doctors. I could remember holding an ice pack to his face after he'd taken a blow in a tournament, arguing with him about needing stitches.

He was so damn stubborn.

I put down the towel and went to answer the door. I could tell with one look that he'd had a rough day. There was tension in his gaze and his dark eyes were stormy.

Without a word, he stepped inside, shut the door, and wrapped his thick arms around me.

Breathing him in, I held him tight. It had been two and a half months since his release, and I still hadn't lost the deep sense of wonder and gratitude that he was home. In a way, it was almost like being twenty again. Like the days when I could sense things changing between us. He'd been my best friend for most of my life, but suddenly the mere sight of him had sent butterflies fluttering through my stomach.

I felt the same tingly excitement now. He was here with me, no longer kept away by barbed wire and steel, and I still felt the same rush of relief every single time.

"Is everything okay?" I gently rubbed the back of his neck.

With his face in my neck, he took a long, slow breath. "Yeah. I just needed you."

I loved hearing him say that. Not because I had a desperate urge to be needed, but because this was how things had been before. We'd relied on each other, sought comfort in each other's arms. No matter what else had changed, this never would. He would always be my safe place, and I would do everything I could to always be his.

He took my hand and led me to the bedroom. I followed more than willingly. Standing next to the bed, he ran his hands through my hair, his face close. His dark eyes held mine and his brow furrowed, his expression fraught with both passion and tenderness. The storm still raged inside him. I could see it in his gaze, feel it in his skin.

I wanted him to know he could share it with me. Soothe it with my body. That I was his and I always would be.

With his hands still in my hair, his fingertips massaging my scalp, he brought his mouth to mine. I welcomed his kiss, relaxing into it. Savoring the feel of his lips. His tongue caressing mine.

He reached down to lift my shirt over my head. Running my hands along his skin—feeling the hard planes of muscle—I pulled his off too. He was both commanding and unhurried as he gradually undressed me, his mouth hardly leaving mine. His calloused hands roamed over my skin, strong and warm.

I unfastened his jeans while he kissed down my neck, and plunged my hand into his pants. A satisfying groan rumbled in his throat as I gripped his cock. He pushed his pants down and kicked them away, giving me full access to him.

Licking my lips, I stroked him a few times. His abs flexed and he looked down between us. His steel-hard cock was thick in my hand, practically pulsing with need. I loved the rush of pleasure it gave me to make him feel good. To hear the primal growls my touch could elicit.

I stroked harder, squeezing the shaft. He grunted, his breath coming faster. Lightly dragging my fingertips down his torso, I lowered myself to my knees in front of him. Flicked my tongue across the tip of his cock to taste him.

He groaned again and gave my hair an appreciative caress. My lips curled in a little smile. Meeting his eyes—I wanted him to watch this—I took the tip in my mouth.

The smooth skin tasted clean, just a hint of his arousal hitting my tongue. His eyes were fixed on me, his dark brow furrowing deeply. The sharp lines of muscle leading down to his hips stood out and his thighs flexed with tension.

Holding the base, I drew him in deeper, letting the tip slide across the roof of my mouth. He growled, the intensity never leaving his face. When I pulled out again, I used my tongue to toy with him, tracing the ridge around the tip.

"Fuck, I love you," he said.

In answer, I plunged down on him, taking him as deep as I could. His thickness made it a challenge, but I'd never been a quitter. Settling into a rhythm, I drew him in and out, caressing him with my tongue as I sucked his cock.

His hips started to jerk and his hand fisted tight in my hair. His growls were deep and desperately arousing. As much as I was enjoying the way this made him let go, my inner walls trembled with desire.

He thrust hard into my mouth, then pulled back. "Fuck. Sorry."

God, I loved how strangled and breathless his voice sounded. In reply, I met his eyes again and kept going, moving his thickness in and out of my mouth. He watched with undisguised lust, still jerking his hips. His cock thickened and his breathing grew ragged.

So often, he stopped me here. Threw me on the bed and buried himself inside me—which I loved. But this time, I wanted to finish him like this, on my knees and vulnerable.

He started to say something, but I cut him off with a deep plunge. His voice broke into a rough growl. I could feel his control slipping, his guardedness falling away. I kept going, my rhythm relentless, determined to make him come.

"Fuck," he said again. "Please."

Nothing he'd said to me had ever been sexier. My jaw started to ache, but I didn't care. Cupping his balls with my other hand, I kept plunging down on his cock. He was close. I could feel it. His body tensed and he grunted with each thrust, holding my hair in a tight fist.

With his eyes locked on mine and his jaw clenched tight, he gritted out the words. "I'm coming."

Feeling triumphant, I welcomed his release. His hand gripped my hair and he growled while his cock pulsed between my lips. The hot liquid hit the back of my throat as he watched, like he needed to not just feel this, but see it too.

When he finished, he released his grip on my hair. I let his cock slip from my mouth and quickly swallowed. He stared at me, breathing hard, his expression finally softening.

"Fuck," he muttered under his breath.

Biting my bottom lip, I stood. "Did that feel good?"

His only answer was another deep growl as he manhandled me onto the bed. Without a word, he pushed my legs open and attacked my pussy like a hungry predator.

The feel of his tongue was so abrupt on my already sensitive clit, I gasped and arched my back. He was merciless, licking me with expert precision, lapping up my arousal into his mouth. His deep groans vibrated through my entire body. In almost no time at all, I was racing toward climax.

He slipped a finger inside me and I almost came undone. I writhed against the sheets and slid my hands through his hair. He devoured me like a man starving, groaning as if I was the most delicious thing he'd ever tasted.

We'd learned everything we knew on each other, so every skill he possessed was perfectly attuned to me. He was an expert. Sliding in a second finger, he focused his tongue right on my sensitive bundle of nerves. I closed my eyes, lost in sensation. In the heat building in my core, the exquisite pressure rising to a breaking point.

His voracious assault on my clit intensified. I couldn't think, couldn't see. All I could do was feel. My eyes closed and I threw my head back, succumbing to the dizzying combination of pressure and friction.

Ripples of pleasure burst through my body as I tumbled over the edge. The orgasm swept through me, my inner muscles spasming around his fingers. He slowed his pace, so attuned to me and what I loved, that he naturally rode out the waves of climax with me, drawing it out until I was practically panting.

I relaxed against the sheets, my eyes still closed, the heady rush of euphoria consuming me. He crawled up the bed and scooped me next to him, tucking me against his body. I nestled in close, relishing the warmth of his skin and his intoxicating scent.

"Thank you," I said, my voice dreamy and soft. "That was amazing."

He kissed my ear, then my neck. "Thank *you*. I still need to fuck you, though."

Letting my eyes flutter open, I giggled. His cock was hardening again. He pressed it into my ass, as if to prove his point.

"Do you need a minute?" he asked, his voice low in my ear.

"No."

Without wasting any time, he rolled me onto my back and climbed on top of me. I didn't know how he was ready again so fast, but I certainly didn't mind.

Coming in my mouth hadn't diminished his intensity. If anything, it had only served to whet his appetite for more. His thrusts were powerful and relentless, his grip on me tight.

"God, I love fucking you," he growled into my ear.

"Don't you dare stop."

"No?" He thrust himself in deeper. "You like this cock, don't you baby?"

All I could do was whimper breathlessly.

Another low groan rumbled in his chest. "Your pussy feels so good."

My fingers dug into the tense muscle in his back and my inner walls tightened around his cock.

"Fuck yes, beautiful. I love this pussy. I'm going to come in you so fucking hard."

The combination of his thick cock pounding me in an unrelenting rhythm and his low growly voice murmuring in my ear was almost too much to bear. I held on, drawing my knees up to take him in deeper.

"Harder," I managed to get out.

"Tell me."

"Fuck me harder."

He groaned again, and with one hand gripping my hip, he drove into me. Every thrust was like magic, drawing me toward another climax. He was rough and hard, fucking me like he finally knew I wouldn't break.

My second orgasm of the night was different. Instead of quick and intense, the pulses rolled through me like slow waves. They were deep, stimulating places I'd never felt before, overwhelming my senses.

Asher's body tensed, his muscles flexing, and he buried himself inside me as he started to come. Long, low groans accompanied his climax, and his hips thrust his cock in deep with each pulse. The way he throbbed inside me felt almost as good as my own orgasm. I held him tight while he came, the last tremors of my climax making me tremble.

He relaxed, keeping just enough tension in his arms so he wouldn't crush me beneath him. I kept my arms around his back, not ready to let go. The connection between us was so deep and profound, I needed this moment. Needed him to stay inside me, sated and motionless.

As if he could read my mind and knew exactly what I needed, he held there, breathing into my neck. He nuzzled his nose against my skin and placed soft kisses near my ear and across my cheek. Our heartbeats were in sync, our bodies warm and satisfied. I held him tight for a long moment, for the first time no longer grieving for what we'd missed.

Now, I was simply hopeful for everything that was to come.

37

ASHER

*A*lthough it wasn't very late, Grace and I didn't bother getting out of bed. She lay tucked against me with her head on my shoulder and one arm draped over my chest. I traced idle shapes on her skin with my fingertips, only half-awake. I was warm and sated, more relaxed than I'd been in days.

By her slow, even breathing, I could tell she'd fallen asleep. A part of me wanted to talk to her. That hot coal of anger still smoldered inside me, a red and black mass that could flare at any moment. Levi had stoked it, but for now, its heat had been tempered. I'd let her sleep.

I WAS DIMLY aware of the creak of metal. A thin, hard surface below me. The darkness was so thick, I couldn't see clearly. Vague shapes, nothing more. I turned my head, trying to make sense of my surroundings.

Bars. I was back in a cage.

Fuck.

There was movement and I tried to jump to my feet. My hands balled into fists, but unseen pressure held me down. My legs were lead weights, my arms useless. I couldn't move. My chest heaved as I thrashed against the invisible bonds crushing me to the ground. The bars were gone, but I still couldn't move, as if a dozen hands held me, pinning me to the cold, hard floor.

A hand clamped to my forehead, forcing me to watch. I saw a body curled inward, arms and legs tucked close to protect himself from the worst of the beating. Legs kicked him over and over, their merciless blows landing on the helpless form. I could hear the cries of pain. Feel every bruise as it bloomed across his body. Every rib being cracked, every blood vessel broken.

The pressure holding me threatened to crush the air from my lungs. I had to get up. Had to get free. I had to help him before they—

"Asher."

Released from the grip of the unseen hands, I shot up, completely disoriented. Something touched me and I reacted before I'd even opened my eyes. My elbow cracked backward, connecting with something hard.

The sharp scream of pain woke me completely. The room came into sudden focus. Grace's room. No bars. No inmates. No one holding me down. But I'd just—

Oh fuck. Oh god, no.

I whipped around to find Grace holding her face, her legs pulled up as if to shield the rest of her body.

"Oh my god, Grace. What did I do?"

Her eyes were squeezed shut, her hands cupping her nose.

"Did I hurt you?" I could hardly grind out the words.

Without opening her eyes, or moving her hands away from her face, she nodded.

My chest broke wide open. I felt like I was going to die right here at her feet. I carefully reached out, but I was terrified to touch her.

Fuck. What had I done?

She took shuddering breaths, like she was trying to get a hold of herself. It took me another second to realize I was doing nothing, just staring at her like I was fucking helpless.

"Hang on, baby. I'll be right back."

My hands shook as I got out of bed and hurried to the kitchen. I grabbed towels out of a drawer and an ice pack from her freezer.

Her eyes were open when I got back. She sat cross-legged on the bed, the sheet in her lap, still covering her face with her hands.

There was blood everywhere.

She seemed to notice it at the same time I did. With a gasp, she moved her hands out to look at them. Blood streamed down her nose, over her lips, dripping from her chin. Her hands were smeared with it and red drops had splattered over the sheets.

"Oh god," she said.

With horror pouring through me, I handed her a towel. I wanted to help, wanted to fix this, but I was too afraid to touch her.

Because I'd done this. She was bleeding everywhere because of me.

"Grace, I'm so sorry. I don't know what happened."

She gingerly held a towel up to her face. Her eyes were already red-rimmed and bloodshot. "I think you were having a nightmare." Her voice was muffled by the towel. "I tried to wake you."

"Fuck. I'm sorry."

She shifted the towel to wipe the blood beneath her nose and winced, sucking in a sharp breath. "Holy shit, that hurts."

Sick with the realization of what I'd done, I did my best to help her clean up. Eventually the bleeding stopped. Without a lot of conscious thought, I stripped the sheets and bedding and replaced it while she went to the bathroom. When she came back, she put on her pajamas, then got back in bed. I wrapped the ice in a towel and handed it to her.

I couldn't bring myself to touch her.

She leaned her head back against the headboard and took a deep breath. "I think I'm okay."

Nothing about this was okay. I'd had a stupid fucking nightmare and when she'd tried to wake me, I'd elbowed her in the nose.

"It might be broken." The necessity of those words gutted me, but I said them anyway.

She nodded. "I know. Nothing we can do right now."

"Grace, I'm so sorry. I..."

I had no idea what to say. How could I apologize? I felt like I was still in a nightmare. I'd hit her. I'd made her bleed.

"Asher, don't do that." She lowered the ice. "Don't. It was an accident."

It had been an accident. She was right. But that didn't matter—didn't change anything. I'd still done it. She'd been trying to help, and I'd—

"I need to get some air."

"Don't go." She reached for me. "Asher, please. Come to bed."

"Can't." I felt like I was going to crawl out of my skin. "Keep the ice on it. I'll be back."

She started to say something else, but I couldn't stay. It

felt like the walls were closing in on me, the invisible hands from my dream pushing me down. I knew if I closed my eyes for even a second, I'd be right back in the nightmare. Only this time, it would be Grace on the ground, and the one hurting her would be me.

I scooped my clothes off the floor and stumbled out of her bedroom. Somehow, by the time I reached the front door, I was dressed. Everything was hazy, a maddening swirl of horror and raw guilt. It clawed at me, shredding me from the inside.

The cold night air hardly registered. Neither did the fact that my feet were bare. I wandered outside with no idea where I was going, my head a mix of images from my nightmares, and the all-too-real sight of Grace bleeding all over her bed.

It was worse than my worst fear. I'd been afraid I wasn't safe, afraid the darkness inside me would hurt her. But never like this. I never would have thought I might injure her physically. Intentional or not, it had happened. I'd been so out of control, I'd probably broken her fucking nose.

Everything I'd been telling myself had been a lie. That I could do this. I could make this work. I just needed time.

I didn't need time. I needed to be kept away from everyone. They probably should have stuck me with the murder charge. Kept me locked up forever. At least then I wouldn't have been a danger to anyone except the pieces of shit who deserved my wrath.

The urge to hit something filled my gut and made my chest tight. I was so fucking angry, and I had nowhere to put all this rage. Because I was angry at myself. Furious that I'd hurt her. That I was so fucking broken, I couldn't even sleep safely beside her.

I didn't know how long I wandered. Hours, maybe,

walking in circles around the streets of her neighborhood. The stars began to fade with the first hints of dawn before the chaos in my brain eased. My heart rate finally slowed and my breath wasn't so ragged. Clarity, and at least a modicum of rationality, started to return.

I still felt like I'd stabbed myself in the heart and was in danger of bleeding out, but at least I could think. I needed to get back and check on Grace. Hopefully she'd kept the ice on her nose for a while and gone back to sleep.

As the rational part of me returned and panic retreated, I calmed myself by making a plan. I'd let her sleep, then take her to the doctor as soon as she was ready. I'd stay with her while she got it checked out. I'd get her whatever she needed to feel better. Clear my schedule so I could take care of her. And hope and pray that I hadn't hurt her too badly.

And that she could forgive me.

After that? I didn't know what I was going to do. How to deal with the fact that I'd lost control and hurt her.

I quickened my pace, suddenly anxious to get back. Something pricked at my instincts, a sense of urgency filling me. It was different than panic. That was a vague sense of impending disaster, a feeling I couldn't place, even though it was strong. This was different.

And then I realized I smelled smoke in the air.

I broke into a run and rounded the corner onto Grace's street. A column of black smoke rose into the pre-dawn sky.

Grace's house was on fire.

38

ASHER

*M*y feet pounded on the pavement as I sprinted toward her house. There was no haze of panic in my brain. My training was there. Everything was clear. In the seconds that it took to run to her house, I'd already visualized what I needed to do depending on what I found when I got there. I had one objective.

Save her.

I slowed when I got close and did a quick visual sweep of the front. No Grace. But a lot of smoke.

Half her house was still unfinished. Did her smoke detectors work? Were there enough of them? I didn't remember seeing one in her bedroom. The smoke could suffocate her before she had a chance to get out.

I also didn't have my phone.

Fuck.

The front door wasn't hot but when I opened it, smoke billowed out. I crouched low to get beneath it. So far, it hadn't filled the front room, but it wouldn't take long. In the low light, I could make out the hazy gray, flowing across the ceiling like cloudy liquid.

No alarms sounded. The house was eerily quiet except for the growing roar of flames.

Smoke was filling the hallway. My eyes stung and I could taste it in the air.

I had to get her out.

Moving quickly, I ran in a crouch to her bedroom. The door was closed, but smoke was leaking inside through the crack at the top.

"Grace!"

I felt the door with the back of my hand and touched the doorknob. Cool. No fire inside.

Thank fuck.

But Grace wasn't answering.

"Grace," I called again, throwing the door open.

She lay in bed, her head resting on the pillow. One arm hung over the side, her palm up. The ice pack I'd brought her sat on the floor next to the bed, like it had fallen there. I coughed; smoke was quickly filling the small bedroom.

I rushed to her side, bundled her in one of the blankets, and tucked my arms beneath her. "Grace, honey, wake up."

Her eyes stayed closed, but she mumbled something. She was alive, but the fact that she wasn't waking up was a bad sign.

Without a second to lose, I picked her up in my arms. I took a breath, held it, and ran for the front door.

A smoke alarm started to sound as I raced outside. Fucking finally. I rushed her out toward the street, my head swirling with next steps. I needed to call 911, but my phone was inside the house. I'd set her down, make sure she was still breathing. Run to the neighbor's and call for help. Get back to Grace and stay with her until paramedics arrived.

Carefully, I laid her out on the ground. "Grace, honey, I need you to wake up."

Her eyes fluttered, like she was trying to open them, and coughed. "What?"

"Stay still. Just breathe."

"Is everything okay over there?"

I looked up at the voice. One of Grace's neighbors looked out his front door.

"Call 911. Now!" I barked.

"Oh my god." He disappeared back inside, his door still open. A second later, he was back, talking on his phone. His head tilted up as he watched the smoke billowing out of her house.

"Help is coming." I stroked her hair back. She was breathing, but she was disoriented and having a hard time waking. She needed oxygen. "Stay with me."

Panic started to rise in my chest. I was helpless. I'd gotten her out, but what else could I do? She didn't need CPR, but she needed help. My training didn't matter. All I could do was wait.

Come on, guys. Get here. Please.

Every second felt like an hour, every breath I took labored. I talked softly to her, stroking her hair, trying to keep her awake. Wishing I could breathe for her.

"Stay with me, honey. Stay with me."

"Asher," she murmured, then coughed again. "What's happening? I'm so dizzy."

"Shh, you're okay."

The bridge of her nose was swollen and the skin around her eyes was purpling. It did nothing to ease the sick feeling in my gut to realize she was going to have two black eyes. Did she have a concussion? That could be why she was so disoriented.

I'd blackened her eyes, possibly broken her nose, and

now her fucking house was on fire. Vaguely, I wondered if Jack would be the one to arrest me. Someone was going to.

Shrill sirens rang in the distance. In seconds, the sound grew. The ambulance arrived first, pulling to a quick stop in front of us. The engine followed, its lights flashing.

Suddenly, people were everywhere. Paramedics. Fire-fighters rushing to the house. The whole street was a riot of activity. I watched, helpless, while the paramedics attended to Grace. They asked questions and I tried to answer, but it was hard to think.

"I don't know how it started," I heard myself say. "I was out walking. I came back and saw smoke."

Levi ran past. Or maybe it was Logan. In the chaos, I couldn't tell them apart.

Paramedics loaded Grace on a gurney. She had an oxygen mask on her face, but her eyes were open. She kept trying to talk, but I didn't know what she wanted to say.

A hand touched my shoulder and I flinched.

"Whoa, son." Chief Stanley kept a steadying hand on me. "Are you okay? Were you inside?"

"I went in to get her out."

"You need to let us take a look at you."

"I'm fine. Grace needs help."

"She's getting it." He patted me on the back and spoke to someone else, but his words didn't register. "Ride with her to the hospital. You did good, Asher. She looks better already."

Did good? I hadn't done anything good. I'd hurt her, and then left her alone. She could have fucking died. I'd gotten her out in time, but I hadn't done anything heroic.

No man was a hero if it was his fault someone needed saving.

39

GRACE

*M*y tests had all come back fine, but the ER doctor wanted to monitor me for at least six hours before letting me go. I felt all right, other than a headache and a bit of a cough. Plus the throbbing bruise that had once been my nose, but that had nothing to do with a mild case of smoke inhalation.

My nose wasn't broken, but I looked awful. It was swollen and I was well on my way to sporting two black eyes. I'd made the mistake of looking in the mirror when they finally let me up to use the bathroom. I had regrets.

Asher sat in a folding chair a few feet from the hospital bed. His forearms rested on his knees and his eyes were fixed on the ground. He didn't seem hurt physically, and he'd redirected any questions about his well-being back to me. *Just take care of Grace*, or, *I'm fine, Grace needs help*. For a while, it had seemed like that was all he knew how to say.

Now he stared at the floor, glancing up at me now and again as if to make sure I was breathing.

I still didn't understand exactly what had happened. After he'd left, I'd iced my nose for a while. My eyelids had grown heavy and eventually, I'd lain down to go back to sleep. The next thing I remembered, I was on the ground outside my house with Asher saying my name, telling me to stay with him. I had no memory of him carrying me out, although obviously he had. No memory of smelling smoke or feeling the heat of the flames.

If he hadn't been there, I probably would have died.

I hadn't died in a house fire, but his brothers were going to kill me. I'd taken down the smoke detector on that side of the house to fix some ceiling damage last week and hadn't put it back yet.

Big mistake.

"You doing okay over there?" I asked.

Asher glanced up at me. "I'm fine. You?"

"Bored. Worried about the house."

His eyes flicked away. "Yeah."

I reached my hand out. "Come here."

He scooted his chair closer and took my hand. If his eyes had been stormy before, they were raging hurricanes now. He held my hand gently, like he was afraid he would hurt me, and his gaze moved from my face to the floor. He was having a hard time looking me in the eyes.

"It's not your fault," I said quietly.

He just shook his head.

"You saved my life. If you'd been there sleeping, we both could have died. If anyone's at fault here, it's me. I should have put the smoke detector back up immediately."

"It's not your fault," he said.

"Well, it isn't yours, either."

He still wouldn't look up at me.

"Asher—"

"Oh my god." Cara burst through the curtain into the room, dressed in a loose white t-shirt and distressed jeans, her thick hair in a ponytail. She glanced around the room, like she was shocked to find herself here, then looked at me again. "No, really. Oh my fucking god. Who do I have to kill?"

"No one. This was an accident." I pointed to my face. "And I don't know why there was a fire, but—"

"*What?*" she shrieked. "There really was a fire? I thought Logan was lying."

"You talked to Logan?"

"Prince dickhead isn't important. What fire?"

"There was a fire at my house. Asher got me out."

"You saved her life *again*?" She launched herself at Asher, almost knocking him out of his chair, and threw her arms around his neck. "Thank you. Oh my god, thank you. I swear I will love you until the day I die. Thank you."

Looking mildly horrified, he awkwardly patted her on the back. "You're welcome. Just... stop."

Her shoulders shook with sobs.

"Cara, sweetie, calm down."

"Sorry." She straightened and swiped her fingers beneath her eyes. "But he pulled you out of a fire? I still don't understand why you look like you got in a bar fight with a bitch named Bertha, but I'm so glad you're alive."

I glanced at Asher, knowing I was going to make him flinch like I'd slapped him when I said it out loud again. I'd already had to explain the black eyes to the paramedics, the doctor, and every nurse who set foot in this tiny little curtained-off room. Of course, they had to ask, and they had to follow it up with questions about whether I felt safe at home or needed help.

"I tried to wake him from a nightmare and got bonked on the nose." Every time I told the story, I tried to avoid saying Asher had sat up and elbowed me in the face. *Bonked on the nose* sounded more like he'd accidentally bumped into me.

She winced. "Ouch."

"It looks worse than it is."

"So, your house?" she asked, her voice softening. "You don't know what happened?"

"Not yet. I have no idea what started it."

"Probably an electrical fire," Asher said, his voice oddly monotone.

Cara started to say something else, but I shook my head at her. An electrical fire had killed Asher's parents. This wasn't a topic for idle conversation.

Fortunately, she seemed to understand. "Wow. I'm just so glad you're okay. How long do you have to be here?"

"A few more hours for observation. I breathed in enough smoke to get pretty disoriented, so they have to watch me for a while."

"Why are they keeping you down here? This room is terrible. I can go take care of this."

"No, really, I'm fine. I just have to wait a little longer. The sooner I can get out of here, the better."

She crossed her arms but didn't rush off to insist I be given a private room with a view. "Well, obviously you'll come stay with me until we figure out what to do about your house. But I'll put you in the guest room that's farthest from my bedroom so I won't hate you for getting some when I'm not."

"That's very thoughtful. And practical."

"Thank you. But you don't have to worry about a thing." She got out her phone and started typing something. "We might not be able to get in the house right away, so I'll order you some clothes, toiletries, maybe an overnight bag."

"I can just wear your clothes for a day or two," I said. "You don't have to buy new stuff."

"Let me do this, it makes me feel useful." Her eyes brightened. "Oh my god, these pajama pants have wine glasses all over them. Clearly you need these. God, why can't I get same-day delivery out here?"

I smiled at her ridiculousness while she furiously ordered things for me. "Maybe we need matchy wine glass pajama pants."

"Aw, we haven't had matchy clothes in forever." Her eyes flicked to Asher and her smile faded. "You sure you're okay, big guy?"

He rubbed his hands over his face. "Yeah, fine. Grace needed help, not me."

She shot me a concerned look and I mouthed, *I know.*

He wasn't fine.

40

GRACE

*M*y heart fluttered and my stomach felt like it was doing back flips. I hadn't seen my house yet, and I was dreading this first look.

Asher glanced at me, a quick flick of his eyes. The veins in his forearms stood out as he drove and he worked his jaw. He was nervous, too, and the tension in his body wasn't doing anything to help me calm down.

I'd been out of the hospital for two days with no signs of lasting injury to my lungs—thanks to Asher getting me out so quickly. The swelling in my face had gone down considerably, but I still looked like I'd been in a fight. And lost. It made me want to avoid people so I didn't have to keep explaining that it had been an accident.

I saw the looks on people's faces, and I knew what they were thinking. Asher had been a fighter, and he'd done time in prison. And now his girlfriend had two black eyes? What had *really* happened?

Their unspoken questions made me furious. I could only imagine how they made Asher feel.

He'd been unnaturally quiet since the fire. I'd been

staying with Cara and taken a few days off—she and Asher
had both insisted—so I could recover. He'd rescheduled his
jobs and spent most of his time with me, although he went
to Gram's at night to sleep. But everything was different. He
held me, touched me, comforted me. He jumped up to get
me anything I needed, sometimes competing with Cara to
play nurse.

But he was also distant and too careful. He touched me
like he was afraid I'd break—hesitant and overly gentle.

It was driving me crazy.

A vague sense of dread had been building in the pit of
my stomach since the fire. There was so much going on in
Asher's head and he wasn't telling me any of it. I could see it
in his eyes, feel it in the way he treated me. He was trying to
help, but also pulling away. Keeping distance between us.
And no matter what I said, I couldn't coax him into talking
about it.

When he parked in front of my house, I was almost
afraid to look. But the front seemed remarkably normal.
They'd managed to contain the fire and keep it from
spreading through the entire structure.

The fire inspector had determined it had indeed been an
electrical fire. A previous owner had installed an outlet in
the kitchen and hadn't wired it properly. No one could have
known. I'd had the house thoroughly inspected before I
bought it, but no one could see through walls.

Asher was still quiet as we got out and went to the
front door. With a deep breath, I unlocked it and went
inside.

The front looked untouched. The inside did not.

Yellow tape blocked off the kitchen at the back of the
house, but I could see straight out to the backyard. Much of
the wall was gone. Scorch marks showed the fire's path as it

had spread before the firefighters had contained it. The smell of smoke and ash hung heavily in the air.

All that work I'd done. So much of it was ruined.

"Well," I said, taking a few tentative steps inside. "At least I hadn't remodeled the kitchen yet."

Asher didn't laugh at my attempt at levity.

We walked through the house, checking the other rooms. Everything smelled like smoke, but the worst of the damage was limited to the kitchen and surrounding area. The bedrooms were fine, although I didn't know what it would take to get the smell out. Primer and new paint on the walls for sure. Maybe new flooring, but I hoped the hardwoods could just be cleaned. They were all original. It would have been a shame to lose them.

When I'd seen everything, I went back to the front room. I'd grabbed some clothes, hoping I could get the smell out in the wash, but for now I left everything else. I'd have to start going through each room, figuring out what was salvageable and what needed to be replaced. But not today.

"Ready?" Asher asked.

"Yeah." I looked around again, feeling oddly calm. It was upsetting, but I also knew it could be fixed. Aside from the gaping hole in the back and the fact that the kitchen was completely useless, the house had been in worse shape when I'd bought it. It would be a lot of work, but at least it hadn't burned to the ground.

It could still be saved.

My stomach still churned with anxiety and my limbs felt jittery. But it wasn't my house making me so uneasy. It was Asher.

He drove us back to Cara's, but when he stopped in the driveway, he didn't turn off the engine. He shifted into park and waited.

"You're not coming in?" I asked.

"I have some things I need to do."

"Will you come back and stay with me tonight?" I asked, my voice soft.

He didn't answer. His body went still, as if he'd suddenly been frozen.

I let a long moment pass while the sick feeling in my stomach spread. Something was very wrong. "Asher?"

"No."

That one word hurt more than his elbow cracking into my nose. Because I knew what it meant. I knew exactly what he was about to do. He wasn't going to tell me no to tonight, he was going to tell me no to everything. To us.

"Asher, don't do this."

"I can't, Grace." His voice was that horrible monotone— the same voice he'd used when he'd told me he was taking the plea bargain and going to prison. When he'd told me it was over and I had to let him go. "I can't keep pretending this is going to work. It's not fair to you."

I gripped the clothes I held in my lap. "Asher, don't."

"Don't what? Tell you the truth?"

"What truth? The fire was an accident. It wasn't your fault. Not only that, you saved my life. Again. How can you twist that around and turn it into a reason we can't be together?"

"Have you looked in the mirror today?"

"Also an accident."

"Exactly. I had no control over myself and I gave you two fucking black eyes. I could have done worse. And then I left you there, bleeding all over the goddamn bed, and your house caught on fire."

"The bleeding had stopped and if you'd been inside, we could have both died."

"Or I could have gotten you out faster."

"This is ridiculous."

"You should have listened to me," he said, his voice low. "I told you before I left that this wouldn't work anymore. That you had to let me go and move on. You should have fucking listened."

"Asher—"

"No. I'm not the man you think I am, Grace. I keep trying to be, but it's a lie. All I want to do is fucking hurt someone." He clenched his hands into fists. "I try so hard to keep my demons locked away, but I can't do it forever. They're going to get out. This time I didn't break your nose, but next time it could be worse. I'm not safe."

"It was an accident."

"You don't understand. It doesn't fucking matter. You want our life back—the life we were planning before some piece of shit dragged you out into an alley. Do you actually think I can give you that life now? That we could get married and go to work every day and just live like normal, happy people? Do you think we could have kids? Jesus, I can't be someone's father."

"No one said right away. There's no rush for anything; we have plenty of time."

"You're kidding yourself. I don't need time. I need to face the truth about who I am, and so do you. I'm not cut out for this. I love you, and I always will, but I can't marry you. I can't be your husband, and I can't father your children. That's the life you want—a life with a good man and a family. I can't give you that. I can't be him, no matter how much you want me to."

Tears welled in my eyes and my throat felt so thick, I wasn't sure I could get any words out. "You're wrong."

"No, I'm not. I'd be wrong to try to keep you when I know I can't."

"So that's it?" I sniffed, trying to hold back my tears. "After everything we've been through, you just want to quit?"

He closed his eyes. "Don't make this harder. Please."

"You can't—"

"Please," he said again through clenched teeth. "I told you, you should have listened to me. I should have come back and found you married to someone I'd have to hate for the rest of my life, but love for taking good care of you."

"Fuck you, Asher," I snapped. "You keep trying to tell me I don't understand, but neither do you. You don't understand a fucking thing if you think there could ever be anyone else. Even if I had listened to you and taken off your ring, moving on was never an option, even if I'd wanted to. That's the part of this you're refusing to see. If I tell you fine, it's over, I'm done with you, are you going to go out and find someone else? A few years from now, do you really see yourself living with some other woman?"

"No."

"Try to tell me it's because you're too fucked up to be with anyone and that's the only reason."

"I am too fucked up to be with anyone."

"But even if you decided you weren't, no one would ever be right for you the way I am. You know how I know that? Because no one will ever be right for me the way you are."

"That's not enough," he roared and smashed his fist into the dashboard. His knuckles came away bloody.

I grabbed a shirt out of my lap wipe up the blood, but he jerked his hand away.

"Get out of the truck."

"Let me just—"

"Get out of the fucking truck, Grace."

His tone left no room for argument. I gathered my purse and the small pile of clothes I'd retrieved, holding them close to my chest, and got out of the truck. As soon as I'd closed the door, he tore out of the driveway, leaving me behind.

41

ASHER

I left Grace at Cara's house and went looking for a fight.

The need to hurt someone was so acute, I couldn't control it anymore. I didn't give a fuck who it was. I needed to punch someone. My knuckles were already raw, but the fist to the dash hadn't been enough. I had so much pain burning inside me, I needed to get it out—inflict it on someone else.

I drove straight to the Timberbeast Tavern. It was mid-afternoon on a weekday, but if I didn't find a goddamn Haven there, I'd keep looking until I did.

As the truck rumbled to a stop in the parking lot outside Timberbeast, I told myself those assholes needed to pay anyway. I was only there to deliver what they already had coming. It was about fucking time.

With my blood pounding in my ears and my vision hazy with rage, I stalked into the tavern.

It was mostly empty. A few barflies hunched over their afternoon beers and a grizzled bartender wiped down glasses with a white towel. His eyes narrowed at me, as if he knew exactly why I was here and wasn't going to take any of my shit.

Fortunately for him—or maybe for me, but I wasn't exactly thinking clearly—no one I wanted to hit was here. So I left.

I was only thinking half a step ahead, like my mind was fixed on the present moment and couldn't see past it. I got in the truck without a clear idea of where I'd go next—just turned on the engine. Maybe it was a subconscious attempt to keep me from thinking about the real reason I was losing my shit. It was like being in prison again. I couldn't even think her name.

The ease of slipping back into survival mode probably should have alarmed me. I was cut off from the rest of the world, untouchable. It was empty and hollow, but it was better than the alternative.

I drove out onto the street and someone walked out in front of me, right in the middle of the road. I slammed my foot on the brake, making the tires screech against the pavement, and cranked the wheel so I'd avoid hitting him.

The truck came to a stop and my heart felt like it was going to rip through my ribs. What the fuck had just happened?

Gavin stood in the middle of the road, his arms crossed, a shit-eating grin on his face.

Fury burst through me like gasoline on a fire and I flew out of the truck. "What the fuck are you doing?"

He didn't move. "Stopping you."

"You jumped out in front of me, you dumbass. I could have fucking killed you."

He scoffed, like that was both ridiculous and amusing. "You weren't going to hit me. Plus, I walked very calmly into the road, I didn't jump."

Surging in, I grabbed his shirt at his throat. He didn't even flinch. I wanted to shout at him. To tell him how stupid he was. That I could have killed him, and how would I ever have lived with myself if I had. But his lack of reaction took the wind out of my sails. He looked at me like nothing was wrong.

I let go of his shirt and he shifted his shoulders to straighten it. "You can be a scary motherfucker when you want to be, you know that?"

"I didn't think you were scared of anything."

He grinned at me again.

"Are you done?"

"Nah, bro, I'm just getting started."

"With what?"

"Keeping your scary ass from going to prison again." He patted my shoulder. "Let's go."

He climbed into the passenger seat of the truck. I gaped at him for a second or two. A car approached from the opposite direction and honked. I was parked diagonally across the street. With a groan, I got in, put it in drive, and got back in my lane.

"You jumped out in front of me on purpose?"

"Obviously it was on purpose. Do you think I'm stupid?"

"How is walking into oncoming traffic *not* stupid?"

"Hey man, I'm not the one who just dropped by the Timberbeast by himself."

"How the hell do you know about that? And how did you know where I'd be?"

"It's a small town, dude, everyone knows everything."

I glared at him.

"Grace activated the Bailey alert system. She said, and I quote..." He paused to get his phone out of his pocket. "'Asher just left Cara's and I'm afraid of what he's going to do. He looked like he wanted to go kill someone and I don't use that phrase lightly.'"

"Seriously?"

"Yeah, man. I was closest, so I said I'd head you off."

"And your solution was to throw yourself in front of me so I'd almost run you over?"

"It was a rush, dude, I'm not gonna lie. Don't go that way, turn left."

"Why?"

"I just risked my damn life for you, turn left."

I had no idea why I was listening to him, but I turned. "I'm probably going to regret this, but where are you trying to make me go?"

"The Arena."

I looked at him like he must be crazy.

"Come on, man, I'm terrible at interpreting nonverbal communication. What does that look mean? Because in my head, it could mean you're surprised that the Arena is still there. Or maybe it means you don't remember it, but that seems less likely."

"I remember it."

The Arena had started as a thing, rather than a place. It was what we'd called the boxing matches Gram had resorted to when we'd fought too much as kids.

When we'd gotten older, it had turned into an aggressive version of rock, paper, scissors. And to keep Gram from finding out, we'd taken it to a clearing out near the lake. By then, we were all taking martial arts. Teenage boys with fighting skills squaring off was a lot different than an eight- and nine-year-old, or seven-year-old twins, throwing some punches with big padded boxing gloves. But whenever a big enough issue arose between any of us brothers, we'd taken it out to the Arena.

There was no way I was going toe to toe with any of them now. No fucking way.

"Unless you tell me someone's dragging the Haven brothers out there so I can beat the shit out of them, the answer is no."

"This isn't a Haven problem, Ash. This is Bailey business."

"The fuck it is. I don't have an issue with any of you."

"Yeah, well maybe we have a fucking problem with you."

"I'm not fighting out there."

He chuckled, his demeanor still completely nonchalant. "It's so funny how you think you have a choice."

"I'm not going."

"Let me make something perfectly clear." He shifted on the seat so he was facing me. "We're going. You can drive, or you can try to get out of it. But if I have to knock you out cold, hog-tie you, toss you in the back, and handcuff you to the truck, I'll do it. You think you're stubborn? I'm fucking relentless."

His eyes were wild, the sort of crazy a guy couldn't fake. He wasn't kidding.

Without another word, I drove us out to the Arena.

Levi and Logan were already there, sitting on the tailgate of Logan's truck. Evan stood with his arms crossed next to his motorcycle. I parked beside Logan, and we got out.

"Damn it." Logan jumped off the tailgate and dug his wallet out of his pocket. He threw a bill at Gavin and it fluttered to the ground. "Didn't he even put up a fight?"

Gavin scooped it up and cheerfully tucked it in his pocket. "I'm very convincing."

"You bet on whether I'd come?"

"We bet on whether I'd be able to get you out here by myself," Gavin said. "Easy money."

"I'm fucking disappointed in you," Logan said, pointing at me. "Did you even make him work for it?"

"What the hell are we doing out here?" I asked, squinting in the bright sun.

The Arena was in a flat clearing surrounded by scrubby pines. The low undergrowth gave the ground a little padding. Not as much as a real ring or training mats, but enough that when a match inevitably went to the ground, we were less likely to get hurt. Fallen branches we'd stripped and sunk into the ground years ago still stood in the four corners, marking the boundaries of our makeshift ring.

"We're keeping you out of trouble," Logan said.

"Your fuse keeps getting shorter." Levi hopped off the tailgate. "We've known this was coming for a while. You want to get some shit out? Let's do it here where it doesn't end with you in goddamn handcuffs again."

"No."

"So we should just let you rampage around town looking for a fight?"

I crossed my arms, but that was exactly what I'd been doing. What I still wanted to do. "How the fuck do you know what I was doing?"

"You went to the Timberbeast, right?" Levi asked. "Like I said, man, we saw this coming. You've been acting like a psycho since the fire at Grace's house."

"Don't fucking talk about her."

Levi gestured at me. "A ringing endorsement for your stability right there."

Evan took a few casual steps closer. "When a wolf starts going rogue, the pack has to deal with him. I hate those asshole Havens, but you go after them now, like this, and you'll start a war. We're not letting that happen."

"Who brought the gloves?" Gavin asked.

Levi reached into a duffel bag in the bed of Logan's truck and tossed a pair of fingerless padded gloves to Gavin, then another to me.

"I'm not doing this. You guys don't get it."

"So it's cool if you lose your temper and go try to pick a fight—by yourself, I might add—with guys who won't hesitate to hurt you," Logan said. "But you can't spar with your brother out here?"

"No."

"To be fair, we probably shouldn't call it sparring," Gavin said, adjusting the strap on one of his gloves. "Because I'm going to fucking hit him for real."

Logan laughed.

"Your funeral," Evan said with a skeptical glance at Gavin.

"I can take him," Gavin said. "And now you'll all know."

"Gav, you're nuts, man," Logan said. "I still say we should do this two on one."

Gavin eyed me with that wild-eyed expression. It was unnerving. "Nope. I got this."

Logan nudged me with his elbow. "I'd put my gloves on if I were you. He's dead serious."

"I'm not fighting him."

"Yeah, well, he's going to fight you. I guess you can decide whether to fight back, but I would. He's good."

"Hold up." Evan raised a hand. "Rules."

"We don't need rules," Gavin said.

"We always have rules," Levi said. "No bare knuckles. No cheap shots to the nuts. No knock-outs. Submissions only."

Gavin tapped the pads of his gloves together and bounced up and down on his toes a few times. "Fine."

I stared Gavin down. I did not want to do this. "Do you have any idea how many fights I won in prison?"

"How many were knock-outs?" he asked.

"Most of them."

He shrugged. "Can't knock me out. That means you gotta make me tap out. You might look scary, big brother, but you're out of practice. And I'm not."

Anger and fear vied for dominance inside me. The rage was hot and addictive. Even though I wasn't angry at Gavin, I knew it would feel good to let it out.

But I was afraid of what I'd do to him. Afraid I couldn't do this without losing control.

In all those fights I'd won in prison, I hadn't stopped a single one myself. It had always been guards or other inmates pulling me off my opponent.

Did I have enough control left to grapple with my brother?

Blinking, I realized Evan was shoving the gloves on my hands.

"Let's get this over with. I have shit to do."

I jerked my hands away and finished strapping them on. I flexed my fingers a few times. It had been a long time since I'd done this with gloves on.

"Come on," Gavin said.

The rest of them backed away. We weren't quite in the marked-off area, but apparently Gavin didn't care. He took a quick step forward and popped me right in the nose.

"What the fuck?" I roared.

"Oh shit, he actually did it," Logan said.

Gavin backed up past the corner markers and beckoned for me to follow.

"Fine. Fuck it."

I stalked toward him and threw a right hook. He put his hands up to guard his centerline and dodged. I stayed on the offensive, harassing him around the Arena, making him back up and change directions. Although I threw punches, I wasn't really trying to hit him. Gloves or not, I wasn't going to punch my brother.

He had no such qualms. His fist landed below my chin in a swift uppercut, making my teeth rattle. He hit me again, scoring a punch to my ribs. I absorbed the blows, barely flinching.

"Is that all you've got?" I asked.

Gavin smiled.

Putting my arms up to guard my head, I twisted back and forth while he tried to land another punch. He hit hard, but I could take a lot of this. I'd always been able to take a hit, but prison had hardened me. I lured him closer, answering with a half-powered punch for every three he threw.

With a burst of speed and power, I surged in. I wrapped an arm around his torso and pressed my head against him. Before he could react, I hooked his front thigh, yanking it up while I drove hard with my legs. We rolled to the ground, but I had control.

Logan shouted instructions at Gavin from the side. We grunted as we pushed and pulled against each other, gaining holds, breaking grips, constantly shifting positions. Just when I thought I had the upper hand, he twisted away. The little shit was making me work for it.

Clarity started to flow through me as I grappled with him. My anger ran deep, but something about this primal struggle for physical dominance filled a need I'd been desperately trying to suppress. As if my very bones and muscles craved it. I'd been denying what this did for me, but out here, in the clover and scratchy grass, I gave in to it. Fought against an opponent trying to control me.

And it felt really fucking good.

Gavin was right—I was out of practice, and he was not. I teetered between restraint and anger, trying to hold on to myself while I fought. The longer we grappled, the more I tipped toward rage. Toward unleashing everything I had, overpowering him at any cost.

He got his forearm around my throat, close to trapping me in a choke. For a second, I couldn't get any air. Like a switch had flipped, my survival instinct exploded. I broke his grip, turned into him, and manhandled him to his back.

Less than a second later, I found myself on top of him, my body weight holding him down, my fist flying toward his face.

I pulled back the punch, stopping myself before I could break his nose. Or worse.

He took full advantage of my hesitation. A few perfectly executed moves later, he had me in a blood choke. I could breathe, but with the pressure he was putting on my neck, I had about ten seconds before I'd pass out cold.

I tapped his arm with my free hand and he immediately released.

Breathing hard, I rolled onto my back and stared up at the cloudless blue sky. My knees were scraped bloody and I was covered in dirt and sweat. Gavin caught his breath next to me and to his credit, he didn't gloat. He didn't jump up and celebrate his victory.

That wasn't how we did things.

Instead, he got up first and held out a hand to help me to my feet. I stood and he wrapped his arms around me, hugging me tight.

I hugged him back, feeling no shame at my loss. I'd deserved to lose today. They'd been right to bring me out here, and the outcome was as it should have been. Evan had said it best. When one of the pack went rogue, the others had to deal with him.

I wasn't going to cause more trouble for my family. From now on, I was going to do what I could to make sure I didn't cause more trouble for anyone. It was the only thing left I could do.

42

GRACE

I didn't bother Cara after Asher left. She was busy in her office doing who knows what, so I fired off an emergency text to his brothers, letting them know he was on the loose and I expected the worst. The look in his eyes when he'd driven away had been terrifying. For now, I had to trust them to get him through whatever this was. I hated doing it, but I had to let him go—for the moment, at least. I knew him well enough to know there wasn't anything more I could do.

Besides, he'd just broken up with me. Again. And I was pretty fucking angry about that.

So I went to the kitchen and helped myself to a drink.

She came down about an hour later, while I was mixing drink number three.

"Oh shit. Is this good drinking or bad drinking?"

I added another splash of gin to my glass. "Take a wild guess."

"He freaked out, didn't he?" She rolled her eyes. "I knew he was going to freak out. I don't know how you've been able to stand him the last couple of days. I was this close to popping a Xanax every time I had to be in the same room with him for more than five minutes."

"Yes, he freaked out. Royally freaked out. It was an epic freak-out of gigantic proportions."

She sighed and started mixing herself a gin and tonic. "This would be so much easier if I didn't like him. Then we could just bitch about what a dick he is and how we hate his guts."

"I know."

After dropping a slice of lime in her glass, she hooked her arm through mine. "Come on."

She led me upstairs to her bedroom and we got in her bed, nestling ourselves under the covers.

"Your sheets are like clouds of butter." I rubbed the fabric against my cheek.

"Who says money can't buy happiness?"

"Right? God, how do you ever get guys to leave this bed? If I was naked in these things, I'd never get up."

"You'd be surprised." She took a sip and set her drink down. "On a scale of *babysitting a watered-down vodka club* to *blacking out at a frat party*, how drunk are you?"

I held up my glass. "I'd say by the time I finish this, I'll be at *definitely take my phone away*."

"Good to know. Where is your phone?"

"Downstairs."

"Noted. So what happened?"

Tears instantly flooded my eyes. "He broke up with me. Again."

"What?"

"We went to the house to look at the damage and when we got back here, he said he had to go. So I asked if he'd come back and stay here with me tonight. He told me no."

I sniffed and tried to wipe my eyes. Cara deftly took my

drink.

"Then he said I need to face reality. He can't do this. He can't be a husband or someone's father."

"Well, not with that attitude, he can't."

"He's so convinced he's broken beyond repair."

"Why?" She tilted her head. "I know the basics. He killed a guy who was trying to rape you and then went to prison for it. That's heavy stuff. But I can't help but think there's something else going on here."

"I know. I thought he'd get better when he got used to being home. I swear, I read everything that's ever been written about inmates transitioning back to their lives and none of it prepared me for what it would really be like."

"He needs more therapy than I do. Have you talked to him about that?"

"Yes, but he's so skeptical. And stubborn."

"A stubborn Bailey? You don't say."

"God, I know. It's genetic with those boys."

She adjusted her pillow. "Honest question. Are you sure you should reproduce with him? I thought you were the most stubborn person I knew until I met him. And now it's a toss-up. I'm afraid of what might occur if your DNA is allowed to mix."

"Stop trying to make me laugh."

"I'm being completely serious."

I slumped back against her headboard. "I love him, Cara. I love him so much it hurts."

"I know you do, boo."

"But it used to be so easy. When we were little kids, it was like we'd always been best friends. I never questioned it. And when we got older and started to drift apart, it felt so wrong. I didn't understand why until the night he told me he loved me. Then it was like everything fell into place. We were happily dating, and I knew we were going to get married, even before he proposed. And it's not that every second was perfect. We had our little arguments like anyone would. But everything was easy. It was simple."

"And now it's hard."

My eyes filled with tears again. I didn't bother stopping them. "So hard. I feel like I've had to fight for ground every day since he came home. I'm tired, Cara."

She tucked a strand of hair behind my ear. "I know you are."

"You're right, this would be easier if we hated him. If he was just some guy I'd met who turned out to be a jerk."

"Don't let my outer calm give you the wrong impression. I'm furious with him right now."

"That's good to know. I was starting to worry."

"I never thought I'd say this, but I get why you waited for him. You were right when you said I would have understood if I'd known you before—if I'd seen you together. Because I'm telling you, I used to think that whole soulmates thing was sentimental bullshit. A charming fairytale naïve girls would tell themselves to make themselves feel better about being alone. *Oh, I'm waiting for my soulmate.*" She rolled her eyes.

I laughed softly through my tears.

"But I think for you two, it's real. You're actually soulmates. And it's nothing short of a goddamn tragedy that you're not happily married and making babies right now."

"I don't know what to do." I twisted my ring around my finger. "How many times does he have to break up with me before I get it through my thick head that he means it?"

"The problem is, he doesn't mean it for the right reasons. If he wanted to go find some tattooed biker girl with a record to suit his new ex-con persona, that would be one thing. And reason for me to murder him, just so we're clear. But he loves you just as much as you love him."

"Why does he keep thinking he knows what's best for me?"

"Because he's a guy."

I wiped my cheeks. "I'm so tired of it. He's wrong."

"Okay, don't get mad or cry harder because I already feel bad for saying this, but I think I'd be a shitty friend if I didn't." She pressed her lips together for a second. "What if he isn't wrong?"

"Not wrong about what? You just said we're soulmates."

"Yeah, and in a perfect world you would have become Grace Bailey a long time ago. But he'd still be the old Asher. The reality is, he's not. He's all kinds of fucked up and we both know it. His brothers know it, too. We've all been watching him like a hawk lately, waiting for him to self-destruct. If he doesn't get that under control, maybe he's right. Maybe he shouldn't be a husband and father."

Glancing away, I chewed on my lower lip.

"I don't want that to be true any more than you do. I know how much you want him, and I want you to have him just as much. But what if you want something that's not good for you because you've wanted it for so long you don't question it anymore?"

I felt like crumpling into a ball and falling apart. I didn't want her to be right. But I knew she might be. And I hated it.

"Maybe I should have listened to him the first time," I said, my voice deceptively quiet, a stark contrast to the torrent of grief clawing at my chest. "He told me it was over, but I refused to listen. If I'd accepted it then, none of this would have happened. The worst would have been over a long time ago."

He wouldn't have had to break my heart a second time.

43

GRACE

*T*he air conditioning in my car had barely begun to cut through the scorching summer heat when I turned onto my street. I was more than a little bit hung over after yesterday. Cara and I had stayed in her bed, but around dinnertime, she'd brought the bottles upstairs for easier drink mixing. Hours later, we'd both fallen asleep in our clothes, sprawled out on top of her covers.

Now I was hot and dehydrated, but determined to start the slow process of salvaging what was left of my house so we could start rebuilding.

We being a generic term. It would mostly be me, I presumed, although I'd have to hire a contractor to redo the roof and outer wall. Insurance would help, but this was going to be so much work. And so much money.

I pulled up to my house and a confusing flash of hope and annoyance ran through me. Asher's truck was parked outside.

What was he doing here?

I didn't want to see him right now. My wounds were still too fresh. I was aching and raw and the last thing I needed

was a face-to-face reminder of how much this hurt. I probably should have turned around and left. But instead, I went
inside.

I found him near the kitchen, picking through the
burned-out debris.

"What are you doing?"

He stood and brushed his hands together. "Figured I'd
help clear things out."

"Why?"

"Because it's a lot of work and you need the help."

Maybe I should have been grateful, but the man had
broken up with me yesterday. I wasn't in the mood for gratitude, even if I did need the help.

"You don't have to do that."

"I'm going to anyway. It's the least I can do."

I clenched my teeth. God, he was so stubborn. "What is
this, a way to ease your guilt? You're still convinced this is
somehow your fault, so if you help clean up, that'll make
everything better?"

He didn't answer. Just looked at me. Which only made
me angrier.

"I don't need your help. Go home."

He flinched like I'd slapped him. "Grace—"

"No. I don't need you."

"Just let me help."

The pain in his eyes reflected mine. This was killing us
both and it made me furious.

And I snapped.

"I waited for you for seven fucking years." I knew it had
nothing to do with what he'd just said, but the words
tumbled out just the same. "And now I'm realizing everyone
who thought I was crazy or stupid was right. I should have
listened to you that day in the sheriff's office. You laid it out

for me. You told me the truth. You said it had to be over. But did I listen? Nope. I dug my heels in and convinced myself this was just a bump in the road."

I paused to swallow and wipe my cheeks. It was hard to speak clearly but I couldn't stop this avalanche of emotion.

"I used to imagine your release day. When things were hard or I was missing you more than usual, I'd stare out the window and picture it. They'd open that big gate and you'd come walking out. And I'd be standing there next to my car, wearing something cute I'd picked out for the first time you saw me again. I'd run right into your open arms and you'd hold me and it would mean we'd never have to be apart like that again. But that was just a stupid fantasy."

"I tried, Grace. I wanted to make this work for you, but I can't."

"You didn't try," I shot back.

"What else do you expect me to do?"

"Get some fucking help. Would it have killed you to just talk to someone?"

He crossed his arms and his jaw hitched. "You never have."

"We're not talking about me."

"Maybe we should. I know I'm fucked up, but you can't even admit that you are."

"What is that supposed to mean?"

"When was the last time you went out in public by yourself?"

I clenched my teeth, getting angrier by the second. "It's not that big of a deal. I'm not the one sabotaging my relationships."

"Maybe not, but don't get after me to talk to some fucking therapist when you can't even acknowledge that you have a problem."

"Fine. You don't need therapy. Or maybe we both do. I don't care anymore. You don't want to be in my life anyway, so it doesn't matter."

"Grace, I—"

"No. I'm done. You said it's over, and I'm listening to you this time. Because I can't keep doing this." Reality was hitting me square in the face. This was really it. I twisted his ring off my finger. "You have to go. This house isn't your responsibility. I'm not your responsibility. You can't be with me? Fine. Then we're done."

His dark brow furrowed and his hands clenched into fists. He looked down at the ring pinched between my thumb and forefinger.

He'd hurt me. Deeply. I'd put that hurt away, believing in the very deepest place in my soul that he would heal that wound someday.

And then he didn't. He tore it open again, leaving me raw and bleeding.

So I looked down at that ring, opened my fingers, and watched it fall to the debris-littered floor.

Then I turned and walked away.

I WAS TOO angry to cry. Or maybe I'd cried myself out last night. But I drove into town feeling hollow, like I had a gaping hole in my chest.

Which I did. It was where my heart used to be.

Pain and grief were exhausting, so I clung to anger. He'd had the audacity to say *I* needed help, when he was such a disaster? He was right, I hadn't been out in public alone. But I was going to prove to myself, once and for all, that I could. Asher was wrong.

I drove to the hardware store and found the closest parking spot to the entrance. No lingering in the back area of the lot where I had an easy escape. No changing my mind and deciding I needed lunch first. I was going inside.

And then the fear stormed in.

It didn't slip through like smoke creeping in the cracks around a door. It barreled into me so hard it took my breath away.

But it was not going to win.

Gritting my teeth, I got out and slammed my car door shut. I marched through the automatic doors, hearing their soft whir as they slid open.

It smelled like freshly-cut wood—such a familiar scent. I'd been here dozens of times since I'd bought my house. Usually with Cara, but sometimes one or two of Asher's brothers. Jack had come a few times, too. I'd always found a reason to bring someone along.

A customer was checking out, keeping the one cashier busy. The rest of the store seemed quiet. I knew from experience there were probably other customers wandering the wide aisles, pushing carts, loading them with tools, hardware, and household supplies.

This was fine.

I took a deep breath, swallowed hard, and kept walking.

My hands shook, so I shoved them into the too-small pockets of my shorts. I wanted to buy something—to force myself not to run out the front door—but I couldn't think of anything I needed. Which was ridiculous, because I needed just about everything. I had a house to rebuild.

Cabinets. Maybe I'd look at the kitchen displays. I could even snap a few pictures for ideas, if I could hold my hands steady enough to take a clear shot. Then I'd grab a few things on the way out, make my purchase, and call it a success.

I could do this.

I turned down an aisle lined with countertop samples. My heart beat too fast and my hands wouldn't stop trembling. The shelves went so high, all the way to the ceiling. Like a wall.

The walls of an alley.

The alley where I'd—

I gasped and clutched my stomach. It felt like I might vomit. I looked around, firmly telling myself where I was. That these were samples of marble and granite, not the sides of buildings bathed in the dirty light of a single bulb.

But it didn't matter. I was vulnerable. Alone.

I had to get out of here.

The automatic doors slid open as I raced outside. It probably looked like I'd just shoplifted something, but I didn't care. I had to get away—had to outrun this feeling. This fear. I was so alone.

I got in my car, slammed the door shut, and locked it. My hands shook violently and tears streaked down my face. What the hell had just happened? What was wrong with me?

I never thought about that night. Not that part, at least. I could see the rest. The moment when the cops had led Asher away in handcuffs. But the alley? I'd blocked it out. Gotten rid of those awful memories.

Oh my god. I had blocked it out. But I hadn't gotten rid of anything. It was all still there, deep inside me.

The realization hit me as hard as the fear, like a storm breaking in my chest. I'd been assaulted, and I'd never dealt with it.

How could I be oblivious for so long and then see it so clearly in an instant?

I'd ignored the fact that a group of men had been seconds away from raping me in an alley. It had seemed insignificant in the face of everything else. Asher's arrest and detainment. The murder charges. The plea bargain. His eight-year sentence.

Once he'd been sent to prison, I'd kept my focus on him. After all, I hadn't actually been raped. He'd stopped it from happening. He was the one suffering, not me. He was behind bars, living through hell. I was out here, free to do as I pleased. I was fine.

And I'd found a million ways to ignore my own trauma. Finishing college. My friendship with Cara. Work. Martial arts training. Remodeling my house. Crocheting. I'd filled my time thoroughly, never leaving room to face what had happened to me.

Spreading the fingers of my still-trembling left hand, I looked at the bare spot where Asher's ring had been. At the indent left behind. And I wanted to punch the dashboard just like he had yesterday. I wanted to scream, and cry, and rage at the world. Because none of this was fair.

I wished I could go to him now. I craved the solace of his arms around me with a desperation that I could hardly bear.

But I couldn't do that to myself. Even if he comforted me tonight, tomorrow he'd break my heart again. And there were only so many times I could put myself through that. Only so many times I could live through the wound in my soul being ripped open before I broke apart completely.

44
———

ASHER

*P*rison had made me an expert at compartmentalization. I was able to focus on one thing almost exclusively, putting everything else away. I'd kept my attention on the present, whether it was one of the useless group therapy sessions, or watching the guys most likely to start trouble out in the yard. Everything else had been put away, tucked into a separate place in my brain where it couldn't interfere. Couldn't make me weak.

In the aftermath of ending things with Grace, I drew on that skill. I put her away and focused on work.

Or I tried to. Now I sucked at it.

No matter how hard I tried to keep my mind on the fence I was building for Mrs. Dickerson so her yippy dog could run around without terrorizing the rest of the neighborhood, I couldn't stop thinking about Grace.

I told myself, for the millionth time, that I hadn't overreacted. I'd been calm and collected. No longer panicked from the stress of hurting her, or the fire. It had been days. My head had been clear. It had been the right thing to do. The only thing I could do.

So why did everything feel so horribly wrong?

There wasn't another alternative. Although it had gutted me to leave her the first time, and it was gutting me to do it again, I couldn't keep pretending I was fine. I wasn't.

I finished for the day and let Mrs. Dickerson know I'd be back tomorrow. She offered me a cookie, which after yesterday, I knew to politely decline. I was pretty sure she'd mistaken salt for sugar, and it had been all I could do to swallow the bite I'd taken so I didn't hurt her feelings. Today I just told her I wasn't hungry.

My truck was parked out front. I took off my tool belt and tossed it on the passenger's seat. It was hot as fuck out today, and I'd been working in the sun for hours. I downed the rest of my water and wiped my forehead on my arm. I needed a shower, and then a cold beer.

A truck pulled up behind mine and parked. I almost groaned out loud when I saw who it was. Josiah Haven.

Great. Just what I needed today.

He got out wearing a dark t-shirt and dusty jeans, and he had a light sprinkling of sawdust in his facial hair.

My jaw tightened. "What do you want?"

He held his hands up. "Can we parlay?"

"What are we, fucking pirates?"

"I'm trying to wave the white flag here, Bailey. I just want to talk."

"Fine. What?"

He took a deep breath and glanced around, like he wanted to make sure we weren't seen talking to each other. "The thing with your grandpa's truck was out of line. We shouldn't have done it."

That was a surprise. No Haven had ever apologized for a prank—nor the other way around. At least, not in my lifetime.

I furrowed my brow, but gave him a short nod. "Okay."

"It's one thing to put a beard on Lola or run a Haven flag up the flagpole in front of City Hall or whatever stupid shit we come up with. But Grace was right, that was too personal. I don't want to start a war over it."

I hesitated a beat before answering. I didn't want this to escalate any more than he did. "Neither do I."

He held out his hand and I shook it.

"Thanks." He turned to go back to his truck, but paused and looked over his shoulder. "By the way, any of us would have done the same thing if it had been our girl. It sucks you had to get locked up for it."

That really took me by surprise. "Thanks, man."

He tipped his chin to me and got back in his truck.

Well, holy shit.

I glanced down at my water bottle. I'd gripped it so hard, I'd put a dent in it. I really needed to get a handle on my anger.

As if that wasn't the understatement of the decade.

I checked my phone, stupidly hoping I'd have a text from Grace, but knowing I wouldn't. And knowing that it was entirely my fault.

I'd thought once I broke things off, I'd at least feel a sense of closure. I wasn't leading her on, letting her believe I could be someone I wasn't. All I'd done was tell her the truth. That was supposed to have helped.

But I felt worse than ever.

I did have a text, but it wasn't from Grace. It was from Chief Stanley, asking if I had time to get together. I replied and we made plans to meet at the Caboose in an hour.

≈

WALKING into the Caboose was a stark reminder that I couldn't go anywhere in this town without encountering Grace. She wasn't here, but the restaurant was filled with memories of her. Playing pool. Snacking on greasy bar food. Meeting up with friends, or my brothers. We'd been here together a hundred times—both before my prison sentence and after—and now I couldn't associate this place with anything but her.

The entire fucking town was like that. She was everywhere.

The chief was already here with two beers on the table. I tried to ignore the onslaught of memories, the relentless pull that Grace had on me, and joined him.

"Thanks for the beer," I said and took a sip.

"Sure. Thanks for meeting me. I wanted to see how you're doing."

I looked away. That was a loaded fucking question. "I'm all right."

He scrutinized me for a few seconds, then nodded slowly. "Okay. How's work?"

"Busy. I'm holding my own. I'll be back on my feet soon."

"Glad to hear it."

I had a feeling he was one step from asking me about Grace, so I quickly tried to change the subject. "How's Skylar?"

"She's good. Moved back in with her mom about a month ago."

"Oh yeah? Have you seen them recently?"

"I have, actually. I drove out there last week to spend some time with Skylar. We had a good visit. Wound up taking them both to dinner, which I hadn't exactly planned, but..." He trailed off, lifting one shoulder in a shrug.

"Do you get along with your ex these days?"

He made a noncommittal noise in his throat and took a swig of beer. "Yes and no. We seem to do all right in small doses, but more than that is asking for trouble. I do my best to behave myself for Skylar's sake."

I wasn't sure why, but I suddenly wondered if Chief Stanley only missed his daughter. Maybe he missed his ex-wife a little bit, too.

A server brought a large basket of onion rings and set it on the table.

"Thanks," I said.

"I was hungry and didn't want to wait, so I ordered before you got here," he said with a quick wink. "Now tell me how you're really doing."

"I told you I'm fine."

"That's a crock of shit." He cracked a smile, but I could tell he'd come here with an agenda, and now he wasn't going to let it go. "I was at the scene, Asher. I saw what happened, and I saw you. If you're doing fine after that, there's something wrong with you."

"Why? I went in and got her out. Firefighters do that kind of thing all the time. You don't take your guys out for a beer every time they answer a call."

"I would if they'd pulled their girlfriend out of a fire. And if they'd looked like you did afterward."

"I'd been up half the night. I was tired. And yeah, I was stressed. I was out walking, and when I got back, there was smoke pouring out the back of her house. It was crazy."

"And why were you out walking before dawn?"

I stilled, looking him dead in the eyes. "I didn't hit her on purpose. She startled me awake and my elbow hit her nose."

"I know. I wasn't implying you hit her. I'm wondering why you're so jumpy when you sleep."

"It was just an accident. Her face was too close."

He raised an eyebrow.

I took a drink of my beer.

"Word travels fast in this town, Asher."

"Yeah, I'm aware."

"Then it won't surprise you that I know Grace Miles no longer wears an engagement ring."

I ground my teeth together. "With all due respect, Chief, that's our business."

"You're right. And I don't know the whole story. But I see the road you're traveling down and I can't help but worry you're setting yourself up for a heap of regret."

"I live with regret every day."

"So why add to it? Look, I'm not here to tell you I know what's best for you. Or that I know the reasons you two are having problems. But I do know you. I've known you since you were born. I've also been around the block a few times, and I'd like to think I've learned a few lessons along the way. Just be careful. Hindsight is a powerful thing, and I'd hate for you to look back and realize you made mistakes that can't be fixed."

Right now, I felt like my entire life was a mistake that couldn't be fixed. "Yeah, okay."

He eyed me like he wasn't sure I was hearing his message, but he didn't press it further. And I knew there was truth to what he was telling me. I already had to live with a shit ton of regret. But there wasn't anything else I could do about that now, except learn how to live with the burden, and the demons that still haunted me.

45

ASHER

*A*nother day went by and the emptiness inside me only grew.

I finished building Mrs. Dickerson's fence, avoided having to eat another questionable-looking cookie, and decided to go to the gym. Even after working hard all day, I had too much energy. I needed to burn some of it off or I'd never get to sleep tonight.

The slight tang of sweat in the air and the sound of gloves hitting bags greeted me when I walked in. My hands twitched. Ever since I'd grappled with Gavin, I'd wondered if I'd been wrong. I'd gone into it angry, and that choke hold had set me off. But I hadn't lost control. If that had been a fight in the prison yard, I would have pummeled his face until someone dragged me off him. But I'd stopped.

I glanced at the caged-in ring at the back. At the practice mats with students and coaches working together. Was there a chance that I could take this up again? That maybe I could relearn control?

My body craved it. There was something about pitting

my will against someone else's—the struggle to defeat an opponent. Grappling with Gavin had been cathartic. I'd felt better afterward, even though I'd lost.

Working with Elijah had felt good, too, but in a different way. It had been satisfying to pass on what I knew, especially to a great kid like him.

I'd been so afraid to unleash the darkness inside of me. I still was. But I had to face the fact that burying it hadn't worked.

Could I accept it? Live with it as a part of me?

I didn't know.

Jack Cordero was on one of the practice mats. He was dressed in a gray t-shirt and shorts, and he wasn't working with another adult. It was a kid.

Holy shit. That was Elijah.

I watched as Jack corrected his form, then took him through a short sequence of moves. They finished and Elijah jumped to his feet, his hair damp and messy. He held out a hand for Jack.

Jack took it and stood, then patted him on the shoulder.

I was totally unprepared for the rush of emotion that filled my chest. Looking away, I cleared my throat.

"Hey, Asher." Jack came toward me and raised his hand in a greeting. Elijah either hadn't seen me, or didn't want to. I saw him disappear into the locker room.

"Jack," I said with a nod.

"I'm glad I ran into you. I need to thank you for working with Elijah the way you did."

"Yeah, of course. Sorry I didn't ask you or Naomi first. I just figured I could show him a few things."

"That's all right. Under normal circumstances, I think Naomi would have wanted to know. But this was obviously what he needed."

"Good to hear it helped." I rubbed the back of my neck. "Did he... did he ask you to bring him here? Or was this your idea?"

"Both, I suppose. He piped up one night at dinner and told us you'd been teaching him to grapple. He started naming moves and telling us about things you'd talked about. I think he said more to us that night than he'd said in the last year. It was like you broke him wide open. He was afraid we'd be mad, but he seemed to relax when he realized we weren't. Then he said something about me working out here at the gym and I had this feeling he was giving me an in. So I went for it. Anyway, I hope I'm not stepping on your toes. You were basically his coach and I didn't mean to take over."

"No, not at all. I'm glad you did. He needs this. He needs you."

"Thanks, Asher." He held out his hand and I shook it. "I appreciate that."

Elijah came up next to Jack and shoved his hands in the pockets of his gym shorts. "Hi."

"Hey, big man," I said.

Jack patted him on the shoulder. "I need to go grab my bag. I'll be right out."

Elijah nodded. He wasn't exactly effusive, but he made eye contact.

"How've you been?" I asked. "Learning a lot?"

"Yeah." He glanced down at the floor for a second, then back up at me. "I saw those kids again."

"The little shits?"

His mouth twitched in a smile. "Yeah, them."

"What happened?"

"It was weird. They tried to start trouble, but I wasn't really scared of them. I just thought about what I'd do if one of them got close enough. And then none of them did. They stopped and left."

"Assholes like that try to prey on the weak. They could see you're not."

He smiled and the pride shining in his eyes made my throat feel thick again.

"So, thanks for teaching me stuff. And, um, I was wondering if maybe I could still come over sometimes. If you need help working on your truck or anything."

Damn it, this kid was going to make me cry. "Yeah, bud. Anytime."

"Thanks."

Holding my arm out, I beckoned him closer. "Come here, kiddo. Baileys always hug it out."

I expected him to give me a quick side hug, but he wrapped his arms around my waist. I squeezed him and let go. He gave me one more smile, then ran off to find Jack.

I GOT HOME and found Gram on the back porch, sitting in her rocking chair. Her hands rested on the sides and she tipped it back and forth with her toes, the wood creaking with her gentle motion. She hummed a song, a wordless tune I'd heard countless times.

She met my eyes with a smile. "Come sit."

I needed to fix myself some dinner, and a shower wasn't a bad idea either. But I went outside and lowered myself into the chair next to her.

"What troubles you, Bear?"

My first instinct was to say *nothing*, or *I'm fine*, but I didn't bother lying to her. Instead, I stared out at the darkness for a while. At the chicken coop and her gardens. At the way the land sloped toward the creek, and kept right on going up into the mountain peaks. At the dim shapes of distant pines, barely visible in the darkness.

"I didn't want to hurt Grace again," I said, finally, my voice quiet. "But I told her I can't marry her. If I didn't do it now, I'd only be delaying the inevitable."

"It probably feels that way. But there's not much that's really inevitable."

"Like death and taxes?"

"Oh, sure, there's that. But I'd say love is, too."

"I wish it were that easy. Just love someone and the rest takes care of itself."

She laughed softly. "It's never that easy, Bear."

"It was for us."

"Until it wasn't."

I shifted in my chair. "That's what I mean. Back then, all I had to do was love her. And now, no matter what I do, I can't win. Either I hold onto her and she suffers because of me, or I let her go so she at least has a chance at happiness, but I lose her."

"If that's how you see it, then that's how it is."

"What's that supposed to mean?"

"It means you're convinced you see things the only way they can be seen. Tell me something. If I asked you to describe a tree, what would you say?"

"I don't know. A tree has a wooden trunk that grows out of the ground. The trunk has branches spreading out from the center, with leaves or needles on them."

"If an eagle could talk and I asked him to describe a tree, what do you think he'd say?" She paused for a second. "A tree looks awfully different from above than it does from the ground. But even though his description might sound nothing like yours, neither of you would be wrong."

"I've tried to see this differently. But every time I do, I *am* wrong."

She went quiet for a moment, the only sound the creak of the wood beneath her chair. The rhythm of it was soothing, calling back to deep memories from my childhood. Evenings like this spent with her on the back porch, listening to stories told by moonlight.

"You know, Grandad and I almost didn't get married."

I looked over at her. "What?"

"Mm hmm. It's a good thing he didn't believe in no-win situations."

"What happened?"

She looked down at her hands in her lap. At the wedding ring she still wore. "Frank Bailey was a man who never hesitated to go after what he wanted. That will of his would not be denied. As a child, he terrorized his mother because of it, but his parents knew better than to try to break him. They simply did their best to teach him to use his powers for good."

"Really? He always seemed so laid back."

"Oh, he was. He was friendly and easygoing. But that didn't mean he wasn't determined. Once that man got something in his head, that was it." She paused for a moment, tipping the chair with her toes. "And then one day, Frank Bailey got it into his head that what he wanted was me."

I watched her, fascinated. She'd told plenty of stories about Grandad, especially since he'd passed. But I'd never heard this one.

"That could have been simple enough. A man falls in love with a woman and she falls in love right back. They decide they want to get married. Easy. That's how it's done. But there was a problem."

"What problem?"

"Frank Bailey was a white boy. And in those days, white boys didn't date Indian girls. And they certainly didn't marry them."

"Really? His family didn't want him to be with you?"

"Oh, it wasn't just his family. We got it from both sides. The Baileys were not too keen on Frank fraternizing with Miss Emma Luscier, with her dark skin and long black hair. And my family was furious at me for running around town with a white boy."

"How old were you?"

"Eighteen. Frank was nineteen. We were old enough that we could have just run off and eloped, to hell with everyone."

"But you didn't?"

"I wanted to. I was positive that was the only solution. His family would never accept me, and my family would never accept him. And not marrying Frank Bailey had ceased to be an option for me. Come hell or high water, I was going to marry that man."

"I thought you said Grandad was the determined one."

Her mouth twitched in a smile. "We both had it in us, but he wasn't just determined to marry me. He was determined to marry me in front of the whole town. And everyone, including our parents, would be nothing but over the moon with happiness about it."

"So he wouldn't elope?"

"He flat-out refused. I said we only had two options. We could make our parents happy by going our separate ways, which of course neither of us wanted. Or we could elope, and deal with the fallout, whatever that might be. Neither of us really wanted that, either, considering we knew we'd probably be disowned by both families. The way I saw it, we could keep our families, or we could keep each other, but we couldn't have both."

"But Grandad didn't agree?"

She shook her head. "He most certainly did not. I don't know if there was anything in the world that could rile him up like the feeling of being caught between a rock and a hard place. He simply refused to accept that we had to choose between our families and each other."

"So what did he do?"

"A better question would be, what *didn't* he do. He courted me openly, for all the town to see. But he didn't just court me—he courted my family. Some of that was simply showing them the sort of man he was by treating me like a lady. But when he sent me flowers, he'd send some to my mother, too. He found out the sorts of things that interested my father, and he learned all about them, so they'd have things to talk about.

"Eventually he was going on hunting and fishing trips with my father and uncles. He was stopping by to share tea and frybread with my mother. And he worked his Frank Bailey magic on his parents, too. He started by enchanting them with stories about the forest and the mountains, then springing it on them at the end that they were the tales of my people. He brought me to his house for tea or for dinner so they could get to know me. He seemed to know, intuitively, that both sides needed to see the other in a new light. See each other as people, same as them."

"How long did that last?"

"Three years."

"Are you serious? You already knew you wanted to get

married, but you waited three years so both sets of parents would give you their blessing?"

"Yes we did. For three years, we chipped away at the deeply ingrained prejudices both our families held against each other. And let me tell you, Bear, the day I wed Frank Bailey, I knew every minute had been worth it. The whole town turned out. We held it in the park because there wasn't anywhere else that was big enough for all our guests. And right up front, while the minister led us through our vows, stood my mother and father, side by side with his. Our mothers cried together. Our fathers shook hands in friendship."

I blew out a breath. "Wow."

"Frank knew there was another way of seeing our situation. He soared on the wind like an eagle and looked down, instead of staying stuck on the ground. And he was willing to do whatever it took to make things right. To find a way out of that rock and hard place. Do you know why?"

"Because he was stubborn?"

She chuckled. "He was that. But no. It was because he believed in love. More than anyone I've ever known, he believed that love was more powerful than anything. And Frank loved me big. He loved me so big, he was convinced that it would be enough."

"And he was right."

"He was, although it wasn't just his love that was big enough. The real magic was in our love together. That was what made us unstoppable. What allowed us to turn a no-win situation on its head."

"That's amazing, Gram."

"He was an amazing man."

"He really was. It must be hard to live without him."

"I miss him every single day. But like I said, his love was

big. He left me with enough to last until the day I'm called home and get to see him again."

I let out another breath to ease the tightness in my chest. Gram grew quiet, her chair coming to a stop. I thought she might be getting ready to go inside, but instead, she spoke.

"Grace's love is awfully big, Bear. For a long time, it was big enough for both of you."

"I love her too, Gram. Me not loving her isn't the problem."

"Of course not. You've loved her since you were a boy."

I scrubbed my hands over my face. She wasn't wrong.

"The problem is, you're carrying around all that anger and pain. Your wounds are deep, and the first was inflicted a long time ago."

"I know, but losing Mom and Dad hurt everybody."

"Yes. Losing them wounded all of us. But now you have more hurts—and those new wounds, they're painful. The thing about pain, whether it's physical or not, it demands our attention. A lot of the time that's as it should be. We move our hand away from a flame to avoid being burned, or we treat an injury so our body can heal. But when that pain doesn't go away, and it's not something we can easily fix, it starts to dominate our life. Add in a hefty dose of anger, especially anger at things you can't change, and it's easy to forget how to feel anything else."

"It's hard to remember there is anything else."

"But there is. Grace has been trying to show you the only way she knows how. By loving you through this. She's a bit like Grandad. She doesn't see your anger and pain as an obstacle that can't be overcome, any more than he saw our parents' prejudice as something we had to accept. You have your feet on the ground and you're staring at the trunk of the tree. But she's soaring above it. You're both looking at the

same thing, but she sees a side of it that you don't. So maybe you need to look at it through her eyes."

"Gram, I don't know if I know how."

"Sure you do. Imagine what life would be like if your love for each other was bigger than anything else. What would you do? Because I can assure you that it is. You just have to open your eyes and see it."

"What if it's too late for that?"

"Maybe it is. Maybe it isn't. There's only one way to find out." She did get up, then, smoothing down her clothes. Pausing next to me, she put her hand on my shoulder. "Goodnight, Bear."

"Goodnight, Gram. I love you."

Her eyes crinkled with her gentle smile. "I love you too."

I stayed outside on the porch until well into the night, staring at the darkness. Sitting with my thoughts.

Maybe Gram was right. Maybe my anger and hurt had kept me from seeing things clearly. In prison, I'd believed that I'd lost Grace forever, and part of going home would mean learning to live with that loss. I'd already been convinced I couldn't be with her.

And when I had come home, I'd come face to face with all the ways I'd changed—none of them for the better—and all the things that had changed here. None of it had felt like it could ever fit together again.

But was that the truth, or just the way I'd seen it? And what did Grace see that I couldn't?

What would life be like if our love for each other was bigger than anything else? And what would I do if I believed that were true?

I pulled out my wallet and phone. I had a handful of business cards stuffed inside. Declan's was at the back. I slid it free and eyed it for a long moment, letting that possibility play out in my head.

I'd believed I couldn't fight again. Couldn't even train. It was too dangerous.

But I'd taught Elijah. I'd grappled with Gavin, and even in the face of losing, I hadn't lost control. So maybe I'd been wrong. I knew Declan's offer still stood. I could leave Tilikum. Train to fight professionally. Maybe make a lot of money. Give Grace the space to move on.

It wasn't a real option, and I knew it; and not because I couldn't be a fighter. I tucked his card back inside and pulled out the one I'd really been after.

Grace had quietly left me business cards for several therapists. This one specifically worked with transitioning prisoners. Their office was closed, but I didn't want to put off this call until morning. I needed to act before I could go back to being a stubborn idiot and talk myself out of it. I left a brief message and ended the call, feeling a sense of control beginning to return. Control I hadn't quite realized I'd lost.

I was still skeptical about anyone's ability to help me. But the truth was, refusing to try wasn't any better than giving up.

And Baileys weren't quitters.

Stubborn determination rose from deep inside me. It had been there all along. I'd just let it become twisted and focused on the wrong things. Gram had said nothing had riled up Grandad like being caught between a rock and a hard place. I knew that feeling. That restless drive to see things through. To go through any obstacle. To win.

In prison, I'd done what I felt I had to do to survive. But I wasn't behind bars anymore. I couldn't keep retreating into myself and pushing people away. I couldn't fight my way through life, because in the end, the only person I was really fighting was myself. No wonder I felt like I was going crazy.

What would I do if I believed our love was big enough?

With a deep breath, I got ready to make one more phone call, this one risky. I was going way out on a limb here, but at this point, I had no other choice. I had to go all in. So I brought up Cara's number and hit send.

46

GRACE

*C*ara's car flew down the open highway. She hadn't told me where we were going, but that was typical. It was probably some new spa she wanted to try. In fact, I was hoping it was a new spa she wanted to try. If I had to put on pants and leave the house, I wanted a massage and a facial out of the deal.

Also wine. Plenty of wine.

The last week had been agonizing. It was so much like the beginning of Asher's prison sentence, it almost felt like I was having flashbacks. When they'd first taken him away, the grief of missing him had been sharp and acute. Over time, it had dulled, becoming easier to live with.

Now it was as fresh as the day he'd been led out of the courtroom in handcuffs.

When Cara had first declared that we were going on a spontaneous road trip, I'd told her no. I wanted to spend my day off in pajamas eating junk food, binge-watching the trashiest TV shows I could find, and drinking too much. Usually she was totally supportive of that kind of self-therapy. But she'd forced me to shower, made me put on real clothes, and dragged me out to her car.

I was still deciding how I felt about it. Especially because, so far, there had been no wine.

"You're so fidgety," she said. "Will a manicure get you to stop picking at your fingers?"

I stilled my hands in my lap for about three seconds. My finger felt naked and uncomfortable without the ring I'd worn for so long. I couldn't stop rubbing the indent where it had been.

"I don't think a manicure will help. I'm not messing with my nails. Plus, why do you care?"

She shrugged. "Just an observation."

"Where are we going?"

"You'll see."

"Normally I like it when you surprise me, but I don't think I'm in the mood. I'll enjoy this a lot more if you just tell me what we're doing. To be specific, I'm looking for reassurance that something delicious and highly alcoholic will soon be in my hand. I've had to work, and be sober, for the last five days. I'm over it."

"Don't worry," she said, her tone soothing. "I have it covered."

I leaned my head back against the seat. "Did I tell you I tried to go to the hardware store alone?"

She gasped. "No. What happened? Was I wrong and you were totally fine? Because, for the record, I'd be very happy to be wrong and to discover that you just love me so much you never want to do anything without me."

"Unfortunately, no."

"Damn."

"It was awful. I was terrified. I knew where I was, and I

knew it didn't make any sense. But I ran out of the store and locked myself in my car. How messed up is that?"

She sighed. "My baby's growing up and discovering her neuroses."

"I started looking for a therapist because clearly I need it. Do you have anyone you can recommend?"

"Oh my god, I thought you'd never ask. I have three in mind who I think would be perfect for you. Private practice, but don't worry about insurance or anything. I've got it."

"You're not paying for my therapy."

"Yes I am. It's at least fifty percent my fault that this went on as long as it did. Maybe sixty."

"Cara."

"Don't argue. You won't let me rebuild your house, or buy you a new one. You never let me do anything. Give me this."

I shook my head. "You're so weird."

"I know. I honestly don't know why you like me so much."

"Because you're my person."

"Should we get married?" she asked, glancing at me. "I'm serious. Have you considered it? I wouldn't even make you sign a prenup, which would make my family go insane. Put that as a checkmark in the pro column. And we don't have to have sex or anything. I tried it once with a girl and honestly, it didn't do anything for me. I was bored off my ass. Besides, you're the only woman I've ever known who I can stand to be around for more than like five minutes. Except Gram and the Stitch and Bitch ladies. I can do a couple of hours with them."

"It's Stitch and Sip."

"Whatever. Seriously, though. Maybe we should just put

our own rings on it and be platonic same-sex companions for the rest of our lives."

"That's weirdly tempting. But then you'll meet a man you actually want to marry and you'll have to divorce me. Sounds messy, because without a prenup, I'll definitely take half of everything."

"Meet a man I want to marry?" She threw her head back and laughed. "Oh my god, you're so cute. No. That isn't happening. We do need a provision for dick-getting, though. But since our marriage won't be sexual, that shouldn't be a problem."

I was about to say, *well, since I'm not marrying Asher, I'm never marrying anyone, so why not marry you?* But suddenly it wasn't funny anymore.

We passed a large sign, the words catching my attention from the corner of my eye. I whipped around to look, but we were driving too fast.

I must have read it wrong.

Except...

"Cara?"

"Yeah?"

"Did that sign say *Correctional Facility*?"

"What sign?"

"Cara."

She shrugged. "I didn't see a sign."

"Don't lie to me."

"I'm not lying." She held up her hand, like she was swearing an oath. "I didn't see a sign. I was watching the road and mentally planning our non-lesbian platonic same-sex life-partner wedding. Do you think that's too much to put on the invitation? Also, can I take your last name, because I really like Miles and I don't want to hyphenate."

I narrowed my eyes at her, then glanced around at our

surroundings. I hadn't been paying attention to where we were going. Cara surprised me with little day trips all the time. But this stretch of highway was starting to look oddly familiar.

"Where are you taking me?"

She kept her eyes on the road, and her lips pressed closed.

Another sign came up on the right. Cara pressed the gas, like she'd race past it before I could read it. But it was too late. I'd been right. It said *Washington State Correctional Facility*.

I swallowed hard, a sick feeling spreading through my stomach. "Why are we out here?"

She refused to say a word as she pulled off the highway.

I'd been here before. It had been a long time, but I remembered it clearly. I'd come to visit Asher. I'd gone through the background check and gotten clearance. Waited for what had felt like hours for them to take me into the visiting area. Only to be told Asher wasn't seeing any visitors. He wouldn't come out.

We drove into the visitor parking lot. The tall concrete wall topped with barbed wire loomed over everything. A watchtower jutted above the wall, making the place feel even more harsh and ominous.

I hated this place. It made me sick with rage just to look at it. This was where I'd lost him. Where they'd taken him from me.

"Why are we here?" I asked again, my voice barely a whisper.

She stopped and pointed out my window. "That's why."

Asher stood near the wall, dressed in a dark t-shirt and jeans. He didn't come toward the car, just waited with his thick arms at his sides.

"Go," Cara said.

Thoroughly bewildered, I got out of the car. Asher took a few steps forward and stopped.

"What are you doing here?" I couldn't believe he'd come back to this place willingly.

He cast a quick glance at the watchtower, like it made him nervous. "It's a do-over."

"A what?"

"A do-over. You weren't here the day I was released and you should have been." He looked over his shoulder. "Although I'm not going to ask them to let me in and then let me out the gate again. If you really need me to, I could try, but I don't know if they can. I obviously won't pass a background check."

"No, god, don't go in there."

One corner of his mouth lifted in a smile. "Good. Grace, I'm so sorry. I doubt I could have made this any worse for you if I'd tried. It might be too late, and if it is, I'm going to have to figure out how to live with that. But if it isn't, if there's even the tiniest chance you could forgive me, I have to try."

"I thought you couldn't be with me. Isn't that what you keep saying?"

"Would it make any sense if I told you an eagle sees the trees differently than a man on the ground, but they're still the same trees?"

"Gram?"

"Yeah."

"Kind of, but what are you trying to say? Because right now, I don't know whether to run to you or get back in the car and go. After everything we've been through, you were adamant this can't work. And now, what? You changed your mind?"

He rubbed his chin, then met my eyes. "I need to tell you what happened in there. Everything."

"Okay."

"Within a day or two of being transferred to this facility, word got around why I was doing time. Among some of the inmates, it earned me a certain level of respect. I'd stopped a rapist, and even other criminals tend to hate rapists. But there were other inmates who basically just wanted to fuck with someone, and they picked me. They wanted to know if I was really tough enough to do what I'd done, or if it had been a heat of the moment kind of thing."

I had a feeling I knew where this was going. I'd seen what he looked like when he'd been released. Battered knuckles. A gash above his eye.

"That was how it started. Guys would attack me just to see what I could do. And even after they realized I'd win pretty much every time, it didn't make them back off. It made it worse. I became the guy to beat. Everyone wanted to be the one to take me down, because no one could."

"Oh my god."

"So I fought a lot. But the thing was, I started to want it. I looked forward to it. As soon as someone would jump me, I'd get a huge rush. I knew how messed up that was, especially considering why I was doing time. But in the moment, I didn't care. It was like I had this demon living inside me and letting him out felt really fucking good.

"Then a few years ago, I got a new cellmate, a guy known as Switch. He was a hacker who'd gotten caught up in some drug trafficking stuff. I don't know who thought it would be a good idea to toss him in with the guys in my cell block. He was this skinny computer geek. They were going to eat him alive, so I made it clear that if anyone touched him, they'd have to deal with me.

"That worked for about a year. But the other inmates were getting sick of seeing me win all the time. They'd started betting on my fights and some of them kept betting against me and losing. It pissed them off. They decided it wouldn't be enough to go after me. They went after Switch." He looked down at the ground for a few seconds before continuing. "They held me down and made me watch. And they beat him so badly, he almost died."

"Oh, Asher."

"I wasn't really the same after that. It took me to a really dark place. I started picking fights instead of just defending myself. I thought about doing things to get more time added to my sentence because I didn't want the people who'd known me to see what I'd become. I'd turned into a monster."

"You're not a monster."

"That's debatable. I didn't come home and start throwing punches at everyone. But stuff started coming out in other ways."

I nodded. "The nightmares."

"Yeah. And panic attacks, apparently. I had an appointment with a therapist a couple of days ago and it was eerie how well he described everything I've been going through. The feeling of being watched when I wasn't, all of it."

"You went to therapy?"

He rubbed the back of his neck. "Yeah. It was stupid to not even try it."

"I started looking for a therapist too."

He gave me that half-smile again. "Well, aren't we a pair."

I nodded. "I guess so."

"I didn't want you to know about everything that happened in there because it was bad enough that I knew."

He flexed his fingers. "My hands remember exactly how it feels to break a bone and knock a guy out cold. I have a lot of shit I have to live with, and I didn't want you to know that part of me existed. I think deep down, I thought you could move on and remember the old Asher, and pretend I'm someone else."

"It doesn't work that way."

"I know." He took a deep breath. "The wrongness of living without you is killing me. I think it's killing us both. I really thought I was doing what was right. But I was wrong. I was so fucking wrong and I'm sorry it took me so long to realize it.

"You've been fighting for us since the night I was arrested. And I failed you. I should have been fighting by your side. I never should have left you. I should have put my faith in you the way you put your faith in me. I should have believed in us. I'm so sorry I didn't."

Tears welled in my eyes, but I didn't know what to say.

"Grace, I'm fucked up and broken, and I can't lie, I'm scared as hell. I'm scared I'll ruin your life and someday you're going to look back and wish I'd never come home. But I love you. I love you with every molecule in my body and every shred of my soul, and I will until the day I die.

"I'm standing here before you, a man who was stripped of his freedom, his future, all his plans. This whole experience brought me to my knees. But there was one thing they could never take, and it's all I have left to give you. My love. I don't know if it's enough—I don't know if anything could ever be enough after what I've done—but if you'll have me, it's yours."

My lip trembled and it took me a second before I could get any words out. "Asher, that's all I've ever wanted from you."

His brow furrowed and he tentatively lifted his arms to the sides.

I didn't hesitate. I ran to him and jumped, throwing my arms around his neck and wrapping my legs around his waist. He held me tight, crushing me against him.

"You'll never have to fight alone again," he murmured against my neck. "I'll always be with you. I swear. I'll never leave you. Do you hear me? I promise."

It was hard to stop sobbing long enough to answer. "I hear you."

"I'm so sorry. I love you so much."

"I love you too."

He held me for long moments, eventually letting me slide down to the ground. Gently cupping my face, he kissed me, slow and deep. We were undoubtedly being watched by the prison guards, but I didn't care. This was the moment I'd wanted—the moment I'd missed.

We both had a lot of healing to do. But wrapped in each other's love, there wasn't anything we couldn't face. I believed that down to the very bottom of my soul. Asher and I belonged to each other.

He pulled away slightly and kissed my forehead.

I reached up to touch the sides of his face and looked into his deep brown eyes. "Welcome home, Asher."

47

ASHER

*G*race traced her finger over my mouth. "You're going to have to wipe that smile off your face if you're going to pull this off."

She was right, but it was hard to stop. "I know, I know. I'll be serious."

"Good."

"What about you? Are you sure you can make this call and be convincing?"

"What do you think I am, an amateur? I've got this."

I leaned close to kiss her. "Of course you do."

We waited in the gym lobby, both sweaty from our workouts. I'd spent the last hour sparring with Jack. I might have been twenty-five years younger, but the guy was a beast. He made a great workout partner, especially because he had such good instincts. He could tell if I was getting too riled up and needed to step away for a few minutes.

My therapist had pushed me hard to start training again. So had Grace. Even Gram had told me to suck it up and put my gloves back on. So I'd talked to Mark, the head trainer here, and booked a few private coaching sessions. Since then, I'd been working with him once a week, and sparring with Jack or my brothers in between.

Jack and I also took turns working with Elijah. They didn't have a kids' program here anymore, but he'd really taken to his training and wanted to continue. He was getting damn good, and he didn't have trouble with little shits trying to bully him anymore.

It turned out I didn't need to bury my demons. I needed to control them. Training again and working with Elijah were good for me. Really good.

Making Gavin tap out a few times hadn't been bad, either. He'd beaten me once, but I wasn't letting him get away with it.

I wasn't letting any of them get away with anything.

Since I'd come home, my brothers had teased me relentlessly about my prison time. I'd found more things with files or materials to make fake prison shanks baked into them than I could count. I could admit it was funny. I laughed every time.

But I also had to answer back.

"What's Jack doing back there?" I asked. "Shaving or something?"

Grace glanced toward the locker rooms. "I don't know. I'm sure he'll be out soon."

Mark came out to the front. He was in his fifties and had owned this gym since I'd started coming here years ago. Like any trained fighter, he was lean and fit.

"You looked good out there," he said. "Your skills are coming back fast."

"Thanks, man. I picked up some bad habits, but I'm working through them."

"Yeah, you've got some brawler in you that wasn't there

before. But don't worry. Focused skills practice will work that out of you. It's already making a difference."

"Thanks."

"Listen, I wanted to talk to you about something. I don't know if this would interest you, but I've been looking for another coach, someone who can also work with kids. I've seen you with Elijah and you're a natural with him. I know you've only been back in the gym for a little while, and you'd need to go through a coaching certification. But if you're interested, we could make that happen."

"Coaching?" I asked, not sure what else to say. I'd actually thought about it—more than once. Coaching would give me purpose. Fill a need I knew I had.

"Yeah. You're a natural. It's hard to find coaches who can work with adults as well as kids. I know you're probably pretty busy with the handyman gig, but I'd love to convince you to come work for me instead. You're a born coach, man. I can see it."

A born coach. Declan had said I was a born fighter. I liked this take on it a lot better.

"You know what, let's talk about what it would take," I said. "I'm interested."

Mark shook my hand. "Great. We'll set something up."

Grace bit her bottom lip through her smile as Mark went back into the gym.

I slipped an arm around her waist. "You look awfully happy."

"I'm just so proud of you."

I kissed her forehead. "Thanks, Gracie Bear."

Jack finally came out, dressed in his uniform. "Are we ready? I checked in with the station. They're good to go on their end."

I met Grace's eyes and we both nodded. "We're ready."

"You sure you want me to cuff you?" he asked. "I could just meet you down there."

"It's fine, I can take it. And this will be more convincing. They know I'm overdue in answering back, so they're suspicious of everything right now. Pictures will sell it."

"Okay, let's do this."

Jack grabbed his handcuffs and I held out my hands. They snapped down over my wrists with a metallic click. It did give me a quick hit of adrenaline to feel them there again, but it wasn't anything I couldn't handle. That was part of why we were doing this after a workout. I'd burned off a lot of energy already, so this stunt shouldn't set me off in a way I didn't want.

I met Grace's eyes. "You okay?"

"Yeah. It's weird seeing those on you again." Her lips turned up in a smile. "But the boys are going to lose their minds."

"Come on, Bailey," Jack said, his voice deep and serious. "Let's go."

He put his hand on my shoulder and led me outside. His car was parked up the street. Grace followed behind, snapping photos. We walked slower than necessary, giving her time to text the pictures and make the first call.

We'd agreed to leave Evan out of it; we didn't have any evidence he'd been in on the prison pranks. And Chief Stanley had let me know when my other three brothers would all be off duty, so I knew they were around.

"Logan, oh my god," Grace said behind me. "One of the Havens showed up at the gym and Asher lost it. Jack broke it up, but he's taking Asher in. I don't even know what to do right now."

Damn, her voice was convincing. My girl was good.

"I don't know, he ran off. And then Jack said he was

sorry, but he had to take Asher in. I took a picture because I didn't think you'd believe me. Jack's putting him in the car now. Oh god, Logan, what are we going to do? I can't believe this is happening."

"Jesus," Jack muttered. "She's merciless."

"She's the sweetest girl you'll ever meet, but she's got an evil streak. Especially when it comes to pranking. The best part is, most people have no idea. Some of the best Bailey pranks have been all Gracie Bear."

Jack chuckled. "Here, she got her pictures, I can unlock these. You're going to need both hands."

"Thanks," I said as he released the cuffs. "You're not bad at this yourself. Any chance we could get you to fake an arrest on one of the Haven brothers?"

He scowled at me. "No."

I just chuckled.

"All right, in the back," he said, and I could hear the humor in his voice. "And if Naomi gets me in trouble for this, I'm blaming you."

"Fair enough, I'll take the heat."

Jack drove us to the sheriff's office with Grace following behind. With any luck, my brothers would be down here in a few minutes. I hoped they'd burst in and make a stink. The louder they were when they got here, the funnier this would be.

We went in and Grace hurried into the lobby behind us.

"Are we ready?" Grace asked.

Rebecca Roy, a girl Grace and I had known since kindergarten, was at the front counter. She smiled and gave a thumbs up. "All set."

"Good," Grace said. "They're on their way."

"You're planning on cleaning this up when you're done, right?" Rebecca asked.

Jack chuckled. "Don't worry, Bec, that's part of the deal."

"Good." She jerked her thumb toward the back. "I'll just wait over there so I don't get caught in the crossfire."

Grace glanced out the front. "I think that's them."

Jack rushed me around to get behind the front counter. Rebecca had our supplies all ready. I had no idea how Grace had convinced Jack and the rest of the sheriff's office to let us do this. That was my girl for you. Jack waited just behind the barrier so he wouldn't be seen in the lobby, and I ducked down behind the desk.

The lobby doors flew open and Logan's voice boomed, "Grace? What the hell is happening?"

"Where is he?"

"What's going on?"

"Thank god you're here," Grace said.

"Jack, where the hell are you?" Logan called toward the back. "Where's Asher?"

I slid two of the chocolate cream pies from Rebecca's desk into the palms of my hands, making sure they were steady.

Three.

Two.

One.

I popped up, slid one pie across the counter toward Grace, and palmed the other one. Hesitating long enough for them to see me—really see me—I gave them my best Bailey shit-eating grin. "Hey, bros."

"What the fuck?" Logan asked.

I tossed the pie right in his face.

Grace slid the second pie off the counter and a second later, Levi had chocolate cream pie dripping down his shirt.

Gavin's eyes went wide. "What the—"

I cut him off with the third pie, hitting him like a bullseye.

Logan doubled over laughing so hard he gasped for breath. Levi swiped pie filling and whipped cream out of his eyes and flicked it to the ground. Gavin stood still, like he was too shocked to move.

"Oh. My. God," he said through his pie-face. "That was fucking amazing."

Then Gavin started to laugh, and Logan kept laughing so hard he couldn't wipe the pie off his face.

Levi shook his head slowly, but even he laughed. "Okay, we deserved that."

Grace had her hands over her mouth, her shoulders shaking as she giggled at them.

Logan wiped a handful of pie from his face. "G, you set us up? That's it."

She squealed and tried to run away, but Logan got her with a blob of chocolate. I heard someone mutter *oh shit* as I jumped over the front counter, and all-out war began.

Gavin and Levi attacked me with handfuls of pie filling as I tried to throw myself in front of Grace. Chocolate and whipped cream flew, splattering everywhere. I scooped up a blob off the floor and hurled it at Logan. He answered back with another handful that smeared over my shirt.

"Hey, Baileys." Jack's voice boomed across the lobby.

We all stopped and looked at him. He and several deputies grinned at us, all with pies in their hands.

Oh shit.

I grabbed Grace and threw my arms around her, turning my back on Jack and the others to shield her from the onslaught. Cream pie—smelled like banana—splattered across my shoulders. I couldn't stop laughing. Levi and Logan immediately started scooping up more pie and hurling it back toward our new attackers. In seconds, we were all embroiled in a pie fight in the lobby of the sheriff's department.

Just a typical day in Tilikum.

The deputies finally ran out of pie and the battle died down. Everyone put their hands up in mutual surrender. The whole place was a disaster—splatters of pie and whipped cream everywhere.

Gavin was covered from head to toe. He'd foregone any sort of cover in favor of going on the offensive. Levi and Logan had taken their share, and Grace and I were both a mess.

So were Jack and the other deputies.

We cleaned up, and with this many hands, it didn't take long. I gave Jack props for the extra pies. We'd gotten my brothers and he'd gotten us all. Pranks with layers were the best kind.

Still sticky, but no longer dripping pie filling, my brothers followed me and Grace outside.

"I can't believe you did that," Logan said. "I seriously thought Jack fucking arrested you."

"I can't believe Jack attacked us with more pie," Grace said. "I never want to smell banana cream again."

Gavin was still smiling. "Well done, bro. That was epic."

I smiled and hugged it out with him, then Logan.

Levi shook his head at me, then held his arms out. I bear-hugged him tight.

"Sorry about what I said that day." Levi's voice was quiet. "I'm glad you're home."

"Thanks, brother. Me too."

"Okay, broca colas," Logan said. "I need to go shower."

"Shower?" Gavin asked, scoffing. "Let's just go jump in the river."

"Why would I do that? The river's cold."

"Baby," Gavin said.

"You're a baby."

Levi shoved Gavin's shoulder. "I'll dunk both your asses in the river."

"I'd like to see you try."

Grace grabbed my hand and tugged me away. "Quick, let's get out of here before they try to rope us into jumping in the river with them."

We paused outside her car and I hooked my arm around her waist, hauling her roughly against me. "I'm thinking shower. But maybe I'll lick you off first."

"It's so weird how I got pie *everywhere*," she said, emphasizing the word.

I covertly brushed my fingers between her legs. "Everywhere, huh. Yeah, I'm definitely licking you clean."

48

ASHER

I found a spot about a block from the bar and parked. The street was quiet. Most of the college students were still gone for the summer, and it was ten o'clock in the morning. Too early for the bar crowds. But that was the point.

"Are you sure you're ready for this?" I asked.

Grace reached over and squeezed my hand. I wasn't sure if she was seeking reassurance from me, or offering it. Maybe both.

"I'm sure. I need to do this."

"We both do."

Neither of us had been back here since the night our lives had gone sideways. Grace had admitted she'd avoided this entire street for years. Both of our therapists had suggested we consider revisiting the bar when we felt ready. We'd talked about it and decided we wanted to try.

I'd called ahead and talked to the owner. He'd been surprisingly cool about it, offering to meet us here before it opened so we could do what we needed to do without the pressure of a crowd of customers.

We got out of the truck and I let Grace take the lead. She took slow steps toward the front, but it wasn't as if she were forcing herself to move forward. Her body was alert, but not tense. She was simply taking the time she needed.

She'd already made incredible progress. After a few sessions with her therapist, she'd started asking me to take her places so she could try going inside alone. Her first attempt had been a little rocky. She'd spent about five minutes in the Sugar Shack, the little corner store we'd frequented as kids, before she'd needed to come out. But she hadn't run out in a panic. And she'd said knowing I was outside waiting for her had helped a lot.

I'd sit outside every store in town for as long as she needed if it helped her feel better. I'd do anything for her.

Since then she'd worked her way up to actually buying groceries by herself. I was so damn proud of her.

She reached the door to the bar and glanced over her shoulder. I was right behind her.

"Ready to go in?" she asked.

"Yeah. Let's go."

My heart rate kicked up, so I took a few deep breaths. I braced myself for the assault of memories I was sure would hit me, but as we walked inside, images of that awful night didn't take over. The bar hadn't changed very much from what I remembered, but I wasn't overwhelmed. I felt the edge of unease, but no loss of control.

The owner, a fit middle-aged guy with a lot of gray in his beard, came out from the back. "You must be Asher and Grace."

Grace and I shook his hand.

"Thanks for this," I said. "We appreciate it."

"No problem. Miss, I never had the chance to apologize for what happened to you here. We've tightened up our security and have cameras out there now. That never should have happened."

"Thank you," she said.

"Feel free to have a look around. I hope it helps."

He retreated to a stool behind the bar, giving us space.

Grace moved slowly, her steps deliberate. She made her way to the pool table where it had all started and trailed her fingers along the edge.

I remembered every moment of that night, even clearer now than I had in the immediate aftermath. Then, I'd been mired in shock and the aftereffects of adrenaline and rage. Now, I could recall that night without the same overwhelming level of emotion.

It still hurt. My life had taken a terrible turn that night, and it had started right there at that pool table. But I wasn't swept away in violent recollections. For the first time, I faced what had happened to us, and the choices I'd made, with calm acceptance.

I'd protected Grace, and I'd paid a price for it.

Wordlessly, I walked through the bar, taking it in. Grace lingered near the pool tables, then went straight for the back. I hadn't been sure if she'd want to go out there, but if she did, I was going with her.

Next to the door that led outside was a sign warning that recording was in progress. Without hesitation, she opened the door and walked out.

This was harder.

The alley had been dark that night, but even in the midmorning sun, the sight of it hit me square in the chest. For a second, it was hard to breathe.

But Grace wasn't pinned to the ground, seconds from being brutalized. She was standing in the daylight, her hair moving in the breeze. Beautiful and perfect.

And, despite everything, mine.

Which was something of a miracle.

I took a few steps, looking around. Letting this place do whatever it was going to do to me. I would probably never come back here, but I'd needed to face it. Needed to face what had happened and what I'd done.

I'd never been proud of the outcome. It wouldn't have been right to glory in someone's death, no matter what he'd done. But it would have been a lie to say I regretted it. I'd have done anything, even sacrificed my own life, to save hers. And I'd do it again without question.

If that made me a monster, so be it.

Grace threaded her arms around my waist and rested her head against my chest. I wrapped my arms around her, holding her securely in my embrace. Felt the soothing reassurance of her heart beating with mine, and breathed.

"Thank you," she said softly.

"For this? Of course. We both needed it."

"Yes, but..." She paused and lifted her face to meet my eyes. "Thank you for what you did here. For saving me."

I brushed her hair back from her face. "Thank you for saving *me*."

She smiled up at me. And the fact that she could do that here—with her blue eyes shining with true happiness—lifted some of the weight off my shoulders. Some of the power this place, and that night, had held over me was gone, dissolving into the air and blowing away on the gentle wind.

"Do you need more time?" I asked.

She took a deep breath. "No. I'm finished."

I was too. Finished and ready to move on.

~

PARKED cars already crowded Evergreen Street when we got to the house.

"I guess they're not wasting time," Grace said, nodding to the wide-open front door.

"How did they get in?"

She sighed. "Your brothers all have keys."

"Oh, I didn't realize you'd done that."

"I didn't."

"Then why do my brothers have keys to our house?" I asked as we walked in.

"Because they're your brothers?"

I shrugged. That was probably as good an explanation as any.

Voices greeted us when we got inside. Today was a big day. The house had been inspected for safety, the insurance company had done their thing, and we'd been given the all clear to begin repairing and rebuilding.

It was going to be a hell of a lot of work. But we had a lot of help.

My brothers were here, of course, as were Jack and Elijah. And most of Grace's family on the Miles side were already here as well. Naomi and their mom Shannon had offered to babysit all the little ones while the adults came to help get us started clearing out debris. Someone had already gotten people organized and work was well underway.

Grace and I had rented an apartment to tide us over until we got the house in livable condition again. Cara had tried to talk us into living with her, and although her house was pretty amazing, we'd agreed we wanted our own space. Even if it didn't have a spectacular view of the river.

Our place was nice, and coming home to Grace every

night was amazing. But I was anxious to get this house back together so we could move in. Make it ours.

Our new favorite dates were trips to the hardware store and browsing through home and garden magazines looking for ideas. We were currently in the middle of a debate about kitchen countertops. She wanted granite. I wanted composite quartz.

I was pretty sure I was wearing her down.

Cara emerged from the back of the house dressed in an old Tilikum College t-shirt, knotted at the waist, with shorts and what looked like a brand-new pair of work boots. She had leather work gloves sticking out of a pocket.

"There's my darling little cuddly bear." She hugged Grace.

"Look at you," Grace said. "Nice boots."

She shrugged. "I have no idea what I'm doing, but fake it till you make it, right?"

"I love it. Thanks for coming."

"Of course, boo."

"This is unrelated, but have you talked to Libby Stewart lately?" Grace asked.

"From the library? No, not in a while. Why?"

"She stopped by the coffee shop yesterday to tell me she couldn't help us with the Eliza Bailey search anymore. Which is fine if she's busy or whatever. But she told me I should stop looking because she's positive there's nothing else."

Cara's eyebrows knitted together. "Really?"

"Yeah, it was strange. She almost seemed upset. Who knows, maybe she was just having a bad day. But she was really adamant about it, like she was sure it was a waste of time."

"That is odd."

"Isn't it? Anyway, I was just wondering if you'd seen her."

She tapped a finger to her lips. "No, but now I'm curious. Maybe I'll go to the library and do some digging myself."

"You're like a cat, you know that? Dangle a bit of string and you ignore it. Move the string around a corner, and suddenly you have to investigate to find out where it went."

"That's probably accurate." She glanced around the construction zone that would eventually be our house. "Anyway, like I said, I don't know what I'm doing, so I'm just letting your brothers boss me around. Speaking of, next time, could you please try to gather a crew that isn't made up entirely of Baileys and hot but very married men? I'm absolutely basking in the insane amount of masculinity on display out there, but it's torture. Your brothers are brutally hot and the fact that they're all happily married is making them exponentially hotter, which is messing with my head in ways I don't know how to deal with."

Grace laughed. "I have no idea what you're talking about right now."

"Do you see them out there? Smiling at their wives with those looks that say, *woman, you're the only one I'll ever love and even though I watched you push a baby out of your vagina, I'm still as hot for you as I've ever been, and when we get home, I'm going to show you.* Why is that so hot, Grace? Tell me, because I'm so confused right now."

"You're really surprised that being openly in love with their wives and committed to their families makes men attractive? Everyone knows that's a thing. Its why women love to ogle pictures of male celebrities being cute with their spouses or holding their babies."

"Do women really do that? I've never done that."

Grace patted her on the shoulder. "It's okay, sweetie. I know this is new, but it's perfectly normal."

I went out back while Grace continued reassuring Cara. I didn't really understand what they were talking about, but that was typical. Those two had their own language, a lot like Levi and Logan's twin language when they were little.

I checked in with everyone, wandering through to see how things were going. They'd gotten off to a good start. Our lumber delivery arrived, and with so many people, we got it all unloaded and moved around to the back in no time.

It didn't take long before things started to look a hell of a lot more manageable. We braced the back wall and shored up the roof supports to make sure it was stable. Cleared away most of the burned debris. Sorted through things to figure out what was salvageable, and cleared out space so we could rebuild the outer wall.

"This is like one of those home improvement shows where they build a whole house in like two days," Logan said. "You guys will be living here by next week."

"I can't believe how much progress we've already made," Grace said.

"Couple more weeks and we'll be neighbros." Logan lifted his hand to fist bump mine.

I just looked at him. "What?"

"Didn't I tell you? We're moving in next door."

"What?" Grace squealed. Her *what* sounded a lot more enthusiastic than mine. "Next door to us? Here?"

Logan looked entirely too proud of himself. "Yeah. Since Gavin obviously isn't going anywhere, we figured we should get a house with a third bedroom. The one next door was available, so we snapped it up."

"You've got to be kidding me," I said.

"This is going to be so fun," Grace said.

"I know," Logan said. "It's gonna be lit. The backyard is huge. I'm already working on a design for the fire pit."

Grace smiled.

I shook my head. "If you're living next door, you need to give me all the keys you have to our house."

"Why would I do that? What if I need to borrow something?"

"That's why I want your keys."

Logan laughed and patted me on the shoulder, then walked away.

"Aren't you excited?" Grace asked. "It'll be fun having them right next door."

I glanced around at my brothers. Levi was working in the kitchen alongside two of Grace's brothers. He wouldn't be a bad neighbor. But then I caught sight of Logan snapping his shirt at Evan, earning an angry growl. Gavin was on the roof and I had no idea if he was up there for a reason, or just using the work party as an excuse to do something dangerous.

But Grace was probably right. It would be fun.

About an hour later, Grace took a few people with her to get food and drinks for everyone. The work party was winding down as the sun sank lower in the sky. We'd gotten so much done, it looked like a completely different house already.

Dinner arrived, along with Gram, who brought pie and cookies. We stuffed our helpers with food, which was the least we could do for everything they'd done.

The work party gradually turned into a regular party. There was food everywhere. My brothers produced a case of beer, and Grace's siblings had brought wine from their winery. Her brother Cooper and brother-in-law Chase joined Logan and Gavin in crafting a makeshift firepit out of rocks. Soon there was a nice blaze going—a safe distance from the house—and someone turned on music.

It had been a damn good day.

I stood with Grace near the fire, my arm around her shoulders, a beer in my hand. Her arm was locked around my waist and she had a plastic cup of red wine. We were tired and dirty. Her cheek was smudged with soot and there was dust in her hair.

She was perfect.

Gram picked her way across the rocky yard. After handing out slices of pie to everyone, she'd spent the last hour chatting with Grace's sisters-in-law. I drew her in next to me with my other arm and gently squeezed.

"Thanks again for bringing dessert."

"Oh, sure. I like feeding people. It makes them happy."

"Especially when it's pie."

"Isn't that the truth." She tugged on my arm. "Come out front a moment. I have something for you both."

We followed her around the house to where she'd parked. She fished a box out of her backseat and handed it to me.

"I've been saving this for a wedding gift, but I decided it was time."

I opened it and drew out something flat, wrapped in tissue paper. I could tell right away it was a picture frame.

Grace pulled back the tissue, revealing a collage frame with four photos. In the top left was a picture of Gram and Grandad. They looked exactly as I remembered them from my childhood. They were standing together on the back porch, smiling, and Grandad had his arm around her shoulders.

Next to that was a photo of my parents, Charles and Helena Bailey. They were looking at each other, rather than the camera. Smiling in a way that made my chest ache.

Below that was a picture of me with my brothers from

when I was about nine. We were all sitting in the bed of Grandad's truck, a bunch of dirty, messy-haired boys. We looked like trouble.

Finally, a photo of me and Grace. I was about eleven here, Grace ten. We were standing in the creek with our pants rolled up to our knees, looking at something in Grace's hands. Our heads were close together, our expressions excited, like she'd just found a treasure.

I remembered that day. She'd found a rock that had a streak of something gold-colored in it. It hadn't been real gold, of course, but it had sparked weeks of imagining, the two of us pretending to be prospectors, panning the creek for riches.

Grace traced her fingers lightly over the frame. "Oh Gram. This is amazing."

I swallowed hard, waiting for the rush of emotion to pass before I could speak. "Thank you."

"You're welcome. I chose the photos I thought you'd enjoy the most. I know the house isn't ready for you to put up pictures yet, but it felt like today was the right day to give it to you."

Grace swiped under her eyes. "I don't even know what to say."

"That's all right, Mama Bear, I hear what your heart's saying." Gram glanced back at the house. "Things are looking good in there. You'll be hanging this on the wall in no time."

"Yeah, we will," Grace said. "It's such a shame there was a fire, but it could have been so much worse."

"Sometimes these things happen just the way they're meant to," Gram said. "There's meaning in the two of you bringing this house back from the ashes together. Making it a home."

I looked at Grace and she met my eyes. Gram was right. This house was full of meaning for us. It was a link between our past and our future. A representation of the life we'd both wanted, and the life we were now working together to build.

That life didn't look like the one we'd been expecting the night we'd stood outside this house and shared our first kiss. We'd faced hardships and challenges we never could have predicted. There was no magic that would instantly heal the wounds we'd suffered. Like this house, it was taking hard work for us to rebuild what we'd had together.

But we were rebuilding. Because love was bigger than tragedy. It was bigger than pain. I'd lost sight of that for a while, but Grace had been here to show me the way. Her steadfast love and loyalty had taught me so much. She'd saved me from the darkness, from the demons I'd never thought I'd escape.

Her love was that big. I never should have doubted her.

But somewhere along the way, I must have done something right, because this beautiful woman was mine. Forever.

And soon, I was going to make that official.

49

GRACE

I leaned back in my chair at Gram's big dining table, feeling pleasantly full. I still had some dinner left on my plate, but I'd already eaten too much. If I kept going, it wouldn't be long before I was wishing I'd worn pajama pants instead of jeans. Gram's cooking was like that, and it wasn't even a holiday. Just a Tuesday night in October.

The table buzzed with loud conversation. Logan and Levi were arguing with Evan over something to do with old muscle cars. Gavin was telling jokes to Elijah and making him laugh hysterically. Jack occasionally added his two cents to the muscle car debate, and my mom and Gram chatted about chickens. My mom was apparently thinking about getting some for the fresh eggs, and Gram was heartily encouraging her to get her own peckers.

Asher sat quietly next to me, his arm around the back of my chair. He leaned close and placed a soft kiss on my temple.

We'd moved into the house on Evergreen Street several weeks ago. In between coaching an ever-increasing number of clients, and the kids' grappling class he'd started, Asher had been working hard on the house to get it livable again. The outer wall and roof were repaired, and we had a functioning kitchen. Not much cabinet space yet, but we had a sink and refrigerator.

There wasn't a stove or oven, but even though the cooler fall weather had settled in, Asher insisted he could just grill food until we got a new one.

Living in that house together, even with work left to be done, was everything I'd ever dreamed of, and more.

Sometimes I still woke in the night, and in the haze of sleep, stretched my arm across the bed, reaching for him. But now, he was there, sleeping beside me.

He still had nightmares, but their frequency had lessened. Therapy was helping. But it was more than his sessions with his counselor. He had purpose again. Gram would say he'd found his mission. Training in martial arts gave his body something it craved, and working as a coach gave him meaning and direction—something a man like him desperately needed.

Things weren't perfect, but they were improving. And I was so, so proud of him.

He inspired me every day, and I'd been working on myself just as hard. Processing what had happened to me hadn't been easy. It was difficult and uncomfortable. But Asher had been with me, supporting me, every step of the way. It felt good to know I could go where I needed without Cara as a crutch. That I was no longer letting the past rule my present. I was in control.

Asher brushed his nose against my temple and kissed me again. "I'm going to get some air. Want to join me?"

"Sure."

I grabbed my sweater and we went out to the back porch. It was chilly, with the fresh scent of fall in the air. We stood next to the railing and Asher put his arms around me to keep me warm.

"Have I mentioned lately how much I love you?" he asked.

"Yes, but you can say it as often as you like."

He moved so he was facing me and picked up my left hand. "You know, it's October. It's not summer anymore. We haven't talked about that."

"I guess we haven't."

"When I asked you for a summer all those years ago, I think we both knew that wasn't what I really wanted. A summer with you would never have been enough. When you asked for the same from me a few months ago, I knew that was still true. But I still needed it to be that way, and somehow you understood that."

"You needed time."

"Yeah. I'm sorry for all the ways I made things harder. I'm trying to make it up to you, but I don't know if it will ever be enough. You waited for me for so long. That still blows me away."

"It's simple. I waited because you're my best friend and I love you. Because you sacrificed everything for me. And because I knew you'd be worth the wait, no matter what."

Idly rubbing my ring finger, he tucked my hair behind my ear with his other hand. "Grace, you're worth everything. And there's something I need to ask you."

My heart fluttered in my chest. His eyes were intent on mine, holding me captive.

"The first time I did this, I made a big show out of it. And that was fun. I'm glad I did it that way. But this is different. This question, this moment, isn't about a grand gesture in front of the whole town. It's about you and me."

Swallowing hard, I nodded.

"Grace Miles, I've loved you my whole life, and I'm going to love you until the day I die. It would be my greatest honor if you would spend those days with me, as my wife. I promise you, I'll spend the rest of my life loving you with everything that I am." He leaned closer, brushing his nose against mine. "Will you marry me?"

Closing my eyes, I melted against him. His arms wrapped around me and he buried his face in my neck.

"Yes," I said softly in his ear.

He squeezed me tight, almost crushing me against him. "I love you so much."

"I love you too."

After long moments in each other's arms, he let go and dug into his pocket. He lifted my hand and slid a ring on my finger.

The same ring I'd worn before.

Biting my bottom lip, I gazed at my hand through the tears filling my eyes. It looked so perfect. Like I'd never taken it off. "You kept it."

"Of course I did," he said. "I'm sorry I ever gave you a reason to take it off. That won't happen again."

"I know."

I let out a long breath and he pulled me in close. Wrapped his thick arms around me. A few tears leaked out of the corners of my eyes.

Everything was right again. Asher and I were together. We were whole.

The back door opened and Gavin poked his head out. "Gram said to quit making out back here or you're both grounded."

"I said no such thing." Gram's voice carried from inside. "You kiss that girl all you want, Bear."

Asher's shoulders shook as he laughed. "Thanks, Gram." He looked down at me. "Should we tell them?"

"They didn't know you were going to ask me again?"

"No. Like I said, this was just for us."

I tilted my chin to meet his kiss. His lips pressed against mine. Gavin made gagging noises from the doorway, but we ignored him.

"Yeah, let's go tell them," I said.

Taking my hand, Asher led me inside. Gram caught my eye and her mouth twitched in a smile. Maybe he hadn't told them, but I had a feeling she knew.

"So, Grace and I have something to say." Asher glanced down at me and winked. "We're getting married. Again. Or still."

"How about still," I said, holding up my hand.

Everyone jumped up from the table and the next thing I knew, I was being hugged by a seemingly endless stream of people. My tearful mom, then Jack. Elijah, who seemed like he'd grown two inches since last week. Logan squeezed me so tight I had to beg him to stop and Gavin lifted me up and twirled me around. Levi hugged me almost as hard as Logan had. Evan held back at first, but still hugged us both, offering sincere, if gruff, congratulations.

Ten minutes later, Logan and Levi had gone to the store for drinks, Gavin was building a bonfire outside, my mom brought over several bottles of wine, and Asher and I found ourselves on the brink of an impromptu engagement party.

I stood on the porch watching Gavin stack more logs on the fire. Gram wandered over and slipped her arm through mine.

"Well, Mama Bear, seems now you have a wedding to plan."

"I sure do."

"It's about time, isn't it?"

I laughed. "Yeah, it's been a long engagement."

"That it has. But I always knew things would turn out all right."

"You really did, didn't you? Are you sure you're not psychic?"

She chuckled softly. "No, nothing like that. I've just been around a while. Besides, you've always belonged to us. You've always been a Bailey. Now we just get to make it official."

I put my hand over hers and squeezed. "Thanks, Gram."

Asher came over and gave her a light kiss on the head.

"You did good, Bear," she said, patting his arm.

"Thanks. For everything."

"You're welcome. But it's nothing. You're my cubs. This is what I do."

She patted his cheek, then went back inside.

Asher moved next to me. "So when do you want to get married? Soon as possible?"

"I don't know, maybe we shouldn't rush into anything."

Chuckling softly, he drew me in front of him and put his arms around me. "Suit yourself. But I don't want to wait too long. I keep thinking about how much I want to put a baby in you. Kinda want to marry you before I do that."

"Oh my god, did you just say *put a baby in you*?"

He put his mouth next to my ear. "Yeah. Why? Too caveman for you?"

A tingle ran down my spine. "Actually, no."

"Beautiful, we can get married anytime. If you want a nice wedding, we'll have a nice wedding. If you want to get married this weekend down at City Hall, we'll do it. I'll give you anything you want."

"Including a baby?"

He kissed my earlobe. "Absolutely."

"We don't have to have a baby right this second, but I'm not going to lie, you murmuring in my ear about getting me pregnant is really hot."

"Yeah? Maybe we should go home and practice."

I giggled and he squeezed me tighter, trailing light kisses down my neck. "We should probably stay for our own engagement party. At least for a little while."

He groaned. "Okay. For a little while."

I watched the sparks from Gavin's fire rise into the night, wrapped in Asher's strong embrace. Loved. Happy. At peace.

The roads we'd traveled had been unexpected and hard. But our struggles had made us who we were. We'd been tested and challenged. And ultimately, our love had prevailed. I'd always believed, deep down, that Asher and I were meant to be together. Our souls were inextricably intertwined and there was nothing that could tear us apart.

Together, we were unbreakable.

EPILOGUE
EVAN

*T*he cold night air rushed past me as my bike raced down the empty highway. The scenery flew by, unseen, save for the patch of road illuminated by my headlight. I wasn't sure where I was going. Away, mostly. I was too restless to go sit at home. I needed to drive. To cut through the wind and lean into the turns. I needed speed.

The highway curved and I had to slow down when I got into Pinecrest. I could drive right through and keep on going. There wasn't much to do in this little town. But the Crooked Owl Tavern caught my eye. A beer didn't sound bad right about now. I'd been here before; it was a dive, but the beer was always ice cold.

I parked outside, took off my helmet, and went in.

The light was dim and classic rock played in the background. The rough-around-the-edges crowd hung out here. A few biker types—I'd seen their Harleys outside—and guys with thick beards and work boots. There was a group of twenty-somethings playing pool, a few girls who eyed me when I walked in, and a couple of grizzled old-timers at the bar.

I picked a stool away from everyone. I wasn't here to talk about the weather, or sports, or whatever the fuck passed for news in a shit hole town like this. I was just here to kill time and get a drink.

The bartender came by and I ordered a beer. True to form, it was ice cold. Had a nice bite to it. I hunched over my drink, bored. Restless. Dissatisfied. But that was how I felt most of the time, so it wasn't exactly new.

My phone buzzed in my pocket, so I checked my messages. It was from a client asking about the car I was restoring for him. I'd get back to him later. Taking another swig of my beer, I flicked through a few things. I'd been waiting to hear about a lead on a forties Dodge Power Wagon I was hoping to get my hands on. It didn't look like much, but if I could get it for the right price, I'd flip it and make a shit ton of money.

I accidentally hit the contacts icon and a name I didn't recognize flashed on the screen. Jill? Who the fuck was that? Why did I have the number of some girl I didn't know?

Oh, shit. She was pink cardigan girl, the one Luke Haven had been hitting on. That made me crack a smile. Fucking Luke Haven. As a Bailey, I was obligated to hate the Havens on principle. Truthfully, I didn't really give a shit about the feud, or the Havens as a whole. But Luke Haven? I'd keep that goddamn feud going just to feed my hatred for that piece of shit.

I selected Jill's contact info and hit delete. It wasn't like I was ever going to call her. She'd tasted sweet when I'd kissed her in front of Luke, and sweet was a hard no. A girl like her looked harmless, like a kitten. But kittens had sharp claws, and they were damn good at convincing you it was your fault when you got scratched.

My younger brothers hadn't learned that lesson yet.

Asher... he was another story. But he'd always been the exception to most rules. And Grace was no kitten.

I was happy for my brother. Glad he'd gotten his shit together enough to work things out with Grace. I didn't envy him the demons he'd had to battle, nor the time he'd done in prison. The whole thing still pissed me off. But there wasn't anything I could do about it. And he was home now.

But fuck, this meant there was going to be a wedding. I'd probably have to be in it. And if not, I'd certainly have to go.

I fucking hated weddings.

The beer wasn't putting me in a better mood. Neither was thinking about weddings. I'd left my brother's impromptu engagement party hoping to outrun the hollow ache I'd been feeling. It was irritating how it kept trying to follow me.

A beer wasn't going to cut it. I'd go home and drown it in whiskey.

Leaving my bottle half-full, I was about to get off my stool and cut out of here, when someone sidled up next to me.

A girl in a black leather miniskirt and a leopard-print top that barely contained her tits perched at the bar. "Hi."

My brow furrowed. "What?"

The corner of her mouth lifted. She was pretty, even though she wore a lot of makeup, and she had flower tattoos on her shoulder. "You look a little lonely over here all by yourself. I thought maybe you could use a friend."

My eyes swept up and down. She was about my age. The type of girl who knew exactly how hot she was. Definitely not sweet. By the way she watched me, I could tell what she wanted. Girls didn't openly stare at your dick like that when they were hoping you'd ask them out to dinner.

She wanted a night. Maybe a string of them.

"A friend?"

"Yeah, although who am I kidding? I could use a friend, too. I've had a shitty week."

I grunted and took a drink of my beer.

Her eyes flicked to my crotch again. I followed her gaze, making it obvious I could see what she was doing.

"I'll just cut to the chase. Do you want to get out of here?" she asked.

I raised an eyebrow. "Aren't you going to buy me a drink first?"

She licked her lips. "I was thinking of something better than just a drink."

I looked away, considering. Usually if I was going to grab a girl to take home with me—or more accurately, take to her place, because I never took girls to mine—I liked to be the one on the prowl.

But this girl was hot, no denying it. And she was right, I was fucking lonely. A little company didn't sound half bad.

Plus, it had been a hell of a long time since I'd indulged in this kind of thing.

"Look, I know I'm being really forward," she said. "But I'm the type of girl who isn't afraid to go after what she wants."

"I see that."

She lightly traced a finger down my arm. "A guy like you —tall, thick, rugged—is like crack to me. I can't resist. And I really did have a shitty week."

"So did I."

"See? This works out for both of us."

She had a point. There was no doubt this girl looked like trouble, but at least she was up front. I knew what I'd be getting into. And damn it, it really had been a long time. Why the fuck not?

I put my beer down. "You live nearby?"

"Yeah. Just up the road."

"Let's go."

We left, and I got on my bike. Followed her up the road to a little house tucked behind some apple trees.

She didn't turn on the lights when we went inside. Just led me straight back to her bedroom.

This aggressive thing wasn't bad. No forced small talk. No bullshitting. No games. She'd brought me home to fuck, so why waste time pretending we were going to get to know each other first? She hadn't even given me her name, and I didn't want to know. Didn't care. It was just sex. Just a release.

Just a way to feel a little less empty for a while.

AFTERWARD, she lay sprawled out on the bed, like I'd fucked her unconscious. I had no interest in staying, so I got up to deal with the condom and clean up.

She had a bathroom right off the bedroom. I shut the door and flicked on the light. Tied off the condom and tossed it in the trash. I caught sight of myself in the mirror and quickly looked away. I wasn't exactly a fan of what I saw there these days.

I washed my hands and splashed water on my face. When I turned off the faucet, something on the counter caught my eye.

I stared at it, a sick feeling erupting in my gut. If that was what I thought it was—and it sure looked like it—there was no part of this that was okay.

Fuck.

EVAN'S BOOK, **Unraveling Him**, is now available!

DEAR READER

Dear Reader,

Well, here we are. The end of Asher and Grace's story, and the beginning of this new small-town family series.

What a ride.

It's no secret that I wrote a draft of this book three years ago, and let me tell you, there is a reason that draft was shelved. I wasn't ready. The differences between that old manuscript and the story you just read are many. And honestly, this one is so much better.

I've learned a lot as an author in those three years. And I tried to take everything I learned and pour it into this book, and this series.

I'm really proud of the result.

This story was a huge undertaking. I had so many layers to weave together, while always making sure that their relationship was the focus of the story. The town, the Bailey-Haven feud, the Eliza Bailey mystery, plus a cast of important side characters (you'll see more from all of them).

But the focus is still Asher and Grace, and working

through their rocky reunion to their happily ever after was a big challenge.

Writing about wounded people is totally my jam, and also an exercise in balance. Although their story deals with some big issues, I didn't want this book to be too heavy. And at the same time, Grace was assaulted and Asher went to prison. I had to be willing to dig into that.

My mantra for this book, and really this entire series, has been, "What would you do if you weren't afraid." Every time I questioned myself, wondered if I should tone it down or not take a certain risk in the story, I asked myself that question. What would you do if you weren't afraid? (In fact, it's a note on my bulletin board by my desk.) My answer to that question guided every choice I made. Every word you read was the result of me letting go of my fear and letting this story unfold as it was meant to, regardless of the consequences.

Yep, even that epilogue.

Maybe especially that epilogue.

I hope Grace and Asher's story was everything you hoped it would be. I feel like it's some of my best work and I'm so excited to continue with this series. There's a LOT more to come from these brothers. We're just getting started.

Love,

CK

ACKNOWLEDGMENTS

A heartfelt thank you to everyone who helped make this book possible.

Lori, you absolutely nailed the covers for this series. Thank you for your time and talent!

Thank you to Elayne for a superb editing job and to Erma for being kind enough to proofread and find those pesky little mistakes that try so hard to slip through.

A huge thank you to my team of admins and beta readers: Nikki, Alex, Jessica, Emily, Joyce, and Tammy. I couldn't do what I do without all of you!

A special shout out to Nikki for helping me keep my head on straight, and brainstorming me out of all those dark and scary corners. And for believing in me since the beginning.

To my family for your love, support, patience, and understanding.

ALSO BY CLAIRE KINGSLEY

For a full and up-to-date listing of Claire Kingsley books visit
www.clairekingsleybooks.com/books/

For comprehensive reading order, visit www.
clairekingsleybooks.com/reading-order/

How the Grump Saved Christmas (Elias and Isabelle)

A stand-alone, small-town Christmas romance

The Bailey Brothers

Steamy, small-town family series. Five unruly brothers. Epic
pranks. A quirky, feuding town. Big HEAs. (Best read in order)

Protecting You (Asher and Grace part 1)

Fighting for Us (Asher and Grace part 2)

Unraveling Him (Evan and Fiona)

Rushing In (Gavin and Skylar)

Chasing Her Fire (Logan and Cara)

Rewriting the Stars (Levi and Annika)

The Miles Family

Sexy, sweet, funny, and heartfelt family series. Messy family. Epic
bromance. Super romantic. (Best read in order)

Broken Miles (Roland and Zoe)

Forbidden Miles (Brynn and Chase)

Reckless Miles (Cooper and Amelia)

Hidden Miles (Leo and Hannah)

Gaining Miles: A Miles Family Novella (Ben and Shannon)

Dirty Martini Running Club

Sexy, fun stand-alone romantic comedies with huge... hearts.

Everly Dalton's Dating Disasters (Everly, Hazel, and Nora)

Faking Ms. Right (Everly and Shepherd)

Falling for My Enemy (Hazel and Corban)

Marrying Mr. Wrong (Sophie and Cox)

(Nora's book coming soon)

Bluewater Billionaires

Hot, stand-alone romantic comedies. Lady billionaire BFFs and
the badass heroes who love them.

The Mogul and the Muscle (Cameron and Jude)

The Price of Scandal, Wild Open Hearts, and Crazy for Loving You

More Bluewater Billionaire shared-world stand-alone romantic
comedies by Lucy Score, Kathryn Nolan, and Pippa Grant

$\sim$

Bootleg Springs

by Claire Kingsley and Lucy Score

Hot and hilarious small-town romcom series with a dash of
mystery and suspense. (Best read in order)

Whiskey Chaser (Scarlett and Devlin)

Sidecar Crush (Jameson and Leah Mae)

Moonshine Kiss (Bowie and Cassidy)

Bourbon Bliss (June and George)

Gin Fling (Jonah and Shelby)

Highball Rush (Gibson and I can't tell you)

Book Boyfriends

Hot, stand-alone romcoms that will make you laugh and make you swoon.

Book Boyfriend (Alex and Mia)

Cocky Roommate (Weston and Kendra)

Hot Single Dad (Caleb and Linnea)

Finding Ivy (William and Ivy)

A unique contemporary romance with a hint of mystery.

His Heart (Sebastian and Brooke)

A poignant and emotionally intense story about grief, loss, and the transcendent power of love.

The Always Series

Smoking hot, dirty talking bad boys with some angsty intensity.

Always Have (Braxton and Kylie)

Always Will (Selene and Ronan)

Always Ever After (Braxton and Kylie)

The Jetty Beach Series

Sexy small-town romance series with swoony heroes, romantic HEAs, and lots of big feels.

Behind His Eyes (Ryan and Nicole)

One Crazy Week (Melissa and Jackson)

Messy Perfect Love (Cody and Clover)

Operation Get Her Back (Hunter and Emma)

Weekend Fling (Finn and Juliet)

Good Girl Next Door (Lucas and Becca)

The Path to You (Gabriel and Sadie)

ABOUT THE AUTHOR

Claire Kingsley is a #1 Amazon bestselling author of sexy, heartfelt contemporary romance and romantic comedies. She writes sassy, quirky heroines, swoony heroes who love their women hard, panty-melting sexytimes, romantic happily ever afters, and all the big feels.

She can't imagine life without coffee, her Kindle, and the sexy heroes who inhabit her imagination. She lives in the inland Pacific Northwest with her three kids.

www.clairekingsleybooks.com

www.ingramcontent.com/pod-product-compliance
Lightning Source LLC
La Vergne TN
LVHW090305070225
803198LV00023B/161